Shards of Glass

By
Jeremy Varner

Shards of Glass
Book 1 of the Agent of Argyre Series

Second Edition

Copyright 2011, 2019 by Jeremy Varner
All rights reserved.

www.jeremyvarner.com

First Edition Published in 2011
Second Edition Published in 2019

To Christi for her patience and gentle prodding, Dawn for encouraging me to start, Earlaine for provoking me into debates and Shirley for telling me to find something I'm good at and stick to it.

All were vital contributions.

Table of Contents

Prologue

Lying on the floor, surrounded by a small sea of blood and glass, I finally started to understand. Scattered fragments reflected small parts of myself as I realized my mistakes in full. It hurt to know that people died because I fell short, because of my inability to accept the darkness inherent in everyone. It hurt to know that, when the darkness was staring me in the face, I couldn't see it. And as I drifted off, blood running across the floor, I found myself dreaming of a night in front of a television, dreaming of a different world.

It wasn't that far outside of Seattle, in a suburb called Burien. I was too young to remember much of what the place was like, but memories of that night were clearer than most. Shadows of tall trees rose over my house, blocking the light of a setting sun. My mother passed behind me from time-to-time, patting me on the head. At least, I assumed it was her hand as I never looked up, staring obliviously at the screen, entranced by colorful characters singing off-key.

In the kitchen my grandmother had hastily thrown together dinner since neither of my parents were particularly gifted cooks. I didn't mind that my parents weren't any good at it since, at that age, microwaved hotdogs were enough for me. Still, the house was warm and filled with a pleasant smell despite the haste. For what has to be my earliest memory, I could have done worse.

I was content in that little world as my dad stepped in.

He moved unnoticed beneath the sound of my tone-deaf fictional friends. Through the living room he snuck over to his old comfortable chair, resting behind me without a sound, ruffling my hair before I was any the wiser. It was probably the dozenth time someone had patted my head that night, but the hand was bigger, heavier, and came with a different smell. Surprised, I looked up with glee at the seemingly giant hand atop my head, crying out, "Dad!"

Gently chuckling, he lifted me into the air and gave me the greatest hug. It made me feel like he was the strongest man in the world. And, in my eyes, he was. As a police officer, the "best" as far as I knew, he was a hero to me in more ways than one. But, strong as he was, he was tired and soon sank back into the old chair. The well-worn chair even smelled like him: a mix of pine trees and whatever the cologne mom liked was supposed to be. He nudged me off his lap as he eased into the old grooves and waved towards the television with a simple request.

"Turn on the news, kiddo."

Long forgetting where I'd put the remote, I charged ahead and slapped my hand against a touch screen. I had no idea that a simple motion like swiping my fingers across the channel control would change my life, my world, forever.

Tired, haggard, a reporter appeared on the screen standing in a place I'd never seen before. Wearily, she said, "It's two-thirty AM here in front of the UNESCO Headquarters in Paris. Representatives have told us a statement would be released by the UN shortly. While we don't know the nature of the discussion, we do know that several of the world leaders have been called for an emergency meeting, including all member nations of the UN Security Council."

At the time, most of that flew over my head. I didn't know what a UN was, or a Security Council. I didn't know why anyone would be meeting that long after bedtime or why anyone cared. Maybe if I were older, the moment would have seemed more important right from the start instead of when I saw it again in history class years later. But it wasn't what was said that caught my attention back then, it was what I saw.

People in suits walked out, their faces a sea of emotions ranging from horrified to strangely accepting. Some were afraid, defiant and angry. Others were perfectly accepting, at peace. But they left the building and started to scatter across the stage all the same, making way for a man that I'd somehow known was coming before I could see him.

Tall and broad at the shoulders, he cut a sharp image in his dark suit, complimenting his bronze skin and golden hair. Every step he took seemed to float, his body moving weightlessly. The video distorted as light shone from his skin and when it cleared silence fell over the crowd. He stood at the podium, soon joined by a mysterious entourage in black suits.

I think we all felt it. Whoever this was, he radiated something powerful to everyone. Even as a kid, I felt my heart pounding in my chest. It was a primal reaction, instinct. Something about him was different.

"My name is Alexander Neumann," he said in a deep, powerful voice. "I came to speak with you, the people of the world and your leaders, about the birth of a new nation: The Republic of Argyre."

Alexander hesitated for a moment, glancing at the people beside him, before saying something that changed the world. "You deserve to be told the truth. You are not alone. A people, not unlike your own, have lived without safe haven for centuries. We do not come today to ask for land or resources. We have what we need. But we are not foolish enough to believe that we can organize without frightening you."

It was the opening of the most monumental event in human history. He told us about his people and, in turn, about ourselves. We were not being invaded by aliens; we were being shown something we'd always known in one way or another. They'd been called Nephilim, Demigods and "The Fairy Folk". We'd whispered about Witches, performed exorcisms and burned people at the stake. They'd haunted our dreams, captured our imaginations and defined who we were. And now they were standing there, declaring themselves to the world and accepting, once and for all, the title of "Alters".

By the time there were eight billion people on the Earth two billion were latent, inactive Alters going on with their lives thinking they were like everyone else. They were our friends, families and coworkers while we never even noticed. Every day you could meet at least a dozen of them. But until they go active, even they don't know for sure.

And the active ones, the ones that aren't "normal"? Eventually there were nearly fifteen million of them across the planet. Through simple luck of the draw these people became something else. There's a ten percent chance if you're terminally ill or come in contact with their fluids. Statistically, it's usually the former. Cancer, AIDS, Malaria and even conspiracies around reality television have all been cited as a cause – some with less credibility than others. Then, if you're in that ten percent, you become like them, leaving behind your life to join others of your kind or possibly becoming a judge on one of those shows that supposedly pushed you over the edge.

How else do you think they always find the angriest people on the planet?

Whatever cause you believe, they were there. On that day, November 16th, we were told the truth. I don't exactly remember the speech from that day, not clearly, though I saw it repeatedly throughout my school years. Instead, what I remember was that room I was in and what it felt like. We stood there, my family and I, watching this unfold as Alexander told us everything.

"Some may call us monsters," he said, innocently enough.

I didn't understand what he was saying at the time. Sadly, all I understood was "monsters". Startled, sobbing, I turned and started running for my mother as fast as I could before powerful hands caught me. Lifting me into the air, dad brought me back to that smell of pine trees and cologne.

"Don't worry, kiddo," a strong, calm voice said reassuringly. "They're not monsters."

I lifted my chin, looking into my dad's peaceful blue-green eyes. He squeezed my shoulder and hugged me close while watching the screen.

Watching over our shoulders, mom muttered behind us, "This has to be a hoax."

"Seems a bit large to be a hoax," dad replied firmly.

She paced the room, a look on her face I couldn't understand, and growled. "What kind of idiot would admit something like that to the entire world?"

She looked so upset, so unsettled, and I couldn't fully understand why. I just remember climbing off of dad's lap, walking over and hugging her legs. "It's okay mommy," I said. "Daddy will protect us from the monsters."

Mom glanced across the room to him, running her hand through my hair. Quietly, she said to him, "People won't lie down and accept this."

"I know that, Marion," He said, idly gazing down at his uniform. "If this is true, things are going to start changing. But I'm in a place to do something about it. The police are going to need to make sure people understand that the law applies to *everyone* equally."

Mom muttered back, "When has that ever worked?"

He walked over to us and gave her a hug. I looked up at them, unsure if this was just how my parents reacted to "monsters". But I looked at his badge and heard what he said clearly. Even at that age it meant something to me.

He was a smart man: everything he said came true. Our world changed and his job changed with it. We moved to Seattle, dad taking a job trying to keep the peace between the mainstream humans and the Alters. And mom was right too: they didn't take it lying down. Riots, lynch mobs and Witch hunts started to spring up across the world anew. By the time the dust settled, my family was gone and I was alone.

Luckily, we were never really alone. Those men in the black suits revealed a history of their own. They'd been urban legends in their own right: men in black spiriting away people and creatures that needed to be kept secret. They were in the room at that meeting, forming a pact with the nation's leaders for the good of us all. An "Alter Control Task Force" was founded in that room, using their organization as its backbone.

The ACTF isn't meant to hunt the Alters, only keep the peace. Not that it's easy to do that. One side believes they're oppressors and the other side believes they're sympathizers. But, like the regular cops, everyone likes them just fine when they're needed. The rest of the time no one likes them, even the other cops.

Despite all of that, years later, I joined up with the nudging of a friend. At the time I didn't have many other options. But now here I am, Nathaniel Leone of the ACTF. I hope to succeed where my father failed and live up to his ideals.

Right now, I'm not off to a very good start.

Chapter 1

"Morning" Hours

I started my month in a pet store, wearing a "specialized uniform", waiting for Werewolves to tear me apart. The thing was hot, heavy, and hard to move in. I could barely see and every sound was muffled except for one. Though others were in the area, I was the only agent standing out in the open, guided by voices over a radio from a safe little van outside.

"Hit the button, Nate," one of the voices demanded.

Taking a quick glance around, I groaned and muttered, "Do I have to?"

"Wouldn't want to blow your cover," another said, chuckling.

"Why did I even have to pretend to take this job?" I grunted. "Couldn't we have just told them what we were doing?"

With a strained but controlled tone, obviously stifling back laughter, one replied, "Human owned store chain, it's technically out of our jurisdiction."

Sighing, I reluctantly reached up and pressed the nose of a big cartoon head. The character's voice bellowed from the big mouth with a giggle, "Come on, be civil, buy me some kibble!"

"These kids don't get paid enough," I muttered. "It doesn't even *rhyme*."

"Now, now," a voice said past snorts and laughter, "'tis not our place to critique the poetic stylings of Sir Chester B. Wolfendown."

I swallowed my pride and tried to ignore their snickers while taking the long march down the aisles. As miserable as I was, I knew my tormentors were right.

"Chester's" mascot, me at the time, had been under siege in recent months by Werewolves. The chain advertised to Alters, even had some special products for the dog who could groom themselves, but their choices were a bit off the mark. "Chester", in the opinion of some Werewolves, was a racist depiction. The criticism was fair enough, but we couldn't just let them haul off and take their aggression out on some underpaid teenagers. Not long ago, the biggest wolf pack in Seattle could have helped us smooth it over, but the Third Avenue Hunt folded under "unfortunate circumstances". So, I had to walk around as bait and, honestly, part of me was starting to look forward to getting attacked by Fido with 'roid-rage.

Walking around in the get up was bad enough, what with it being hotter than Hades and having an animatronic tail sweeping around my ass. But to listen to those awful sayings every 10 minutes while children would occasionally throw dog treats at me was too much. I was feeling sympathy for my attackers: even I wanted to kick my ass at that point.

The saving grace was seeing interesting people wandering through, shopping for the few things anyone with some fur could use: hairbrushes, fur grooming tools, were-tiger cages. Don't ask me what they use that last one for. I'm not sure I want to know. But people *were* buying them.

One of the interesting people to pass my way was someone I'd known already, sort of. I'd seen her in the neighborhood and admired her from afar, but never actually screwed up the courage to ask her name. Though I was easily capable of facing down Werewolves, it was hard to approach her. I'd only known her as "The Ahab's Girl" from the local coffee shop. I wasn't even sure if she was there for a pet, a friend, or herself. But, even if she didn't realize I was there, and even if it was a bit "creepy stalker" of me, I kind of enjoyed watching her walk around. Not that I was about to actually approach.

It's not that I'm a bad looking guy: I'm in great shape, average height, pretty good hair. I may be a little pale from years of night shifts but I'm not sickly looking. I'm told my eyes are nice from time to time: a shade of aquamarine I inherited from my father. But, watching her, I still felt like she was way out of my league.

I knew she was an Alter of some sort, with sky blue eyes and a subtle glow to her ivory skin, but not what kind. Not that it mattered much to me. I was probably biased, like some teenager or a flighty nitwit citing love at first sight, but she seemed so perfect. She was elegant, practically drifting through the aisles. And, though I'm sure I should have stopped looking, it was a nice moment that I got to have to myself, standing there with a wagging tail.

Of course, that's when the Werewolf tackled me.

In a flurry of fur, teeth and claws I was crashing to the ground while my goofy head went flying off like a beach-ball. Strangely, in that moment I wondered how the Seahawks were doing that night. But by the time I hit the floor, watching Chester's head ricochet down the aisles, I figured, "Probably as bad as I am."

I wrestled with the wolf as Chester's head continued to bounce, nose triggering once in a while, the sound of his ridiculous voice echoing off of the shelves.

"I'm really not fakin', I loves me some bacon."

The mass of fur and muscle on top of me kept the rest from view as I heard my backup start dropping Werewolves throughout the store as fast as "Fido" dropped me. Knowing they'd come soon, I wanted to spare myself the embarrassment of being rescued. Controlling his arms and using them to hold his head back, I managed to buy some time and avoid being shredded by razor sharp claws and teeth.

I was hoping to find something to knock him out in that moment but quickly found nothing and, giving up the search, I opted to fight dirty. A quick lift of the knee turned his snarls into pathetic whines as he rolled off of me, wheezing for air. I scrambled to my feet, ripping open the front of my stupid costume to reach for my weapon.

Catching sight of the badge, he bolted from me as fast as he possibly could, barreling towards "The Ahab's Girl" at the far end. Knowing I couldn't start firing that way, especially at her, I was forced to give chase and tackle him, the same sort of cheap shot he'd taken at me. The two of us crashed to the polished floor and coasted along into a rack, chew-toys cascading over us.

Pinning the struggling wolf, I looked at her cowering by a rack next to the decapitated head of Sir Wolfendown, staring at me as though I were crazy. The Werewolf snarled and snapped and she screamed and ran away. It wasn't exactly the best first impression.

My assailant was thrashing a little more than I expected, his heart racing fast even for a Werewolf. Yet, he wasn't as strong as they normally are. He was more winded than anything. I'd even say he was out of shape.

As I cuffed him, the fur moved just enough for me to see an unusual rash along his skin. It was familiar, what I could see through the thick carpet of hair. I briefly thought at the time that maybe their tirade started from an allergy to the shampoo. Whatever the rash was, though, I didn't have time to examine it.

We dragged the suspects outside, other agents trading jokes at my expense and comparing which of us got the biggest catch. But as we reached the exit we came face to face with a small fleet of police cars and news vans.

As cameras flashed in our face, one of the other agents chimed in, "busted."

***

My face was all over the news for quite a while right next to Chester's. Even weeks later, I awoke to the sound of my alarm mixed with people debating whether the ACTF overstepped its jurisdiction from the next room over. I'm never quite eager to start my day, let alone start it with a reminder of my infamy. So I turned away, hoping to ignore their opinions and drift off to sleep again. Unfortunately, the golden glow of the sunset over Seattle reminded me that I needed to get up if I was going to make my shift.

I stumbled out of my room on the prowl for anything I could shove into my toaster or microwave. The TV in the next room was still on in the background providing a steady white noise of things I really didn't pay much attention to. There were occasional Alter-based blurbs from the local news, a few talking heads giving their opinions on our work, but otherwise not much else that concerned me.

I sat on my old wood stool in the kitchen, staring out at the TV across a room full of furniture I never used: my grandmother's old couch, my mother's old rocking chair and a beat-up recliner in the corner of the room. The only thing in the room I used regularly was the TV on the wall, now showing loud and obnoxious people telling me how I should feel about the news.

They were excited that night over rumors of a possible mayoral bid by an Alter. I wasn't quite as enthusiastic. As long as they've been around in secret, Alters have been in charge of almost everything at one point or another. Leprechauns tend to manipulate gold markets, Sirens tend to be pop stars, and you'd be amazed what some world leaders have been. The idea that one of them would run for office wasn't exactly newsworthy to me.

It did interest me, slightly, that he was active and made it clear to everyone that he was. I didn't catch what exactly he was, being half-awake, but it was still unusual. The media was fascinated with the idea that someone who had the luxury of hiding what he was would give that up and let everyone know. Obviously, that meant he wasn't a Vampire, Werewolf or anything else with an interesting night life. Though, it wasn't like that would have mattered much to the mainstream population – he still stood a snowball's chance in the upper levels of hell.

As far as the media was concerned, it was a sign of a coming revolution. Never mind that their hype and buzz had about as much substance to it as the soggy frozen waffles I was eating for "breakfast". Alters are too much like everyone else, aside from one hell of a smile. But it gave them the sort of controversy and conflict they needed to draw an audience. Unfortunately, I wasn't their audience – I didn't even catch the guy's name.

When the topic went away, they lost what little of my interest they had. There were a few other stories worth listening to: an anti-Alter protest on Harbor Island, the Seahawks getting hammered and rumors of an Alter-driven drug ring. But slowly I realized I couldn't force myself to fake interest in some of their other stories like which star was in rehab. Sometimes I think that's just how they take a vacation.

I turned away from the TV to my "breakfast" for the day: a plate of waffles from my freezer that smelled and tasted like wet cardboard. Somehow, they were still partially frozen, squishy, and burnt along the edges all at the same time. Somehow, I'd forgotten my old toaster needed to be fixed – or replaced. I was sure some Goblin in the Undercity could piece the thing back together, but I wasn't quite sure why I was still trying to use something older than me. Grandma said it belonged to my mother, but for the life of me I've never figured out when the thing was made.

With a heavy sigh, I gave up on my soggy, burnt waffles and pushed them aside. There was nothing left to do but get up and get ready for my day

As I walked into the bedroom, my black and silver uniform sparkled at me from my closet, the sun reflecting off of silver plates and the Vesperadin weave. Though the material's been around for some time, not many get to see it like that. Even I never got a set of clothes made with it until I joined the force. Friendly as they are, the ACTF techs don't like to share their toys.

Vesperadin is as thick as denim, smooth as silk and always has a subtle sheen. Rumor has it that it's some sort of organic thread laced with nanotech. Whatever it is, it's better than Kevlar: resistant to bullets, fire, stabbing, blunt trauma and, sometimes most importantly, stains. Over the years I've been stabbed, bitten, and hurled through windows and every time I've come out of it intact save for modest dry cleaning bills and the occasional concussion.

It isn't perfect, "resistant" never means "foolproof". If it couldn't fail, there wouldn't be armor inserts tucked into pockets inside. You also wouldn't need armored boots or gloves, even if they double as weapons. Even with those, nothing is perfect. Sometimes, when you're dealing with something that could possibly rip you in half, nothing can stop it. I try to remember that fact every time I put on the suit and badge as a daily reminder not to get sloppy.

When I stepped into the hallway, my landlady's apartment was bubbling with activity. Her voice murmured beyond the door as a bit of smoke rolled under the gap. Barbara Zdunk had always been a spooky woman with a bit too much time on her hands. At all hours of the night a mix of world fusion music and her laughing for no apparent reason could be heard throughout the building by those listening closely. Together with the smell of incense and liquor, I often got the impression she could be a Witch – either by blood or by practice.

Even considering that, my rent's fair and the location couldn't be beat. At best, I just had an eccentric woman living across the hall. At worst, she could try to put a curse on me for missing the rent. With the place being two blocks from headquarters, about the same distance from the courthouses and, blissfully, right next to a coffee shop: I just made sure to pay the rent on time. Curses be damned, a good deal is hard to find.

By the time I reached the front door I could hear the steady fall of rain and walked out into a drizzle from clouds that rolled in while I wasn't looking. Outside, Alters were out in force, most of them having the sixth sense to know to bring an umbrella, going along with their lives now that the sun had set. They weaved around under the hazy shine of neon lights and glow-in-the-dark paints adorning the walls of their little village etched out of the heart of Seattle: "Fangtown".

The name of the place wasn't exactly their choice, given "Fang" was a slur at the time, but they embraced it for all it was worth. One look at the dentist office under the welcome sign was enough to say that. Once upon a time, my neighborhood was part of the "International District" before the mass migration of everything abnormal. Seattle was pretty prime real estate for Alters given the near constant rainy season and the proximity to a border that can be jumped in a pinch. And the people of the International District were traditionally welcoming of others, which is how a place you'd normally call a Chinatown would end up with people from all over.

Though, I doubt anyone expected it when the local Jiangshi invited all their friends.

Given I was a kid when they first showed themselves, it sometimes got lost on me how much progress they'd made. In a relatively short time they'd blanketed part of the International District, Pioneer Square and a small part of the Downtown area with covered walkways for daylight travel and nightclubs that stayed open straight to dawn. But one thing always stands out to me, especially in the right light.

Murals, visible only when it starts to get dark, cover Fangtown like a warm aura. The history of their people and the community stretches across the walls in dramatic portraits blending into each other effortlessly like a river of time. And, as I walked to the coffee shop that night, I couldn't help but take in the view of those walls through the mist. Even though I live right across from it, there are some times when you just have to take it in or be depressed by how mundane a place like this can still be.

People from the outside would probably be surprised by how many office buildings there are in Fangtown. In the past there was a myth that Vampires who came across grains of salt or randomly dropped objects would have to stop and count each and every individual piece. It turned out they're mildly autistic, have a knack for numbers and a bit of an obsession with completing a task. Now, the number one occupation among Vampires is accounting and two minor accounting firms, plastered with bright neon paint, sat across the street from me. Without the mural, I'm sure I'd be depressed by the concept of an army of pale people being perfectly content crunching numbers.

Not to say the town doesn't have its unique charms. They're just charms that are far more subtle than the décor. The businesses that Alters open cater to each other in ways that seem almost sarcastic. I can't think of anywhere else in the world but the Fangtowns and Argyre where you could find a Bat's Belfry or Howler's Fur Suits. And I *know* there's nowhere else in the world that'd have a Zomboner Club.

But those things were nowhere to be seen on the short walk from my apartment to the coffee shop – aside from the coffee shop itself. Ahab's: a coffee franchise with a tongue-in-cheek name that they refused to apologize for. In fact, anyone who understands their little joke is rewarded a cookie by tradition – a tradition I freely abused. But, despite their horrible sense of humor, they're almost as popular among the locals as their infamous predecessors thanks to one quirk. Ahab's is a coffee shop… and blood-bar.

And that's exactly the smell that greets you when you enter: roasted coffee, chocolate chips and the sweet scent of blood drifting from the red brew specials. I never understood the red brew, myself. Vampiric creatures, despite their frequency in lore, actually make up less than fifteen percent of the Alter population. Yet you'd be surprised by how many people decide to drink the blood coffee. I guess it sounds interesting enough to intrigue you between the involuntary shudders you have over the concept. I've tasted blood before, typically my own, and it has never been my thing. But every day, I walk into this place for my "morning" ritual and see at least a dozen people downing it without a hint of hesitation.

For Vampires, it makes sense since their metabolism is through the roof. You can stow away more food on a liquid diet and digest it much faster than solids. But, even then, I could never understand why anyone would favor drinking blood over something else that tasted less like...*blood*.

Strangely, this thought continues to haunt me after living here for the better part of three years.

As I contemplated the blood and waited in the never ending death march for coffee, I found myself being stared at more than usual. I imagined that after a while they figured out I wasn't some random visitor to their little corner of the world or had seen the reports about Chester.

It was funny watching some of these people and the way they reacted to my presence. From the guy looking like the Freemont Troll brought to life in a five foot, four inch caffeine junkie, to the Cyclope man who couldn't help making his stares obvious: I was getting some strange looks. Hell, in the back, a Banshee woman shattered her glass with inaudible sounds she made out of reflex.

I glanced over my shoulder at the breaking glass and was met with a sea of unnaturally bright eyes turned my way.

I was used to being eye-to-eye with Alters, it's even required to identify them most of the time, but every man has his limits. Seeing that many staring eyes, several bordering on neon, was mine. Nervously, I put on a pair of mirrored sunglasses from my pocket.

The world outside my shades lit up in an explosion of colors. The pheromones and biometrics of everyone in the room were laid out before me, painted out as colorful digital auras. The auras were filled with information on what races they were, what they were feeling, even what they were thinking to a degree. And as I stared at them, practically seeing into their souls, I didn't see many friends in the crowd.

The sunglasses, what we call "the visor", often get strange looks from people who don't understand what they are. People walking around in black and wearing mirrored sunglasses at night likely seem a bit out of place. But they're one of the most useful tools at our disposal with night-vision and chemical analysis built in. Nanocrystals in their surface amplify ambient light and display information on even the slightest physical or chemical abnormality. At that moment, the room was looking pretty abnormal and only one person had a calm aura.

My friend Trey, Trevor Taylor Thompson, always shows in a dull shade of blue.

Though it was the friendliest color in the room, it was also the one that said the least. Only mainstream humans and people with extreme control could manage such a color. But Trey has eyes that shine far too brightly to belong to a run-of-the-mill human. For as long as I've known him, we've played a single game almost without exception.

"You're a Tanuki," I said with a tone of triumph, watching his aura for even the slightest change.

Trey laughed, shaking his head while he quipped, "No, but thank you for noticing."

He wasn't just my friend, he was my favorite puzzle. In three years I had yet to identify what exactly Trey was. I knew he had an Alter ID, one I'd glanced at but couldn't read, and his eyes were green enough to practically glow in the dark. Aside from that, the man was a question mark. Yet he knew me and my routine almost too well, getting my orders ready often before I'd even have a chance to say them anymore.

Without a word between us he produced two cups of different sizes and placed two lids of different colors next to them. Besides the smaller cup sat a black lid while the larger lid was red. It was probably bad form for him to do it without checking if my mind had ever changed for even the slightest moment. But it wasn't as though my order was ever any different. It made his job easier, letting him work without even needing to look up from the counter, only glancing up to make one request.

"Take them off, Nate," he asked quietly.

Despite the auras, I'd forgotten "them" until that moment. Reaching up, I pulled the visor off and put it on the counter. "Sorry about that, Trey," I whispered back.

The visor becomes second nature after long enough. You wear it so much on duty that you start to forget just how unnerving it is to see someone wearing sunglasses in the middle of the night, your own reflection shining back at you. But for Trey, it seemed more. Though I never understood it, he was acutely aware that it stared into his "soul". Perhaps the reflection was too much for him.

"Vampire?" I asked with a grin.

Sliding the cups over to me, he merely shook his head and chuckled at the notion. "You've guessed that before."

Frowning, I picked up the cup with the black lid, careful to avoid the red, and tapped my fingers on the counter. "Oh well, call me Ishmael."

His shitty grin grew wide as he produced a cookie and placed it on the counter. "We need to stop giving these things out," he said, "or at least cut you off."

"Just give me my cookie," I grunted, taking a quick, scalding hot sip, "and be happy Starbucks doesn't try to sue."

"Not my problem," he said, "I just work here."

I smirked and picked up my consolation prize and the coffee it came with, ready to depart for my corner. But as I prepared to leave, Trey whispered one last comment.

"She's here today."

Looking over my shoulder, I saw the bright sky blue eyes set against an ivory face. "The Ahab's Girl" sat there, looking like she was made of white gold and silk, her skin practically glowing under the dim shop lights and the murals beyond the window. Her dark hair was, so far, untouched by the rain outside and pulled back into a bun.

She was as much of a mystery as Trey, coming every few days with a book, sitting in the same corner every time. I knew she worked in the area, never showing up in anything that didn't look like office clothes. But aside from that I knew almost nothing else. Her aura was always guarded, like she was repressed, shy or ashamed of herself. Given the book, I always went with shy, but I never saw anything to be shy about.

Maybe a shy cat lady, given I'd seen her in Chester's only a few weeks before. Perhaps even a crazy cat lady. Of course, that was not a downside: crazy's never exactly stopped me in the past. But, considering our last encounter, I just hoped she wouldn't recognize me as I slinked to my corner of the shop.

I was curious if she was okay – don't get me wrong. But was I brave enough to talk to her? No, not really.

The others smiled now that they'd seen the dumbfounded look on my face. One would think they'd have noticed it one of the dozens of other times I'd had it on my face when she was in the room. But I suppose I was never quite as interesting as I was after my brush with mascot glory.

I pushed aside the embarrassment and sat down, trying to lose myself in the strange Alternative Jazz you could only hear in Fangtown. The music was an interesting blend of conventional style with the subtle feeling of something more flowing through it, much like the girl. I've heard they have notes in the music inaudible to a normal human. Whether that's true or not, it was the perfect music for admiring her from afar.

I turned away after a moment of observation, feeling a bit creepy by then, and watched the rain slowly thicken into rolling sheets refracting the glow of the city into an ethereal haze. The cars passing by turned puddles on the street into a field of mist, deepening the natural reflections of the glass. Had it not been for that momentary reflection, I may have never seen the pair of sky blue eyes staring into the back of my head.

A moment of panic washed over me. Should I turn and acknowledge it? What if the glance wasn't meant for me? She never looked out the windows or at anything other than her books as long as I'd known her. And yet, she was looking at me – or at least in my general direction.

I peered over my shoulder to realize it was more than just my imagination. She'd moved across the room to sit at the next table, smiling at me and my stupid expression. I choked on the endless options of things I could say just then, narrowly managing to ask, "Can I help you miss…?"

She smiled at my trailing voice, practically lighting the room and gesturing lightly to the uniform. "You know there's a coffee shop a couple blocks outside Fangtown with a police discount."

I wasn't used to being spoken to by anyone but Trey, and definitely not by her. So I wouldn't be surprised if I appeared a little awkward while replying, sheepishly, with an ironic, "I'm more welcome here than with the SPD."

"Really?" she asked, grinning. "Are they upset about Chester, or did you do something else to piss them off?"

I winced at the mention of our fuzzy friend. Obviously, she recognized me. But she did have a good question – one I never had the answer to myself. As far as I figured, we were just there to help the local cops. Still, in the end, there was only one real answer to her question.

"I sided with the wrong team."

She stunned me with a quiet giggle. "Janice Gray," she said, walking over with an outstretched hand. "And you, Officer...?"

"Devotee," I corrected, staring at her hand like a moron before finally taking it, "Devotee Nathaniel Leone."

She slipped into the chair next to me, still smirking at me like she knew I'd been looking all this time. "And what, exactly, is a devotee?"

I looked into her eyes, baffled she wanted to speak to "Chester", and tried my best not to stumble on my words. "It's kind of like a deputy without any actual authority or... will of my own."

Another giggle crossed her lips and another heartbeat skipped in my chest. "So then who's will do you answer to?"

"My lancer," I said.

"Lancer?"

Normally, I like to think I keep my cool. In fact, I'd say I was pretty calm for a guy in his 20s. But the whole situation clearly had me off my game as I could feel a blush coming while replying, "We like to be a little different."

"So," she said, taking a long look at me and raising an eyebrow ever so slightly, "you're a rookie."

"No, no, not a rookie!" I stammered. "We just stay close to more experienced officers for the first three years."

She continued to look at me, seemingly measuring me up. I hoped, prayed even, that the uniform did me some good and could wash away the one encounter we'd had before.

And as she finished, to my relief, she smiled and said, "It still looks better than the talking dog."

Relief wasn't even the word for it. I'm not even sure I know the word for it. The closest I can think of, off the top of my head, is exuberance. But, despite the joy, I tried my best to play it cool and only say "oh, really," as if I weren't in the least surprised.

"Sure," she said slyly, "much less like a dog."

"Well, I do get to fetch coffee for my lancer every night," I said, somehow more at ease.

She laughed again. At least she thought I was funny. But, as the ice started to finally break, I glanced out the window and saw a black and white car that sent the chill back over me as it rolled to a stop by the curb. I gave her a quick, disheartened glance and nodded out the window.

"And that'd be my ride."

I hesitated to get up but knew better than to leave the boss waiting. Starting toward the door, she stopped me with a hand on my sleeve. Confused, I watched her carefully place a slip of paper on the lid of my cup. It was a simple, yet profound gesture.

I nearly didn't realize the significance of it. But as I saw her smile again, it dawned on me what it was. Grinning, I walked back out of the Ahab's, practically strutting despite the harm it could do to what little was left of my image.

My night had started on a high note and I was sure it was going to get better.

Chapter 2
Yelling Idiots

Outside, I walked into the rain and came face-to-face with the sleek and strange form of my lancer's car, which we call "chariots" for the same reasons I was a "devotee". Beads of rain followed the curves and waves of its near alien frame as the four wheels below glowed and hummed. The light and sound of their dedicated motors purred in unison like a chorus of unearthly beings holding the car aloft. And the car itself, lights pulsing in the dark, shone under an ethereal glow from the roof.

Unlike the "red and blues", local cops, the lights on our cars are purple with a faint UV behind them to draw an Alter's attention. With them on you could see the white parts of the car glow from a distance without having to mount floodlights to the roof. But, even with half of it outside the visible spectrum, that light normally wasn't on while parked. He was letting me know we had somewhere to go that night.

The near seamless form of the car opened up before me, lights streaking across previously unseen gaps in the side as the seemingly handle-less door opened. Beyond that door, in his well-pressed uniform, sat Lancer Lucian Descartes. He looked at me, visor shining, and held out a hand like Charon requesting his dues. Handing over the red-brew coffee and free cookie as my toll, I climbed into the passenger seat.

Sniffing the cup and cookie to see if they were fresh, he glanced to me and mumbled, "Is it red?"

"Trey knows your order," I replied absently, shuffling in the seat while trying to figure which pocket would keep Janice's number safe.

He nodded approvingly and ate the cookie while I watched. It was his prerogative to eat the cookie since, as his devotee, I was there to kiss his ass while he was there to keep me breathing. It was a symbiotic relationship I didn't dare to question aside from one that'd gnawed on me for months.

"Do I get to drive tonight?"

And, like always, he glanced to me with a smirk and replied coolly, "When you grow up, kid."

A tall man, at least six feet, and having a lean, yet muscular frame, you'd think he'd be intimidating at first sight. But with a fair complexion and sharp, yet subtle, features, he almost looks feminine. Overall, he's a strangely unassuming figure in uniform, despite the gold differentiating it from mine, and often I would imagine people believing he was a pushover. But feminine features and a lean figure belie an easily missed truth: Lucian is a Vampire, a very old one at that – something I made a point to use against him from time to time.

"I just think I should get some practice," I said, dryly, "before they figure out you're too old to drive."

He brushed that off with only a quiet snort and returned to enjoying his bloody coffee.

Though we jabbed at each other, it was nothing personal. I'd be a bit insulted being referred to as "kid" by anyone else. But Lucian's old enough to call just about anyone "kid" and get away with it. No one on the force is exactly sure how old – he's just always been there. Legend even has it that he was one of the original "men in black" and that he would leave the force occasionally to "find himself". Considering his age, and the fact he helped found the organization but hadn't made it higher than lancer, I sometimes think it'd be easier for him to find Waldo or Jesus.

Still, riding with him, I knew I was in the best hands. Lucian's record speaks for itself. No one has been with us as long as he has and anyone with us longer than a few years has seen his work in action. We've all known the kinds of people he's put into the cold depths of the ACTF's prisons. And here I was, his devotee, a fact never lost on me – though I was sometimes a little sarcastic about it.

He was also the man who recruited me into the force. According to him, I was from a legacy of people who'd worked with the ACTF's precursors long ago. And somewhere in my family line there was a hunter good enough that Lucian felt I was needed here. In a way that was reassuring, but also kind of terrifying.

As we sat quietly with our coffee, the time rolled over to 7:30 and an image shaped like an abstract human face lit up on the dashboard terminal. Our shift started not with a bell or a whistle but the cold hum of lights shining across the dashboard and the eyes of a mechanical woman staring at us, through us, as she said, "Welcome to the Oracle System."

A strange kit-bash of technology and genetics, the Oracle System isn't much understood by outsiders. The canopy around us lit with a vibrant display of maps, reports, memos and real time activity monitors. Psychic beings linked with the best in satellite technology and computer networks give us a real time read on the city, on the world. On the screens we could see everything from crimes in progress to criminal records of people walking past us. On a level, I could understand the fears people had of such a system. Big brother, as far as I've seen, has fangs.

But the technology has long been justified to me. The display just in that moment was showing a fairly active night: a few muggings, a jewel theft, a couple drug busts and the like. But while Lucian seemed to know what we were going for he didn't let me in on it at all. Instead, we made our way out of Fangtown and out toward the waterfront. I kept careful watch on the screens, wondering what awaited us that way.

He must have seen me looking at the map and made an off-hand gesture. "It's not on the screen," he said, nodding. "I got word of something last night just before heading home."

"A tip?" I asked, getting my visor back out, "What kind of tip?"

He replied with an eerie smirk, "The kind of tip that gives me a chance to run you through the courses."

"Oh joy," I said sarcastically, "the courses."

'The courses' was Lucian's code for 'we're probably getting shot at'. Every night I've heard the term required a trip to the doctor. So, of course, as we started crossing the Spokane Street causeway, traveling through the shadows of the Jeanette Williams Bridge, I remembered mention of protests on Harbor Island and started to feel some dread.

The island's had a lot of purposes over the years. Companies used the land for ship building, smelting, storage and a laboratory or two. In the last few decades there was a tendency for homeless people to use the place as "beach front property". But rarely did you hear of Alters straying that way.

It was only recently that a company on the island got the bright idea of creating a graveyard shift. A shift staffed by people who wouldn't demand extra benefits for working after midnight, or even complain about the late hours, would have doubled productivity without drawbacks. That is, unless you count pissing off the local unions as a drawback.

But the protest wasn't because these new employees were non-union and breaking up the benefits – they could have been unionized at any time. The thing that usually infuriates people is that they're "inhuman". Since the day Alters went public, over 75% of active Alters have lost at least one job because of something to do with what they are. From there it breaks down into four neat little subcategories: relocation, light sensitivity, discrimination and "other".

I've always been of the opinion that "other" was a nice word for "ran for their lives".

These people had been organizing for weeks before that rainy night. We could see them from quite a ways, standing shoulder-to-shoulder with their umbrellas and their soggy signs as they carried on despite the cold. Though the group looked like a giant brick of waterlogged fabric, they sounded ready to riot. From under the wet canopy of umbrellas we could hear the crowd chanting, "Jobs for humans, not for Fangs!"

They filled the air with their indignant cries. I could hear it all the way back from the causeway over the steady beat of rain against the glass and the hum of the car. As we rode up to them it gave way to a single voice that rose above the rest.

We pulled up silently between the warehouses and approached from behind. The man on stage, a rounded, balding fellow that seemed vaguely like someone I'd seen before, stood there screaming hateful things through a megaphone. It was hard to tell what he was saying with the crowd roaring to life every time he finished a sentence. But, given the chant I'd heard before he started talking, I wasn't encouraged that he had something inspiring to say.

They were too busy screaming like idiots to notice us as we rolled in. Lucian blared the sirens to give them a shock. All of a sudden, the once unruly crowd opened up like the Red Sea and allowed us to coast through. The few who stayed close to the car beat on our windows while we calmly rode by, the rest migrating away as though they'd started to fear the backlash.

But it didn't faze the man on stage, a fellow with no apparent respect for our unorthodox lights. It just made him scream louder while his blood pressure visibly rose. His eyes were practically ready to pop from the back of his head, his face turning a shade of red the visor reserved for the mentally disturbed, and he screamed, "Here comes the long arm of the *Fang law*!"

I grimaced at the phrase and looked to see what Lucian intended to do from there. I only saw the back of his head as he climbed out of the car right into the lion's den. A thunderous roar rose from the crowd as the man continued to scream through his megaphone, "And here's the Fang!"

They sounded like a group of chimps surrounding the ever-calm Lucian. From my position in the car, it was like looking at a zoo behind glass. But Lucian took it in stride as he walked ahead, acting without a moment of doubt, beckoning me to join him without a word.

So I did.

The man watched me get out and bellowed, "And his Fang-bitch!"

Instantly, I knew where we stood with this man. It was one thing to use Fang in a chant: it was short and rolled off the tongue like any good slur. But yelling it like that, three times, there was no question we encountered someone who would've picked up a pitchfork and a torch in another age. It made me feel better about the idea we were stomping all over his little demonstration.

Sure, I'd known there'd be a few of them by the nature of their protest. But it's hard to identify whether it's part of the rhetoric, mob mentality or personal character until someone's screaming the right words with such conviction. The Fangtowns may try to embrace the labels, try to take some of the power away, but it's just a defense - a scab over a wound that hasn't quite healed. After all, we were standing in front of a man willing to scream at a tall, silently pissed off Vampire.

I waited for an explosion that never came as Lucian merely smiled. It was a strange smile, not showing his teeth and yet being too broad to be a simple smirk. It was like he was trying to stifle back powerful laughter and yet not making a sound. In fact, I could see more activity in his aura than I could in his body-language as he stood almost perfectly still with that strange grin.

It bothered our bald, screaming friend almost as much as it disturbed me. Voice straining, he shouted one last time, "You have no jurisdiction here!"

He was right, we had no reason to break it up and the US laws have always sided with the right to protest. We were just rattling our sabers to let them know that we were watching. They knew that as well as we did and started to smirk right back at us, mocking the fact we were even standing there in the rain with them. But Lucian knew what to say and, like the news had been pointing out, it never really stopped us before.

In the calmest, eeriest tone I imagine they've ever heard, he spoke loud enough to hear over their own chuckles and the rolling rain, "One, you're protesting about Alters, so it's within our rights to make sure you don't do anything stupid. Two, there's Alters in the crowd, so we have to make sure you don't turn on each other."

The crowd fell silent under the sound of the rain, the river and the sea. A quiet, uneasy murmur rose among them. It didn't take long before one of them cried foul from the back of the group and the ringleader tried to scream us down again. Unfazed, Lucian raised a hand to wave off their objections and turned to me with a question.

"What do you think?" he asked. "Dwarf?"

I had no clue what his angle was at first. Looking at the faces around us, though, I realized his motive: divide and conquer.

"Well, he's short, broad shouldered and has stubby fingers," I said, gesturing at the loudest man before trailing off.

"But?" Lucian interjected.

"Well," I continued, crossing my arms to try to look even the slightest bit more confident, "while the nose says Dwarf, the eyes tell me Leprechaun. Notice the way they're sparkling like emeralds in the dark."

The crowd found new life after that little accusation. They roared and balked at the idea that one of their own wasn't "one of their own". But the reaction of the bald man – that was the best of all.

I don't know if you've ever made someone so angry that they lost the ability to speak coherently for a while. It was awkward but amusing to watch the man stutter over himself as he seethed. If the red aura coming off him was heat, the rain would have rolled off in clouds of steam.

"How dare you?" he finally screamed at us, "I'm a good Christian man! I'm not one of those monsters!"

I nearly burst out laughing. I couldn't tell you the number of people I met who believed the stories of Alters and holy ground. Never mind that genealogy studies show that three of the last seven popes were Alters. If that doesn't prove crosses and funny hats don't do anything to them, nothing will.

Lucian, a Catholic himself by some accounts, ignored the silly comment and snapped right back at him, "So you've been tested?"

The bluster and rage faded away from the man's face as he stammered, "W-well, no."

"Have any of you been tested?" Lucian cried out to the crowd. "If you haven't, you might be protesting yourself."

It didn't sway them much, an angry growl swelling under hushed voices. Still, Lucian was undeterred by the sound of the pack sizing him up. "If you're going to do it, we're going to need to check all of you to see who is and isn't in our jurisdiction."

Following a cue I was never given, I grabbed a blood monitor from a pocket and raised it for the others to see. It was too good to pass up. Looking at me, he gave an approving nod and pointed my way. "Just present yourselves to Devotee Leone and let us get this sorted."

A voice rose to protest, "Testing us like that is a violation of our rights! You can't do that!"

"Unfortunately," Lucian replied to the confused faces of the crowd, "I'm legally required to."

All of a sudden, that riled crowd became a timid brood of chickens. I lifted the monitor and waved it around like a crucifix in an old movie. It was like we'd asked them if they had an STD and offered a free public screening for everyone. For all of their boisterous attitudes they became gun-shy awfully fast.

The crowd started to thin and move away. Lucian had played some half-truths and assumptions in our favor and used that "one in four" chance to turn the crowd around. I wondered as I watched them if that might have been my lesson for the night.

"Well," I said with a touch of hope, "that was interesting."

But Lucian looked at me, smiled and replied, "That wasn't even what we came here for."

Chapter 3
Nasty Giants

Sitting in the dark, watching the new workers pile in, it was hard not to think about why Lucian would break up the protest. A lot of personal reasons came to mind off the top of my head but none that felt quite right. Lucian's usually had a reason beyond being petty. It was more important that we maintained balance and supported the local laws in the long run. So I found myself wondering why exactly I'd just helped scare off a screaming bald man and his minions.

I wouldn't have my answer for another few hours. After the workers reported for their shift, Lucian took our car to the far end of the island and shut it down. Our lights, all the identifying digital markers and everything that could be used to spot the car were off, leaving us sitting silently in the dark. We'd gone into stake-out mode.

Stake outs have never been enjoyable to me. They've always been like an endless mind-numbing road-trip. You sit in a car for hours on end but there's no listening to the radio, no new scenery and no bathroom breaks. Instead, it was just me, the sound of the rain and a Vampire humming show tunes for three hours. By the time he'd gone over "Seasons of Love" for the third time I was slowly fashioning my coffee cup into a sharp spike. I wasn't sure what I was going to do with it, but whatever it was I was probably going to do it five hundred twenty-five thousand six hundred times.

I was only stopped by a glimmer in the dark – one of the warehouses, a run-down, abandoned hole, was suddenly busy with activity. Something was going on that wasn't supposed to in a building that hadn't been used for some time. Before I could even ask, Lucian was out of the car and on his way. I followed his cue and climbed out after him.

We crept through the shadows to avoid being spotted by the people gathering inside the old crumbling heap. The constant drizzle didn't do much to stop us from seeing the auras from a distance as we weaved through the darkness. They were mostly blue, either Alters wanting to avoid detection or possibly regular humans. I couldn't be sure at that distance, but it made me wonder about our jurisdiction again.

"Is this ours?" I asked quietly, peering around a corner at the people marching through.

Lucian glanced my way and whispered confidently, "I'm sure of it."

I was ready to protest, opening my mouth to question him again. He silenced me by pointing at the doormen of the little gathering. Standing there at the warehouse was a pair of tall, muscular men with the auras of Werewolves.

I shut up and followed him around the edges, the dark shades of our uniforms blending with the stormy night. Around the back of the building we scaled crates as quietly as possible and peered through one of the old dirty windows.

It was strange and confusing at first. The crowd of at least a hundred people, both human and Alter side-by-side, encircled the entire building. Gazing over them, I saw the old familiar sight of a cage erected in the center of the room.

Seeing it brought me back to what seemed like another lifetime. The smell of blood and sweat washed over me, memories of tape wrapped tightly around my fists, the sound of people rattling the chain-link fence we'd used as a cage. These people were there for the same thing I was all those years ago.

They were there for a fight.

Lucian nodded, stroking his fingers along the side of his badge as the center lit up. It linked with the Oracle and placed a mark on the map signaling to the rest that we'd found something. Whispering to the badge, he filled them in on the details as the Oracle started to sweep the area and signal for backup.

I wasn't listening very closely just then, instead watching the situation and wondering just what exactly he expected to see here. The audience was technically our problem, but the best we could get them on would be a few misdemeanors that hardly seemed worth the trouble of removing baldy and the gang. I'd help bust up Werewolf "dog fights" under my previous lancer and the audience usually made it ten times worse for half the gain. Watching the fight was criminal mischief but hardly the big score of engaging in organized crime and aggravated assault. For a moment, I even doubted the tip really paid off. But then I saw the fighters…or at least the reaction to them.

The audience cheered and parted to let the men through. I couldn't see what they were looking at, just an aura through my visor that told me it was huge. Blood pressures rose rapidly in waves through the crowd as hearts started to race and hormones ran wild.

When I finally saw the reason behind our visit I could only say one thing: "Holy shit."

Once, I'd been a fighter myself, before Lucian recruited me. But not once had I ever run into what was walking to the cage just then. They were Giants. Not the Giants you'd picture in a fairy tale. No, these were ten foot tall, seven hundred pound modern day Neanderthals wearing crude boxing gloves made of old towels and duct-tape. And Lucian apparently thought we should try to arrest them.

This seemed like a silly idea to me.

For their part, they didn't seem to be pleased to be part of a sideshow. But strange Alters have rarely had it easy. Latent Alters occasionally emerge through diseases and quirks of the human body like acromegaly, gigantism, porphyria and a slew of other genetic hiccups. So they end up in sideshows, professional sports, street fights and acting. Great heroes like Andre the Giant paved the way for these two guys to beat the hell out of each other in front of a roaring crowd. And, sadly, I imagine they thought this kind of thing would actually go somewhere – I know I used to.

Instead, we would only see two people with aspirations for the lime light beat each other senseless. But these guys, they were way outside of my weight-class, they were a class all of their own. And now, while slightly smaller giants of the past got to have fake fights, these guys were getting ready to legitimately bludgeon each other with the clubs they called fists.

A makeshift bell rang and two massive men charged across the buckling platform. Their fists smashed into each other with sickening crunches over the bloodthirsty roar of the crowd below.

I watched on conflicted as the two sides of me debated the situation at hand. One side figured Lucian wanted to give us an advantage. It'd be easier when we had backup and one of those giant men was out cold. But the other side wondered if it was ethical to let these guys pound each other to spare my ass a whuppin'.

Watching their faces distort under each other's fists helped settle the debate. I ran my tongue across bridgework where natural teeth had once been to remind myself of how it felt. For that moment, it seemed best to let wisdom preside over morality. At least, I called it "wisdom" at the time.

"I'm not getting in there yet," Lucian commented, echoing my sentiments.

The fight lasted a few rounds despite its ferocity. Giants, true giants, are very dense and constantly healing under the stresses of that much weight on a human frame. It was to be expected that they could take that kind of punishment but shocking to actually watch it happen. I'd seen men fall to pieces under a fraction of the abuse…yet here they were, standing tall.

As the fight continued, ACTF vans approached in stealth, only producing faint UV pulses for our visors to pick up. They flashed in sequence to identify themselves, shining across our visors like signs floating over their heads. Those signs, however, weren't very promising.

Three vans of clerics, rookies, green as they could possibly be, stuck in groups called lances so that their large numbers could compensate for their inexperience. Clerics are the last guys you'd send to handle a giant crowd… or a crowd with Giants. Every lance had a lancer, thus the name, but it was five rookies to a lancer: a total of eighteen people with fifteen of those having no clue what they were doing. The Oracles must have figured crowd control was a good training exercise. And sure, it may have been good experience, but it meant Lucian and I had to handle the heavy lifting.

"You handle the loser," Lucian said calmly, hopping down from the crates, "I'll take the one still standing."

Nodding, I followed him and ran a finger along the contact strip of my left glove. The normally black gloves and boots shifted rapidly as nanites across the surface flipped around, exposing the opposite face. In an instant, my protective gear was silver plated offensive gear. It's like spraying mace on my

35

knuckles for most Alters, probably fighting a little dirty. But I knew I'd need the edge after seeing the nature of our reinforcements.

The vans caught the attention of the guards as Lucian and I moved in, silently taking them out with a few well-placed blows. Though Werewolves have higher endurance, they're easier to drop before they start to change. This was fortunate, given the train-wreck unfolding back at the vans. The clerics clambered out with about as much grace as a herd of drunken elephants before running down the block of warehouses mostly unprepared.

Even from where I was standing, I could see that only half of them had switched on the silvers and fewer were wearing their visors. Silently, I signaled them by swiping two fingers across my eyes before clenching my fist – a gesture we have for "visors up, silvers on". A couple of them reached for their field manuals while the others stared on blankly.

My optimism after talking to Janice was fading: this was going to be a very long night.

Lucian spotted the same thing I did as he came back from securing the guards behind the building. He palmed his face and grunted "FNGs" while their lancers did their best to straighten them out. They were the freshest of the bunch and obviously only days out of the academy. If we were going to make it work we were going to need to approach it differently.

The warehouse had one exit as far as I knew, so there was a chance we could do it even with a pack of raw clerics. All we needed to do was catch them off guard and bottleneck them into the right place. Memories of my previous lancer's orders when I was a cleric seeped back into my brain.

"Lucian," I said, "I think we can Halo it."

He looked at me for a moment then laughed. "Yes, I don't suppose even the rookies should be able to blunder that."

I wondered for a moment why he paused and laughed the way he did. But, having his approval, I went to the men we'd dropped around back. Kneeling by the one that seemed the most coherent, I realized on examination it was the one I'd punched. His broad cheekbones and heavy brow, along with the red rash rapidly spreading across his face, confirmed he was a Werewolf.

He wasn't very alert, but he was definitely more so than the one Lucian had knocked into next week.

Making sure his gag was secure, I backhanded the hell out of him. He yelped, jolted up, and glared with a burning hatred as a new rash formed across the opposite cheek.

I greeted that glare with a nod and a smile, "Good morning starshine."

He growled and tried to kick me – obviously not a musical fan.

"Look," I said after pushing away the half-assed kick, "you've got two options here. You can go furry on me and we can get into a pissing contest that probably ends in me shooting you. Or you can tell me how many guards are walking around inside that building."

Golden eyes related to me a desire to avoid being shot. They stared on as I held up fingers until eventually he gave me a nod when I got to six.

"Including you two?"

He nodded again, rash starting to swell from the silver tap across his face, and I signaled to Lucian with a circling motion by my head. The signal was relayed down the chain through the other lancers: our plan for a "Halo" was on.

The Halo is an Alter-proof crime-scene tape. The bastard child of mace and a spike-strip, they would keep anything remotely unusual from crossing unchecked. That is, of course, if the clerics could find them.

They fumbled around in their equipment and gave each other blank looks like they were hoping the next guy knew what to do. At a certain point someone did, usually the rightfully pissed off lancer at the end of the line.

We left it in the lancers' hands, returning to the back of the warehouse as the roar of the crowd continued. The Giants were listlessly shuffling around by then, glazed looks in their eyes. They were punch drunk and winded, losing stamina and the will to fight with every blow. It was only a matter of time before one of them keeled over.

I reached behind my belt and waited for that moment, heart starting to race, while counting heads to see just where the guards were. Everyone was on their feet, screaming their heads off, except for the isolated ugly guys staring on stoically for any signs of trouble. I found three of them easily, but one wasn't sticking out like the rest. With three fingers I gestured to Lucian and pointed out the guards I could see, hoping he could spot the fourth.

He held up four fingers, waving to the last one by pointing out the "official" for the fight was wearing the same black shirt as the rest. Whoever was running the fight was too cheap to even pay someone to declare a winner and keep it civil. Though, being armed in this sort of fight probably couldn't hurt. I guess it all balanced out in a strange way.

Just after spotting the fourth, it came: a punch that split the air with a crack as it landed. A hush fell over the crowd again as one of the men started to fall, eyes rolling back into his head and his aura going black like someone hit a light switch. The platform groaned and cracked while the man dropped and the cage shook. It continued to creak as the cage rattled and the supports settled into the form a half-ton mass forced it to take. Silence gave way to murmuring that built to cheers and jeers from the crowd as they rose to their feet one last time.

"Damn," Lucian muttered. "I was kind of rooting for the other."

I chuckled and pulled a device from my back. "Throwing a banshee."

As I prepared the device with a twist and got ready to chuck it, Lucian put in a pair of earplugs and braced himself. Banshees, beautiful little tools, are specifically built for riot control and disorientation. Ultrasonic frequencies and a good shockwave are a great way of clearing out anyone with a pair of ears. More importantly, anyone with better than human hearing feels like they're being put through a blender. And, on top of that, there's a mild boom when they first go off.

No one looked up at the sound of a breaking window drowned out by the noise of the crowd. It wasn't until the silver rod hit the platform, bouncing lightly across the cage, that anyone even noticed it was there. Most of the humans glanced toward the window, oblivious of what was coming. The Alters, however, recognized it and ran like hell. The humans fell into two groups at that point, people run over in the stampede or people who joined it without knowing what the hell was going on. Not that it took long for the blanks to fill in.

The rod split open, a glowing blue core blasting out the sound of something like a screaming firework trapped in the room with them. Full disclosure: the "mild boom" shattered the rest of the windows. Not that anyone would have noticed the windows with the rod soon shifting to the sound of children screaming through megaphones while scraping a thousand chalk boards with industrial wire brushes.

I love Banshees: they're like the Fourth of July without the risk of dismemberment.

We jumped through the windows, pulling our side-arms, The Helios PPG, as the crowd stampeded for the doors. With a few quick, quiet pops, bolts of light shot across the room into the knees of a guard. He screamed, wounds glowing with a violet light that faded as he collapsed to the floor.

Thanks to being mostly an energy weapon, the Helios has a setting for situations like this: "crowd control". Tracking every shot we take, the gun fires stun-scale shots first and ramps up if it's clear we need stopping power. But even in "crowd control" the cocktail of charged chemicals and the UV light was like shooting a flesh-searing ball of toxins into his kneecaps. The heat, combined with the allergens in the bolt, left nasty little wounds he clutched while rolling around in agony. It would heal, eventually, but he wasn't going to be happy in the meantime.

The rest heard his howls and saw the tell-tale light, running to intercept us. But if the Halo was going to work I needed to follow the crowd. Holstering the gun and taking off, I dashed through the warehouse, vaulting over a few of the straggling humans. Rushing the door, I whipped out a strip from my belt.

One of the guards caught sight of this. He took aim from across the room with a 9mm I barely saw. Luckily, the visor saw a lot more than I did, highlighting his aggressive intent with a blood red that told me to get the hell out of the way.

He fired a shot as I hit the deck and rolled to get clear, pulling my gun to fire back. But as I leveled it his way he was already lining the next shot. Quick blue bolts struck his shoulder and ribs as Lucian picked him off for me.

With a sigh of relief we exchanged a quick nod from across the frantic room and I returned to the door.

Outside the clerics had done exactly what they were supposed to do. The crowd herded right into a wall of light rising from a ring of strips. As expected, humans were getting through with no problem, running right into the waiting arms of officers past the strip. I threw down mine in the meantime, kneeling and turning it on at the door, completing the circle and preventing anyone from backtracking into the warehouse.

Gunfire continued as Lucian tried to drop the last guard, who'd crouched behind the benches to cover himself. Lucian was so focused he didn't even notice the ten foot tall fighter charging at him. Shooting at the guard myself, I bought Lucian a moment and shouted to him, "Paul Bunyan on your ten!"

There's a funny thing about bodies that constantly regenerate: they tend to overcompensate when they're healthy. Giants are never fully healthy, but Vampire bodies are constantly improving themselves as much as possible. And Lucian's age meant that the next thing I saw was fully expected.

With a deft movement he went low to the floor, taking a knee and flipping the half-ton man over his head with a shoulder block to the shin. It was like the guy got clipped by a boulder while running downhill.

Even though I know how it worked, it never failed to impress.

The other lancers radioed in and let us know that it was all contained outside. They called a team of porters, our prisoner transport specialists, to start cleaning it up. Lucian let me respond to it while he stood over the Giant with the gun leveled at his face.

"Looks like we're good," I replied. "Though we're going to need ambulances for the four wounded in here."

A light groan emerged from the loser of the fight, reminding me he was there. I studied him for a moment, taking in the sheer size of him from much closer than before, musing, "And maybe a forklift."

Lucian chuckled. "Perhaps a crane if we can find one?"

Though it was a joke, I seriously considered it. Who doesn't want to swing a Giant out of a building with a crane, after all? Unfortunately, I had to decline.

Things started to calm and Lucian managed to restrain the other fighter. He used a set of ties since there was no way we could get cuffs on the man. Approaching my own, I looked him over again and wondered how we could even try to move him without the heavy equipment we joked about. But what troubled me most was a metallic patch lying on the floor next to him.

It had fallen off of the big man when he hit the floor, his arm smudged with silver, surrounded by a bright red contact rash. The arm, if not his whole body, was now noticeably twitching. I'd seen the effect before and recognized it from bad memories. But I had to see one last thing before I could confirm my suspicions.

Taking out my flashlight, I opened his eyelid as much as I could and shined it into a completely dilated pupil. Shining back at me was an eerily reflective silver where the retina should have been. Reflective eyes like a cat or other creatures of the night are common in nocturnal Alters, but Giants weren't nocturnal and they'd never reflect silver even if they were.

Only one thing could have caused it, and even saying the name gave me a chill: "alchemist blue".

Hermasin, alchemist blue, is an Alter brewed synthetic drug. Addictive as hell with an incredible high but an even worse crash – everyone I'd ever seen use it insisted it made them stronger. It provides a range of effects that make it desirable for athletes and junkies alike. And as I looked at the crap on the floor I wondered which group the fighter fell in. Was he taking it to boost his physical abilities or just taking it to get his next fix?

Given past experiences, I realized that line was pretty thin.

Cursing under my breath and standing, I looked around the room for more, hoping to find nothing. But my hopes were quickly dashed as I spotted a tiny glint of silver under one of the stands. It sat there, mocking me, laughing at me as it oozed off another discarded patch, seeping into the cracks of the floor around it.

One thing I knew as I kneeled by the stands was, even if the fighter took it to get an edge, a second patch meant that his supplier was probably in the warehouse. It looked used, probably ripped off while running so the clerics wouldn't have noticed it. Knowing how green they were, if they had seen it they wouldn't have known what it was anyway. So I made my way for the door hoping to catch someone with silver eyes and pockets full of poison.

But the third year is the year where a lot of agents do something remarkably stupid. I was knowledgeable, prepared and alert for the most part. But I hit the danger zone: I was comfortable in this environment – too comfortable. I had come up with a solution, cleared the room, helped my lancer and discovered drug use in the crowd. But my head wasn't where it should have been: I took my eyes off the big man.

"Nathaniel," Lucian yelled, "behind you!"

But it was too late. I turned and saw the big man, amped on the blue and up for round two, making a beeline for me. I reached for my gun but couldn't have pulled it out before he was right on top of me.

Being punched by a Giant is like standing in front of a wrecking ball that doesn't like you. I remember getting out "oh shi-", before everything went grey and I exhaled as if a truck had parked on my chest. When my vision cleared I was a foot off the ground, blowing a hole through the warehouse wall. I tumbled across the pavement outside, my visor continuing on, without me, for a good twenty feet.

Dazed and confused, I did my best to stagger to my feet while my lungs burned, trying to catch my breath. Everything was fuzzy and my head felt like I'd spun in circles until I couldn't do it anymore. The sound of a screaming Giant and the rapid pulses of Helios guns going off were a distant echo through a long tunnel. Had I been a little clearer I would have been helping the others with it. But, as I stood, my legs felt like they had separated from my body and melted like butter under me.

It was as I stared into the sky, wishing someone would make the buzzing stop, that the behemoth walked over me with a hateful look in his corrupted silver eyes. The blue had made him resistant to pain. He was harder to drop even as they pumped him full of UV phosphors, silver nitrate, allium extracts and whatever else was peppered into the bolts. Getting pummeled, he simply shrugged off the burning holes in his back as if they were mosquito bites.

My gun was out, as much good as it did me before the punch, and I did the only thing I could do. Lifting it towards him, I aimed for the center of the three I was seeing and shot for the one thing I could make out: those shining eyes.

He grunted as the blast passed through his eye and into his skull cavity. A ghostly light shone faintly through his ears and nostrils. Still looming above me, he let out one last rasping breath. His remaining eye rolled back as he suddenly went limp.

I was too dazed to feel anything about what happened at the time. All I knew right then in my hazy state was that I'd shot him and all of that weight, dead weight, was now falling my way. My eyes started slipping closed as Lucian came into view, shoving that massive frame away with relative ease.

As I was coming back around, I could sense people hovering over me. A seemingly distant voice said, "He didn't break anything but I don't think he should be on patrol for the rest of the night."

Out of the darkness another voice replied, "I'll take him in to do paperwork after we're done here."

My eyes started to work again, a light shining into them. Grunting, I sat up and pushed the light away. Everything felt intact, aside from the killer headache and the feeling of being hit by a truck. I couldn't tell you how long I was out, but I was in one of the ambulances now as clerics outside looked surprised I woke up.

And one of the geniuses asked, "Did it hurt?"

Staring at these beautiful minds, I wondered if I'd been that dense only a couple years ago. And, staring right back at me, they still waited for an answer to that question. I shook my head and climbed out of the ambulance without saying a word, limping back to the warehouse I flew out of.

Lucian chased me down, grabbing my arm with a firm, inescapable grip. I met his stern, authoritative gaze as he said, "We're going back to the headquarters. Let the others handle the warehouse."

I knew any answer but "yes sir" was reason for him to throttle me. So I took the smart road and staggered back with him

43

to the car. As we passed the building I stopped to look at the aftermath and assess what happened.

The hole in the wall was at least 12 feet high, the metal peeled away from the building like a banana peel and trampled. Some feet away, the body was covered in a tarp collected from one of the other warehouses.

The large mound that used to be a man caught my attention and I remembered the look in his eyes before I fired. I'd shot people before, but never from so close. It was a strange, hollow feeling to have actually seen the expression he had as it hit him. I couldn't help but wonder if he'd be alive if I hadn't been looking away.

Lucian patted me on the back. "He would have killed you with the first punch if it wasn't for the coat. That didn't leave you much of a choice."

And I knew he was right. But it didn't help to calm me any as I thought about how close it all came. My personal feelings about alchemist blue had made me sloppy and it was enough to cost this guy his life. I knew it was him or me but I don't think it had to be that way.

Lucian, watching me, turned for the car and said off-handedly, "But I'm sure you'll never make that mistake again."

Chapter 4
Afraid of Elves

Watching the world roll by my window, I could only think of that man lying on the cold, damp ground as investigators studied the last minutes of his life. Would they find more drugs or evidence of a dealer? More importantly: would they find that I could have prevented what happened?

I didn't know what had already been found. I couldn't have known. But I couldn't shake the weight of it. The only one who had any answers was the man sitting next to me. And Lucian said nothing as he quietly navigated the glowing streets of Fangtown.

In my altered state, under the hazy rain, the cityscape was haunting. Dazed, confused and guilt ridden, I could see layers to the city that hadn't been there before. I watched as Alter children ran down the sidewalk, covering their heads from the rain. Sometimes, I think, I forgot they had children too.

"You shouldn't do that," Lucian murmured. "Hate yourself, I mean."

"But," I hesitated, staring at the strange children skipping through the water, "I screwed up."

"That you did," he replied as we came to a stoplight. "But I saw the patch too. I know why you were distracted. Everyone out there has been caught off-guard before."

I looked out and watched the variance of humanity strolling by through the crosswalk. As different as they were, they were all fairly similar in the way they moved as they tried to avoid raindrops and cars. Beneath the fur, fangs and fins they were just like each other – and probably just like me. He was right. Everyone could have made the same mistake I had.

"And everyone in here?"

He chuckled as the light turned green. "Of course not, I'm perfect."

Sometimes, I hate that man.

We didn't take long to pass through Fangtown to the station. Officially, the headquarters is located in the International District, across the street from Kobe Terrace Park on South Main

Street. But the Fangtown residents have a different name for the station's little corner of the world: "The Garden". It isn't hard to see why.

A black tulip-like complex of tinted glass and black lights rose against the backdrop of Kobe Terrace. The lights inside, shining through the dark, mirrored windows, gave the appearance of small points of light across the surface. Between the "petals", an eerie black light rose to the sky. From a distance it's as though it were a cursed, unholy flower.

Designed to be a fortress within the city, no flat surfaces were left for someone to scale or land on. No spaces were to be unprotected, a hostile field of ultraviolet light and gas jets exist between the tightly layered buildings. Everything was meant to avoid losing control without scaring the "normal" people.

In the daylight it has a much more welcoming appearance. But to the people who had seen it like this, in this light, it has an apt nickname: Hell's Tulip.

People buzzed all around "Hell's Tulip" at that hour, making it the busiest location in the city after midnight that wasn't a bar or court house. Either they were coming in through the front entrance to file a report or driving into the underground parking structures to bail out their friends. But, for whatever reason they were there, it became a world unto itself. And a little less than half an hour after I climbed out of the ambulance, we joined that bustling activity.

We pulled into the west end of the underground complex, where we bury our little secrets and prisoners, and into a parking structure that straddles 7th Avenue South. The west end, reserved for patrol vehicles, was mostly empty at that time of night. Everyone was gone, patrolling the streets, where we would have been had I not been throttled by stupidity and the jolly drugged giant.

We parked close to the agents-only entrance on the bottom level. Lucian climbed out of the car and walked off as I stared vacantly into the dim lights of the Oracle displays.

The pain had finally caught up to me – that first burst of shock and adrenaline fading, the full weight of the impact settling into my chest and everything else that hit the pavement. It was a bit like waking up the next morning after a really rough time in the gym. I hadn't felt this bad since my days in the cage, and I couldn't decide if it was more like trying to get back in shape or recovering from a loss. Either way, my ass hurt and I didn't quite want to stand up yet.

"You look like shit," Lucian muttered from above, having come back when he noticed I wasn't moving. "Perhaps you should visit the doctor."

Pathetically, I looked up at him. "I think I'm okay, but my ass is starting to hurt and I don't think I can walk without a limp."

Softly chuckling, Lucian shook his head and replied, "Then you will limp and no one will judge."

Looking at the entrance, considering that judgment, the image of a single face crossed my mind. "*She's* in there."

He laughed, the bastard, and rested a hand on my head as if I were a child.

"She's not that intimidating," he said. "Besides, she's probably heard everything about it anyway. Suck it up and move your ass."

Impressed by Lucian's sympathy, or lack there-of, I made the effort to move with a grimace and a sigh. My hip was a bit stiff and had a warm, dull pain radiating through it as I straightened my legs. It reminded me of one thing the uniform lacked: padded pants for when your ass literally bounces off the pavement. Maybe someday the R&D would take suggestions. But in the meantime I had to accept the minor limp I was going to have for the rest of the night.

The control panel on the entrance lit up and synchronized with our badges. Lucian pulled off a glove and placed his palm on the panel to identify himself. The computer cross-referenced his hand against the badge and lit up with little confirmation signs, displaying his name and a photo where he obviously posed too much for the camera. Though you'd be forgiven for thinking no photos existed of the man, the inability to show up on photos has long been disproven by many a narcissistic Vampire.

It seems a bit redundant to some that we use the badges and a hand scan to get in, but the concept is pretty sound in my opinion. The way I see it, someone could easily steal a badge but if they have your hand they deserve to get in on dedication alone.

Don't repeat that to anyone else in the force and, if you do, don't tell them who said it.

The scanner ionized after the match was confirmed, burning away any residue that would leave a palm print on the thing. The doors opened and we heard the same haunting voice that greets everyone as it cheerfully announced, "Welcome back Lancer Descartes and Devotee Leone. We are happy to see you return safely."

I never had a good grasp on who the "we" represented in that statement. Did it mean that the cameras were being monitored or was it just a general statement from the organization? Either way, it always made me a little nervous to hear the voice's surprise that we hadn't been dismembered or something. And I couldn't help but notice that the cheerful voice didn't seem to recognize that I'd been beaten senseless. So obviously it was either pre-recorded or the people behind it had a very generous definition of "safe return" I didn't quite share.

Regardless, the next voice we'd hear wouldn't be so oblivious. In fact, I figured it'd torment me for my fate. Even after all the redundancy for automated security, there's still a doorman operating an elevator with no buttons inside. Our security engineers were obviously Alters, driven by a level of OCD hard to find anywhere else.

I imagine the doorman position is a relatively comfortable and boring task for whoever is stuck doing it. I've yet to meet the doorman and have recently come to the assumption that either he, the front door, or both were handled by the Oracle System. Though it made me wonder, as we stepped into the elevator this mysterious watchman controls, just why the Oracles would choose a goofy old-man voice for that particular task. Maybe they were feeling nostalgia for that little doorman in the Wizard of Oz.

"Nate! Your flight came in," the warm, goofy voice chuckled. "Welcome back to terra firma."

Oracles are rarely so annoying, which was evidence the man was real. Still, you could never be sure since there was no face to his disembodied voice and I had no idea where he'd be watching from. Wherever the voice was coming from, I glared into the camera with the sourest look I could muster, hoping the entity on the other side would take the cue to back off. But there was no response aside from Lucian's chuckle.

"See," he said, amused, "news travels quickly and gossip travels even faster."

He was right, of course. The lift operator wasn't the only one waiting for us. The guards posted at the other end of the elevator applauded as I passed by without a word. I could hear Lucian apologizing for my lack of humor through the light laughter everyone exchanged. I didn't care if I looked rude as I hoped to maintain what little dignity I could while limping my way through the doors. All I wanted to do was find a desk to hide behind for the rest of the night. Maybe I'd even get a couple ice packs to sit on if I could do it quietly. I was just hoping there wasn't going to be another row of fans awaiting my arrival.

Luckily, they weren't on the other side as I opened the door. Unfortunately, *she* was.

Standing there was the tall, slender, yet curvy figure of an Elf named Dulaf. Sporting a short black skirt and combat boots, she was completely out of uniform. Yet with that she also had the lab coat to show she was part of our science division, a paradox I could never quite figure out. Despite an only half-serious appearance, she's the head of our lab's dayshift and a resident of the Tulip's sanctuary levels. Making me miserable is just her hobby.

"I've got a gift for you," she announced in a sing-song tone, grinning from ear to ear, producing a copy of Jack and the Beanstalk from behind her back. "It's a survival guide!"

I dryly faked a laugh and took the book from her, limping along to the office spaces. She followed with that cat-like grin on her face, a delighted tone to her voice. "It's the story of an idiot who got duped into meeting with a giant and making a complete ass of himself."

Normally, a guy could get the idea that people didn't like him. But I knew the group was laughing so I wouldn't be crying. It's harder to feel guilty if you're too busy being embarrassed. Regardless of their intent, I shot a look of death her way. It was a pointless gesture that she shrugged off with a smile and a flick of her ears.

Elf ears, for those who haven't seen them, are surprisingly mobile. They flex, bend and twist independently of each other – signaling emotions like the subtle motions of creatures in the wild. And her ears told me, more so than her smile, that she was incredibly amused – yet slightly cautious. She was like a cat toying with a mouse.

"Poor Nate," she giggled, "You need someone to rub something on your butt?"

I stopped long enough to respond, glaring back into her emerald eyes. "Look Dulaf, I've had a rough night and I'd like to just sit down, get some paperwork done and try to forget the whole thing ever happened."

Bad move on my part.

Encouraged by my efforts, she hugged me as tightly as possible, nuzzled and whispered in my ear, "I could help you relax."

It was a chilling statement for many reasons. First of all, she was my superior, even if we were in different divisions. Second, no matter what I answered it was assured she would use it against me. And third, while she sometimes looks like a teenage girl she's almost as old as Lucian. None of these were good for me.

All I could do was mutter, "I wish Elves were allergic to silver."

"But then," she said, playfully tugging the silver on my collar, "I wouldn't be able to touch you."

"What a loss that'd be," I said with a sigh.

There've been times I've wondered why Dulaf devoted so much energy to me. Of all the people I've worked with, she's been the most helpful and most taxing at the same time. Sure, everyone else was joking and laughing, but she'd gone out of her way to find me a book – a brand new copy from the crisp spine and clean pages. Once, I heard that she knew my ancestors and felt that she owed my family. But "owing" my family had so many meanings that it didn't really answer anything one way or another.

We made our way through the weaving tangle of corridors and randomly assorted rooms toward the inner complex. I'd been hoping she'd break off her pursuit as we passed the science division's wing. But her shift was over, we passed it, she kept following and I accepted she wasn't going to leave me alone. And Lucian, ever helpful and following from a distance, thought it was amusing and could be heard snickering in the background.

He was still getting a good laugh out of it by the time we made it to the great multi-story room we consider office space. Acting on some sort of strange sense of efficiency, the same designers who made the redundant security system also turned one large room into an office for up to thirty people at a time. The first thing you always see as you walk in, aside from the sea of desks, is the great array of monitors hanging from the ceiling.

The monitors, always on, always shining above us, give every detail we can get on Alters and crime around the world. Every time a new Alter is born, commits a crime or gets run out of town, they appear on that monitor. Sitting in the large, cavernous room in the core of the building, with the catwalks and staircases weaving around like the frame of a cage, you could almost forget the outside world if not for that constant reminder.

Not all of us were doomed to being herded together like sheep, however. Lucian broke away and headed to the kind of private office I'd get one day if I made it to lancer. But in the meantime he was abandoning me with Dulaf, her grin somehow broadening as I winced while sitting.

I don't know if she actually had anything planned or if she was cooking something up as we walked. In fact, my best guess now is that she was smiling to make me torture myself. I wouldn't have put either past her. But as I sat down, dropped the book and looked at the polished black glass surface of the desk I realized I needed to fill out a report on what happened. No matter what she might have planned, I really didn't feel like focusing on her crap at the time.

I reached for my visor and found it wasn't there. Vaguely remembering it bouncing along without me, I realized it had to be on the island. Sighing, I pulled a spare from the desk and put it on before tapping the glass to turn on the display. Across the glass the familiar abstract face of the Oracle shined in front of me before relaying the information like a hologram off of my visor. Most of what I needed for the report was already sorted for me, including the fact the Giant I shot had absorbed almost two dozen rounds before I fired. Despite that, I couldn't quite bring myself to look directly at his profile.

Dulaf watched me as I went about typing my report on the desk's touchscreen, ignoring her to the best of my ability. She must have noticed I was suddenly able to tune her out, because the grin soon faded and her ears twitched. Maybe she was wondering how I managed to stop giving a shit about people giving me a hard time. Or maybe…

"It wasn't your fault," she whispered, hugging me lightly.

The visor caught a silver aura radiating off of her, calm and almost reassuring, glowing with a soft, steady light that showed she was at peace. I looked up to see it shine around her face like a halo and thought about how unpredictable Elves could be.

"You couldn't have known he wasn't really unconscious," she continued. "How could anyone guess he took a dive?"

I shook my head and muttered, "He didn't take a dive. He was amped on blue."

"Alchemist blue?" she asked, perching on the edge of my desk, peering down at the beginnings of a report on its surface. "You're sure?"

I nodded and whispered, "No mistaking it. I'm familiar, remember?"

We stared silently, awkwardly at the screen on my desktop. I have no idea what was going through her mind at the time, but I was beginning to wallow in doubt. Despite Lucian and Dulaf's support, it was too hard to shake the thought. It weighed on me like a sin that I needed to wash away, like the blood on Lady Macbeth's hands.

But Dulaf ruffled my hair, reassuring, "If he was hopped up on that stuff there was really nothing you could have done. You know that."

"Yeah," I replied, resting my chin on my fist. "But there's still something I can do."

"And what's that?" she asked.

"Figure out how he got it," I said with a rising voice, "so it doesn't happen to anyone else."

Chapter 5
Medical Miracles

The walk to Dulaf's lab to look over the evidence wasn't pleasant. I hobbled along with a cramp that wouldn't go away while she mocked me for being too old. Given her ancient nature, that was a burn. But I made it, collapsed into a chair and vowed that I was never going to get up again. I knew from the way I felt while walking that there was really nothing severe about it aside from being horribly inconvenient. Still, my butt was happy there were soft cushions in the lab.

Despite being the dayshift supervisor, Dulaf tends to hover long after hours. For every piece of evidence that comes through our doors there is at least one person that has to take an order from her like a whipping boy. Two of those nervous men were hard at work as I idly looked around the room, spinning in that blessed chair.

They were Elves, young ones at that. You can tell the age of an Elf by the size of their ears. They never stop growing, taking a leaf shape as they continue to extend, becoming long pointed blades. These guys were new, freshly pointed and panicked at every possible instance of pissing her off as they sorted evidence. Everyone, even Elves, seems to have FNGs.

The "Fae", the more harmless class of Alter, make up a great deal of our personnel. Elves, Dwarves and Witches are all quite busy at work in forensic investigations and the department's R&D.

Most Alters are decent people that come across a physical need that makes them a bit less predictable. They may need to survive on a liquid diet, draw in warmth from other people or have a tendency to go berserk once a month. But the Fae are the ones that are physically stable, if not always emotionally.

Dwarves for instance really are stocky, hairy men with a knack for metal work. But what is often missed is the fact their talent with building stems from a severe obsession for problem solving and creation. They're workaholics to the point of never having really hidden from the world. They've always been out there, busy creating, usually showing up on TV building custom motorcycles or remodeling a house while wearing amazingly high shoe-lifts. But, if they hadn't, they likely would have gone insane from boredom.

And that's a common trait of the Fae: boredom. It's what makes Dwarves workaholics, Witches famously eccentric and Elves mischievous. So we keep them as busy as possible down in the depths of the labs.

However, people like Dulaf are prone to stray from work to look for something more entertaining and, unfortunately, they tend to find it. At least for now she was right behind me, staying focused on the matter at hand, working away in the forensics lab.

The room was about the size of a locker room, curved into an arc with a wall consisting entirely of storage cubbies for crap we've collected. And the two rookies were obviously having a hard time with this apparently complicated series of…boxes.

I say this because I watched them repeatedly put things into the wrong box. Even I, a field grunt, knew that they were making a mistake. But it wasn't my place to point it out at the time. No, that was left up to the annoyed sighing woman behind me.

Dulaf looked on at the duo fumbling around and whispered in my ear, echoing the thoughts I'd had only moments before, "fucking new guys."

With a stamp and a growl she stormed over to them and barked out, "New evidence is always in *this* section! It gets moved down the line *after* it's been processed! How many times do I have to tell you this?"

Now, I didn't know the answer myself, but I did know that there was a momentary pause where the rookies had a minor dilemma. On the one hand, you wanted to answer her question. On the other hand, answering a rhetorical question was tantamount to reminding her you were stupid.

Watching them squirm with twitching ears was comical. In fact, it almost made me feel the torturous walk was worth it. After all, they were pissing her off as she had been trying with me moments ago. It was a moment of instant karma.

They quickly begged for forgiveness before starting to point fingers at each other. But I soon started to tune out what they were saying. Looking at the container in their hands was a cold revelation that made the rest of their conversation moot.

I'd left the crime scene less than an hour before sitting in that lab. And yet, sitting there, they already had the evidence in storage. I'd lost a considerable length of time to that punch – long enough for them to give the place a once over. But how much time did I actually lose? I was suddenly afraid to look at the clock.

Dulaf joined me, breaking my trance with a hand on my shoulder as she dropped the evidence container by me. She sat it on the table and began presenting the various items within. A few baggies of materials sat in the box along with photos of the scene, complete with shots of the glorious hole I made doing a back-flip through the wall. Most of it was unimportant to me, just a painful reminder of memories far too recent.

"Any requests?" she asked, glancing my way.

To be honest, I wasn't sure what I was planning to do. I knew that if anything was going to be of help to me it was going to be on the patches – particularly the one off the Giant's arm. But how I was going to make use of them was still beyond me. Still, it'd be a start, so I painfully stood again and peered into the box with her, sifting around for that particular baggy. They weren't too deep in the box, still coated in that silvery substance and a bit of dirt from the warehouse floor.

"Do we know if all of these from the same batch?" I asked, gingerly offering them to her.

"Dunno yet," she said, snatching the baggies from my hands, hurrying to her workstation like a kid with a new toy while I sat back down and stayed out of her way. I didn't want to stray too far, for more than just the fact that walking hurt. There was a need to know if they were connected or a set of isolated incidents. If they were made together, then I had one dealer to handle. But if there was more than one dealer, then blue had come back to the city all over again.

The last time it was in the city was when I was a child. Somehow, by sheer luck or determination, the police, a few in particular, managed to stop it. Not all of them made it out of the situation untouched. In fact, very few did. The idea of having to

55

walk that same road wasn't pleasant to me and I'm sure it showed on my face.

"Leo got that look too," Dulaf mused. "He was always worrying about things beyond his control."

Leo: that was the name of the first hunter in my family line. He lived a very long time ago, though no one would tell me just how long, fearful of revealing their age. But, as my family's name was derived from him, it may as well have been an eternity. Leo to Leone must have taken a few centuries at least. But they wouldn't show all their cards to me even now that I was three years into the fold.

"So," I muttered quietly, lifting my head, "I remind you of him?"

She nodded. "He had no sense of humor either."

I almost responded to that remark before realizing it'd prove her right. All I could do was sit quietly, nod and watch her work.

Watching was a bit confusing. The process was complex and way outside of my field of study. While everyone is required to go to the same Academy for a year, once you pass the basics it all becomes extremely specialized. Dulaf went on to learn how to break down chemicals and figure out the way bullets shatter. I went on to learn how to drop a Werewolf with one punch and shoot someone from across a football field. I had no clue what the hell she was doing and had no legitimate reason beyond impatience to even be there.

Even if I could understand, I don't think I would have had the attention span for it. After keeping myself upright for a while, everything was starting to feel heavy. At first it was a few blinks, gradually keeping my eyes closed longer, before eventually everything just went black.

Your mind wanders in funny ways after a good hit to the head. There was an odd feeling as I drifted off as though someone was watching me. I don't know why I would hear him, but I swear my father was whispering to me right then. I couldn't make out what he was saying, but I felt as though it had to do with the things in the room and the names invoked.

Before I could relive the family history, a voice cut through the comfortable darkness. "You're sleeping on the job."

Dulaf hovered over me as I opened my eyes. Giggling, she patted my cheek as if I was somehow adorable for having passed out and pulled me to my feet.

"It's okay," she smiled, "I'm going to be working on this for a while. How about you go get yourself checked out in the clinic?"

I would have resisted, I did resist for a moment, but the fact her first thought was to send me to the doctor said something about how I must have looked. So I gave up and went on my way.

The corridors of the complex seemed so much longer than usual that night. Passing portraits of knights from the old order, I looked at them for the first time in a very long while. They seemed so iconic in the way they were presented, as if they were superhuman. And some really were, I reminded myself as I walked by the figure of Lucian in his heyday. He was clothed in black and gold, a saber at his side, with his hair hanging past his shoulders and a piercing glare as if he were the angriest man alive. It makes one wonder how he mellowed so entirely over the time between now and then.

There were other faces I recognized: the original agents of Seattle, Dulaf, Alexander Neumann, the founders of Argyre and others of their kind. They were all somehow important enough to be immortalized and placed with care on these walls among the trophies of conquest and memorials for those who'd otherwise be forgotten.

The memorial wall, the place most often visited by anyone, was where we put the names of those forgotten souls. A solid black slab looking like polished stone, it's covered in slightly glowing designs that change shape in a constant rotation. As you watch it, usually mesmerized by the seemingly magical form of the wall, it repeats the same sequence of markings over and over. Agents understand these markings all too well, fearing that we become part of it someday.

Scrawled in the ancient language of the Fae, these markings are the names of everyone to have died in the struggle since the beginning of the old order. The surface of the wall is made of the same material as our visors, layered so multiple streams of data pass by at once as it rotates through a seemingly endless list.

If you know the language and you look closely enough you may catch a name you recognize as it flashes by – quite literally if you touch the wall. I don't know why but I felt the need to touch it that night as I saw the gold letters of Leo's name pass. As I did, it froze in place and "rose" to the surface while the rest continued on without it, as though I'd plucked it from the list like a leaf from a mountain stream.

"Did you ever screw up like that?" I asked the wall as if I expected it to answer.

It wasn't going to, of course, and I had never seen any evidence of *real* ghosts. But I still needed to ask that question to myself at the very least. Did he, in the days of swords and horses, make the mistakes I did? Probably not the exact same ones, but maybe something similar, likely details only Lucian and Dulaf knew. Still, the thought comforted me. I released his name back into the stream and walked on, feeling a bit more confident from the simple gesture.

It wasn't much further to the clinic from there: only about two more turns through the weaving hallways before coming across the eternally smiling face of our local doctor.

"Mr. Leone," he said far too cheerfully. "How nice of you to join us, please have a seat."

Sitting down, I took off my jacket, watching the man hover around the room with his seemingly permanent grin.

"Hear about the incident?" I asked.

"Of course," he said gleefully. "Who hasn't by this point?"

He always leaves me feeling uneasy. His cheerful nature and constant smile belie his true nature. Hiding in plain sight, he's one of the most infamous breeds of Alter ever known. They were men who always seem to age gracefully with a bright personality while those around them wither away and turn into cranky, isolated bastards. We've called them many names and painted them in exaggerated caricatures. They are the Reavers or, as they're known most commonly, Reapers.

I was now sitting with the doctor of death.

The Reapers are a mysterious people, the stigma around them preventing people from looking too close. Some say they feed off the life forces of people around them. The heat and electricity of living things are supposedly absorbed and somehow converted into their own. They're often depicted as parasites without visible attachment…like someone you owe alimony. They go where they can help others recover and, if the stories are to be believed, feed off the life of those individuals. I don't know how much of it is true, but you'd be horrified to know how many doctors in your life have been latent Reapers acting on the instinct to get close to the ill.

Looking at him, it was hard to tell. The doctor looked almost more lively than the twenty-something girl acting as his nurse. For a race literally associated with death, the Reapers have just about every trait we naturally attribute to health and vitality.

He has a fair complexion and bouncy, lively hair that never seems to have a split-end or tangle in it. His teeth are perfect in every way and so white I wonder if he drinks bleach after-hours. In fact, he's the kind of pretty and perky that makes you hate his guts.

Seeing that smile on his face, watching him come at me with those needles, I couldn't help being bothered by it. Reapers got the "angel of death" reputation for a reason, constantly glowing as everyone else was on the ropes. I knew he wanted me to be healthy, because healthy is better, but it didn't help the thought of him being the Grim Reaper with a friendlier face.

"You really should relax," he remarked as I stared uneasily at his nurse taking a sample of my blood.

"Why do you need that?" I asked, watching the needle warily. "I was smashed through a wall. No mystery illness there."

His smile faded ever so slightly. "We have to check for any signs of alchemist blue," he said coldly, "to make sure you didn't absorb any."

"Never making that mistake, doctor," I muttered.

"Given your family history," he replied, smile returning to his face, "we can't be too careful, can we?"

"Yeah," I said, trailing off, "I guess you're right."

I lay back while they ran their tests and took scans of my battered body. I knew they wouldn't find what they were looking for. I'd been too cautious to have touched the patch even a moment. And I didn't think anything was broken since I was pretty sure I'd have been screaming at some point along the way. Rather, it felt like everything had been compressed.

"Looks like you came out of that pretty well," he said after taking a glance at the screens. "I think some pain medications and a dose of omega should take care of this nicely and speed you along your recovery."

I sat up quickly, shaking my head. "I don't need the omega, just give me the pills."

He sighed. "It's harmless Nathaniel; you don't need to worry about it."

Logically, he was right. But, in my opinion, I did.

Omega is probably the greatest discovery in medical history according to many doctors. Most people don't even know the origins of the stuff and happily take what's given to them. But I'm not one of those people.

The Alters, a few in particular, have a bit of need for blood. There's a wide variety of reasons: health, maintaining minions, drinking it, replacing what they lost through stigmata and many more disgusting concepts. So it didn't surprise anyone to find they had been working on perfecting a readily available supply.

Humans had been trying to figure out the inherent problems of donated blood for a long time, usually just reducing it to the components like plasma or experimenting with synthetic substitutes. Obviously, we weren't making a lot of progress. Alters, liking to think outside of the box, opted to do something a little more direct: they created the donors.

Omega's more than O-Negative and more advanced than any synthetic anyone had created so far. It was the end of low donations, supply shortages and the blood typing system.

It's also completely disgusting and kind of haunts me.

I'd seen the factories before, large tanks of blood derived from fleshy spheres connected to elaborate life support systems. Surrounded in crimson, allowed to bleed like a stuck pig, they looked like oozing apples hanging from wires. They drain these tanks from time to time and filter out anything potentially dangerous like antigens and Alter Stem Cells. It was enough to make me lose my lunch the first time I saw them.

They don't die; they just bleed eternally and continue to thrive. Their Alter based genetics are tailored to survive. And they do survive as their blood continues to replenish at an exponential rate, nutrients and oxygen pumped through their flesh. And a chemical cocktail added to the tanks, still left in the product afterwards, allowed the blood to continue to "live" and reproduce on its own.

And they wanted to put that shit in me.

Though it wasn't the disgust I had for the factories that made me reject the concept. At least, it wasn't that alone. One hit of the stuff is like becoming an Alter for a moment, the chemical cocktail and suped up blood working its way through you and making everything run that much better. You hurt less, become more alert, and everything heals just a little bit faster. It's no wonder the same knowledge and materials were used to create alchemist blue.

I could see the benefits of the stuff. But I can't stand that concept. I can't help feeling like it's too close to home. I also can't help feeling the urge to run down the streets screaming, "Soylent omega is people!"

He tried to argue with me a little longer, but it didn't happen. I took a few pills and waited for them to clear me. Lying around on the table was a pretty good break from having to do anything, anyway.

But Dulaf entered not long after that, looking over me as I was staring at the ceiling and counting the tiles. She held up a set of papers, smiled at me, grabbed my cheek and tried to pinch it off. With a yelp I sat up and swatted her hand away, snatching the papers from her.

"Your instincts were pretty right on," she said. "The results say they're definitely from the same batch of hermasin. I even found three sets of fingerprints on each patch."

We exchanged a look and I remember smiling genuinely for the first time since I'd woken up in the ambulance.

She smiled back. "But two sets are the same on both patches."

"We have a dealer," I said, almost excitedly, "and a supplier."

She nodded. "In fact, we have one of them already. He's being processed downstairs."

Up until then I'd been feeling heavy and guilty that night, talking to walls and moping at my desk. But when I heard those words I suddenly felt the weight lifted off of me. I finally knew what to do next. I was going to nail the supplier to a wall… just as soon as I stopped walking like a zombie.

Chapter 6
Emotional Process

They sent me home that night with the whispers of Lucian having to talk to the commander in the air. I wasn't sure what it meant and it scared me that I had been dismissed while my lancer was probably getting grilled for my mistakes. I wasn't really afraid of being in trouble but my gut always told me I should be in the room when it happens. I would have been completely inconsolable if it weren't for the fingerprints. Because of those, I went home with a little bit of hope and the hints of a smile on my face.

Dulaf told me she'd keep watch and let me know when the guy matching the prints was ready for questioning. It was all I could think about that day as I laid in bed and watched daytime television after my surprise nap the night before. And to settle my nerves, after the television lost my interest, I just watched the lights around the room.

The room glittered that day as I surprisingly got to see the sun and watch the light outside shine through the window. But among the sparkling lights was a beautiful but grim reminder of the night before. A brilliant blue light sparkled across the ceiling and walls, the sun shining off the exposed cores of my Helios clips. Watching them, it reminded me that I had to leave one of my clips out in the sun to recharge the energy of the shots I'd fired the night before.

The stone sparkling from the core of that clip is probably one of the greatest discoveries the Fae brought with them: Aurorastin. Just like the Drow and Metamorphs, what we call the fanged ones, the Faelish brought an unorthodox solution or two with them to problems that were important to them: sunlight, armor and killing the dangerous ones. Unfortunately, the clip sitting in the sun was a reminder I'd had to do the latter.

The world was a mess when Aurorastin first appeared. Oil reserves were being depleted, global warming was coming to a tipping point and pollution levels were reaching new heights. But then it started to filter into society: a sparkling blue gemstone that could harness solar power like nothing we'd seen before. It wasn't until years after they introduced it to us that the Alters themselves came out of hiding. But when they did, the fact they'd produced this stone was one of the reasons why people were so willing to take the ACTF's deal.

On the surface it looks like a sapphire but it's so much more than that. It revolutionized power: a nanocrystal compound that manages to tap into over ninety percent of the sun's energy and retain a thermal charge even after sunset. Suddenly getting our energy from sunlight made sense to everyone and it made a damn good lasing material for our weapons too. With a chunk of that stuff you could do just about anything, right down to killing a Giant…

It was still soothing to watch the light though, like the sun reflecting off ocean waves on a peaceful day. Somehow that was enough to put me in a good place by the time my phone rang, startling me out of my lava-lamp trance. I nearly fell out of bed scrambling for the phone, certain Dulaf was calling with the promised news.

Instead, a totally unexpected voice greeted me.

"Nathaniel," Lucian said, "we need you to come to the station."

Whatever good mood I was starting to have promptly sunk from my chest to my gut, settled into a nice pit, curled up into a fetal position and died. The earlier rumors echoed in my head as I wandered to my closet with the phone, absently confirming I was hearing Lucian as he continued to talk. And I'm sure he noticed the repetitive "yes" and "okay" response he was getting as I drifted through the room. Who knows what I was actually agreeing with.

Was I under review? Did my mistake catch the attention of the Commissioner? I could picture so many ways to be screwed as I put down the phone. I'm not even entirely sure I hung up at the time.

It didn't take long to get ready and make my way to the station. Living rather close, I didn't have to take a very long trip. But I have to admit I took longer than usual that day, ditching the usual shortcuts through the neighborhood in favor of the scenic route. Despite my best efforts, I arrived before sunset.

Headquarters should have been somewhat less intimidating in the twilight hours. The light of the setting sun reflected off the windows towards the peak like a crown of stars sitting on pointed rooftops. The green of the park wrapped around the base, refracted through the odd prism. It was as pleasant as it could possibly be while I felt like hurling.

I entered the surface doors and walked through to be greeted by the station receptionist, a seemingly human girl with a rather thick collared uniform. She stood behind a wall of bullet-proof glass decorated with the station emblems, the ACTF's crest to her left and the Cascadia-Seattle crest to her right. All the while she smiled broadly through her heavy glass shield.

In the same soft, calming voice that welcomes everyone to the entrance below, she said, "Welcome Nathaniel Leone."

I stopped to look back at that moment. Knowing what she was, who she was, the greeting disturbed me. Looking back at her, seeing her simply projected against that bullet-proof glass, knowing she wasn't actually a person, I was extremely uneasy. It wasn't because she was a hologram since I'd talked to her many times before. No, what troubled me was that she called me "Nathaniel" instead of "Devotee".

Only one thought occurred to me: *Holy crap, I've been fired.*

Staring at the edge of the glass, outside what I assume was her line of sight, I considered if it was okay to question a hologram. I'd already talked to a wall the night before, so it wasn't too much of a stretch to do it twice in a day. What would I even ask her? Would she even be allowed to answer?

But before I could say anything to the fictional girl, Lucian cleared his throat behind me. I looked back to see the ominous sight of him staring from shadowed rooms beyond. He had been standing at the door I'd turned away from, watching me as I stared at glass like an idiot. Then with a low, calm tone he summoned me. "Right this way, Nathaniel."

They were all calling me "Nathaniel" and it was telling me something wasn't right. It was like I was a child again and my mother was saying my full name. But there was no way to escape whatever fate was awaiting me and, considering it may have been my last moment as an agent, I refused to hide from it. I turned, nodded and walked through the doors.

The other side was worse than the reception. Several higher officials in the Seattle branch stood there in well-pressed uniforms. Considerably more elaborate uniforms than my own were adorned with medals, patches and tassels as if it meant anything more than intimidating lower ranks like me.

I recognized the Commissioner, Omero Alston, one of the original agents of Seattle like Lucian. He was a tall, wide man with broad shoulders – nearly large enough to be considered a Giant. His skin was thick, dry and grey like he were crafted from stone given life.

After all, Commissioner Alston is a Golem.

He isn't really a "rock monster". Golems are large men with extremely thick skin like a rhinoceros. But when you look like that it's very hard not to look like you're made of stone. Alston is like a walking statue. His glass-like eyes were piercing and slate grey as he stared on at me.

And I stared back, impressed at the towering man before a flash of light caught the corner of my eye. Dulaf, broad smile on her face, stood there with a camera. I could feel the blood drain from my face in an instant.

Lucian stepped between us, calm as always. But, this time, there was a sadness behind his eyes not normally there.

"Nathaniel," he said, "we've been discussing your behavior last night. I've been informed by Commissioner Alston that I will be reassigned to a special detail starting tonight. You will no longer be riding with me."

I stammered, "I know I made a mistake, but I swear I won't do something like that again. Dulaf and I found something big and I'm going to make up for the whole thing!"

"There's no need to argue young man," Alston said in his deep, booming voice. "The decision has already been made and nothing is going to change it. Take off your jacket."

I removed it slowly without protest, unable to find the right words to say. It was surreal to watch Lucian take the jacket and remove the badge. I averted my eyes to avoid seeing it as I proceeded to start removing the gun from my belt.

"Now," Lucian said, stopping me from surrendering the weapon, "Take your new jacket."

I stopped, staring at a new jacket in his hands and gawking like a twit. Frowns turned to smiles and a polite applause as I put it on, even from Dulaf. The left shoulder now had a silver patch with a golden shield bordering the crest of the ACTF. The Aegis: a protective blessing for those granted the right to walk alone. I had been promoted to a full agent.

I closed up the jacket and Lucian replaced my badge as I stared speechlessly at them. My breath was taken away.

"But," I started, hesitating as I recollected my thoughts, "I blew it last night."

"All of the reports say you did what you were supposed to do up until you became distracted," Alston said, reassuringly. "As you know, every time an ACTF weapon is fired the Oracle forwards all information to an independent investigator in Argyre. If there was any reason to think you could have done it differently, we would be suspending you instead."

He lifted a large, rugged hand and gestured to the patch with a wave that would have been subtle from a smaller man.

"Last night was the final night of your evaluation period," he continued, "we were either going to promote you or consider letting you go. Your service over the past year has shown you've got a good head on your shoulders. As it stands, the only mistake you made was taking your eyes off a Giant you believed to be unconscious. Your evaluating lancer has decided you're ready."

I looked to Lucian, still dumbfounded by the whole thing.

"Like I said last night," Lucian replied, "we all screw up like that. I probably wouldn't feel safe letting someone go until they've made that kind of mistake. They're not lessons you want to learn alone."

"But," I stammered, "after this and Wolfendown, won't everyone be watching me?"

Alston's heavy hand landed on my shoulder like someone gently handing me a brick to carry. Coolly, he replied, "It's true. In any other organization that might be a problem, but in our situation it might be an asset. As terrible as it sounds, the locals still see us as monster hunters so last night probably helped offset Wolfendown."

"What about the Alters?" I asked, pensively.

"The Alters know you were cleared by the Oracle," Lucian answered over my other shoulder. "They might not like it, since you're human, but most Alters trust the Oracles even if they don't quite respect them."

I scanned the faces around the room. Everyone nodded along with Lucian, even Dulaf as she filmed with that damned camera. I didn't mind her at that moment, my tension starting to release as I finally started to feel comfortable wearing that new patch. As their words sunk in, I felt somehow validated by it.

"Welcome aboard Agent Leone," Alston said, finally lifting the hand and releasing another source of tension. "Make us proud."

The group saluted, applauded one more time and started to scatter. Only Lucian and Dulaf stayed behind with me. Dulaf was grinning like an idiot again. But Lucian? I couldn't always tell, but I think he was actually going to miss me.

"You're really letting me go solo?" I asked, half teasing.

"We're understaffed," he replied matter-of-factly, dodging my tease. "The Oracles cleared you of wrong doing and the doctor cleared you medically."

I studied him for a moment, wondering if he really missed the point or if he was just playing cool again. His expressions always felt just a touch distant, above it all, but as he stood there I could almost see a spark of genuine emotion in his face. He glanced up and made eye contact with me, a softened look for such a sharp face, and continued with a lightly snarky tone, "You're bruised but not broken. I think it's about the best we can do."

Hearing the tone, knowing what it meant, I asked, "So what are you doing next?"

He sighed. "You know Benjamin Hale?"

My blank expression answered for me.

"Still don't pay attention to the news, do you?"

Dulaf chimed in from behind the camera, "He's that Alter looking to run for Mayor."

Vague memories emerged of hearing this while cursing my busted toaster. "The guy no one can shut up about?"

Lucian frowned and nodded. "Guess who's stuck watching him now that he's making it official?"

I cringed. Guard duty is the most loathed job in the ACTF because it involves so much sitting on your ass. But Lucian doesn't sleep much, a logical choice for a twenty-four-seven hellhole assignment. Sure, he couldn't go into the sun, but he could lurk in the shadows. Still, one thought was hard to ignore...

"Penance for being involved with me?" I asked.

He laughed and patted the shoulder Alston just released. "No, I think they felt less would happen if they knew exactly where I was going instead of having me follow my mysterious leads."

I shrugged and nodded, unable to argue with the logic. He dragged me into enough in our time to make it sound reasonable to keep an eye on him once in a while. Sure, he got things done. But I can't imagine the bulk of paperwork and public relations nightmares they go through for things like busting up the protest. I still wasn't completely sure if I was going to have to answer for my part in it... or the hole my ass made in that wall.

I hesitated for a moment at the thought, looking at them and asking quietly, "The investigators are sure?"

Dulaf nodded and finally spoke up with a surprisingly solemn tone, "The footage from the cameras showed how close you were to dying. They said you were lucky it was a body blow because if you hadn't been wearing the coat, you might've died."

Mirroring her tone, Lucian remarked, "In that situation, you did the only thing you could do."

"Still feels dirty," I muttered.

Squeezing my shoulder, Lucian whispered one last piece of advice, "Always check the suspect's status before you take your eyes off them. It may save your life, it may save theirs."

I nodded along, considering it might be my last piece of advice from him ever. He smiled again, released my shoulder and walked away, stopping to look back before he turned the corner. I'd never seen him smile and frown so often in a single day. And with that smile he said, "I expect you to follow my example and make their lives interesting."

I smiled back and waved. "You can count on it."

And just like that, Lucian was gone and I was standing there, flying solo. The confusion and excitement faded and gave way to a sudden rush of nerves. For the three years I was hoping to get to this point I didn't fully realize what it meant to actually get here. The devotee training wheels were off and I suddenly felt very exposed.

Chapter 7
Interrogating a Revenant

A flash of light and the sound of a shutter broke me from my haze. Dulaf's grinning face peeked from behind her little camera.

"Gonna wet yourself?" she asked.

"No," I quipped, "unlike you I was raised in the era of indoor plumbing."

She winced and feigned a wounded expression. "I see we didn't get you away from Lucian soon enough."

It was true; I did pick up a lot of irreverent attitude towards Dulaf from Lucian. In fact, though I was once cocky as hell, Dulaf used to terrify me due to an incident in boot camp. And for the first time in a long time I was about as nervous as I'd been back then – I really did feel a little like "wetting myself" even if I wasn't going to admit it. Flying solo, without someone to watch after me and make sure I wasn't screwing up was a frightening experience. A year ago, I would have been full of confidence and yet completely unprepared. Now, I was seasoned enough to realize how unseasoned I used to be, and I had no clue if I was really ready as I started walking down the hall.

"He wouldn't have let you get promoted if you weren't ready," she idly commented. "He would have been the first to kick you out."

It was lines like that which confused me about Dulaf. She'd be there to film me looking like a twit, hand me books about Giants and do her best to say things that make me squirm. But then, on rare occasions, she'd say something like that and make me feel better. I wonder sometimes if she just torments me for some ulterior motive in her grand scheme. But for now she was on my side… apart from the camera she used to document me pleading for my job.

I nodded, made a futile attempt to grab the damn thing and continued deeper into headquarters. And she followed, shift apparently over once again.

"Where are we going, Nate?" she asked, ears flicking.

"Is he ready?" I replied quietly.

She shut off the camera and tucked it away, her demeanor unusually serious, and the giddy energy gone. "It didn't take long to process. Matching the fingerprints off the pads was a little tough but we've definitely got one of them."

"Tough?" I asked.

A uniquely Elven expression crossed her face, an eyebrow raised, ears folded back like a cat. "One of the sets didn't exist."

I stopped, wondering if she could be serious. "What do you mean 'didn't exist'?"

Any doubt she was serious was erased by her tone as she replied, "I tried the Oracles, the conventional networks, the FBI and even Interpol. You name it, I tried it. Those fingerprints do not exist on anyone's system."

It was hard to swallow. With the sophisticated networks we'd set up since the Alter revelation it was nearly impossible to disappear. They'd have to somehow avoid ever being in contact with the system. But how could that have happened? How could anyone who created enough drugs to supply others not have priors? Scarier still: how could someone avoid the Oracle system of all things?

Hell, every Alter living in a country that signed the pact is legally required to register with us. And that thought left me with two very intimidating prospects.

"Either they came from somewhere outside the system," I whispered. "Or they found a way to break it."

We fell silent, walking through sterile corridors running under the compound until we reached the final bridge to the holding area. There, where walls and floors were plated with silver, the word "Acheron" was etched into a sign.

The River of Pain, one of the rivers of the underworld, chosen by our designers to describe the prison they built deep beneath the Earth. Under the headquarters and part of Kobe Terrace across the street, we bored a hole into the earth and created a spiraling structure that holds prisoners, patients and refugees for the Cascadia ACTF.

Walking on, the lights slowly changed from white to a violet-shifted blue and back. The smell of flowers drifted past us and the quiet sound of a babbling brook echoed off the metal walls. It started to build as we got closer and the light shifted ever more towards a pale white glow. As we cleared the opening at the far end we stepped onto a moon-lit balcony overlooking a serene garden with a stream running through it.

We'd reached the place above Acheron, what we would consider Limbo. Not everyone wants to live a life with the outside world once they change. From that balcony I could see a boy with a pair of large black eyes like something seen in an alien movie. He chased a girl, a girl who had a tail, around the garden until she pushed him into the stream. As she laughed, her tail wagged.

It was a calming scene under the illusion of an open sky. Kobe Terrace, the area above, has so many stones that people walk over every day never knowing they've been laced with tiny cameras. The information trickles down through a series of relays to seamlessly linked monitors covering the cave's ceiling. It's like water through sand.

As the children played we could see the moon above shining through light clouds, trees and small plants that seemed to float overhead on small islands of earth. I watched that sky, taking in the beauty of it and forgetting what sort of engineering went behind it. It's always been like magic to me.

We walked down a flight of stairs into a security office at the base, broad stone steps moving down a rock wall. Elaborate markings carved into those walls were allowed to be overgrown with vines that coiled around the supports beneath. Below, we could see the children's parents discussing literature as a small impish man juggled apples overhead. They seemed so at peace with their fate and their tiny little world.

The stream wound through the garden every way it could. As it drops over tiny waterfalls and rolls through smooth, polished rocks, it provides a sense of a natural world under the unnatural sky before disappearing into the far wall.

Security guards allowed us through and waved us on to Acheron at the far end. Unlike Fangtown, my uniform drew no scorn here. The few that noticed me smiled. To these people the ACTF are protectors and they appreciate the home we'd built for them. I was sad to leave that place because I knew the sentiment wasn't going to be shared by the people behind the steel gates we were about to enter.

We passed by half a dozen heavily armed and armored men sitting in booths about six feet apart. It was what we called the "firewall".

In the event someone escapes from the prison below and manages to reach this area they would meet with a series of three giant metal shutters in the spaces between those booths.

The guards, curates, are sworn to prevent anyone from getting through. If the time came, two would step out of their booths, hit the button for the shutter behind them and do their best to handle the situation alone, giving the next two rows time to prepare and close their shutters as well. It was essentially a suicide pact to prevent the evil inside from escaping long enough for the rest of the department to swarm the sanctuary. I didn't have it in me to become a curate, another path I turned down in favor of being an agent.

So I couldn't help but show respect for these guys with a small salute as I passed into the sounds of torment beyond their room. We made our way through the asylum section, hearing the ever-present wailing of the disturbed residents.

Not everyone who becomes an Alter has such a clear-cut division between the natural and supernatural. Some of the sounds were hardly even human, belonging to those that had lost themselves to the more savage nature of their transformation. The howling was the most haunting, like wolves separated from their packs. It was a sad, lonely sound, echoing through the hallways from somewhere deep below as we continued on the short path to the next section of "Limbo".

I think it disturbed Dulaf more than me. She watched for each sound, a frightened look in her eyes like a small animal in a forest. Her ears folded back, her body tensed and she edged closer to me, doing her best to get me between her and the distant sound of lone wolves. I chose not to torment her about it for just that once. Maybe she'd return the favor someday.

Fortunately, we passed through the next armored gateway and found ourselves in the much more mundane holding station. The room immediately beyond, with only a desk and a single curate, is sterile and boring after the beautiful garden and troubling asylum. A let-down for most visitors who take the scenic route, I'm sure.

I'd been to this section quite a few times but I always expected something busier when I arrived. Behind the desk a corridor lead to the holding cells, to the far side was the route to the prison, and across from the desk was a secured elevator for prisoner transports. As far as the station was concerned this was the hub of activity, a place where you would expect to see dozens of people at any given moment. Instead, it was only Joe, the curate, who looked about as bored as you'd expect in that room.

"Hey Joe," I greeted, breaking the silence of the room, "mind if we borrow one of your house guests?"

He chuckled after a light startle, took notice of my new patch and said, "Wouldn't mind at all, *Agent* Leone. And Sage Nénharma is welcome to join."

It was always a little strange to hear someone refer to Dulaf by rank. Nénharma was a name she chose for herself since she'd been born when surnames were uncommon. But combined with her rank it made her sound so... proper. Maybe it was just me, but *Sage* Dulaf Nénharma sounded like a much more controlled and measured person.

Apparently, she thought so too. The moment she heard it she stood a bit taller, stepped up to Joe and said in the same tone she used in her lab, "We need to interrogate Martin Clay."

Joe nodded along while heading for the door behind his desk. "I knew there was something up with that one. He's been looking like he was going to get staked for something."

The word "staked" made Dulaf subtly cringe. It was clearly meant to be a version of "nailed" but had connotations for Alters that didn't quite gel. Joe, an old beat cop from before the ACTF went public, came from a time when that was all a work of fiction. I watched Dulaf for a moment to read her reaction. She glanced back my way, shook her head, and rolled her eyes.

We followed him into the guards lounge and past a few curates on break. Most of them seemed laid back, watching reruns on TV and trading stories of prisoners they'd dealt with for the day. One of them in particular was murmuring about a Zombie looking like he had the munchies. Overall, it was just another day for them despite the tremendous surge of people brought in from the warehouse.

With their helmets off, I could see the scars on some of their faces from years of being down in the prison. Despite the best efforts to make it the most secured place possible it was still reliant on these guys to be there to maintain it all. Though they were laughing, I imagine their jobs to be more stressful than mine... and I'd just been punched through a wall the night before.

Joe opened the door to the male detention center and led us through. It was about like you'd expect of a regular jail, barred cells with angry men roused to their feet to yell a few choice words our way. The only real differences were the flavor of prisoners and the specialized bars we were forced to use for them.

Walking by, I saw one prisoner decked out in green. Given the fact he fit the profile, with the reddened hair and the sparkling emerald green eyes, I could tell what he was. He was a Leprechaun, three and a half feet tall, at most, with a beard as red as fire and a nose almost as bright. Given his posture and the slight sway as he moved through the cell, I could wager a guess what he was there for. The old stereotype of the drunk and disorderly Irish stems mostly from the little men with the big attitude.

Leprechauns are related to Dwarves and Gnomes, a group of eccentrics to be sure. But, while their cousins are obsessive, they're often prone to addiction. Despite all their talents, the Leprechaun have a temper that can't be settled and an urge to find ways to escape. Even now, watching him, I saw a shot of rage behind those bright green intoxicated eyes. Studying him closely, I was just kind of relieved they weren't silver.

His well-pressed and somewhat expensive suit told a whole different story, though, with legends of the "pot of gold" being pretty damn accurate. Every Leprechaun I've ever heard of has a sixth sense about where to dig for coal, oil, gold, diamonds or whatever else you might find. And as a result, most of them are loaded... in more ways than one.

Within moments, a shoe flew at the bars and bounced off, a field of electricity sparking between them. The fields were meant to keep the more flexible prisoners from escaping without having to the design the cells with glass walls. It was a bit of a stop-gap measure, but one I was happy to have as the little angry man glared at me. The opinion, however, was not entirely shared.

"Aww," Dulaf squealed, "how cute!"

Suddenly, the angry little man was disarmed, smiling broadly as he said, "Why, hello there. Would you like to see my lucky charms?"

I stifled my reaction, a subtle mix of groaning and a gag reflex, as Joe and I left Dulaf behind with the tiny alcoholic and continued on to the group holding cells.

While the humans had been filtered out of the mob and delivered to the waiting hands of the Seattle PD, the Alters were all ours. Looking into the cell, I realized how many we'd caught in that stampede. Even without the humans on hand we managed to fill two cells to capacity.

Joe tapped the bars with a rod, lighting the fields for an extra dose of security. The cell was so crowded I was even tempted to reach for my gun. But, as Joe ran the back of his glove across the locks and we heard them open, no one made a move. Maybe they saw where my hand was or they knew the next room over was flooded with guards, but they didn't budge an inch. Only the lanky figure of Martin Clay stood as Joe called for him.

Martin was a sickly man with graying skin, salt and pepper hair, very little body-weight and yellowed eyes. You could see at one time he'd been a tall, lean black man with strong features. But now, as he walked by me, he was twisted and withered. He looked like the walking dead and with just cause: Martin was definitely a Zombie.

Alters come in three distinct varieties based on the Alter stem cell, the A-Cell. The passive type, constantly running at a regular pace, doesn't fix anything that isn't broken and give rise to the tamer Fae who don't react violently to allergens or go feasting on people. The reactive types, meanwhile, change only when they're stimulated like a Werewolf. But the aggressive type cells, like the ones in Martin, run at a constant, accelerated pace that never stops.

For a Zombie, aggressive A-Cells meant his body refused to die. Every organ in him could fail, and likely would with time, but he wouldn't die until the cells simply couldn't keep up anymore. For a long time we thought that such a thing was impossible. After all, it was a hard concept to swallow. How could the body survive without something like a heart? The answer: grow a new one.

Martin was in his late 30s but could have easily passed for much older. Enough of his body had failed to make him look like he was standing on death's doorstep already, likely thanks to alchemist blue. Worse, his metabolism had eaten away at every bit of fat in his body, leaving him with a hungry look the guards murmured about as I passed earlier.

Zombies really can turn to cannibalism if pushed long enough. Their bodies, constantly burning at an accelerated rate, consume enough food to feed small elephants. A Zombie could eat its weight in a day if agitated and, despite the best efforts of the ACTF to feed and sedate him, I could see the hunger in his eyes.

It was important to note what he was as we entered the interrogation room. I couldn't use the same tactics I'd use on someone else. He was in a constant state of decay and pain that would likely last forever – so what did he care if he spent a little time in jail? He wouldn't suffer any more in there than he would outside. There'd be no point for him to cop a plea to shave a couple years off of his sentence, especially not with the free food.

Joe saw to it that Martin was chained to the floor, likely seeing the same look I had. I kept my eyes on the withered form in case he tried to attack the curate. It's not so much that we expected him to do something, but it was better to be ready in case he did. Thankfully, all he did was stare at me with those jaundiced eyes. Even as Joe stepped aside and I took a seat, our eyes never broke contact.

Martin, absolutely silent before then, finally spoke in the lazy, slurred tone you'd expect from someone so obviously burnt out, "What're you guys tryin' t' pin on me now?"

I activated my gloves and replied casually, "What do you know about alchemist blue, Martin?"

He watched the gloves shift, breaking eye contact for the first time. I couldn't be sure what he thought it meant, possibly that I was going to start hitting him. But it was simple policy, saving me from sitting in a dangerous room with a holstered gun and no other weapon to use if he snapped those chains.

He looked up with a tinge of disgust and said, "I don't know shit, man. Why're you even askin' me?"

"Your fingerprints were all over the patches," I said.

A grin crossed his dried, cracked lips. "So what? You goin' t' toss me into the pit? I'm not sweatin' that shit."

"Yeah," I muttered, clasping my hands in front of my chin, "I didn't think you would. But, you see, while your fingerprints are on both of the pads, you don't have any rashes on you right now. That sounds like you weren't the one using it."

"Fine," he grunted, "you got me, man. I was Max's corner man an' I picked up a patch for the match. The other was my friend an' I snagged an extra for him. Two patches, just two. S'like, what, a couple months? Shit, I'll do a couple months."

He was brushing it off like I thought he would. Though I didn't think he'd brush off the fact Max was dead. If I actually had credible evidence we could have threatened him with something bigger. A life sentence is a harsh thing for someone who won't die. But he knew we only had two patches; he was the only one who could know.

"Y'know," Martin spoke with a rasp, "jail wouldn't be so bad 'bout now, actually. It's been forever since I had a good meal."

Mind games: a stupid move by people who watch too much television. Everybody thinks they can start screwing with the head of the officer because they saw some really creepy man do it in a movie. Every interrogator's been trained no to take that bait.

"Thing is," I continued without reacting to his ploy, "that friend of yours said you sold it to him. That sounds like a dealer to me. You might be eating around Acheron for a very long time."

In an instant he jumped from his seat. Throwing his body against the table, the chains caught him with a clang, a slight crack forming in the concrete floor. And he stood there, against the weight of the chains, screaming, "They're lyin' through their teeth!"

I didn't expect that to get so deep into his skin, but it did.

79

"Well if you're not the dealer, Martin, who is?" I asked, pretending not to notice the fact our floor was breaking. "We've got two sets of prints and you're the only one that was actually on the scene!"

He twisted slightly against the chains and I could hear them strain as his torso was pressed up against the frame of the table. I continued to pretend I didn't notice the groaning of metal ready to bend. I'm not entirely sure what he thought he could manage to do by attacking me or trying to intimidate me. Even if he managed to break the chain and take me down he'd only have walked right into the waiting arms of a lot of guards. I think he figured it out himself after a moment or two. Like a lion in a cage, he was only roaring for the show of it before sitting down and accepting his fate.

He settled into his chair and said with a low rasp, "I swear t' god I never tried t' deal the shit, man."

"You mean you got two patches for your friends and none for you?" I asked, watching for any tells. "You're a pretty generous guy, Martin. That's expensive stuff."

He growled, "I got it cheap."

Looking into his eyes, I realized I normally would have been using my visor at a time like this. But it was gone from the moment Max sent me flying. Somewhere out there a homeless guy or a factory worker had a real nice pair of sunglasses. For now, I had to rely on my gut, which told me he was telling the truth.

His posture and agitation told me he didn't expect to be accused of dealing. Even if they're lying you can see the difference between shock and denial. He was shocked. But that meant I had to get him to reveal his supplier with only the looming threat of a lie.

"We've got your fingerprints on two patches and an eye witness," I said, "if I can't find the actual dealer then I'm going to have to assume it's you, Martin."

He sighed and leaned back in the chair, fully rested against it for the first time since he sat down.

"I have dealers in New Skids," he muttered, groaning. "I talked to 'em before the match and asked 'em t' bring a couple by."

"Why only two?" I asked. "That doesn't make a whole lot of sense to me."

He shook his head and met my gaze. "No, I was buyin' it for me an' a friend. But after I handed the patch over t' my friend I realized I could bet on Max and give 'im what I had. Would've bought a lot more of the stuff if I'd won."

He sighed and looked down at the table, leaning back again while I watched on. He was telling the truth as far as I could tell – after all, greed is universal. But even knowing the dealer was in New Skids didn't mean much. The place has enough druggies and dealers to spend a year clearing it out and still not catch the right guy.

I leaned forward. "So where are they?"

"They cut me a deal," he muttered, "I can't snitch on 'em. Wouldn't be right."

"You know," I said calmly, "giving Max that patch was a felony."

We made eye contact again over the table as he probably gauged if I was serious. I think he was sizing me up about then, sensing the threat coming down on him before I could even say it. I could see the hunger and frustration mingling in his eyes and feel him about ready to jump again. I wasn't sure if the chains would hold if he tried again, but I couldn't exactly turn back now.

"A death that occurs during a felony goes to first degree," I said. "If we can't cut some sort of deal I don't know if you'll ever walk out of here."

He averted his eyes, lowering them to the table, whispering, "Like I said, I have people in New Skids. Don't know any names but I can tell you where they run everythin'."

I offered a subtle nod and a smile to let him know I wasn't going to squeeze anymore.

"That works just fine for me, Martin."

Chapter 8
Skid Row

Martin gave me the address before Joe locked him away again. I dragged Dulaf away from her new Leprechaun friend on the way out, updating her and taking a moment to grab a replacement visor. I walked out of the headquarters as a full agent for the first time. But not before stopping for something far more important: my keys.

Every new agent gets issued a car, "the hearse", when promoted. Sitting somewhere in the secured garage was my personal vehicle, a vehicle I'd been deemed worthy of. It was an honor I'd been granted.

I just hoped I wouldn't scratch the damn thing.

They wouldn't tell me which car it was, of course, as that would make life easier and that isn't how you treat the new agent. So I pulled the keys out and started pressing the alarm button repeatedly, wandering aimlessly through the garage, listening for the car to react.

It wasn't long before I walked by the nice, new unit a few rows down as it flashed its lights. I'd found my wheels, my own personal car. I was "a man" now. Lucian couldn't stop me from driving this one. I can't say I didn't stop to appreciate the moment as I stared at it. In fact, I probably spent a little too long appreciating it.

It was essentially the same type of car Lucian drives with a few modifications for someone working solo. There's no back seat on "the hearse". No way would you want a prisoner in the back if there was no one to keep them from strangling you. Instead, they give you what they like to call "the box", which I got a real good look at as I got in.

A heavily modified passenger seat, the box has a set of restraints enclosed in a shell, like the seat of a roller coaster in a casket. Sit a prisoner in it, lock it down and it lies down and slides partially into the space under the dashboard. There wasn't an engine up front, each wheel having a dedicated electric motor.

Thus our cars had a lot of storage space and a little sports car could be called "the hearse" with a straight face.

It was surreal sitting in the driver's seat, looking over the restraint frame. For three years, I'd been sitting in the passenger seat of one vehicle or another. Now only passengers and prisoners would be stuck on that side. It was more than simply surreal, it felt completely unreal.

Maybe Max put me in a coma.

As I pushed that feeling aside I started the car, feeling the humming vibrations roll through me, and pulled out as cautiously as possible. I navigated my way out of the garage, protecting the car like it were my child, and set off to New Skids.

New Skids isn't a pleasant place to go. Pioneer Square had once been the so-called "Skid Road". It was once just associated with an old logging tradition, something about skidding logs, only to eventually take on the same connotations found everywhere else. But by the turn of the century, thanks to revitalization in the 1960s, it was a lively place with cafes and nightclubs, more popular than ever when the Alters started to come out of hiding. The neighborhood we know as Fangtown started out of the areas with these nightclubs and slowly started to extend east into other districts.

But there was a negative backlash to the migration. A lot of mainstream humans didn't want to live next to the Alters and the Alters didn't want to feel unwelcomed. Though a lot of people in the International District were fairly accepting and the clubs in Pioneer Square were more than happy to take the money, it was hard to shake the old legends. People started to abandon the areas around the edge of Fangtown to form a weaving string of empty buildings and failing businesses, a new "Skid Road". By the time people were comfortable moving back into these places it was too late: the criminal element had long infected it like bacteria in a cut.

So it came to pass New Skids was born. It's a scar on the city and no efforts to remove it have worked to date. It's the only real defined border of any district in Seattle that I know of. It didn't completely surround the place, if you avoided it you could pass through Pioneer Square, the International District, and Fangtown without a clue, but take a wrong turn in any of the three and you'd notice the change. When you pass through it you could almost believe you'd entered a zombie movie by the way everything suddenly turned grey and ugly around you.

Martin's directions to his dealer were pretty straight forward if slightly vague. I just had to get to New Skids and follow it inland for a couple minutes. Eventually I'd come to a building with a neon purple sign of a waving hand. He said I'd recognize it fairly easily: broken lights meant the waving hand was presenting only the middle finger. According to him, the locals called it "The Birdie".

It was my first time traveling through New Skids alone. It was an interesting experience, watching figures scatter like roaches into the shadows. Most of the street lights didn't work on certain stretches – broken repeatedly and on purpose. Alter criminals thought it would give them some sort of advantage to be in the dark. But the visor leveled the field as I stared through the shadows at their creeping auras lurking in the alleys and hiding inside apartment buildings. I could only imagine how oblivious I would have been without it.

Five minutes into my drive I spotted the waving purple finger bobbing above a run-down hotel. Ironically, the building's style made it clear the place had been built a little before or during the first rush of migration when real estate was at an all-time high. Someone sank a lot of money into this place, only to have it go bust a couple years later. The windows were now boarded up and most of the sign had been stripped away except for that hand, which flickered and hummed as though it were ready to give out entirely as I stepped out of the car. It was the only defining feature, aside from the near invisible marking of St. Peter's inverted cross bound by a pentagram, the sign of an Alter drug house.

Most Alter races can see in the infrared spectrum. So they tried their best to use it, writing hidden messages to each other. Normally it would be enough to hide it from anyone they didn't want to catch onto their little secret. But they always seem to forget the visor when they're high. Not to mention the fact the Cascadia ACTF is almost forty percent Alters.

I let them know it was a stupid idea as I passed it by, taking out my gun and unloading a shot into the center of it. The quiet hum and pop of the energy discharge did little to disturb the neighborhood, but the scorch mark left through the emblem ingrained itself into the wall. A bright blood-like red smear was visible through my visor as if the building were a living thing I'd wounded.

The thought of living stone gave me pause on the steps, making me look to the rooftops with a sudden curious feeling. Are Gargoyles real? I haven't met one or seen them listed on the databases. But Alston's a Golem and stranger has happened. I watched for an aura along the rooftops, surprisingly finding quite a few. Even if they weren't Gargoyles, the place was crawling with activity.

Realizing how surrounded I was, I opened the door to the building and moved through as quickly as possible with my gun still drawn. I walked into the dim, flickering light of an empty lobby, long abandoned despite the lights being on. Though that sign still shone and waved its finger at the world, it wasn't really clear who was still paying the bills to keep that bird flying. The reception desk was coated in a thick layer of dust that could be smelled through the room on horribly dry air.

Cobwebs had weaved through every corner of the room and firmly dominated the space behind the desk, indicating no one had stood there for ages. It was so thick that opening the door caused what looked like a silhouette of a person to form in the mass as a light gust breezed through the room. The illusion of a ghost was standing as the innkeeper, like the hologram of the girl at the station.

Deeper into the lobby, toward the abandoned desk, I could hear chattering and hissing from somewhere above. Many buildings look abandoned in New Skids, but appearances were deceiving, even ones like this were at least populated by squatters. It's hard to imagine how many people were actually there and what sort of people they were. Were they all Alters or were a handful of brave, homeless humans living there as well? Whatever they were, I could hear deranged laughing as I walked up the stairs, echoing from somewhere out of sight.

Room three-nineteen: that's where Martin told me to go and I made no effort to wander away from that path. I couldn't risk walking into a coven or a pack just yet. Even if I won the exchange, I would have tipped off the dealers long before reaching them. So I took every corner carefully, double-checking each time I turned and looking over my shoulder at any noise that might have come. I passed doors extra quietly, hearing sounds beyond, and did my best to walk softly at all times. I tried to fade into the background noise, hoping not to be picked up by superhumanly acute hearing.

Sounds of burnouts became ever clearer as I weaved through the building, sometimes right past the rooms they were in. The hissing became low, angry whispers echoing in the darkness. Other sounds became incoherent twitchings of the ones strung up on their drug of choice. I thought back to the Academy videos of the effects of drugs on Alter physiology. I remembered my own experiences with this world and the things I had seen from it. The voices permeating the building were all too familiar.

But three-nineteen was silent. Close to the outside wall, it stood within feet of a window facing out into the gloomy skyline of New Skids. The numbers had mostly fallen off, leaving behind only a crooked three next to the faded imprints of the one and nine. Standing outside, I could hear nothing beyond that door.

Maybe, I thought, Martin lied to me after all.

But there was some credibility to his information: the door had been rigged to be "always invited". The doorknob had been removed, replaced with a simple push plate with no lock and the engraving of the Alter letters for "welcome friends". It was a sign to other Alters that they were always invited to enter.

The legends Vampires couldn't enter a house uninvited are partially true and extend to more than just their kind. Mild autism that prevails in the Alter community causes quirks of behavior including a surprisingly extreme fear of the unknown behind unfamiliar doors. Like agoraphobia in reverse, they fear the closed spaces that they don't know, but they're fine once they're inside.

There have been studies on why it occurs and very little cause has been found. My theory for some Alters is that they aren't really afraid of the space itself but what they might do beyond it. Just because you need to do certain things to survive doesn't mean you have to like it and for a long time people didn't realize they had a choice. But I didn't have that problem, I was very happy with the thoughts of what I'd do inside that room.

As I entered, it was pitch black on the other side. My visor amplified what little ambient light it could get, but it wasn't much. What could be seen wasn't encouraging. Plastic bottles and surgical tubing weaved across the surface of a table in a complex arrangement, chemical residues floating from it in a thin green haze.

The acrid smell of ammonia, like cat urine, flowed across my face. I could see the bottles of it on the floor next to a variety of other chemicals, ground up pills, sheets of tinfoil and vials of colloidal silver. Nicotine patches were strewn about, used to deliver the drug instead of easily detected needles or pipes. It was like walking into a twisted, demented drug store.

Alchemist blue, despite its relatively new grip on the city, is based in the same science as synthetic drugs of the past. The Alters who got sick from their drug abuse were still hooked when they went active. But to their horror, the drugs they once used were no longer strong enough to work for them. They took the ones they could make at home and tooled with them in every way possible. It was a darker example of Alter ingenuity.

As I walked around the room I could see that Martin had led me to the right place. There wasn't a lot there, but the empty boxes for the nicotine patches were more than enough to make twenty or thirty doses alone.

It took a moment to acclimate to the room's odor and the effects the chemicals were having on me even as I kept my distance. I couldn't imagine how people could stand in that room for longer than a few minutes. I didn't even make it that long before I couldn't stand it anymore. I drew my gun and fired through the wood planks to burn through, smashing out what was left of a window with the handle of my gun. The wind started to pull away the toxic fumes, a new unpleasant smell taking their place.

It was a thick stench that caught in my throat as I tried to breathe. The ammonia, as bad as it was, was actually covering a far greater evil. It was a sickly, distracting smell with a tinge of sweetness to it like rotting wet sugar sprinkled over old bad meat. I knew what it was from back in the Academy and dreaded it as I made my way to the adjacent room.

Opening the door slowly, I was greeted with a stronger wave of the odor. It was like a tangible force that made me step back as it rushed from the room and flowed to the open window. The mingling of the two smells was almost too much for me as I turned away from the door. I gladly moved away from the bathroom, and the smell inside, to try to find a light switch in the dark.

It took a moment of blindly grasping at the walls to find the switch, the fumes and odor disorienting me a bit too much to see it even with my visor. I flipped it on and pulled the visor off to let my eyes adjust in that slightly altered state. The air was so thick with crap that I think they were starting to dilate from being there. It was already clear I couldn't stay much longer even with the busted window. Trying to clear my head with a couple shakes, I staggered back to the restroom.

A tub half full of water contained a partially submerged corpse. His mouth and eyes were wide open, head thrown back and face frozen in screaming agony. He had turned silver-blue, sores burned through his skin, covered in deep black bruises that looked like ink stains spreading across his body. The bruises weaved along his blood vessels, reaching the point where a patch loosely hung from his shoulder. His eyes were now a steel grey as the pupils had disappeared.

This was the face of a blue overdose, "silvering out". It wasn't the first time I'd seen it.

As I backed away from the room and closed the door in a futile attempt to trap that stench, I found myself standing in the main room fully lit for the first time. Without the lights, I could make out shapes and objects around me but not details. So it was quite a surprise to see the walls clearly for the first time. Photos of dozens of people and newspaper clippings plastered the walls like wallpaper. Large X's were drawn across photos and clippings in marker, some of them people I knew to have died in recent months. It was enough to make me step back again, breaking a fragment of glass under my heel.

I looked down, surprised to find glass from the broken window so far into the room, only to find that it wasn't window glass. The shard I stepped on was one of dozens of mirrored pieces reflecting my splintered image back to me. A shattered mirror stood nearby, smashed like almost every reflective surface in the room. The floor was practically carpeted in shards of glass.

Like the door, legends of Vampires and other creatures not having reflections because they were "soulless" was just human interpretation of strange behavior. It wasn't that they didn't have reflections but that many of them refused to look at themselves. Broken mirrors are usually a sign of someone who had destroyed their own images in disgust. I'd seen it before, but never to this degree. Whoever ran this lab was seriously disturbed.

Taking my attention away from the glass I noticed a second desk in one of the corners too dark to see before. Now it was clear that a vanity mirror on it had been shattered away from its frame, likely in a fit of rage. But something else caught my eye there. Sitting atop the desk were two items important to the operation: an old weathered journal and professionally packaged omega.

The process of turning these chemicals into blue required running it through omega as a filter of sorts. The blood components and chemicals in the pack would change the substance as it mixed. I remembered watching people connect tubes to these packs with special outlets and running the chemical cocktail they brewed through it, letting it soak until all the organic parts dissolved. Once the blood had been thinned out, they'd run it all through one last filter, mix the result with the colloidal silver and apply it to the patches.

It was such a simple damned process when you had one of these packs. They were rare, thankfully, outside of hospitals. Only a handful of people were crazy enough to supply them. Fortunately, or unfortunately, I knew one of those people.

For now, however, the journal was far more important. We had fingerprints that technically didn't exist and a room in an abandoned hotel. The journal was the closest thing we had to identification for these sickos. I cracked it open carefully and thumbed through the first couple pages to find what appeared to be a shopping list with food items next to a series of numbers. Commentary was scribbled in a panicked fashion across the edges of the pages saying "not enough" and "too much". I wasn't sure what exactly it meant except maybe it was a sign they sold the stuff to buy groceries.

Before I could look any deeper, however, my head started to spin and everything blurred. I'd stayed too long.

I escaped into the hallway and let the door close behind me, gasping for air while choking on the toxins. It wasn't exactly the freshest I could get, but anything was better than what I had just saturated in. I sank to the floor in the corner while keeping my gun ready on the crowd control setting in case anyone showed up while I was still in a haze. Down there, I waited for my head to clear so I could call back to the station.

It took a minute but I tapped the badge, cleared my throat and called in. "This is Agent Leone; I've got a confirmed hermasin lab and an indigo body. Home in on my beacon, I'll set up a halo. Don't send the clerics, this place is swarming."

They acknowledged my call and sent a response I didn't quite catch as I pushed myself back to my feet. My head cleared enough to stand and see straight, aside from a few fuzzy auras around the lights. One benefit I did recognize as I walked down the hallway was the sudden lack of pain I had been feeling since Max launched me through the wall.

I think I might have been a little high.

Luckily, I wasn't too altered by it mentally. If I had been, I likely wouldn't have noticed strange scraping marks across the door's surface. Despite the fact it was set up as "always invited", something was missing from the door. I stopped and looked it over with my visor once more.

Normally, a mark would show the room to be a drug lab for "visitors". But, with that scraping, the mark was completely gone like it'd been clawed off with fingernails.

Confusing as it was, I couldn't take the time to investigate further. I imagined the others would figure it out when they got there with hazmat suits and coworkers to drag them drooling out of the toxic cloud. I, on the other hand, needed to get the hell out of there while the getting was good.

Walking away from that dump and down the stairs, my strength started to return. I heard plenty of people whispering and growling to each other along with the sound of some of them lighting up. I could even hear a couple doing things I prefer not to repeat in mixed company. But, finally reaching the ground floor, I was almost out the door when a woman's scream pierced the building.

I didn't even stop to think about what I was doing as I sprinted up the stairs and drew my gun. Her panicked voice carried through the halls, crying for help. Without a care for the sound I might have been making I sprinted along the hallway, heavy boots and all. If anyone wanted to come and get a piece of me while pain free, they were welcome to try.

Her voice weakened as I closed in, subsiding as I ran up. The mark that had been missing from the lab door was now emblazoned across one on the floor below the original. I paused when seeing it but quickly pushed the thought aside as I heard one last weak gasp behind it.

With a quick kick I knocked the door open to see a group of powerful auras over a nearly lifeless one on the floor. I fired a warning shot toward the strongest aura, hoping to scatter the group. They scrambled, one hissing and screaming in the darkness as a wound blistered across his arm. The victim looked to be some poor strung out human junkie, but they were a small coven of four Vampires, all of whom rose and glared through the dark with shining eyes. The auras shifted colors as they ran the gambit of emotions about an agent outside their door.

I took the momentary pause to announce with authority, "Everyone to the floor, hands behind your head!"

The wounded one moved into the light coming from the hallway, blood trickling down the side of his chin and light reflecting off his nocturnal eyes even brighter. As silent signals moved between them, far out of my range of hearing, their auras synchronized. Unfortunately for me, the color they settled on was blood red. Two nights, two beatings, no waiting.

They rushed me with blood-curdling, inhuman screams. I took a brief glance at the victim, judged her status, clenched a fist and let the lead Vampire have a mouth full of silver. He reeled back and collapsed, the second leaping past him. I ducked and shoulder checked into his legs, letting him sail right over me before whipping up my gun and firing into the right shoulder of the next one. A flare of light streamed out of the wound as he collapsed, shoved aside by the one taking up the rear.

The fourth, whom I mentally dubbed "Bubba", was a big boy who plowed through his falling friends and rammed headlong into me. Just rising again from the duck, I was nailed around the waist with a full-weighted tackle. Thoughts of frequent flier miles crossed my mind as we barreled past his friend into the hallway and smashed into the opposite wall. The wind, my sarcasm and every thought in my head were knocked out of me all at once.

Squeezing me like a tube of toothpaste, he was a strong one. I punched him in the head to no avail – he didn't flinch even with the silver glove. But a pistol whip to the temple was another matter. His grip faltered and I got him upright, pushed him back with a shoving kick, and unloaded a couple rounds into his knees while he staggered. He fell with a grunt, his injured knee making a disturbing crack as it hit the floor. Screaming, he was stunned long enough for me to crack him over the head with the pistol one last time as hard as I could. With a thud, he fell to the floor.

Taking a moment to confirm he was alive through the visor, I felt momentarily thankful I didn't have to fire to kill. Human organizations train to aim for center-mass and ensure stopping power. But with crowd control on and visor assisted targeting I was fortunate enough that everyone went down clean.

Too bad it wasn't enough to stop someone like Max.

The gurgling noise from the trembling girl drifted out to me and broke me from thought. I lowered my gun slightly and edged into the room. Unsure of what was inside, I couldn't rush in. I had to walk in cautiously, checking corners to make sure the room was secured.

She was in her twenties at most and dressed like a prostitute. It wasn't too surprising for someone in a building like this. They'd got her good, several wounds ripped into her shoulder at the base of her neck. Her eyes were starting to glaze over, not giving her a whole lot of time for the ambulance to come.

I reached for my badge but then hesitated, suddenly remembering I'd only hit three of the four. A foot hit the floor behind me and I whipped around to see the jumper coming back for round two. I caught his wrist, hip tossed him to the floor and stepped on his face while twisting his arm. Lucian was right: I didn't make the same mistake twice.

The groaning from the group was soon drowned out by the sounds of sirens and rapid footfalls. The Special Operations Lance ran into the room in heavy armor, carrying Helios rifles. The cavalry had arrived.

As they gathered up the girl and our future tenants, I took the time to examine the marking on the door and take in what happened. The teams spread through the building and started scouring it for evidence of where the lab owner went. These guys and the girl were all the evidence I needed, though.

They were scavengers, a group of feeders that found a good lure for people that wouldn't be missed. They scraped the emblem off the door and marked a new one. They moved fast, the lab must have been empty for only a night. But regardless of how fast they actually moved there was only one truth to all of this: the dealers were long gone.

Chapter 9
Refreshing Beauty

The sweep of the building took the rest of the night. We gathered up about twenty drug addicts from both sides of the gene pool and cleared the area of the criminal element for about two hours, tops. And the evidence we stripped from the building was enough to give us…absolutely nothing. The place was covered in fingerprints and DNA from enough people that it was like trying to figure out who last pissed in a urinal.

We did know the dead guy wasn't a dealer, though. I was a little ticked off about that actually. But I heard the scavengers' victim was stable and they stopped the bleeding in time, so I still considered the night a win.

I started a new routine that day, similar to the old one except I got to drive to the shop instead of walking down the block in the rain. The patrol car seemed strangely out of place in the parking structure behind my building where I kept it overnight. Sitting next to tiny electric cars and the occasional van, my car, with its cat-like curves, looked like a beast. My car could eat theirs and it felt good.

Still, the routine wasn't all that different after that point. I stood in the long line for overpriced coffee and once again found myself the subject of much attention from the locals as I passed. It didn't bother me this time, I had the Aegis patch and knew, at a moment's notice, I could run like hell to my car and drive away like a thief in the night.

I hadn't been there since flying through a wall and no one in that circle had seen the new patch. For some reason I felt like it should have changed something about the way they looked at me.

It didn't.

A pair of Gnomes practically hid behind a table, in fact. I did, however, avoid the urge to put on my shades this time. I was going to need to practice my tough guy look and could take the opportunity to make eye contact with the people glaring at me. A part of me would have liked if they weren't glaring, but I could understand why. At the very least I had a moment to appreciate that no one tried to have small talk with me over the weather.

"Woo," a voice squeaked behind me, "rainy isn't it?"

It was a short lived moment.

I looked back at long brown locks of hair falling from under a soggy, wide-brimmed hat resting atop two long pointy ears. Even with the goofball hat and the drenched coat wrapped around her it wasn't very hard to recognize Dulaf.

"Why are you here?" I grunted, "How'd you even find me?"

She removed her hat with a flick of her wrist that sent a few drops sailing into my face. Her hair was soaked, hanging in thick locks that framed her face and stuck to her skin.

Smiling broadly, she said, "I've moved in just down the street!"

I don't know what my face must have looked like about then, probably a mixture between shock, horror and surreal disbelief. Whatever I looked like, though, she laughed and slapped the squishy hat against my shoulder.

"It was a joke," she giggled. "My shift ended so I swung by to report what we found today. I didn't want to scare you with another mid-day phone call."

I almost frowned at first, but couldn't help smiling anyway. "Okay, you got me. But what do you have from the building?"

Reaching into the coat, she produced a packet of papers showing the results of various tests run across the omega pack found on that desk. It was the same one used to refine the Harbor Island patches. The tests showed that it was far from anything you could legally stick into a red brew special. But two things caught my eye above the rest.

"No matching prints?!" I burst out – the whole shop tensing as if I'd waved my gun in the air. "How the hell could that happen?!"

Dulaf cringed and put a hand on my arm. With the slightest visible force she pinched my arm with a finger and a thumbnail. A broad smile stretched across her face as she spoke through her teeth, "It's okay Nate. Don't make a scene or I'll have to hurt you."

She wasn't kidding. Even through my jacket I could feel the nails pinching into my skin. Elves are technically the passive A-

Cell variant of Vampires. She may not need to feed and she may be immune to silver but she could still snap me like a twig.

My face was getting hot as I struggled to ignore the urge to wince. Aside from the desire to avoid a public Elf beating, I wasn't entirely sure if wincing would count as a "scene" to her.

"You can let go," I whispered painfully. "I'll be good."

She released the hold, leaving my arm throbbing. I rubbed it with one hand and studied papers with the other while she stared at the menu with a quizzical expression. I couldn't believe what I was seeing on that report. No match for the fingerprints at all. How the hell could that have happened? Maybe they wore gloves, but then why not wear the gloves for handing off the patches too?

And more, there was a word on it that I didn't like: Rephaitol.

It was a word that meant a lot about the dealer because it was a mood stabilizer drug designed for Alters. Were they mixing it into the blue to somehow keep themselves calm while on the drug? The implications were pretty severe.

It was almost enough to make me miss my moment.

We reached the front of the line and Trey prepared for my regular order. But I looked up long enough to say something I'd wanted to say for quite a while: "Hold the red one!"

He stopped, second cup already in hand, and stared in disbelief before my shiny new patch caught his eye.

"Whoa, hey there Mr. Big Shot," he said, chuckling. "Who'd you kill for their jacket?"

Dulaf giggled. "He shot a Giant."

"I did more than that!"

"Oh, right," she trailed off, bouncing back with a wicked smile. "He was also punched through a wall!"

I rubbed the bridge of my nose in frustration, listening to Trey fill my cup. But, staring at the floor, it dawned on me that I had something else worth mentioning to Trey. Thanks to the busts, I had some new guesses to make. I pushed past the embarrassment, lifted my head defiantly and took another shot in the dark.

"Zombie?"

He smiled, shaking his head. "Too pretty."

I murmured my frustration and considered the stranger things he could have been.

"Are you a Fairy?"

Dulaf snorted while Trey grinned and passed the cup. "Do I look like a Fairy?"

I accepted my defeat, even if that wasn't an answer, waved and turned to leave the line. But Dulaf stopped me, crying, "Wait!"

I stopped, not wanting to get pinched again anytime soon. Her ears rose in a peculiar way as she clasped her hands together and spoke in the sweetest tone I'd ever heard from her, "I'd like a double mocha triple filtered omega red with ten shots of espresso."

Ten shots...somehow I wasn't surprised. It actually made a lot of sense considering the way she was constantly right there whenever you turned around. Though I couldn't understand why she wanted me to wait for her to make her order.

"And put it on his bill."

"What?!" I barked at her. "You can't be serious!"

Her head twisted around slowly with the same sweet smile on her face that'd been there while she made the order. In a singsong tone she said only one word: "sage".

And, damn it, she was right: a sage is the science division's equivalent of a lancer. She outranked me still and, according to tradition, I had to cover her tab.

I watched Trey fill the cup and sighed while getting the cash to cover it. The two of them were terribly amused about it all.

He finished, smiled and handed the cup to her. "Will that be everything?"

And, for a moment, I was glad he asked. I had forgotten the one perk that Dulaf couldn't take from me. I had finally been promoted: the cookie was mine. I sighed and forced a weak smile. "Call me Ishmael."

Trey nodded, presented the cookie from behind the counter and offered it to me. Smiling, I reached to the precious symbol of my graduation out of the little leagues. However, by the time my hand reached the cookie… it was no longer there.

"Thanks!" Dulaf chirped before chomping down on her ill-gotten snack.

I was stunned and it soon got worse. Ignoring me as I stood there, she casually commented to Trey, "It's good to see one of your kind again."

Trey winked and nodded at her while she shuffled shyly in place and smiled at him. Not only had she eaten my cookie, but she was screwing with me after watching the guessing game.

I groaned. "You can't seriously be telling me you know what he is."

Leaning over the counter, she whispered into Trey's ear quietly while I watched on. He chuckled and nodded confirmation. In one meeting she had guessed what I hadn't figured out in years. I couldn't help but groan a little louder.

Giggling, she hurried off to find a seat. I tucked the report under my arm and followed, grumbling to myself. She took the seat by the window where I normally sit and watched me with a look of amusement like a cat that caught the canary.

Sitting across from her, getting a closer look, I couldn't help but see the crumbs of my cookie on her chin as she brushed them off and took a deep drink of her jet fuel. My demoralization was complete.

"So," she said after swallowing her caffeine, "there are a lot of prints on it. None of them match, but one did line up with your hunch."

Deciding to put aside my annoyance, I asked, "He sold it to them?"

She nodded and turned the pages of the report. Lined up on the third page was a list off positive matches. Staring at me was the face of the man who'd supplied the omega pack.

"Emil."

Thanks to some personal history and Lucian's use of him as an informant, I knew Emil very well. I wasn't too surprised he'd be trafficking professional packs to drug dealers. It was just legal enough for him not to be put away for long while illegal enough for him to turn a profit. He was slick that way.

Dulaf patted my hand. "Guess you get to go have fun with him tonight, huh?"

Nodding, I put the file down, looked out the window and responded, "Hopefully the weasel's not trying to stay out of the rain tonight."

98

It was peaceful watching the rain streak by. The steady fall of the raindrops against the pavement drowned out the sound of chatting and people in line asking for outrageous mixtures. There were no others asking for ten shots of espresso, but I suppose if more than one of those people existed at once the universe would likely implode.

She stood up and patted my arm again. "I can go run a search through the Oracle for him. He's still driving that thing, right?"

"Yeah," I replied, "always does."

"Shouldn't be too hard to find then," she said on her way out. "I'll let you know if I find anything."

I watched her make her way out the door, putting on her goofy looking hat. She didn't seem at all bothered by the potent mixture she put into her cup. I guess she was always running on it. It even made me wonder if she ever sleeps. But before I could chew on that thought very long she was already gone around the corner and long out of sight. You can move awfully fast on ten shots.

And a familiar voice asked, "Was that your girlfriend?"

"Hey, uh…" I trailed off, going blank on her name as I looked back into perfect blue eyes.

"Janice," she said, smiling. "It's good to see you again Devotee-"

"Agent," I corrected, sticking my shoulder out to flash the patch.

"Oh, *Agent* Leone then! Congratulations."

Janice: the girl I finally spoke to the night of my fateful meeting with the Giant. She looked a bit different now, maybe due to the concussions from the last two nights, both of which likely assisting in forgetting her name. Or maybe it was because I was looking at her directly rather than in brief, nervous glances. Whatever it was, somehow she looked better and I was tremendously pleased to have something to brag about.

"Sorry about before," she said past my silent admiration. "I shouldn't have been pushy like that."

"Pushy?"

"The number," she trailed off, averting her eyes.

"The number," I echoed, my fuzzy memory taking a moment to understand. "Oh, the number!"

She squirmed awkwardly, quietly mumbling, "You never called."

The reason I forgot her name dawned on me about then: a Giant knocked me silly. There had been no sign of her number since that night, in fact. There was only one place it could be. It was likely floating in a puddle on...

"H-Harbor Island!" I stammered, feeling my heart flutter in panic, "I lost it on Harbor Island!"

She raised an eyebrow and leaned back with a look of complete disbelief.

"No, seriously," I said, "I was punched by a Giant and..."

As my voice started to trail off, her look changed and she went from unbelieving to amused. The smirk crossing her face over my abuse wasn't exactly the kind of reaction I'd like to see. But she wasn't angry and that was enough for me.

"So it took getting knocked out to forget me," she said whimsically, laughing.

I awkwardly laughed along with her. "I guess so."

"Well then," she said, "We're just going to have to make sure you remember. How about we skip the number this time and meet up on your next day off?"

That question brought a moment of shock with it. An Alter girl, a beautiful one at that, was willing to be seen with an agent. We didn't have such a great reputation thanks to old stories of Vampire hunters sneaking into rooms and driving stakes through people's hearts. But, it wasn't every day I had a beautiful girl ask me out, or any girl for that matter. I would have been an idiot to turn it down.

Happily, I answered, "I have tomorrow off if you want."

She nodded, scribbled down a new number on a sheet of paper and slid it half-way across the table. Then she stopped, raised an eyebrow and pulled the slip away again. I wasn't sure why, didn't really even have the time to figure it out before she grabbed my forearm. Pulling up my sleeve, she scribbled the new information on my arm instead of the sheet. She was a smartass, a quality I appreciate in the right doses.

Putting away her pen, she smirked and remarked, "Can't lose it that way."

My arm was marked with her address, phone number and the time to meet her. I glanced it over for a moment before rolling the sleeve back down. Part of me wanted to stay there and spend more time with her in that quiet setting by the rainy window. Common sense told me better, though. If I stayed there I was bound to say or do something embarrassing.

So in that moment of clarity I smiled and said, "Guess I should get going, still have work tonight."

She nodded, asking, "Another fight to break up?"

"Nah," I said, "I have to meet with a man named Emil about the things he's selling out of his truck."

"His truck?"

I shrugged and answered, "He owns a poach coach."

"Wait, those are in your jurisdiction?" she asked. "Isn't that a health department thing?"

I chuckled. "Only if you're selling food."

"But, if he's not selling food, what is he selling?"

I looked out the window and stood up. "Probably quite a bit that he's not supposed to have."

"I see," she said in a bemused tone, probably trying to figure out what that could mean.

"Yeah, so he'll probably try to skip town soon," I said as nonchalantly as I could. "So I should get going and cut him off at the pass."

I waved to her and patted the forearm she scribbled on, and she waved back with a light smile. Even if Dulaf ate my cookie and stole my thunder for the day, I left the shop feeling good about myself. Meetings with Janice were apparently good for my mood.

Chapter 10
Unacceptable Scum

Dulaf put the Oracle to work on finding Emil, just as she promised. But something was awry. He seemed to know it was looking for him since, somehow, he managed to turn away from my attempts to intercept. Despite my best efforts, even throwing in a few fake turns to see if it was coincidence, he kept avoiding me.

"Emil," I muttered, "where'd you get the DAO?"

DAO, Delphic Apollo Oracles, are Oracle monitors that watch the rest of the system. The bastard bought a high-tech police scanner and was watching my every move. I accelerated down the block and threw on my lights. If he wanted to play cat and mouse games I was going to show him not to do it in a mobile kitchen. With my sirens blaring and lights pulsing I was screaming down the street after him.

It didn't take him long to notice.

The little red spot representing his Poach Coach started to move faster as I chased it down. He was even speeding through red lights and swerving through traffic despite the horrible vehicle he was in. As I approached the same corners I could see food and blood packs scattered along the ground. People scattered too as I drove through, squeezing the contents out of the litter and splashing it like puddles of mud.

He knew something. If he was willing to dump things to the ground, especially the blood supply, there was something important to be running about. He never had a DAO before; he got it for a specific reason.

As I accelerated down the street and took the last corner as hard as possible I could see his truck careening through traffic in the distance. People had to scramble to get to safety as he sped on by in his old busted death trap.

Endangering the public, speeding, fleeing police, resisting arrest, trafficking paraphernalia with the intent to sell – I was tallying them all in my head. It was good enough to taste as I started to close the distance between us.

As I came up behind the truck, I was momentarily close enough to see Emil's eyes in his rear view mirror. He looked like a terrified animal running from a hunter. I have to admit, my blood pumping and adrenaline surging, I felt a little like growling. I could hear the distant sound of red and blues coming to join the pursuit over the pounding in my own heart. I knew they wouldn't get there in time as I looked at the map floating across the windshield. Emil knew this game well; he was headed toward populated zones so we'd have to pull back.

High speed pursuits are dangerous in most circumstances, too dangerous in fact. Most departments were given orders to break off if going into a highly populated zone. At this time of night our chances of hitting traffic were lower than the daylight hours, but Emil knew where to go to force us off his tail. He was going right into the heart of Alter activity, the center of Fangtown: Crepusculum Forum, "Twilight Square".

Everyone involved knew that if we came within 7 blocks of the square it would be impossible for us to follow any longer. It was the center of activity for the Alters like Time Square on New Year's Eve or Bourbon Street on Mardi Gras. If Emil made it there we wouldn't catch him.

The red and blues flashed in a rear view camera feed across the corner of my windshield. They were holding back, already afraid of losing the guy in the Forum. But I knew he was going to try to bolt out of the city altogether if we didn't catch him now. Something was hot under his ass and I planned to be the one holding the torch.

One thing about his vehicle of choice: I couldn't think of how to stop him. Normally we'd be using all sorts of freaky maneuvers designed to throttle the fleeing vehicle like a prize fighter. But with something this size there was nothing we had that could do it. Even the fancier electronic devices conjured up in the last few years would have trouble getting through a larger vehicle like this. Drastic measures were required.

The rat bastard couldn't escape.

Flooring the pedal I pushed the electric motors to the max and accelerated out from behind the food truck. What little traffic there was had pulled to the side when hearing the distinctive wail of the ACTF siren. The red and blues probably weren't as much of a concern, but I wasn't something to be messed with. I had plenty of room to drive along-side Emil's speeding piece of crap and figure how to pull it over.

The side panels flapped up and down as the winds caught them like a pair of wings. He'd uprooted himself when I started coming and didn't even take the time to secure the damn things. Food stuffs and equipment were teetering dangerously on the edge every time the panel lifted from a bump in the road or a sudden gust of wind and it gave me an idea. There was a feature our cars have that most patrol cars don't.

I flipped a switch for my car's ceiling, opening it, exposing me to the rushing winds outside. Emil looked over as I kept pace with him and finally realized who he was dealing with. Scowling at him, I was still thick in the rush of chasing him down.

We barreled toward the Forum and Emil smiled, looking back at me one last time, as if rubbing in my face that he was about to win. But his look morphed from smug to utterly horrified as he set his eyes on what I had in my hand: a banshee.

With a flick of my wrist and a smile on my face I cast that thing into the truck. Emil screamed as it slipped through the opening.

I closed my roof and hit the brakes, letting him speed on past while I came to a screeching stop. The red and blues slowed too, likely thinking I'd given up the chase. But then they found out better as the ear-shattering scream went off inside that truck, destroying the windows, bouncing it around and blowing out parts of the undercarriage.

It coasted to a stop and came to rest just outside the seven block line we'd been racing for.

I shut off my siren while approaching slowly – waiting for a sign of what Emil was going to do. If the banshee was sitting right behind him, he likely head-butted the steering wheel from the shockwave. Admittedly, the possibility of finding him out-cold was a pleasant one.

But he staggered out of the vehicle dazed and confused. He wasn't a pretty sight under normal circumstances, but in his dazed state he was down-right goofy looking. His dark hair had blown up over his head and twisted into funky locks while his clothes were ruffled and messed. Really, it looked like he just climbed out of bed after a real severe bender.

I pulled up and climbed out of my car while he danced around on the street like a drunk staggering out of a bar. He looked across the hood of my car pitifully and pleaded with me in a weak, disoriented voice, "Nate, you can't take me in, bro."

He always called me bro, as if we were somehow family. We went a long way back, Emil and I. I knew him as a child and met him again with Lucian as an adult. I never liked him calling me bro, not once, and yet he never stopped doing it. Somewhere in that head of his, I think he hoped to draw on my sympathy.

Emil's a class four Vampire, only one rung above normal. Most class fours are people who came to the verge of death by way of disease. But Emil came to the brink by way of a needle. Some mutual acquaintances… weren't so lucky.

He was an opportunistic drug dealer who made the mistake of taking his own product. When the alchemist blue craze started, he was right on top of it and rode the wave. Since then he's squirmed around in the shadows, weaseling his way through life and making a buck off of human suffering. He was and always will be a parasite.

"Bro, please," he pleaded.

Silently, I walked over, switched on my silvers and twisted his arm as hard as I could, shoving his face into my hood. I worried for the paint, but hurting Emil, even a little, was worth it.

Partially climbing the car and putting my knee into his back to hold him down, I exclaimed, "Guess what, 'bro', you're going to jail!"

I slapped on a pair of reinforced cuffs and started to recite his rights while he whimpered into the paintjob of my car.

"You have the right to remain silent Emil, anything you say or do can and will be used against you in a court of law or in front of a legal tribunal appointed by Argyre. If you cannot afford an attorney, the Republic of Argyre will provide one to you. Do you understand these rights?"

Emil coughed. "Man, kid, you used to be cool."

I lost my cool and bounced him against the hood, snarling, "Do you understand?!"

105

"Yeah, yeah!" he yelled. "I get it! It's not my first time, damn it!"

The regular cops surrounded us, starting to climb out of their vehicles to assess the situation, some of them even going so far as putting their hands on their weapons. There was a bit of tension in the air while I stood there, Emil's face in my hood and arms twisted behind his back at an awkward angle. I think they were wondering what to do about the chase. Technically, we both had claim to jurisdiction, in some courts they had more.

"Got him," I said, pushing my knee harder into Emil's back. "Thanks for the backup, though."

They started trying to circle around us, responding to me with silence. They couldn't get behind us because of the busted truck, but the other sides were pretty firmly cut off by a small wall of blue. Memories of an incident between the government and ACTF in North Korea came to mind as they closed in. As I watched them I found myself hoping that was only something that happened in some far off country.

There are a lot of reasons for something like that to happen. They could have assumed Emil was innocent or that I was using unnecessary force. They could think one guy wasn't going to handle the big, bad Alter and try to take him from me. They could even want to start a pissing contest over jurisdiction in a territorial show of machismo. But really, they didn't need a reason to start something and I was going to be in the wrong if they did.

All it took in Korea was a guy with an itchy trigger finger firing at an agent. By the time the news reached us, across the ocean, it was too late to do anything: the short-lived attempt at a North Korean branch was gone. The public assumes the ACTF had been annihilated but the world governments knew better: we evacuated the Alters while crippling large portions of North Korea's forces on the way out. We call it Code 88: a last resort if things go wrong.

Every agent across the world has a fairly deep-seated fear we would be the dumbass to set off an 88 in our country. Looking at these tense men wearing another shield, I felt it sinking into me already. I would have given anything to have them step back and relax right then.

Luckily, I got my wish. One of them, "Ramirez", eased up and asked, "Got him covered then?"

I nodded, extremely relieved, and replied, "Affirmative, I've dealt with him before. Thanks for the support, though."

They nodded, starting to back up gradually as they saw I had it under control. A few headed back to their cars while Ramirez examined the truck. I was more relieved than I'd ever been as I realized I wouldn't be the dumbass to break the treaty on my second day.

"We can't let this thing block traffic," he said. "Is it okay if I call in a hook?"

"Sure," I replied, "I was going to have it impounded for evidence anyway."

Emil squirmed as he saw the prisoner's chair and turned to look at Ramirez with unease. He definitely had something in there that I wasn't supposed to see. But there was nothing he could do as I pushed him into his seat and hit the button to lock down. The frame closed around him, laid back and slid forward into the space under the dashboard.

The nearest officers were a bit surprised, watching me like they'd never seen one before. It felt a little awkward to have, basically, put a prisoner in a trunk in front of them.

Surprisingly, I heard a few laughs as they left, one of them saying, "We need to get one of those."

Ramirez lingered for a moment longer after calling in the tow truck and looked over the car. "Did I see right?" he asked. "I swear you had a sun roof on that thing."

I glanced back to him and chuckled, shrugging, "Some of our guys have horns."

He laughed and nodded along, remarking, "I always wondered why your lights were mounted differently."

I have to admit, in three years, it was the first time I'd ever talked to a regular cop without some tension. After all those years of looking up to my dad with his badge, I'd started to see them differently since joining the ACTF. Being stressed out, worrying about jurisdictions and trying not to be mauled, there was a lot of tension I didn't realize I was carrying.

Ramirez looked over the car one last time, patted it and started to walk away. "Maybe I'll have to drive one someday," he said while returning to his own car.

As he pulled aside to clear the street, I took a moment to section off the area with some crime scene tape and a few halo strips while Emil kicked and screamed inside the box. For a guy who probably spent a good part of his life behind bars or in small enclosed spaces, I was a bit surprised to realize he might have been a little claustrophobic. Of course, in Emil's case I didn't feel any sympathy, but it was interesting to know.

Cut off from the rest of the street, I entered the wreck carefully with an Oracle hand-link and started to meticulously take photos of everything inside. Even though I knew there was something in there, it was procedure to keep accurate records so no one could claim I falsified any of the evidence.

Emil's, and any "poach coach" really, is a "roach coach" with a blood pack cooler and a menu geared towards some of the more disgusting habits of Alter food supplies. I've heard some even serve kibble – though that part is usually urban legend and little more. I never dared to eat from the things so I wouldn't know; food trucks are a bit of a roulette game to begin with.

It was a mess, food and cooking utensils everywhere, the counters and floors dented by the spent banshee rod sitting behind the driver's seat. Sure enough, it looked legit from the outside: the blood packs stored in his freezer were alpha, "food source" graded packs, not omegas. The only real thing I found wrong on the first glance, in fact, was the fact his business license was forged. Second glance, on the other hand, revealed a few more interesting details.

I almost missed it actually, walking around and sifting through the mess left by taking a corner at sixty miles an hour in a taco truck. But the banshee had done more than stop the vehicle: it revealed hidden compartments between the seams of the wall panels.

I kneeled by one of the cracks it exposed and snapped a photo of it before reaching in with my fingertips to try to feel for a latch or handle to use. The interior of the compartment was white and misted over like a freezer or an ice chest. When I pried it open I saw this was pretty dead on. Emil was hiding medical grade omega packs in the walls.

I had him.

In moments I was back at the car pulling Emil's seat upright. His eyes went wide and he went pale even for a Vampire as he stared at the pack in my hand.

"You didn't tell me you were offering omegano sauce," I quipped, feeling pretty smug at the time.

"It's all legal," he cried.

"What about the rephaitol?!" I yelled.

"Rephaitol? I don't have that shit, no one does! That's Locusta territory. I'm just selling the blood!" He yelled back. "There ain't no law about having some blood on hand!"

He was right, there wasn't a law about keeping the stuff, just about what you kept it in. There are two grades of omega packs: professional medical type used for transfusions and "food supply" packets used by places like Ahab's. Emil could have the blood, but the pack type was only legal in medical capacity. I couldn't prove he wasn't keeping it for medical reasons with just the truck. Luckily, I had his prints somewhere else.

"Too bad we found a pack in a hermasin lab, huh?"

He paled a little more and looked in my eyes. "I couldn't know they were buying the stuff for that, man, you know that."

I frowned and held the pack closer to his face, clenching my fist, demanding, "I want to know who's been buying these."

One of my silver plated knuckles grazed his skin and made a mild mark across his cheek. He winced while it blistered in front of my eyes. I watched it for a second, amused, before realizing I needed to back off. It was the first time I'd talked to Emil without Lucian there to restrain me. Maybe Lucian was still restraining me even then.

"Emil, you know what this shit does to people," I said solemnly, holding the pack up where he could still see it. "How can you supply people with the stuff to make it?"

"I don't force them to take it," he muttered, averting his eyes from my visor.

I wasn't in the mindset to argue with him. I only asked, "Who are 'they'?"

He chose that time to invoke his right to remain silent by looking away from me and going dead quiet. He didn't want to give up his clients, probably figuring he could get off the hook with this and get back to business when they came back. Lucian's voice was there in my head, though, talking me down from the thoughts of wanting to slap him silly. But then that same voice, my inner Lucian, provided me with an alternative. I put Emil back and walked away.

I went back to the truck and fetched the spent banshee rod. Since I tossed it manually there were a couple things about it useful to me. When launched out of specialized launchers, typically reserved for the SOL members, it would have spent its power supply entirely and taken damage from impact. But, as it was, it still had enough of a charge to fake a countdown before going dead. It wasn't much, but it was perfect for something that, admittedly, I wouldn't do if I hadn't been granted some slightly fuzzy ethics by a Vampire.

And, I admit in hindsight, even if it was legal, I regret what I did... slightly.

As the lid of the box swung back open, Emil screamed as he looked on at the chirping, flashing banshee in my hand. Then I tossed it in with him.

"Ten seconds!" I yelled before slamming it shut, leaving him with the chirping rod and listening to him pound his fists against the lid.

The tactic wasn't exactly cool by ACTF standards. Though the banshee was actually spent and couldn't hurt him, I knew that they wouldn't let his information be used as a statement in court since this was obviously coercion. But I didn't need him to be a witness to this since what I wanted more than anything was to find the dealer in the first place. So long as he wasn't in any real danger, neither was I. So I kept a mental count of seconds as it continued to chirp and opened the lid again in five.

"Four, three, two," I counted down as he panicked.

"Okay!" He finally cried, "I'll talk!"

I reached in and grabbed the rod, letting him believe I turned it off myself as it shut down from using the last ounce of power it had. Relieved, Emil looked up at me, exhausted, and started to tell me exactly what I wanted to know.

"I don't know who's in charge, but it's big," he said. "There's, like, a new guy picking up the stuff every time. They never send the same person twice but they always get the same stuff, every time. A sandwich, two omega packs, surgical tubing, some cold meds and a couple two liters of soda. Always pay in cash. Same order every couple of days."

"Did you catch the name of the last guy?" I asked.

He sighed, looking up at me sad and exhausted. "Daniel Cho, I think."

It wasn't much, but it was all I had to go on. I tossed the rod into the frame again and slammed the door shut as Emil screamed. I know it was mean, but I still didn't like Emil and my mind was on more important matters: I needed to find "Daniel Cho".

Chapter 11
Fantastic Night

Daniel Cho was another lead that only led to a broad wall of crap. Do you have any idea how many Cho's there are in Seattle? I probably had a better chance finding Jesus for Lucian than I did of finding the right guy in a single night. I spent the entire time scouring the city for a Cho that could have been Emil's buyer. I guess it could have been worse: the guy could have been named something even more generic like Smith or Nguyen.

But it failed and I was glad to have the next day off. Even if I wasn't entirely there mentally, being able to take a breather and step back from the problem sure sounded like a good idea. Besides, Janice's number had been staring back at me since she scribbled it on my arm in what I was starting to believe was permanent marker.

If my luck held, tonight would be our first date. I was a bit nervous about it; the last Alter girl I went out with turned out to be a Succubus. She was a charming girl, fun, but I couldn't keep up and she was draining me – literally. However, the worst case scenario at the moment was I got out of the apartment for once and did something other than the usual routine.

Any other night and I would have been sitting there in front of the TV with a cup of ramen watching sci-fi movie marathons. It was always sci-fi for some reason, rarely drama or comedy, but never horror. I get enough creature features in my lifetime for the movies to feel kind of bland. You wouldn't believe how much every version of Dracula ever made loses its impact when you meet the guy in person and figure out that he's really just a dick.

Granted, I only met him once and it was at a book signing when I was only ten. The Alters had revealed themselves and everyone was having a real weird reaction to the whole thing. Dracula was pretty much the only Alter actually welcomed to society with open arms in all circles.

Well, no, that's not true. When they figured out Elvis was alive and well they decided to overlook a few things. Of these was the fact he faked his death and was living in the south under assumed identities while quietly feeding on the occasional person who happened to recognize him. Ever notice those tabloids could never provide a witness afterwards? He always ate a little too much.

But Dracula was pretty full of himself. All the years of being hyped up by the fan communities had gone to his head. They made him king of Vampires when they thought Vampires were fictional and Vladimir Tepes really died through an ironic beheading. Once they found out he was really alive they forgot they made up most of the things they liked about him. At age ten, I told Dracula to suck on some garlic to my dad's horror.

I was an early starter.

Thinking about Dracula and the fact I wouldn't have to watch another bad movie that night, I found myself wondering what to wear. Janice took the initiative but didn't tell me where we were going or if she wanted me figure it out. It's not like I had a lot of wardrobe choices anyway since my closet contained uniforms and the suit I'd wear to weddings and funerals. Still, with that kind of limited choice and no clue what I was doing, there was a definite challenge ahead of me.

I dug through my dresser, looking for widely-appropriate choices. There was a lot of blue and black in those dressers. Surprising how you learn you're in a rut only when you're doing something to get you out of it. I grabbed some slacks, good shoes, a t-shirt and a jacket hoping I'd manage to look presentable enough – or at least not laughed at.

By the time I dug up an outfit and got the damn thing on I discovered there was only half an hour left before I needed to be at her apartment. I gave myself a quick look and decided to shave off the stubble making me look like a b-list action star. It's laughable really, how that look became shorthand for "tough". I know for a fact the strongest men in the world are all baby faced and as rugged looking as a Chihuahua.

After all that, I was out the door with only fifteen minutes to go. It had finally stopped raining despite the lingering clouds. This was good because I wasn't about to take a date out in a car with a seat that locks the passenger in a box. She might disapprove of that, or worse, she might be really excited about it. Either way, I was walking.

She lived next to the Forum in the center of Fangtown just blocks away from where Emil's truck was crippled. It wasn't far from my apartment and for once I got a chance to enjoy a walk through the more eclectic part of the neighborhood.

The Crepusculum Forum, as its name sounds, has a fairly "Rome at night" feel to it. Modern buildings slowly give way to columns, lit by neon to create a pseudo-natural glow. The murals, with their timelines and historical figures, flow toward the center of the Forum like streams flowing into a lake. Despite being the realm of the nocturnal, I'd say the Forum is one of the most colorful places in the city, always alight with a rainbow and bustling with activity.

It's one of the only areas in the Fangtown region that receives human tourists. It was a peculiarity to the outside world: a region with the glow of twilight featuring Roman construction and unique locations. I passed several on the way: the first Ahab's, a Zomboner and the Moirae Club just to name a few. And when I reached the center of the Forum I passed the most visited of the landmarks: The Sunset Fountain.

The fountain embodies the nature of the Forum. It has a design borrowing heavily from the cultures around the ancient world. Yet, it's covered in light-up tiles and hologram projectors from the modern day. The water seems to literally dance as images flash through the mist above. Figures move gracefully through it like ghosts in a fog. Standing by the fountain, I could see the light reflected off a constantly rippling surface, illuminating the area like a sunset colored disco ball.

I stopped in front of it, seeing a mound of coins spread across the bottom. Some people, especially Alters, believe donating a coin to the fountain would help you buy your way into heaven. The old Led Zeppelin song always echoes through my head when I see the glittering floor under the amber light on the water. Sometimes I even felt the urge to toss a few in, though I never did.

Looking up, through the dancing figures hovering on the mist, I saw Janice's building across the square. It was a typical Alter dwelling: windowless yet elaborately decorated. That was your choice, really, if you lived in a world without sun. You either hid behind a wall or you tinted your windows black. Some architects used the technology we did at the sanctuary, making the walls solid, yet seemingly transparent. But, either way, the buildings look like mausoleums erected around the monument to a forgotten civilization.

Janice's building was a lot more welcoming on the inside: filled with warm colors and a gentle light from small glowing crystal spheres embedded in the wall. I could instantly tell her building was better than mine the minute I walked in the door. It was a great place, in fact, aside from the pair of Werewolves howling in the basement while listening to heavy metal. But you have to make a compromise, I suppose.

Up to the point I reached her door I was fine and expecting things to go well. What I didn't expect was the sudden cold wave of fear running over me the minute I arrived. Suddenly, I sympathized with those Alters who couldn't go into unknown spaces. It was easily the most intimidating piece of wood I'd ever encountered before and likely will encounter for some time.

Did I show up underdressed thanks to my limited wardrobe? Was I overdressed thanks to some sort of grand fluke? I sweated every option in those seconds that seemed like an eternity.

Fidgeting at the door, I nearly considered walking off and pretending I was sick so I could back out of the whole thing. In fact, I was only moments from doing just that before the door cracked open out of nowhere. I practically jumped out of my skin while it eased open and my heart started to accelerate until it came to a sudden, hollow feeling stop.

"You're late," she said, smiling.

One look at her showed me the cold truth of my position: I'd be underdressed regardless of what she wore. I've encountered amazing beings in my years with the force, yet I was still a little stunned. In a cocktail dress that matched the color of her eyes and a dark jacket for the cold night air, she was clearly out of my league. Something about the way she was shaped was beyond natural. It looked like she had been refined over the course of ages by some weary artist trying to sculpt a figure from his waking dreams.

"You look nice," I said in the greatest of understatements.

115

She thanked me and we were on our way. Luckily, the girl knew where she was going long before I reached that door, preventing me the honor of looking like an idiot. We strolled out into the eternal twilight of the Forum and down the street toward The Moirae Club.

The Moirae, a well-known establishment in the Cascadia area, was the first of many Alter owned nightclubs in the city. Named for the Greek Fates, it features three floors with entirely different themes. The top floor, of the past, is a refined, classic restaurant with good food and peaceful music. The ground floor, the present, is a modern nightclub with dance floors and a bar. And the basement, of the future, is a neon-lit rave with pounding music filled with drunken orgy of lust, booze and blood.

I'd been to the basement many times before to break up fights or help Lucian kick down the doors of the VIP room in the back. I doubt anyone in the club had ever seen me without a visor on. So I expected a stare or two as people did the math in their heads about why I seemed so familiar. Standing in line, though, I received very few looks, hardly a glance in fact. I suppose it's hard to pick out an ACTF agent standing in civilian clothes. Then again, who'd look at me when they could look at her?

Janice wasn't the only eye catcher. She stood a figure of grace, though, among the sideshow that lined up around us.

Most of the humans were "conners": the type of people who want to be converted into an Alter because it's "cool". Half would dress in skimpy clothes, despite the autumn and an ever impending threat of rain, and wear distracting jewelry at the common points of contact. One girl behind me wore a necklace of brilliant red stones that had to be worth almost as much as my car.

Meanwhile, the others, the "true conners" as they call themselves, were decked out in goth fashion. A lot of people who think about "latent Vampires" or "latent Zombies" start to conjure images of goths who stay to themselves, writing little poems about the sweet embrace of death. But, statistically, most Vampires are good little Catholics who regularly attend church and are pleased to no end that a carpenter, who probably carved a few wooden stakes in his day, apparently loves them. So, thanks to genetics, the goths are left to pine away for the chance to get bitten or catch an STD that'll give them an opening.

I wonder how many of them get conned into thinking another person is an Alter just for a quick one night stand.

The ones who weren't human, the Alters that thrived in this nightlife venue, were actually more dignified than their human counterparts. They came dressed in silk, satin and a dignified style that almost seemed suited to a nightclub of another era. It was like looking through the ages as I watched these people stand next to modern dressed humans. Even I, the fashion novice, could see the drastic difference between a man in a suit with a fedora and another wearing a spiked collar and some sort of faux leather.

Though nightclubs never needed help, they were easily the most heavily impacted industry during the revelation of these new races. Alters aren't all photosensitive, so they don't have to be nocturnal, but most still choose to live at night. The Werewolves I saw there were a good example of this: able to live in daylight like anyone else, they instead chose to gather with their own kind after the twilight hours with distinctive fuzzy hairstyles to identify themselves to the world.

I also saw quite a few Vampires there – most of them eying the closest conner with bloodlust in their eyes. Having experienced these places and these people from the outside I could almost see the course of their nights. Especially the difference between the ones who were going to do it the legal way and which ones were going to be arrested. Feeding on a living human is legal, provided you have their written consent and let them get the right medical care. But like a condom, the right protection is usually an afterthought. Conners only have a one in five chance of converting after a bite. The rest just get sick and some even die.

I've always wondered how someone could hate themselves so much they would rather be something else. How do they come to the conclusion that they're not good enough? Is it the same drive that brings people to do drugs or other destructive behavior? I wonder how many of them consider who's going to find their body and how it'll affect them. Someone would find them. Someone always came around to find them.

117

Probably their kids if they had any…

Janice nudged me with an elbow, interrupting my train of thought. She smiled and hooked an arm around mine – gently reminding me she was there.

"Sorry," I said sheepishly. "I do that sometimes."

She giggled and replied in a sing-song way, "Well I suppose I'll have to try to keep your attention."

"I don't mean to do it," I said. "Sometimes I get lost in thought and do a little people watching."

"And what are you thinking about now?" she asked.

I wasn't entirely sure, to tell the truth. I'd been staring at the mass of people around me and, for some reason, picturing the group behind the drug lab.

"I think I'm a little caught up in my case."

"Can you tell me about it?" she asked with an understanding tone. "Or is it confidential until you finish?"

I thought that over for a second and shrugged. "I don't think there'd be a problem talking to someone not connected to the news. You're not a journalist are you?"

"No," she said, smiling, "only a court reporter."

I chuckled. "Then I guess you'll hear all of this eventually anyway."

"Or type it" she said. "I don't really know if I pay attention to what I'm hearing anymore – so much reflex involved."

"Do you like it?"

"Oh, it's interesting enough," she mused, tilting her head. "I just think I'm starting to fall into a bit of a rut."

"A rut sounds nice about now," I joked. "I'm hunting a drug dealer who doesn't seem to exist."

Her face lit up as if I had said the most interesting thing she'd ever heard. You'd think a court reporter would have seen all sorts of crimes run by those little typewriter things they punch away at, whatever they're called. But she seemed surprised, happily asking, "How can there be no trace at all?"

She might have been feigning interest or even trying to be sarcastic. Surely it was a possibility, but I didn't really mind too much.

"He leaves fingerprints that can't be traced," I answered. "And he doesn't seem to have a record."

She giggled and patted my arm, quietly reassuring, "Sounds fun."

I'd never really thought of things like that. But I suppose I do like my job more than I usually let on. Even when it gets rough I end up feeling a little touch of accomplishment from what I've done. The dealer was bugging me, too much history with blue, but I was usually pretty content with my position. Plus, there was the shiny new car.

"Yeah," I replied thoughtfully, "I guess it can be."

We came to the front doors, allowed in with very little resistance. Janice smiled on as if there wasn't a reason in the world she shouldn't get in and, strangely enough, it worked. The bouncer recognized me and almost gave me a problem. But with Janice on my arm the problems just seemed to melt away.

I leaned closer and whispered to her, "Do you have something on him?"

She laughed, slapped my arm and dragged me downstairs to a room throbbing with music and flashing neon lights.

I've rarely seen the bottom floor of the Moirae without a pair of nanocrystal shades in front of my eyes. It was a thing to behold, the lights in the room coming in every color of the rainbow, backlighting figures as they danced. It was like seeing the visor image in negative. People were dancing to the pulsing beat of some sort of Alter band that could only be half heard by humans but easily felt throughout your entire body. Chills went through me as I entered the field of vibrating air they considered music.

"Beautiful isn't it?" Janice commented over the noise.

I really don't know what she was referring to but nodded along anyway. I figured it was best to agree with my date.

Obviously, she realized I was clueless and clarified, "The music."

"I can't hear most of it," I said, "just the background."

She gave me the sweetest smile and ran a hand over my eyes gently. "Close your eyes and listen."

I allowed myself to relax, not expecting much, and take in the sounds around me. Vibrating through in steady waves was a pattern so easy to recognize I could almost hear it. Gradually, more waves started to come and form a complex pattern. I couldn't hear it, but I could feel the music clearer than I realized. Despite the pounding nature of what I could hear, it was soothing and peaceful beneath. It felt warm, comforting.

"See what I mean?" she whispered.

"Yeah," I replied breathlessly. "I can feel it."

While my eyes were closed, she drew me through the crowds. I opened them to see a come-hither motion and a shy smile. Warm and relaxed by the ethereal forces around us, I lost myself in her eyes. It took me what seemed like an eternity to realize what she was doing. Taking advantage of my stunned state, she had dragged me out to the dance floor.

"Wait," I protested, "I don't dance."

She laughed again. "Everyone dances!"

With the most serious face I could muster I said, "I'm white, straight and mainstream."

A thoughtful look crossed her face, obviously mocking me, and after a second of bad acting she remarked, "You can fake it."

She started a seductive little dance that stunned me stupid again. I scrambled for thoughts on what to do. Fighting, investigating, shooting stuff, and sci-fi trivia: these are the things I know. Dancing isn't in my repertoire. And yet there she was, with her graceful and hypnotic sway, luring me to try to do my best not to look stupid.

I ran through the things I knew, wondering if any of them could have helped. Another time, another place, they could have all been impressive in social scenes. But in the end the only talent I had that could be of any use was my encyclopedic knowledge of old movies and what I'd seen there.

Out of options and running out of time, I did the only thing I could imagine would work: I tried to make her laugh. Locking, popping and swinging around awkwardly I started to mimic the one dance I knew I could pull off. I did the robot.

She stared at me like watching a train wreck for a second, and then slowed down to fully take in the mess that was me. A normal guy would have felt awkward enough to stop about then, hell, I almost did. But years of being in the ACTF teach you one thing above all others: dedication to the plan. Smiling carelessly, I continued my dance until her brilliant smile returned. Before the song was done I had her laughing and joining along – a victory by any standard.

When the music ended, she took the hint and pulled me away from the dance floor.

"You really can't dance," she mused while I did my best to look dignified.

"I think I did pretty well out there," I replied.

She stopped walking long enough to look back at me with an expression that could only be described as "what have you been smoking?"

"Okay, maybe no so great," I said. "But do I get good marks for effort?"

She grinned, patted my shoulder and walked ahead, saying, "B plus for the effort, D for the dance."

Strangely, I felt a little pride about that "D".

Proud of my C average, I followed her upstairs, up to the dignified top floor that I'd never really seen before. The music shifted to a human band, finally letting me hear the full scope of a song at the cost of that constant warm vibe. But seeing her by candlelight was worth such a trade.

Quietly, waiting to be seated, she said, "We'll get you a couple drinks with dinner to relax you."

While I should have been a bit unsettled that I seemed that uptight, I couldn't disagree with her. Even then, standing in the peaceful setting next to her by the light of candles and the sound of soft music, I was still a nervous wreck.

I didn't want to make her regret being here with me or get into some unpleasant situation. There were a lot of ways to do that, especially for me in the Moirae. But then there was the stress of trying not to look stressed in front of her. I was setting myself up to fail. Of course, not all of my fears were intangible. Quite frankly, the biggest fear, as I stood in that classy level of an otherwise wild club, was the tall black man glaring at me from across the room.

Anthony Newton, owner of the Moirae, was an imposing man. Taller than me by at least a foot and black as the night, he's always an impressive sight. His street name is Anubis, an apt moniker for a werebeast with his form. I wouldn't be much surprised if the original Anubis was the same way, a tall

121

Egyptian man who had a few bad days. Once, he was a member of the Third Avenue Hunt, supposedly going straight. But he still had connections to the criminal underworld, especially the Locusta members that gather in his basement, and was looking at me in a way that made me uncomfortable.

I expected there to be an issue, maybe even some form of violent outburst which would scare Janice off. But instead, in a chilling act, Anubis waved us over and pulled out a seat.

Janice looked at me in surprise and asked, mimicking my tone from earlier, "Okay, what do you have on him?"

"Nothing I know of," I murmured, cautiously making my way to the other side of the room.

As we arrived, he held out a chair for Janice, waved for me to sit and smiled as though we were old friends. I hesitated before deciding to sit, curious if he was going to do something once my guard was down.

And as I sat, he leaned down and whispered, "I love it when you guys legitimize my place."

It burned, sitting there and not making a scene while he said something like that. But with Janice right there, it would have been a stupid idea to do something to offend or possibly endanger her. So I swallowed my pride and watched him walk off with that smug grin on his face. The waiter standing by our table had the same look and all I could do was quietly fume.

But Janice seemed to have no clue anything was happening, happily ordering drinks for us and making it clear she wanted mine as strong as humanly possible. The waiter nodded and hurried away, returning moments later with a glass filled with an amber colored mystery fluid I could smell before it touched the table.

"Drink up," she giggled, "or else."

I gave her a questioning glance before taking the first drink. Immediately, I found myself fighting to keep it down and swallow it without crying or throwing up on her. She'd ordered me a drink mixed for Alters – I'd hoped by accident. It went down as smooth as gravel and tasted about the same. Tears rolled from my eyes and a general burning sensation came up my throat. I was in some degree of pain and completely unable to show it without bruising my manhood.

Janice, for her part, seemed all too aware of this. But, like so many women in my life, she was more amused than concerned. Normally, I'd take offence like I do with Dulaf. But with Janice it seemed so much less hostile and more like she was trying to laugh with me instead of at me. Maybe you feel that way naturally around people you've got a thing for. Or maybe Dulaf twists it in a different way. Whatever it was, it didn't burn as much to watch her giggle at my expense.

"So," she quietly started as her laughter faded. "What's your family like?"

I hesitated. For years I've tried to find the best way to answer that without losing my head. But looking at her sweet face, disarmed by her smile, I felt like I could handle the task of spitting out at least a few words on the subject.

And so, I quietly answered, "Gone."

"I'm sorry," she said, lowering her eyes. "How'd it happen?"

"My dad's job," I muttered, taking another drink of the awful concoction. "It got the better of both of them."

"What was his job?" she asked, looking up again.

I choked down another swallow, returning her gaze. It was such an innocuous question from outside. Yet it was the heart of my life, in one way or another, much like Lucian's influence. My father, like Leo, was a ghost in the wall.

Surrendering to the inevitable, I said calmly, "Cop."

Her tone softened, sounding sympathetic as she commented, "So it's in your blood."

Her eyes were understanding and compassionate. I'm sure her imagination filled in blanks with events more dynamic and violent than what actually happened. But in the end it was no less of an impact on my life and who I was. I'd taken up a mantle that crushed my father, banners of protection that could burn through my soul if I wasn't careful. Beyond that, she didn't seem to need to ask for details.

She let it go and we moved on.

The rest of the night was spent talking more about her occupation than mine, a merciful act if anything. It was hard to imagine how she saw herself in a rut; as a court reporter she spent her days listening to some of the most outrageous events to transpire in the city. And yet, sitting there across from me, she

123

bemoaned the time she spent just acting upon reflex to put down all the information without really processing it. Part of me even considered how great a threat an army of court reporters could be if they got hold of a credit database.

Still, she seemed far more fascinated with what I did. Even though the conversation stayed mostly on her, she found ways to make me speak once in a while on life as an agent. Ironically, our worlds soon merged on that very note.

A vaguely familiar man walked up the staircase into the room, passing through my peripheral vision. Who he was and where I'd seen him were complete mysteries. But I could feel that I knew him from somewhere, like a memory washed away from my mind by either concussions or the chemicals I'd absorbed over the last couple days. Despite the fact Janice was still talking to me, I couldn't resist the urge to turn away from her and watch him.

He was a well-dressed and professional looking Asian man in his early 30s, despite shoulder length white hair that made him seem so much older. There was a pallor to his skin too, distinct signs of a man who could not walk in the sun for long. But I'd never met him before even though I knew I'd seen him somewhere important.

Whoever he was, his eyes turned my way and his face lit up as he smiled and nodded in my direction. I wasn't sure if I was drunk or had a worse memory problem than I'd first thought, but whatever it was, he was smiling at me. Or, at least, it seemed like he was smiling at me.

"Daniel!" Janice called out happily, waving excitedly.

My world got very small for a moment as I watched "Daniel" walk over to greet Janice. Could he have been the man I was looking for? If he was, how could I have even known what he looked like? How did Janice of all people know the man? The questions buzzed through my head faster than the glass of antiseptic I had been nursing for the last hour.

"Daniel Cho," Janice said, confirming my fears, "meet Nathaniel Leone, that agent I told you about."

Daniel nodded to me and offered a hand. It was awkward, not knowing who exactly this guy might be, unable to shake the feeling of him being familiar and being told to shake his hand.

But looking at them, it was impossible to refuse the gesture without making a problem. Even if he was the right "Cho", it wasn't exactly the best place to start something.

"Agent, you say," Daniel remarked. "Then maybe you've heard of my case, I hope."

I wanted to practically leap at him and scream about the case I'd been following, the case he was central to. But there was no way we could have been talking about the same case. He wouldn't have been so nonchalant about it.

"What case would that be?" I asked hesitantly.

His face turned cold, unhappy with what I'd said.

"Daniel had his identity stolen," Janice explained, "a couple weeks ago."

Hearing it left me stunned, dumbfounded really. Even if it was the right Cho it was the wrong guy and probably another dead end. All I could do was repeat "identity stolen" with a vacant look in my eyes.

"Not just my identity," Daniel continued, "my face."

"Your face?" I asked, probably sounding a little dim.

"Yeah, my face," Daniel repeated. "Bank statements were showing all sorts of medical supplies, blood packets, cleaners and a lot of other strange things. I went to the bank and told them it wasn't me only to find they had eye witness statements of a guy looking like me showing up with photo ID to clean my accounts out."

And that's when it clicked, when all the pieces fell together and answered my first big question. I remembered where I recognized Daniel: the wall of photos. And from that I knew exactly why so many dead ends were forming. The lack of fingerprints, the faceless criminal and the accounts of multiple people working such a small operation all led back to one conclusion, at least for someone in the ACTF: I was dealing with a Shapeshifter.

"It has to be pretty funny," he said, "seeing someone steal from a defense attorney that would have probably taken their case."

I nodded along, looking at both of them with a stupefied expression. Daniel politely ignored my vacant stares, said a nice farewell to Janice and walked off to be seated at a table. But Janice gave me a look of utter confusion as he turned away.

"What was that?" she asked.

"That," I said, pausing to recollect myself, "was the first break in my case."

As I watched Daniel sit at the far end of the room, I saw Anubis treat him with the same sort of odd respect he showed me. And I felt the sudden revelation that I was sitting in a building with criminal connections while watching what may have been either the first victim… or the first suspect.

Chapter 12
Anubis

The hunch made my night. Even if it was just a guess, it was strange enough to explain away the twisted things I'd seen. I even relaxed enough that Janice got me to dance again and patiently taught me something other than "the robot". But, as great as the night was, in the back of my mind I knew I still had to get back to work the next day.

Realizing the suspect was a Shapeshifter was a bit troubling. They aren't innately evil, no Alter is, but they have problems connected to their abilities. Shapeshifting isn't the magical talent that old folk tales make it out to be.

Changing form requires absolute control of body chemistry, bone structure and muscle tension. It could take anywhere from hours to days depending on how different the form and it's always an agonizing experience. So, of course, they need something to control the pain, usually something illegal, and a lot of it. Rarely could something relatively harmless like marijuana fully take the edge off and prescription abuse was cracked down on when I was a kid. So that meant the Shifter, if it was a Shifter, probably wasn't producing for sale – he was producing it for personal use and selling off the extra for money.

These thoughts were starting to cross my mind as we left the Moirae that night and Janice quickly picked up on the fact I was once again on the down-slope of my personal roller coaster.

"So what kind of break was it?" she asked idly while I stared into space.

For a moment I considered trusting her, telling her what I was thinking. But there was a part of me that realized the procedures to keep tight lips on such things was there for a reason. Still, she felt like someone that could be trusted despite knowing her for only a short time. Maybe it was the way she mocked my dancing or the fact that, despite mocking me, she actually knew when to stop. Though, I knew I could trust Dulaf. Maybe I just liked women who could laugh at me.

Obviously, it was something to talk to a therapist about the next time I was required to take a mental evaluation.

But, in a moment that would reflect badly on me during that evaluation, I cracked and said to her, "Daniel might be connected to my case."

"Oh yeah," she said with a snarky tone, "Daniel Cho's a hardcore criminal."

"I'm not kidding."

She stopped, turning to face me, staring at me in what had to have been disbelief, and said, "You can't be serious, Danny's harmless!"

"His name was attached to a case and I just saw him talking to Anubis," I replied, trying to avoid eye contact, knowing attacking her friend was probably a bad way to go. I made a mental rule not to look, trying to avoid escalating the situation any more than it had to.

"Anubis talked to you too!" she exclaimed, stepping around, trying to get into my line of sight.

"But I'm an agent," I said, breaking my rule only heartbeats after making it and looking up, "and he was just trying to screw with me."

She silently fumed for a moment, making me feel awkward to even look in her direction. It wasn't rage or fury in her eyes – those I knew how to deal with. It was almost disgust. She was appalled at what I was saying, what I was implying. In her position, I suppose I would have been the same.

"You will not hassle Danny," she said sternly, as close to growling as her soft voice could get.

"I have to," I replied.

She stepped back and grew ever so quiet. "Yeah," she said, "you go do your job, then."

It was a horrible moment, knowing that I was quickly losing my footing with her, losing whatever ground was made in our short awkward dance and conversation. Here I was on our first night out and already I was suspecting her friend of being involved in a criminal operation. Worse, I couldn't tell her why I suspected him.

A quick mention of Shapeshifters and how the identity thefts could tie in would have smoothed it all over. She would have understood that anyone could have been involved in a situation like that. At least, I'd hope she could understand it. But it was something I just couldn't tell her. Even mentioning Danny's involvement was too much and probably enough to get myself roasted. I knew that, I wasn't stupid and I wasn't going to risk the investigation to pull my ass out of the fire.

But looking into those eyes and knowing that was still harder to do than anything I've done in a very long time. Especially difficult was when those eyes turned away from me and she stormed off.

Once again I stood alone, exposed and with no one to blame for it but myself. I watched her leave, conflicted as to whether to follow her or leave it alone before I could dig a deeper hole. The wrong word, the wrong sentence and I could have done more damage to it than I could have ever done intentionally. No, sadly, it was a situation I couldn't confront directly.

I walked home alone and immediately did the one thing I felt could help. I ordered her flowers. A cheesier moment I doubt I've ever had. But in the end, what else could I do? Simply talking to her felt wrong for some reason – no doubt the evaluating therapist would have scolded me for avoiding confrontations and explanations. But it still felt like the wrong thing to do.

I strolled through the apartment and looked around at the furniture in the room. Looking at the old, worn out furniture, I thought back to years when they were new, wondering how many fights were had about my dad's job. Running my hand across the back of one of those seats, I crossed to the kitchen and sat on my trusty old stool and checked for the number to the nearest flower shop.

I ordered her some roses and attached the message: "I can't afford to ignore it but can't stand to hurt you. I hope you understand and can give me a second chance."

Part of me reflected on the many domestic disputes Lucian and I had stopped over the years. How many started with both people just trying to do what they thought was right? Maybe most of them do. And if that's true, then the only reason anything gets resolved is because someone, somewhere, decides they're willing to swallow their pride to say they're sorry and step out of the other's way.

God I wish the job would have let me do that.

Glancing over at the old busted toaster, my mother's toaster, I knew the alternative was to just walk away.

I knew I didn't want to do that right now. But in this case, I couldn't afford to back down and claim I was the one who was "wrong" either. Besides, a first date was not worth my career and it certainly wasn't worth letting a blue dealer, any blue dealer, go.

Cho had a high probability of being a victim in the whole thing anyway. Shifters wouldn't likely use their default name and face for anything illegal. I could put out feelers on him and see if he really reported the identity theft and get to him if my leads ran dry. On the other hand, someone else I saw was probably nowhere near being innocent.

And so, the day after the date that should have gone perfectly, I returned to the scene of my own little crime: the Moirae.

Returning wasn't an easy prospect. Being there in uniform by myself was a new experience and I spent a good part of the day doing a mental check of everything I needed to remember to do. Anubis had left the Third Avenue Hunt before it collapsed, but he still had ties to the Locusta in his basement and there was a lot of illegal business going on down there. Straight or not, that meant at least someone in that building wasn't going to be happy with me being there, and I was going to be outnumbered by the dozens. The ACTF is chronically understaffed, so everyone has to be willing and able to enter the lion's den alone unless they planned to make a *lot* of arrests. But, of course, if you can't call for help you prepare for the worst.

Wanting to avoid getting anyone caught in the crossfire, I got up before sunset for once to go to the club before its usual hours. Though I knew the top floor restaurant was open in the daylight hours, the rest of the building didn't see a whole lot of activity before nightfall. I wasn't expecting to start a fight, but if a fight did start I didn't want anyone caught in the middle.

Before I even entered the club, I inserted my earplugs. The earplugs we use filter out only frequencies produced by the

banshee. They were tuned well enough to hold a conversation…
provided I wasn't talking to a literal Banshee. And, of course,
they were necessary to talk to anyone in that room because I
planned to chuck one through the doors before walking in.

Walking past the bouncer, I switched it on in front of him.
He paled, steering clear so fast you'd think he was a cheetah.
With an underhanded toss I let it fly into the room. There were a
few bounces, the scream of patrons and chuckles from me. But
the banshee didn't go off.

I wasn't actually planning to blast them, at least, not unless
they started it. While we typically let the banshee go with a "toss
and forget" setting, there were some *other* options. The one I
chose to use that night was the rarely used "mockingbird".

You see, the banshee doesn't just produce sound, it responds
to it. It could be used to produce a wide range of effects, from
sonic scrambling to cloaking and everything in between. So,
under the mode I set, it wouldn't go off unless it heard something
really loud, like a gun or the sound of a chair smashing over my
head.

I just hoped no one dropped a plate.

But walking in, I was happy to see I guessed right and only a
handful of people were on the ground floor. The few down there
were now backed against the walls or even up on seats and tables
as if it would somehow help them. Given the looks on their
faces, it was fairly clear it wasn't going yet. Not that I would
have heard it or noticed anyway – I was a little preoccupied.

Walking into the den of a Werewolf, or any metamorph for
that matter, is a cautious moment. Invited as I may have been
before, in the uniform I was about as welcome as the plague. So I
didn't go in empty handed and certainly didn't just walk right in.
In my right hand, the Helios, in my left, a little something we call
a "pack-buster". And as expected, while everyone else stared at
the weapons as though I were storming a castle, the staff looked
like they expected me.

In fact, as I walked in, one of the staff directed me to a room
in the back as another opened a door. Making my way through, I
kept an eye on the guards and entered the back office. Anubis
was sitting in there at a table by himself, quietly sipping soup
brought down to him by the waiting staff of the top floor. I had to

admit, I was impressed at how little he seemed to care about me being there.

But Anubis was mostly alone in that regard as everyone else was clearly agitated. Behind me the guards started to close in with a general sense of tension, keeping distance from the banshee on the floor. Meanwhile, the corners of the office were occupied by the epic forms of two very large, very angry guards who showed some signs of being from the same snarling brood as Anubis himself.

"Fetch," I exclaimed, tossing the buster to one of them. He caught it and fumbled around in a state of shock and panic, probably expecting it to go off in his hands. The guards all around the room jumped in fear or sense of loyalty for a member of their pack, not realizing it wasn't set to blow provided I didn't trigger it from across the room. But Anubis was still completely undisturbed, only making a motion for me to sit across from him.

Watching a Werewolf eat is an interesting experience. Normally, you wouldn't notice any sort of difference from any other large man in a suit. But if you know what you're looking at, what to look for, it's kind of eye opening. They eat as if it were a fight, aggressive and defensive, making surprisingly quick motions while staying alert like someone might try to take it from them. It's controlled, subtle enough that you wouldn't notice, but driven by an instinct deep inside. It's not like a snarling beast over a bowl, just the way they hold everything more like weapons than utensils. In fact, it kind of reminded me of boot camp. Only when watching him did I finally see some tension and I knew I needed to resist the urge to screw with him.

"Mockingbird?" he asked, momentarily lifting his eyes from his meal.

"Of course," I replied, sitting back as relaxed as I could. "Wouldn't want to blast anyone innocent."

He nodded along as a steak rare enough to moo was placed on the table by a woman dressed more like a secretary than a waitress. I took note of her since, at that moment, I could tell she was an Alter but not what kind. Her eyes were a shade of green a bit too bright to be normal and yet she was otherwise unassuming. It was a strange feeling, watching as she moved behind Anubis, around the room, and back to the shadowy corners of the bar. She looked back at me while passing, watching me like I was watching her.

Something about her felt…familiar.

"My assistant, Marionette," he grunted. "She's not usually around when you agents stop by."

Whoever, or whatever, Marionette was, she caught the attention of some place toward the back of my mind. And yet, not able to determine what exactly she was, I soon pushed it back and turned my attention to Anubis again.

"You know," he said, aggressively cutting into his steak, "waltzing in here like you just did is more than a little bit illegal."

"A common misconception," I replied, scanning the room to keep an eye on Anubis' understandably upset pack. "Treaty says I'm granted the right to do whatever I need to do to control a situation with or without authority from the local government."

"And what exactly does that bullshit mean?" he snapped at me before taking a bite, baring his teeth for a moment.

"No warrants," I said, "and since my equipment's on standby, none of you are in any actual danger until I am."

A light, choking snort escaped him as he shook his head, practically snarling, "So what the hell do you want? We weren't involved in those pet store hits if that's what you were thinking… Mr. Wolfendown."

The shades hid a good portion of my wince, trying not to show any larger response to the snickering around the room. One guard even had a pretty good impression of the insipid voice from that god awful head. But I tuned it out well enough despite a slightly clenched jaw.

"No," I replied through clenched teeth, "I figure your old friends of the Third Avenue Hunt would have stopped that if they were still around. I'm here to talk to you about Mr. Cho."

The laughter died down, Anubis looking at me as though it was the strangest thing he'd ever heard. Putting his utensils down for the first time, he laced his fingers together and responded, "Danny boy?"

His voice was shocked, or at least something very close to it. Though, why he was surprised to hear it could be debated, it was definitely there. In fact, looking about the room, it was on all of their faces.

"What the hell did Danny do?" Anubis barked.

"His name was dropped in the middle of a blue investigation," I said calmly as possible with that many uneasy wolves watching me.

"No way," Anubis grunted, "Daniel's clean."

"Oh really," I replied, "as clean as you?"

There was a tangible feeling of tension waving through the room as though every muscle within those walls moved in unison. It was the feeling you get when faced with an angry pack, the feeling you get when you know the room is literally against you. And yet, Anubis just smiled.

"Look, Nathaniel" he said easily, leaning back in his chair. "What those guys in the basement do is none of my business. I just know that as long as I look the other way, I stay out of trouble and they make sure no one else tries to start trouble either… usually."

He seemed sincere. And yet, I had to ask, "Then how exactly did Cho get connected to this? How is he connected to you?"

He pushed his plate aside, resting his hands on the table, calmly saying, "The man's a part of one of the few law firms that will represent our kind."

"And what does that have to do with anything?"

"Well," he replied calmly, "even if we were, and I'm not saying we are, connected to something like that, we wouldn't let our lawyer get tied up in it. Because if his ass is in the fire, where's mine going to be?"

Hearing it laid out like that, how could anyone fault the logic? It would be like poisoning his own drinking water. On the other hand, wouldn't that make Cho the perfect decoy?

Giving him the benefit of a doubt, I asked, "Do you know anyone who might be willing to do it?"

"If I did," Anubis commented coolly, "I'd take whoever it was out in a heartbeat."

Part of me understood what he meant. But it wasn't enough to suppress the unease it caused for me. And he saw it so clear I didn't need to say anything about it.

"When you go home," Anubis said, "you take the uniform off and it all goes away. But me, my guys here, we run a legit business here and at any moment of any day we find ourselves facing a whole lot of problems. Someone could fake food poisoning, claim we put hair in their food or whatever they can think of. That man, he's one of us, an Alter. And because of that he's willing to defend us despite knowing, more than likely, we're going to face a heavily stacked deck when it happens."

A silent nod was extended from everyone in the room as I felt like a complete ass.

"So, yeah," he said as I looked at the resolute expressions around us, "we'd take someone out to protect that man. It's the way a pack works."

"I'm sorry," I murmured, lowering my visor, "I saw you with him and he'd been mentioned in this case by a witness. I jumped to conclusions."

Anubis sighed and finally relaxed as I removed my visor, waving to me and shrugging my apology off. "Don't sweat it," he said, "I saw you looking our way last night and assumed we'd be getting this visit since Danny's been having some issues with the law. And," he continued, lightly shrugging, "you wouldn't exactly be wondering about us without due cause. It's no secret we've made some deals with the devil in the pit on a few things."

The devil in the pit: an infamous figure on the street. This "devil" controlled the organized crime in the area intangibly and, by extension, a body of organizations that bordered on a shadow government within the Alter enclaves across the country, maybe even the world.

"And Daniel Cho is the man that lets us keep our souls," Anubis said. "So I hope you find who tried to do this to him."

I nodded and stood again. "That makes two of us."

Walking out, picking up the banshee and buster along the way, I made eye contact with the people in the room without that visor. A small part of me felt like scum, judgmental scum, undeserving of the job for assuming the worst of the people I should be protecting. Reinforcing this was the fact that, even after everything, I found myself stopping to look at Anubis' assistant Marionette one more time, wondering why she disturbed me so.

My gut told me I was missing something. But was that feeling legitimate or was it something that I didn't want to admit to myself?

The fact I was even asking myself that question was disturbing. Why was my first instinct that the dealer was either Anubis, Daniel himself or a Shifter? I wasn't even sure what the person Emil dealt with looked like. Even the guy at the bank could have simply been in a disguise.

And it became apparent why Janice was so defensive of these people. In my zeal, I might have ignored her word and considered her biased. I'd made a lot of assumptions.

But something occurred to me at that time. If the operation in the lab wasn't large enough for a group, how is it that there were so many fingerprints that didn't match? A group of people with no previous criminal record touching a blue lab meant for one person? That didn't sit right.

Maybe I was biased and only realizing it now that I didn't have Lucian by my side to keep me in check. But with a question like that, I couldn't afford ignoring my theories.

Chapter 13
Unusual Witnesses

Luckily, Shifters are surprisingly easier to confirm than you'd imagine. And, if I wasn't making assumptions, I probably would have checked the system first.

Early on, the ACTF began to tag Shifters with identification chips that could be tracked. Some protested the use of technology meant for pets being implanted into people. Surely, there was no ground for treating people anywhere even remotely like animals, aside from the couple that actually turned into them at least. However, they quickly changed their tune when a Shifter "borrowed" a position in the Argyre governing council.

I thought it was funny myself, but I could see their point.

Hopefully, that chip was functional and waving a giant flag in the air for me to follow. Skipping my nightly coffee, I arrived to work at the crack of sunset. Driven in a way that I hadn't been since the incident with Max, I got to work at a desk as soon as I could and brought up the Shifter tracking display.

I got nothing.

Shifters can be scarce, among the rarest of them all, but as far as I knew, unless I really was biased, there was supposed to be at least one on that map. And yet the whole Cascadia area was coming back with nothing. Nothing was in Seattle, up the coast or even in Vancouver.

There was a chance that Cho was making up some elaborate cover to keep himself free of suspicion. But the idea an attorney would need to sell drugs to fund a habit didn't quite click. If he wanted to get high on alchemist blue he could have done it rather effectively on an attorney's salary.

Staring at the map, I had a sinking feeling. It was looking more and more likely that maybe the person involved got used parts and wore gloves. It was looking more and more likely that I wasn't as good of a person as I'd hoped.

Dulaf waltzed up behind me just then, asking without warning, "Date went so bad you need to use the Oracle to find a new one?"

"No," I snapped, annoyed at the accuracy of her guess, "looking for people in your age range."

She peered over my shoulder, resting a hand on it, and saw the screen was blank. Before I knew it, she clamped down with a grip just strong enough to make me feel a sharp pain.

"Now, now," she whispered, "don't make me hurt you, little boy."

Surprised by the sudden Elven strength, as I always was, I hissed my submission while rolling my chair away. She swooped in where I'd been and examined what I'd really been looking for.

"Shifters?" she asked, bewildered. "Why are you looking for Shifters, Nate?"

Idly rotating my shoulder to get some feeling in it again, I replied, "I thought my dealer might be one, but…"

Her ears folded back, a thoughtful look crossing her face as if she was considering the situation seriously. It was one of her rarer expressions: peaceful, considerate, contemplative and a little sad. Some say that's her true self but I could never be sure. All I knew was she'd see the blank map and inform me I was wrong.

"I guess they didn't get tagged," she said, proving me entirely wrong.

"That can happen?" I asked, almost relieved the idea still held some merit.

"Well sure," she said. "I'd think it'd be pretty easy for someone to fake not being a Shifter if they could change their form anytime they wanted."

"But how would they ditch the blood test?" I asked, rolling back into place.

She sat on my desk and stared at the ceiling silently for a bit before lying down across it and commenting, "Not sure, but I bet they give off a unique colored aura, probably bright yellow from the drugs."

I looked at the ceiling to try to figure out what was interesting enough for her to start lying on my desk as if she were comfortably at home. There was nothing up there aside from the lights, monitors and holographic displays. And yet, she stilled stared on at the information running overhead.

"If you could figure out where they'd be," she said idly, "you could bust them with the aura."

I looked down at her on my desk again, completely clueless to what she was talking about, and asked, "How would I do that? I can't even figure out where they've been, let alone where they'd go."

She raised a hand toward the ceiling, pointed at the displays and said in an absent tone, "Ask her."

"Her?" I asked. Whatever she was pointing at, all I saw was the Oracle system busy at work, maintaining the constant flow. It was almost elegant in the way it balanced watching everyone with being able to sit in the background unnoticed. Like a watchful mother, it was involved in everything but tried its best to stay out of the way.

A watchful mother.

Finally, I figured out what Dulaf was thinking. I looked at her with an expression that meant, simply, "duh". And she nodded, patting me gently on the back as she got up and walked away.

I went to see the actual Oracle sitting behind the ever-present face of the system.

It was more than a tongue-in-cheek use of folklore. We had actual Oracles, among the rarest of Alters, sitting in the compound. Oracles didn't hear from gods, they heard from people. Through bioelectric fields and an acute sense of awareness, when placed in the right environment, they could "hear" everything. After seeing their condition, it only made sense to use their talents to create a greater network of information. So that's what we did, assembled a powerful hybrid of biological and technological observation equipment that could do more than watch people, it could read them.

Hopefully it, she, could read anyone.

The local Oracle is located at the highest point of the station, like a psychic radio tower in the center spire. So I took the elevator and went to a floor higher than I was accustomed to, passing even the Commissioner's office. It was eerily quiet up there, virtually barren of activity as I traversed cold metal corridors coiling up the tower. Covered in silver plates and lined with blue lights, it reminded me of the secured areas of Acheron.

In fact, only one person sat in that corridor. Sitting in a control room, just before the Oracle chamber, was a half-sleeping guard, arms crossed, staring at a console. He didn't look up as I watched him – he merely waved for me to carry on as the doors opened.

He was the caretaker, the only person allowed to see her without her permission. That door only opened for him and those the Oracle permitted. The system was so tight that his role was more like a butler than a guard. But I guessed that was probably why he was half-asleep.

The door closed behind me, locking with an electrical hum as I sat in a small space between that and another door, like an airlock. Psychic ability is a tricky thing to work with and requires very controlled circumstances. I've been told it's less like reading someone's mind and more like saturating in the details no one else can see. Chemistry, physical phenomenon, and psychological effects coming together like a code that can be deciphered with a trained eye and patience. You don't see one person – you see them, everyone around them, and how they all got that way. Thus the airlock was a filter to protect against unannounced noise. I imagine it would be overwhelming otherwise.

I stood at that door for what seemed like an eternity, waiting nervously to see what would happen. There was no course at the academy about proper etiquette when meeting the Oracle. I wasn't even sure what the room would look like. All I knew was she probably had a sense of what I was thinking already and that made me pretty nervous about being nervous…if that makes any sense.

The doors opened, a pink light pouring into the small space around me as a translucent deprivation tank was revealed. She floated in the tank, suspended by red liquid, her hair waving softly and her eyes remaining closed. Somehow she was breathing, thriving inside that liquid environment despite being cut off from the outside world. Though, maybe she thrived because she was so isolated from it all.

She smiled at me, her eyes still closed, and the whole room faded into darkness.

Warmth came through the shadows as wisps streaked by, immaterial fireflies that appeared from the ether. I don't know if it was the same for everyone who stood in that room, but I could hear these fireflies whispering strange, unnatural things as they sped by me, like stray thoughts running through a dazzled mind. Each of them had a voice distinct from any other. Together, they were a great chorus pouring from a single point of light in the darkness.

Standing among the flurry of lights I felt others with me. They weren't watchers or observers, nor people standing in the room. For one brief moment, I felt everyone all around me: all of Seattle, all of the Cascadia area as far north as Vancouver. I felt rain across my face, heard the ocean waves crash to shore and the sounds of people laughing and singing together. I heard others cry, scream and question their place in the world. I felt the pain of the sick and injured. I felt the despair of a weary nurse that seemed to stand over me, or her, or someone. But in the end the laughter and singing came across so much stronger than any of those.

For one moment, as the Oracle called to me, I was one with the world. I felt at peace, as if looking on the face of some higher power telling me it was going to be okay. And I understood in that moment how the people could think we would be tempted to abuse this power. I could picture it becoming more addictive than any drug.

My head started to clear, the voices fading and light taking shape. Vague colors and shapes formed into more solid, tangible objects as I was transported to another place. The haze soon gave way to the image of an empty Ahab's. Only the caretaker sat behind me, the shop and city outside looking abandoned.

"You skipped your daily ritual," a new voice said.

I looked over, the Oracle sitting there in professional clothes with her hair back in a bun. I wasn't sure why she chose that outfit, but part of me felt like it needed to be remembered.

"I wanted to get to work figuring out my case," I said, looking ahead at people slowly appearing out of thin air.

141

"And what exactly were you hoping to find?" she asked calmly.

I looked around the room as the sounds of clattering began to rise and the smell of blood coffee drifted through. The familiarity I had with Daniel the night before came with it. Somehow the people in the room were no more or less familiar to me than he was in this dream-like state.

"I need to know if it's a Shapeshifter," I said. "I need to know why Daniel felt so familiar."

"Suppose it's good we're here then," she said idly. "You can't tell why someone's familiar unless you retrace your steps."

"Yeah," I said, scanning the room lightly. "But where do we start?"

The Oracle smiled at me, a new light flashing over me and jumping us to a new dark, dingy environment: the drug lab in New Skids. The photos on the wall were as clear as when I stood in the room and the acrid smells as vivid as the moment I first walked in.

"He was on the wall?" she asked, browsing the photos.

"Yeah," I replied, joining her and glancing at Daniel's photo as if I'd known where it was all along. "But this photo wouldn't be enough to make him memorable to me, would it?"

"Maybe, maybe not," she said.

"Maybe not?" I asked, "What does that mean?"

"Maybe you've seen him somewhere else," she said, running a hand across the photo.

Even the photo was disturbingly familiar, like an image working at the edge of my mind, more so than the memories of this room that she was tapping into. No, this was an element of something deeper, something I knew should be obvious to me and yet wasn't. And then, it struck me.

In a flash, we stood in Ahab's again. But this time I could see the people more clearly than I had before. The people in the shop were from photos on the wall, including a more professional looking Daniel that I never seemed to notice despite him feeling so natural in that shop now.

"They're all customers at Ahab's?" I asked hesitantly, staring into space as the image returned to the grim interiors of the busted apartment.

"Were they?" she asked.

Apparently from her lack of answers this was already something I knew. She was drawing it from my memories, sorting them like a secretary working through dusty filing cabinets. And it was at that moment the photos started to make sense to me.

"No," I said quietly, "not all of them. But I bet there's a link to the others. Can I see one of the system maps?"

She nodded, gesturing to the wall, blowing the photos away and exposing a new screen like the one across the windshield of my car. A map shined across the screen and lit the room, reflecting off the carpet of glass behind us, setting it ablaze like a twisted, ugly gemstone.

"Show me the location of everyone on the wall of pictures, in relation to the local Ahab's shops," I said confidently.

As expected, dots clustered all around the shops in the area, breaking down into three major groups. The one closest to my apartment had the fewest hits, the newest target for "fresh faces".

"Now any with identity theft reports," I continued, watching the field thin out only very slightly.

It was fairly clear the suspect was scouting coffee shops in an area within a mile radius of each other. They were perched on those locations like a vulture waiting to see someone weak pass by. But some were hovering out in places that didn't mesh with this concept at all. Some victims were miles away from their nearest group, hanging in the middle of places that had no real connection to the case as far as I'd known it.

They were too far from the Ahab's shops to be easily scouted and not nearly close enough to be related to the New Skids lab. So the question became: what did those people have in common?

I pointed at one like an icon on a desktop and the case file opened in front of me. Deceased and marked with a red X on the wall of photos – likely not a coincidence.

"Show me only the recently deceased," I said, looking around the room at the crossed-out pictures, feeling uneasy about what I was stumbling on, "and give me photos."

Sure enough, they matched. They had almost no connections, though some were familiar to me from recent trials and juries.

143

Nothing was there to connect them beyond a passing attachment to legal matters. But that in itself left me chilled.

"List the causes of death," I whispered coldly.

They flickered in next to the photos as she processed the request, taking time to sort through what had to be piles of information. But it didn't take long to see a trend. People were hung, hands behind their back, gags in their mouth. Others shot point blank in the back of the head, hands and feet bound. They weren't just murdered: they were executed.

There was only one real explanation for this: the photos weren't just a list of faces to steal; there was a hit list too.

"But it's all speculation," the Oracle said calmly, glancing at me. "Isn't it?"

And she was right, it was. If I was going to get anywhere on the case I was going to need more than that. The Shifter caught stealing a position on the Argyre council made the mistake of becoming too public of a figure, but I knew that wasn't a mistake my suspect would likely make. I couldn't even prove that it was a Shifter in the first place. What I needed was evidence, a witness, anything. At the very least I needed someone who had a grasp of what happened in that building and who was moving through it.

"You need the girl," she said.

I looked at her and asked, "What girl is that?"

The sounds of screams echoed through our shared recreation of the building.

"That girl."

She was right: the Vampires' victim was my best hope of a witness. If you're just starting out on alchemist blue, you don't go to the source. You get your stuff through a dealer, a friend of a friend or that creepy uncle no one wants you to talk to. Logically, if you're walking up to the production lab, a hidden one using invisible markers, you're not a first time customer. Once again I had an assumption: the girl assaulted by the coven was a frequent visitor.

"She's in a coma, isn't she?" I asked, thinking out loud.

"And connected to EEGs," the Oracle added, "Easily read."

I wasn't sure invading someone's privacy to that extent was the right thing to do. If I abused such a power, wouldn't I taint the investigation? Though, I'd already teetered on the edge a few times before, especially with Emil. It was a complex issue, soon made moot as the Oracle decided for me.

The girl appeared before us in a flickering light, lying in a hospital room. Pale, gaunt, cheeks flushed with fever, she was looking to be on the verge of conversion. She hadn't escaped the assault unfazed. Considering her wounds, she was fairly lucky to come out of it so well. Somehow she survived a brutal attack that damaged the blood vessels in her neck. At worst, now, she was going to become one of them, infected with the A-cells and forced to convert to survive.

Thinking about where I found her, I wondered if she'd even care. Time and again I've seen people taking these poisons, destroying themselves and refusing to stop. I've heard it's a disease and they can't help it. Ironically, someone who was so ready to give up her life was going to become virtually immortal. Karma, God, fate or whatever power controlled these events had some sense of humor.

But she rose from the bed, her spirit lifting from her body, a visual representation of the Oracle extracting information from her mind. It was a haunting sight, humbling to realize how easily the system could take anything it wanted. Without effort, the system we constructed, feared by some to be the ultimate invasion of privacy, proved the fears all too well as I stood face to face with a girl who should have been in a coma.

Soon, that dissipated, vanishing like the ghost she was and spreading through the room in a thick fog. The fog, her memories as far as I could tell, rolled across every surface. It engulfed the room, forming the lab as it had been in her hazy mind.

A faded memory rose from the mist: a figure with two-toned skin hunched in the corner of the room. Surrounded in clumps of hair falling from its head, the figure squatted with uneven limbs looking like they belonged to completely different people. Looking at it, you couldn't tell who it was. But it was unmistakable *what* it was. The girl had walked in on the Shifter in mid-change.

The Oracle stepped forward, speaking in another voice, asking, "What happened to you?"

She'd channeled the girl's voice, her memories, into this new world. And as she spoke, the Shifter, grunting and growling in agony, rose to its feet with the snapping and crunching of bones cracking under pressure and shifting under skin. Whirling around, it turned to face the Oracle and glared through the darkness with shining eyes of two different colors.

Then it spoke, cutting through the nearly tangible haze like a wind blowing out the fog. It was a powerful voice yet came through rattling and pained like someone speaking from their deathbed. It left a deep impression, so deep that even the fog of the coma and immense drug abuse couldn't diminish its power. That voice haunted her.

"I'm finding myself," it said. "Now stop being a pest."

It wasn't much, but the sound was profound. It was easy to understand why it would stay with her so strongly. The whole figure was unnatural, inhuman. But to have it combined with that voice, it was impossible to forget such a thing.

I stared into those eyes as the memory of that entity froze in her mind. I tried to imagine what it would look like without the influence of blue and darkness in the way. Was this what it really looked like at the time? Or was it an exaggeration of a far more subtle form? It left me wondering if a hallucination could be remembered with such crystal clarity. Wouldn't she have forgotten it if she were that fried?

I didn't have time to ask these questions or consider the ramifications of the answers. In moments, I was standing in the entrance of the Oracle chamber again, looking out at her floating in the red fluid. She looked up at me, opening her eyes and smiling, before the doors closed in my face.

I'd received all the answers I was going to get. There was a witness to confirm it was a Shifter, albeit a shady witness. At least it was confirmation of my theory even if it couldn't be used in court. Then again, anything you get from a coma victim wasn't totally viable.

Also, a disturbing truth had been exposed. If the pictures on the walls and the investigation files were accurate, the Shifter was more than a dealer and identity thief: he or she was a murderer. Given the style of the murders they were likely a professional.

With the connections they had to trials and what Emil said to me about the Rephaitol supply in the city, only one motive was obvious to me.

There wasn't a whole lot I knew about dealing with an assassin. It wasn't exactly part of standard ACTF operation. So I needed to talk to someone who might be able to assist me, or at least point me in the right direction.

And, really, when thinking of someone I could trust, only one man came to mind.

Chapter 14
Surprising Encounter

Less than ten minutes later, I was sitting in my car down the block from City Hall. Benjamin Hale, being the City Attorney of Seattle, would be either there or in the Municipal Courthouse. Considering he was responsible for prosecuting Alter crimes as well as the human crimes, I couldn't picture him sitting at home. And because Lucian was assigned to watch the guy, that's where I'd find him too, likely with a copy of his favorite book in one hand and a bottle of pomegranate juice in the other, bored out of his mind.

Then again, he might have been terribly busy…

I watched that building for what seemed like an eternity. How was it going to look if I came running to my mentor for help only days after my promotion? But if I didn't go to see him, who else could I ask? Either way, I shouldn't have been distracting him from his work. My head filled with these thoughts until it began bouncing off the steering wheel.

More time passed stressing over the questions than it would have taken to ask them. Realizing this, I sucked it up and stepped out of the car before I could chicken out again. Avoiding eye contact, I walked to the building, rehearsing what I'd say to Lucian that didn't sound incompetent. My best bet, in my opinion, was to say it was merely a "consultation".

Theoretically, it could have worked after he stopped laughing at me.

But once inside I forgot all notion of covering my pride. There were way too many other concerns inside that building. Surrounded by Alters of all shapes and sizes, ranging from typical thugs to polished men in three piece suits, I found it very hard to move.

Despite the fact the lobby in City Hall is huge, it was packed full of people. It was like the depths of the Moirae if you shut off the music and took away everyone's drinks. I found myself wishing some breed of Werewolf would have tried to mimic sheepdogs instead.

With the need to respond to the concerns of "both diurnal and nocturnal constituents", the City Council meets more often than ever. It was once enough to consider only the needs of the mainstream. But quickly Seattle, the whole of the Cascadia region actually, became a home away from home, a haven away from Argyre. So of course, every time they were supposed to meet at night everyone from activists to reporters showed up to see the "historic" Alter related policies. But it didn't help the crowding any that City Hall was sitting right across from the Seattle Justice center.

The two busiest courthouses in the Cascadia area and the state of Washington are right next to City Hall. Those courts are the only ones in the region that could, or would, handle Alter related cases effectively. With Acheron in the city, it was the only place with effective holding cells. That, and the lingering problems of resolving racial tensions, meant I was in the center of one of the most contentious places in the city after sunset. Looking at the wall of humanity ahead of me, it wasn't hard to believe.

Friendly faces were few and far between as I pushed through. There were enough glares and red auras to make me grateful for the metal detectors and the fact my own gun had biometrics so no one else could use it. One stupid move would be enough to set the whole powder keg ablaze. Some of them were members of rival gangs, likely there to either talk to prosecutors or "talk" to a city official over "business matters".

The two key groups I recognized among them were the International District's Jiangshi Tong and Belltown's Locusta. Between them, they split the majority of criminal activity in Fangtown right down the middle. Needless to say, they weren't fond of each other. Really, the only thing they were less fond of than each other was the ACTF.

Guess who walked right between them?

Ever wonder what the matador feels like in front of the pissed off bull? Just go wear an ACTF uniform in front of two rival factions of Alter Mafioso. People around me quickly took notice the area they were standing in was becoming no man's land and started to spread away from me so fast I almost wondered if I'd forgotten to shower.

Looking between the two groups of pale pretty boys, I probably should have been terrified. Instead, I asked, "So, boy band auditions? You guys have a nice gimmick going on."

Lucian taught me to act like the big dog in the face of odds that weren't really in my favor. Something about it said to me that it was the right time to show no fear, as if I wasn't worried they could tear me apart. They responded to the disrespect with scorn, simmering rage and a few threats spoken under their breath. My hand slipped over the grip of my Helios: a gesture recognized by all.

Quiet snickers broke out behind me while the two groups backed away. It could hurt their reputations, running from one little agent, but they couldn't risk it. The Locusta couldn't afford to make another public spectacle, their higher ups taking a beating in the media and on the streets. The Jiangshi Tong, meanwhile, didn't have the manpower to lose after the headquarters opened up right next to their territory and a gang war went a little south.

It was a simple moment, something that could have been missed by the blink of an eye, possibly not even important enough to mention. But it was my first time doing that to such people without Lucian by my side. It was the first time it felt like he might have been right about not needing him. And when I cleared the crowd, prepared to make my way to the City Attorney's office, I again wondered if it was really necessary at all.

But Lucian was standing behind me before I could make up my mind. He was as I expected, holding a bottle of juice and a practically ancient copy of Grendel with tattered edges and a worn spine.

It was never Beowulf, a story that compared to Lucian in age. No, it was always Grendel, the 1970s version where everything was told from the monster's perspective. Somehow Lucian felt more sympathy for that angle on the story. Though, given the age of the original, it may have been the first instance of anti-Alter propaganda.

Grinning like he'd seen the whole thing, he walked ahead and waved for me to follow, asking, "Witness or beggar?"

I wanted to say neither, claim to be there for another task and scurry away as if I were incredibly busy. But then it wouldn't have been long before I was exposed. It was time to bite the bullet and hope it wasn't some sort of deal breaker in the eyes of the organization. Though, that didn't mean the words came out of my mouth easily.

"Ah," Lucian said before I could speak, "beggar."

My reply consisted of uncomfortable groans and a grunt of acceptance – ineloquent, but easily expressing the sound of swallowing one's own pride.

Nerves make you start to forget things: like the way someone watched out for you over the years and told you to come to him if you ever needed help. But his smile and his hand patting me on the back reminded me. I was both eternally relieved and incredibly embarrassed but returned the smile before he could slap the stupid out of me.

"I need advice," I said quietly.

He nodded, leading me out of the lobby, through the executive building to the CA's office. "Good timing, Hale's busy at the moment so I haven't gotten bogged down in the exciting world of babysitting yet."

The sound of his voice was both telling and confusing. He wasn't happy with the job but something about it amused him. It was the kind of amusement that comes by being petty or watching someone suffer. Such amusement was out of character for Lucian, usually a laid back guy, so to say my interest was piqued would be an understatement.

"Why do you," I started to ask, interrupted by an abrupt gesture and a laugh.

"You'll see," he said. Obviously he was amused enough that even he realized it was behind his voice, like he was happy to have me there so he could share it with someone. But, whatever it may have been, I accepted that "I'd see" and hoped it wouldn't take long to catch on. I've never been good with waiting.

"So, what about the case is giving you problems?"

There were a lot of answers to that question. We didn't have fingerprints, the witness was a drug addict and the one suspect

151

could act as any number of other people. Any of these was enough to sink a case, so where could I possibly start besides the obvious?

"I'm chasing an unmarked Shifter," I said with a defeated sigh.

Lucian looked unusually surprised. It wasn't the sort of surprise you could attach to words like "oh you guys" or "oh shit". No, Lucian's surprise is the kind subtle enough to miss and yet unmistakable to anyone that paid attention. Really, it amounted to the visual equivalent of "huh".

"My dealer's connected with an identity theft ring...and several murders."

He laughed and slapped my shoulder, leaning against the wall outside Hale's office. Smirking, he remarked, "I see you got the interesting job this time."

I chuckled half-heartedly with him. "So how do I catch a Shifter?"

"More importantly," he said calmly, "before it can kill again."

It was hard to keep my head up thinking about that. They were going to sell more drugs, steal more identities and kill again at this rate. Until they were caught there were going to be more victims lining up and it was all on my hands. I was starting to feel very small again.

"Nathaniel, you're a smart guy," he said. "I think you can crack this without me. But I can tell you how to get started on it."

"How?" I asked.

"The key is ignoring the fact he's a Shifter for now," he replied.

"Oh sure, easy enough," I quipped. "What's step two?"

"Now, now," he said in a lecturing tone, "I'm serious here. You need to think about what they do and less about how they do it."

"What use is that going to be?" I asked.

"Well, if you were them, how would you behave?" he asked. "How would you decide to start doing some of these things?"

In the moment it took me to think about it, I realized I'd been an idiot all along. Though, rarely do I find myself not feeling at least a little stupid, this was particularly intense.

"Someone would have to order the hits," I said.

"And who orders hits?" he prodded.

"Scorned spouses, angry people, business rivals," I said, rattling off the list.

"And?" he nudged.

Rephaitol came to mind just then, harking back to the angry men in the lobby. Emil said there was only one illegal supply line for that in the city. The Locusta were connected somehow.

"And the Mafia," I said, lifting my head again.

Out of the corner of my eye, a figure came up behind us with a sort of presence I've felt before. It was an old, familiar feeling for more than one reason.

"Well this sounds like an interesting conversation," the vaguely familiar voice said. "What exactly would you be talking about?"

And there he was: Benjamin Hale. I'd heard the name and watched him speak a few times on television, never realizing who he was. But I remembered him now as someone I met in my cleric days. I'd met him when he was merely a witness to a crime, a frail and fragile man on the verge of death.

But now he was tall and strong with dark hair and bronzed skin, as if he'd been standing in sunlight even on these rainy days. Shimmering sky blue eyes reflected my stunned expression back to me as he smiled on, offering a hand to me for what felt like forever. It was a calming, reassuring smile with no sense of judgment or disapproval veiled behind it like so many politicians and lawyers I'd known. It felt honest – he felt honest.

"I think we've met before," he said smiling, waiting for me to move again.

I took his hand after quite a bit of hesitation and felt warmth radiate from him that was entirely unexpected. Looking at his hand, feeling the energy pass through me, it was clear he was not a common Alter. He was something special, rare and unique.

"You're an Empyreal?" I asked in a hushed tone.

He gave me a silent nod and shook my hand with a gentle dip. Staring at him, it was hard to ignore the scope of what was happening. He was an Empyreal, like Alexander Neumann, beings that defied easy classification. But, in the end, I was shaking hands with a creature that folklore had classified many times before – one generally referred to as… an angel.

Chapter 15
Painful Memories

Benjamin Hale wasn't always an Empyreal. Once he was a man like anyone else, sitting under a clear night sky on a curb in front of the smoldering remains of a bar, clutching a glass and stifling the urge to sob. He was bald, withered and gaunt, left ravaged by months of chemotherapy. And I was a cleric, fresh from the academy, one of the green-horned nitwits. He was the witness to my first hate crime.

"The Wildman", the name on what was left of the sign, had been torched, the liquor inside used as an accelerant as the bartender appeared to have been burned alive. And the only one left to tell us who set the fire was the sad, sickly man on the sidewalk.

I'd heard of The Wildman before, even stopped in once with the other clerics after clearing academy exams. It was one of the few Alter establishments outside of Fangtown, owned and operated by a Woodwose named James. It was a rarity, a peculiar little place where the customers were all a little bit strange. And then it was left in cinders.

The room smelled thick of alcohol, ashes and burnt flesh. I walked through that building, surrounded in charred furniture and looking at the body of a man nailed to the floor, still soaked in water from the fire department and trace amounts of alcohol used to set him ablaze.

Fire is the worst thing to happen to a crime scene. The worst part isn't necessarily the burning; nothing is ever completely consumed by the fire. No, it's the fire department: smashing and blasting everything with water and washing away what was there before – even the ashes and remains. By the time the fire is out there's nothing left to examine. So to say we were lucky to have Benjamin Hale would have been an understatement. Unfortunately, not everyone shared that opinion.

"Hey, Nate," one of the other clerics whispered, shifting through the cinders, "Did you recognize that guy out there?"

Of course, never being one to follow the news, I replied, "Not a bit."

"It's Benjamin Hale, scum of the Earth and all around shitty guy."

"Why?" I asked, glancing out the door at the back of Hale's pale head.

Throwing a chunk of burnt wood aside, the cleric snapped, "You honestly don't remember this guy Leone?"

I shook my head and shrugged, vaguely seeing something, remembering nothing solid. The cleric leaned in close, whispering lower than before, "Remember the Satyr trial?"

"Of course I do," I said, "it was…"

And then I remembered. His name and face were forgettable, but Hale's actions were scarred into the memory of every agent. The Satyr case was the first major blow against the rights, even the lives, of Alters on the North American continent. It was, is, one of the greatest travesties to have been carried out in a court of law in the 21st century. Hale had committed a sin that could never be forgotten: he was the defense attorney in that trial.

Satyrs are one of the more unfortunate types of Alter. At a glance you instantly know they're not the same as everyone else. Their legs are formed differently, their body hair particularly thick. From a distance, you could understand the goat comparisons of the past. You could even understand how someone who was raised on such stories would think of the satyrs and demons of folklore. But until Benjamin Hale walked onto the scene, no one considered it a valid defense.

His client, a middle-aged, seemingly harmless man, was on trial for brutally torturing and dismembering a Satyr. The charges against him were specifically regarded as a hate crime. But in a matter of days the case started to fall apart. Hale knew all the angles he had to play. He displayed the man's "deep religious ties" and the stories of Satyrs throughout history, describing them as lecherous creatures tormenting women. The man testified that he did it to protect his wife and kids and that he feared for their safety and their very souls.

According to Hale, it was an act of temporary insanity brought on by centuries of detailed misinformation. In Hale's argument the man was not acting out of racism or hatred but on sheer terror. The prosecution argued anyone living in the modern day should know such people were actually human. But, combined with the knowledge of reality, the man's talk for fearing for their souls only made Hale's case all the stronger.

If the judge decided the case, following the exact letter of the law, he would have been found guilty and sentenced to some degree of a prison term. But when invoking religion and citing the history of Satyr-kind in such contexts, Hale had one ultimate truth on his side: you could never find a jury completely without religion. In the end, the jury decided they could picture themselves losing their own sanity and doing exactly what the defendant had done. In the end, Hale's client walked.

In one fell swoop the verdict opened up a loophole making it impossible for several races to live with the general population. Legally, they could still live anywhere they wanted. But, also legally, someone could off them at a moment's notice for "fear of their soul". It shouldn't have worked but it did.

Hale was a piece of work.

You'd think after all he'd done he would be easy to remember. You'd think that I'd recognize him anywhere. Yet, standing over him outside that bar and watching him clutch that glass, he was so different from the figure at those hearings. He was so weak, on the verge of death. He seemed so much more... human.

I don't know if it was sympathy or morbid curiosity but I couldn't help to ask, "What's a guy like you doing at an Alters bar?"

A tiny, fractured voice replied, "Wandered in a few months ago, been coming ever since."

"You don't look so good," I said. "Get caught in the smoke?"

He rolled the glass in his hand, watching the little reflections off the faceted surface. Sadly, he muttered, "Chemo. I wasn't here to see the fire."

"Thought you were our witness," I said, trying to avoid staring at him.

"I saw who did it," he said, "I just wasn't here to stop it."

It was a pathetic little voice, filled with guilt and self-contempt, half the strength and a faded shadow of what it must have been before. His words couldn't convince anyone, not anymore. Yet I was standing there, being swayed, watching him shiver and shake.

"They killed my friend," he said mournfully, "they killed my only friend."

"The bartender?"

He gave me a light nod and stroked the side of the glass he held onto gently. "I know everyone thinks the bartender is their best friend. But I haven't had a drink since the day I found out I had cancer. I just came to talk to him."

"Why would the defense of the infamous Satyr case dare to come to an Alter bar?" I asked, looking at the glass.

"Because he didn't care," Hale said, looking up from the glass out at the city lights under a starlit sky. "He wanted to talk to me, told me I was a good person despite it all."

A laugh broke through the wavering voice, catching me off guard. "I guess he probably says that to a lot of people. It's probably good for business to make the losers of the world feel better about themselves."

"Maybe," I added, "but he was a Woodwose and they rarely tell anything but the truth."

"What is a Woodwose anyway?" he asked.

I sat next to him, probably not the smartest thing to do professionally. But, even if the rest of the agency loathed the man, I couldn't leave him hanging.

"Well," I said, "a Woodwose is a wild man of the wilderness. They're more alert, aware of patterns and subtle details others aren't. Almost like a scared animal in the woods, scurrying around at every sound. But you put that kind of pressure on an evolved mind and they start to recognize patterns, behaviors, things the rest of us miss."

"Sounds like he should have been a detective," Hale muttered.

"Most are," I said, looking at the glass and tapping a knuckle against it. "He probably was too."

Hale lifted the glass, watching the city reflect and refract through it, saying, "He was always washing this thing. I only saw him use it once."

"Woodwoses have some OCD," I said, looking through the glass myself. "But once it's clean, it's clean. He was probably using it to watch you."

Hale burst out laughing, rocking back and looking at the sky. Chuckling, he said, "So that's why he never put the damn thing down."

"Yeah, Woodwoses can be pretty paranoid," I said, looking back over my shoulder. "Though, who can blame them?"

The laughter died, Hale sighing heavily. "They were so hateful, those two. They came in before and just spat on everyone there like they were nothing."

"Did they come by often?" I asked.

He nodded and said, "Too often by most accounts. They were just around to give hell to the people inside. No one ever expected them to show up when James was alone."

I watched Hale for deception, seeing as he was infamous for bending the truth, asking, "Then how do you know they did it?"

"Because I was there," Hale said, the hint of tears starting to well in his eyes, "before James sent me away."

"Why didn't you call the police?"

"James said he had it handled," he said sadly. "He was such a big guy, thick arms, built like a house. He always looked like a biker or a Viking. I never thought a couple of punks could do that to him."

"I guess," I started to say, hesitating, "it's amazing what people can do when they're driven by that kind of raw emotion."

He nodded, saying quietly, "It reminded me of why I'm so scared of what's coming."

"What's coming?"

Hale put the glass on the sidewalk and looked across the pavement glistening with the water of long departed fire trucks. He lifted his eyes to the windows across the street, which reflected the two of us against the burnt husk of the former Wildman. There was a stark contrast between me in my uniform and his broken, world-weary form.

"They say I'm latent," he finally said in a defeated tone. "Chemo isn't working, but they say the gene activation will."

"So you have a choice between death and conversion," I said, reflecting on the choice.

159

Still staring at the image of us across the street, Hale must have come to realize a sad, disgusting truth. Looking quietly terrified he said, "I don't think I can be one of them."

"Maybe not," I said, shrugging. "But is it worth dying over?"

He took a long look back at the charred building and the crews moving about it. "Not sure."

I couldn't fault his logic, couldn't tell him it was all going to be okay and that being part of the crowd was going to be easy. It would have been like telling a man coming out of the closet to his family wouldn't go over poorly or changing his religion wasn't going to alienate him from his friends. Quite frankly, there was no way anyone could know the answer to any of those things. No one could tell Benjamin Hale becoming an Alter would be the right thing. No one could tell him "being himself" was going to be the right decision.

"Do you think those guys will be punished for this?" he asked quietly.

"Actually," I said, "I think you know the answer to that a lot better than I do."

He didn't reply, didn't even look in my direction. All he did was stare at that glass, stand up and walk away. I didn't try to stop him. I probably should have, him being our only witness, but everyone there knew who he was so we weren't going to lose him.

Before he could leave, he stopped, looking out at the horizon between the buildings and seeing the sunrise in the distance. Rolling the glass in his hand again, he held it up to the light and watched it sparkle. With a small, sad little smile he looked back and said, "Might not be seeing too many more of those, I imagine."

And, just like that, he left.

As an agent you deal with many people who spend a lot of time trying to do everything they can to somehow subvert you. But none really succeeded in a way this man had. A petty thief or a mafia boss never had quite as much power as the people who take part in the legal system itself. But Hale was a broken man, stripped of that power by his mortality and forced to see the truth behind his work.

It wasn't until I stood in front of him in the City Hall that it occurred to me what exactly he meant about that sunrise. I'd watched a man literally step across the line in the sand, and then conveniently forgot his name all over again. For him it was a day like no other. Sadly, for me, I had far too many just like it.

Chapter 16
Living Contradictions

Filled with news clippings, honors and degrees, Hale's office was a memorial of sorts to the man that once was. But at the desk I saw signs that it was a life he was struggling to leave behind. Photos of various Alters standing with him lined the wall behind that desk, surrounding a photo of him, still bald and frail as I remembered, standing in an aura of sunlight coming through a hospital window with his arms stretched wide as if to take it all in. It was a photo of a man that appreciated life, all life.

"You were right," he said, walking around that desk and opening a drawer, "I did know the answer to that question."

We exchanged a look and I knew exactly what he meant before he continued. "And I fixed it."

It was a strange sensation having seen this man both at his best and his worst. But it was a strangely hopeful sensation that made me feel there was a potential in everyone, even the violator of human rights that was Benjamin Hale. The one standing in front of us now, taking up the glass he had fished from the remains of that bar, was an entirely different man in the way he spoke, the way he stood and the way he lived.

"So did you decide to do it based on what I said?" I asked.

"No," he responded with a smile. "The conversation turned me in the right direction, though. I had thought at one time people could be justified in how they felt about Alters, never realizing I was one myself. But then I watched a man like James, who looked so normal and yet had those obvious little things like the way his eyes twinkled and the way his hair and beard weaved through themselves like tree branches. I found myself thinking, 'if that is enough to justify the hate, then I think I might have been wrong'."

Lucian silently nodded out of the corner of my eye, arms crossed, standing at the far end of the room. I couldn't see the look on his face but I could almost feel the lack of enthusiasm he had about the arrangement. Something was off between them.

Yet it was hard to imagine not feeling something marvelous about this man we were standing with. I couldn't explain it, he just felt so… transformative.

"So you're a friend of Lucian's?" he asked.

"I guess," I said, looking back at Lucian's cool expression, "more of a student."

"He doesn't exactly agree with some of my methodology in the last few days," Hale said. "But I'm happy to have him on the team."

Hale grabbed some papers from the desk, heading out the door with us in tow. For some reason I could see the same thing Hale did about the situation with Lucian. The way he walked, the way he talked. For some reason the amusement Lucian had before I ran into Hale was gone, replaced with this silent disapproval. Well, silent for a while at least.

"I still think our security is sorely lacking," Lucian sniped as we walked down the hall. "You walked from the courthouse back to the office without security again."

Hale looked bemused for a moment before brushing it off, shrugging and smiling. "You need to be more trusting of people, Lucian. If you can't step into their shoes and understand their position then you can't represent them."

"I understand their position fine," Lucian scolded. "I don't think you do."

The words weren't very harsh, but the tone was unmistakable. This wasn't a minor difference of opinion between a pair of coworkers. This was something that had boiled beneath the surface for both of them.

Hale's security was obviously a serious issue, being the first active Alter in the entire country to run for any position of power and one of the first to hold elected office. But while being a City Attorney was a major step, it was also one that became easily forgotten. If the rumors were true and Hale intended to run for Mayor, he'd be putting himself in a new spotlight that could lead to severe backlash. Given Lucian's tone, I think Hale either didn't understand that or chose to ignore it.

"Lancer Descartes, Lucian," Hale said with a sympathetic tone. "I know the rumors around my plans have stirred some controversy, but you've seen how I've been trying to reach

163

people and make them understand it's okay. If I were to walk around with security all the time and surround myself with armed Alters like you, they'd think there was some validity to their concerns."

"These people don't need validation," Lucian replied.

"And that's why I have to diffuse them one person at a time to try to spread the good will," Hale said, smiling, "thus hiring our friend Mr. Thompson."

Lucian's smirk returned for an instant, reminding me of his earlier amusement.

"Hey," I whispered curiously, "when do you let me in on the joke?"

Lucian looked at me, smirk broadening into a sly, fang-bearing smile and said, "Wait until you meet Mr. Thompson."

"Mr. Thompson?" I asked.

"My private chief of security, William Thompson," Hale said, chuckling to himself. "For some reason Lucian seems to have a problem with him."

"Several problems with him, actually," Lucian said. "But I'm sure Agent Leone will get a good laugh at it. Where is the negligent bastard anyway?"

Hale tensed a bit, the reaction evident in his posture even if I couldn't see his face. As awkward as the conversation had been, it was definitely piquing my curiosity. This Thompson Lucian thought would amuse me was somehow at the center of their conflict. But, having known Lucian for years, I was at a loss for what exactly could trouble him about one man so openly.

"Well," Hale said, relaxing and nodding ahead, "he's right down the hall, in fact, waiting in the lobby."

I picked up my pace, craning my neck like a child searching for a promised surprise. Thoughts flashed through my head of various things it could be. Maybe he was a particularly strange Alter or a dreg of mainstream human society. The variables were infinite and my imagination ran wild. But never in a million years could I have pictured what was waiting for us at the far end of the hall.

With his well-pressed suit, sunglasses, tie and a radio earpiece that came up behind his ear, Thompson was dressed like a professional. Short, broad, bald and immediately recognizable was the man who'd led the lunatic protestors on Harbor Island.

"That can't be him."

Lucian didn't reply. He just smirked.

"Mr. Hale," I asked, "You do know this man is part of the fringe most likely to try killing you, right?"

Hale stopped, turning to me with a calm, assured expression. His bright blue eyes were so clear, like a cloudless sky on a sunny day, far removed from the smog of the cities. One of the rumored abilities of the Empyreal was the ability to settle anyone's fears with a look. Considering that, I may have been under his spell for a moment. But at the time I didn't really care, I became lost in the serene look in his eyes and the gentle tone of his voice.

"I know," he said, "but that man doesn't actually hate Alters."

Momentarily breaking that trance, I replied in a deadpan tone, "He was screaming it at the top of his lungs in front of a crowd of panicked idiots."

"As the leader of a union for a security provider," Hale said. "A security provider that wasn't sure their night watchmen could handle any problems Alters may bring to the table. It's a feeling shared by a lot of law enforcement."

He rapped a knuckle across my badge, saying with a smirk, "In case you haven't noticed."

We continued down the hall, my head swirling with the possibilities of how bad that could be and how assured Hale was it somehow wouldn't go sour. I glanced at Lucian, smirking while he made a "crazy" gesture towards Hale. But it was hard for me to be amused at the concept of a man like Thompson in charge of such a delicate situation.

Putting Thompson as the head of security was like placing a fox in a henhouse when the farm dog was sleeping. Yet, I could see why Lucian would be amused by such a thing. He had to be amused by something so absurd; it was the only option he had besides being furious.

We joined with Thompson and I put on my visor to avoid the inevitable awkward stares that would have passed between us. The man's aura was peculiar as the visor went on, a shade of brilliant yellow reserved for people under the influence. A drug addict and a possible hate monger given the responsibility of protecting one of the most controversial figures of the last decade: a horrible combination for Lucian's job outlook. But, I admit, the insanity of it all put a bit of a smile on my face too as we walked through the lobby. At the very least, Lucian could keep an eye on one of the crackpots with ease. And if that was Thompson's union, Hale probably hired several of the rest.

Half way through the crowded lobby Lucian commented, "You know there are other ways out of this building less exposed. This lobby was meant to be roomy, not secured."

I nodded, scanning the angry faces and notable mafia figures throughout the room, realizing just how many people could take a shot at the man right then and there. On the one hand, Empyreals are notoriously hard to kill, on the other, that wouldn't stop anyone from trying. In fact, like Lucian, I was left wondering why Hale would be so careless with his own safety as we stepped outside.

We passed an artificial stream that runs through the City Hall and down the side of the steps. Lucian stepped away, possibly a reflex from the Vampires' aversion to water. But Hale was an entirely other matter. Standing at the top of the stairs and looking at the water running downhill, he leapt over the divider and landed on the water. Not in it, not by it, on it. And with a smile on his face, he rode the stream downhill like an escalator, careful to hop down to the next step with every sudden drop and waterfall he came across.

Watching him I came to understand why Hale thought he was secured.

"Think he's betting on a higher power being on his side?" I asked Lucian quietly.

"Probably," Lucian said. "It wouldn't be the first time he's taken that into consideration. But hopefully the same calculation that worked against Satyrs works in favor of men who walk on water."

I turned to watch Thompson pass us, following the eccentric Mr. Hale down the stairs. An uneasy feeling took hold on me, seeing the two polarized figures standing so close to each other on the slope.

"He's in trouble, isn't he?" I asked Lucian.

"Most likely," he said. "But that's my concern. You've got problems of your own."

"Any suggestions on what I do with that?" I asked.

Lucian stopped halfway down the stairs and looked back, raising an eyebrow in consideration, saying, "If this thing has any connections to the mafia, then you're going to have to go to the head of the snake."

"Wait, you don't mean…" I trailed off at the thought of it.

He nodded to me, turning from amused to dead serious in an instant. He didn't need to clarify any more than that. There was only one head to the snake despite all other appearances, attached intangibly to the surface world's crime, a man by the name of Rufus Plagas: the devil in the pit.

Chapter 17
Absolute Evils

I wouldn't have to look very far to find Rufus. Far beneath the ACTF station, deep in the lowest levels of Acheron, Rufus has been in custody since the organization came public. And in what seemed like the blink of an eye I was standing with Joe the curate on a lift as he asked me, "It was the ninth level again, right?"

I nodded, waving for him to throw the switch, listening to the cranking and bracing myself against the long descent. We rode down the coiling, screw-shaped path around Acheron as it drilled into the Earth. Over a mile of tunnel passed by with views of prisoners in their common grounds through observation windows on the way to the bottom. They all looked like *such* friendly people.

Acheron's nine levels stack on top of each other like a great inverted tower. The deeper you go, the more dangerous they get and the smaller the section afforded to them. With each floor having fewer prisoners, the same number of guards can theoretically keep the peace. If that failed, a mile of sloped corridor would make it a long, unpleasant walk. It amazes me at times to think of the kind of effort we went through to secure a few unusual prisoners.

The worst of the worst, though, was housed in the ninth level, a floor with only one prisoner. And, while Joe had always acted as the ferryman to those depths, my escort seemed unsettled. It was a mystery I wouldn't solve for some time, but he had good reason to be disturbed. What I wouldn't give to have been able to read the man's thoughts just that once, like the Oracle did for my comatose witness.

For now, Joe's expression led me to wonder whether the gates of hell would be opening at the bottom of the lift. It was a pleasant surprise to find myself looking into a small lounge-like room with an inconspicuous monitoring station in the corner and a half-dozen guards watching either television or the video of a lone room past heavy doors.

A guard stood and approached while I stepped off the lift, making a gesture to let Joe know he was good to go. They wore beefed up versions of the curate gear, bordering on riot gear. In fact, my visor barely recognized him as alive under all the body armor and the thick, reflective visor of his helmet. Were it not for the humanoid voice bellowing out of the helmet, I never would have guessed I hadn't entered a room of fairly lazy robots.

"Glutton for punishment, I see," the large man said jovially.

He lifted a portable scanner at his side and did a half-assed sweep as if he didn't feel any urgency in the matter. Really, he waved me along in far less time than I imagined it would take. Maybe, I thought, they were getting complacent with their jobs after landing the floor with only one prisoner. But I couldn't imagine ever being that comfortable in the position myself.

Hell, even standing in front of those doors caught up with me: I was about to speak to Rufus Plagas, "the red plague". It was a big deal and everyone who ever went there treated it like one. Sure, it was one guy, but it wasn't just "one" guy, it was *the* guy. We all knew it: he was probably, quietly, the most dangerous man on the planet.

Ancient evils are myths for the most part, fantasies by the people too afraid of the creatures of the night to remain rational anymore. But Rufus is and always has been the real deal. I've long heard the stories and rumors saying the entire place was constructed right on top of his tomb like some old Greek myth.

The doors opened. The guard who'd scanned me barked "clear" and I stepped through. When the doors closed again I found myself surrounded by a dim violet glow revealing the dark figures of four men, standing at attention with large Helios rifles like those of the SOL team.

It was scary as hell but at the same time struck me as the most boring job in the world. They reminded me somewhat of shock troops acting as the British Royal Guard. Could one find a way to stare these men in the eye through the thick black visors and blinding dark, I imagine they would have never smiled or blinked.

And as I walked by them I could only hear the faint sound of music beyond. Piano keys and violin strings echoed off the walls with a distant clarity as if from the heart of a great cavern. The sound of my footsteps grew hollow as I approached the sad little melody. All that existed for a moment, before I cleared the shadowy entrance, was me and that serene, welcoming music.

I stepped out of the darkness into the light coming off a glass structure isolated from the rest of the room. The air smelled, even tasted, of garlic and I could see a wall of vapors rising from a gap in the floor just outside the glass. Beyond the vapors and glass was a garden of fruits, vegetables, and exotic flowers I'd never seen before. The music echoed from within the structure and a voice hummed along with it. Scissors, snipping at leaves, sang counterpoint.

A fifth guard approached me from around the corner of the catwalk, the sound of glass at his feet drawing my attention to light panels surfacing the floor around us. He nodded and waved for me to follow as he walked on by and around the next corner through a cloud of what I now realized was an aerosol allium mace. Chills ran across me as I connected the dots: the entire room, the corridor and the air itself were engineered to slow the prisoner down.

"I'd heard of these," I whispered. "We're in one of the vaults, aren't we?"

The guard looked over his shoulder at me, helmet revealing only a reflection of my own face. He nodded, saying solemnly, "The first, actually."

I knew the Acheron-like structures were common, spiraling prisons buried away from the rays of the sun and the eyes of the people. But the vaults? The vaults were… legend. Vaults are used, supposedly, to store the things the task force couldn't afford to let out: information, weapons and, apparently, people. The thought of standing in one was overwhelming. I'd come to expect a lot of strange things but the idea there could actually be a room holding Excalibur was a bit much.

Of course, *that* part might just be a rumor.

The guard led me around to a bridge on the far side of the room, crossing over the mist to a small ledge. A glass alcove stood at the gates of this apartment they called a cell. From there I could see every room and every object aside from one, presumably the restroom. Momentarily, I wondered whether Rufus had any mirrors.

The guard stepped away from the alcove and I observed the rooms beyond the glass walls. Each room had a specific organization and no two rooms quite shared the same pattern. His den was perfectly arranged with every speaker, monitor and piece of furniture placed at exact angles and parallels while another room, one I couldn't even try to name, was a mess of dominos arranged in a huge, ornate pattern that couldn't be deciphered from the angle I had.

Over it all were the strains of classical piano playing that same slow melody. Lifting my eyes from the dominos to the sound of the music, I finally saw him. He must have been there the entire time. But he appeared to me as a ghost would, materializing above his garden, trimming away at stray leaves.

Rufus was well over six feet tall with a lean build characteristic of many Vampires and Faelish I've known in my life. His pale alabaster skin had a perfectly smooth appearance, matching the long platinum blonde hair flowing to the middle of his back. Despite the comforts of his little home he wore a prisoner's orange uniform. But one look at his environment and the fact he was permitted a pair of scissors told me the guards didn't see it the same way.

Striking blue eyes lifted from a small bunch of flowers and glanced out in my direction. They were piercing and hollow like an unnatural glass, the pupils dilating so rapidly it was as though he'd zoomed on me like a camera lens. By the time I realized he was looking at me he'd already turned away and yet the moment seemed eternal.

He sighed and spoke in a strange European accent that reminded me of the romance languages. And in this strange yet dignified accent he muttered, "Back so soon?"

"What do you mean?" I asked.

He finally lifted his whole head away from his work, studying me from head to toe as he stood fully. One of his eyebrows raised and the corners of his narrow mouth drooped ever so slightly, a micro-expression I almost didn't catch.

"Excuse me," he said, shrugging and assuming a relaxed position. "I saw the uniform and assumed you were someone else."

"Well, I'm Agent Nathaniel-"

"Leone, yes," he said off-handedly, almost to himself. "I recognize the family resemblance."

"Family resemblance?" I murmured.

Separated by two-inch walls and at least 50 feet of space, his keen ears still heard me. "Leo and your father. Though Michael was just Seattle PD, wasn't he?"

"Family tradition," I said dryly, trying not to show the gut-punch feeling that came from hearing the names out loud.

"Poor Michael," he said, grinning with fangs clearly bared. "He tried so hard, didn't he?"

I wasn't prepared for that. How'd this guy, of all people, know anything about my father? Yet he knew the name and it was clear he knew there was something wrong with him. As much as that bothered me, I also knew I couldn't let him know. I could see it in his eyes as he stared at me. He was analyzing, assessing the situation and working the problem through.

"My father isn't why I'm here," I said. "I'm here to ask you about a string of recent murders."

"Murders?" he asked, trying to mimic some sense of surprise. "What murders would those be? I've been down here for ages."

"People have been killed in the last few months," I said, "all identified in photos found on the wall of a room belonging to a Shapeshifter."

I stepped closer to the transparent doors, trying to appear threatening. "And we think you know a lot more about that."

"We?" he asked, smirking, clipping another leaf from a plant before weaving his way to the doors. "Lucian sent you down here I take it. He always accuses me of every little thing."

"The Shifter had Rephaitol," I said. "Everyone knows you still have connections to Locusta and the other crime families. You're the authority on their activities even when you're not directly involved."

His grin faded for a second, upset I deflected his attempts, but was soon replaced with a new slier smirk. Rubbing a finger and thumb against the freshly clipped leaf, he strutted up to the doors and stood face to face with me, only a couple inches of material between us.

"True," he said, trying to stare into my covered eyes, "they wouldn't really know what to do without me."

"So what can you tell me about the Shifter's murders?" I asked. "There's evidence they were hits."

"It's possible the Locusta hired someone," he said calmly, nodding along. "In fact, it could be any number of organizations in town."

"Like who?" I asked.

"Well," he said, shrugging, "It could be the Jiangshi Tong. Perhaps it was another power play or peace offering to settle their recent gang war."

I shook my head. "Don't go there. Everyone knows those guys march to the same orders."

He stared for a moment, probably gauging just what I was and wasn't telling the truth about. It was a gamble actually – I'd had the theory for a while, even told it to Lucian, but could never confirm it. The only group that really lost anything was the Third Avenue Hunt, who never seemed to be attached to Rufus. But I watched the other two groups dance around each other since I joined the force. One would lose territory to the other, only to gain in another location. If one of them lost an operation the other would pick up the slack and yet neither one of them seemed to gain permanent ground.

It always looked like some sort of criminal waltz.

Eerie as it was, the silence lasted only a second before he smiled and rapped his knuckle against the glass.

"I guess some things never change," he said.

Backing up, watching his hand bounce off the surface, I asked, "What's that supposed to mean?"

He shook his head, bouncing his fist against the glass lightly, almost playfully, before answering, "Your father saw those little patterns too. He followed them like a bloodhound while hunting them step-by-step. You know, I started to like him before I sent that little rat Emil his way."

I still didn't expect just how much Rufus knew about us. It should have made sense: Alter drugs led back to Alter makers and that, in turn, would have led back to any number of strings attached to him. I can't say it didn't hurt, but I was ready to

173

shrug it off. Really, I had to at the time. It could wait, it had to wait.

Brushing it off the best I could, I pressed, "Who's ordering the hits, Rufus?"

"Both sides have been using the person in question," he said quietly, looking at the leaf between his fingers again. "Shifters are good at what they do and rather cheap labor considering their only requirements."

"Requirements?" I asked. "What 'requirements'?"

"The chemicals needed for their… 'habit'," he said. "Rephaitol is hard to come by outside of Argyre."

These men brokered one form of death for another. The smell of ammonia overwhelmed me again from memory alone, the sight of the chemicals and medical supplies flooded back as if I were standing there minutes ago. I could see the room as if I were standing there again, hearing the broken shards of glass under my feet.

Before I knew it, a question came out of me that wasn't part of the plan: "Can you look at yourself in the mirror?"

"I think," he said coldly, "I can look at myself much easier than certain other people."

"What are you talking about?" I asked.

The tone of his voice softened as he said, "Could you imagine what some people see when they have to look at themselves? It must be heartbreaking to watch yourself become a shadow of what you used to be. Really, your mother was probably right to leave him after what he became."

I tensed after that one, trying my best not to. He was treating this like it was personal. I'd seen a lot of people try psyche out tactics to make someone back off. But he wasn't trying to scare me: he was trying to piss me off.

He walked away from the door, turning his back to me as he went to one of the inner walls of his cell. Staring into it, I could see him looking for some brief glimpse of a reflection, only finding the crystal clear transparency of the glass-like walls. Frowning, he turned his attention to me, eyes first, head following very slowly after.

"How is she by the way?" he asked while I seethed. "Marion, wasn't it?"

Training took hold finally. He was getting to me but I was able to step back again, an invisible hand resting on my shoulder from people who weren't in the room. Stifling the pain of old memories, I asked, "Who's next, Rufus?"

Something behind his eyes changed – a newfound fire in them that wasn't there in the otherwise cold stares. He held up the hand with a leaf in it and crushed it with enough force to make already pale knuckles bleach white. He marched back to me with that glare, almost intimidating despite the walls and guards. "I think I've told you enough, Leone."

But I held firm, asking louder, "Who's the next target, Rufus?"

"You dare to demand answers from me?" he snarled. "You all treat me like some animal in a cage that you can just gawk at whenever you want!"

"Who's the next target?" I asked, trying to remain focused on the goal.

He continued, growling as he said, "They try to control the world, control me. But I'm the one who has all the connections. The Illuminati, the Gormogons, the original Freemasons and countless others have answered to me! I always made sure I was pulling the strings from both sides of any conflict. And now I'm being used for information by the fucking whelp of someone I scraped off my boot years ago!"

"Who's the next target?!" I shouted, the guards coming to attention at the sudden noise.

He fell quiet, standing face to face with me on the other side of the wall. Without batting an eyelash he said, "He's on the wall."

"Fine, we'll browse through the photos," I replied calmly, coming down off a bit of a rush.

"Not that wall," he replied smugly, "the *other* wall."

"Other wall?" I asked. "What other wall?"

The corners of his mouth slowly rose again as he said, "You'll either find it soon or it won't matter anymore."

"Where is it, Rufus?"

He just grinned, staring as though he could penetrate the visor with his gaze. It was unnerving to see someone, especially an Alter, stare into my visor. His aura was a calm, unnatural blue color a man just yelling shouldn't have. He stayed locked on, unwavering, unaffected as though he had nothing he feared or regretted.

And then, still locked in the gaze with me, he broke the silence. Shrugging, he said, "You're going to have to look for it yourself because I haven't the slightest clue."

As far as I could tell he was telling the truth. His aura was unchanged and his posture was as clean as any I'd ever seen. Considering the nature of the man I wasn't entirely positive he couldn't fake the truth to even the most sophisticated machine. But, as far as I knew, it was the truth right then. So I nodded and turned to walk away only to be stopped by his voice.

"Before you go," he said, "I have a question I'd like you to consider."

I made a rookie mistake then: I acknowledged him and asked over my shoulder, "What kind of question?"

"Well," he said quietly, almost whispering so the others couldn't hear, "consider for a moment your theory is right and I'm fully in touch with my connections outside. Take that for granted and assume I, somehow, have managed to maintain complete contact with my people outside while being at the end of a mile of tunnel."

I nodded and turned around to face him fully again, curious what he could possibly have to say about that "theory".

"I ask you, assuming this fact, one question," he said, stepping even closer to the glass than he had before, beckoning me silently to lean in and hear a great secret.

Momentarily feeling stupid, I decided I wanted to hear this and did exactly as he wanted, leaning in to hear some sort of juicy gossip like some fourteen year old girl.

His smile stretched wider and he looked me square in the eyes again, asking, "Do you see a phone in here?"

I could feel a chill at the implications of what he was saying, what he was implying. There were no phones, there was no way for him to contact the outside, yet everyone knew the man was in contact with the surface. Everyone *knew* he was still the man in charge.

And he punctuated the train of thoughts with another question: "Whose strings am I pulling now?"

Before I could consider the answer, the man whipped up his arm so fast it practically blurred. Light flashed off the steel as he drove his scissors into the door between us with remarkable ease, the glass-like surface fracturing into a spider-web.

I hopped back, hand on my gun the second my back foot touched the floor. The guard lifted his rifle, the charged weapon humming over my shoulder. I hoped, in that moment, he was aiming at the Vampire.

I glanced over my shoulder. The guard was in a defensive posture, keeping the gun as steady as it could be and pointing at Rufus. He wasn't the leak; he was just as surprised as I was.

The screeching of glass drew my focus back to Rufus as he started to drag the blades through the wall, his knuckles white around the scissor handles. I backed away as he started to laugh, his voice carrying above the grinding and cracking of the wall.

"I'm so glad a Leone is working this case," he said.

I ignored it, brushing it off and backing away all the way past the bridge before allowing myself to turn around. The guard next to me kept his aim locked, likely wondering the same thing I did. How long could that wall hold?

But one of the others came, looking us over once and then at Rufus and his impromptu art session. He said in a gruff, matter-of-fact tone, "Transparent Vesperadin, he isn't getting through that."

I glanced at the second guard and nodded. But, despite his assurances, it was hard to feel safe in that room. It wasn't the maniac with the scissors or the possibility the wall could shatter that bothered me: it was the fact one of them could be someone other than who they appeared to be. And worse than that was the unsettling knowledge that, if I was even considering the possibility one of them was the mole, he'd gotten to me.

Even after the sound of it had been muffled by steel doors and a mile of tunnel, I could still hear his laughter following me through the night.

Chapter 18
Gripping Terror

Tired and disappointed, I dragged myself through the door into a pitch black room. I couldn't see anything even with the visor: everything black, empty and cold. I groped about the walls, managing to turn on the lights to find myself standing in the lab once more. It was different now that it'd been cleaned by the hazmat teams and scoured for evidence with the greatest of care. In fact, it was almost entirely empty.

I walked through the room, listening to the skittering sounds of mice in the walls that once again braved this corner of the building. Though, they sounded a bit more around the size of rats than mice. The broken glass had been swept away and the window I'd shattered removed. The wood planks covering the window were gone, replaced by a single sheet of plywood nailed over the frame.

I could never understand that. Why would you board up a window no one's ever going to want to enter? Who or what were they trying to protect from the elements? The only ones who'd been in there in recent times were the rats and the dead guy I found in the tub. Maybe they just thought he got chilly from breezes blowing over his water.

Whatever the reason, it was too damn dark even with the lights on, which made sense since several were broken. I grabbed at the plywood sheet to find it was held on by only a few small nails that shouldn't have been able to keep it up. I ripped it off to get some fresh air and light flowing into the room.

The sky was a shade of lavender with a golden string separating it from the earth. Birds flew by under a cloudless sky and lit up in a brilliant rainbow of colors with a long, winding path of light. I took off the visor to look out at the world without it. It all seemed so peaceful outside.

The wind blew by as I stared off into the dawn. I took a deep breath, letting my chest lift and settle under the jacket. My ribs didn't hurt anymore; I was healing already without the miracle of omega.

A smug grin crossed my face as I turned away from the window and walked back to the center of the room. The walls were cleared now of most of the photos and articles, all of which now safely locked away in the evidence rooms back at headquarters. The ones that remained were of people and places I couldn't recognize, smudged or faded beyond recognition – unimportant except for one with a light scribbling of letters across the bottom corner.

I stepped closer, carefully adjusting my glove before reaching out and lifting that one from the wall to examine the words below. It was hard to make out – written in scribbled, unsteady, even chaotic handwriting.

I snatched the picture from the wall to look closer. But as it came away something slapped to the floor. Looking down, a perfectly wrapped and prepared patch lay at my feet. I guess I'd found the dealer's private stash. It didn't occur to me how strange it was the CSI teams missed it in the sweep.

Sighing, I kneeled and picked up the patch with the same hand used to snatch up the photograph. It looked so harmless in my hands, wrapped and sealed so it couldn't leak out. If I hadn't known what it was, it probably wouldn't have been worth a second glance. Surprising how deceiving appearances can be. I wondered momentarily what it was like for the guys who used them.

Staring at it, contemplating what it was like, I heard a low hissing noise beneath it. Smoke wafted from my hands and I realized the photo was burning. Panicked, I fumbled with the two objects to separate them and take a quick look at the photo before it was too late. I wasn't fast enough, it was already burning apart. Somehow the crap on the patch leaked through after all.

"Damn it," I mumbled, throwing down the now ruined photo and watching it dissolve. The smoke had a powerful smell saturating my every sense for a moment as I breathed. It was almost intoxicating. No, more than that, it *was* intoxicating. I started to feel that buzz I had the first time I stepped into the room.

Was this what they felt? Was that all it could have been? No, I'd seen people start to feel like they were invincible and I sure

179

didn't feel superhuman. It was just a contact high, a warning sign that I was close to becoming a "blue canary" as they were called on the street. A partial taste of what would happen if I wore such a thing...

I couldn't indulge that kind of thinking. I just couldn't. I dropped the patch next to the photo and backed away as fast as I could, staring at it with a horrible hollow feeling like I was narrowly teetering on an edge.

And then the doubts came. I wasn't just thinking that, was I? How did those thoughts get in there? How could I even entertain them for a moment?

Shutting my eyes as tightly as possible and turning away from it, I rushed to the exit. I couldn't risk being in the place anymore, I had to get out. I grabbed for the doorknob and turned it as quickly as possible. The goddamn thing broke off.

Cursing under my breath, I tried to put the knob back together. My hands wouldn't work, my fingers trembling and shaking too much already. I was trapped in that room with the patch and the lingering fumes. I needed to get out somehow.

The gun – I'd forgotten the gun. Pulling it from my side, I stepped back and opened fire at the hinges, kicking it out of the frame and staggering out into the hallway. I tripped on the threshold of the door, shaking too badly to walk straight. Falling to the floor, crashing to cold linoleum, I stared at a shattered mirror over a cheap sink with rusted pipes. It was on that floor I realized I'd ended up in the wrong room. Somehow I'd gotten turned around, stumbling into the bathroom.

I cursed myself and climbed back to my feet, rubbing my eyes to try to get some focus again. Was I already that buzzed by the smoke? Maybe it was just sleep deprivation.

Yeah, that was it; I just needed to go home.

I lifted my head slowly and let my eyes open again, hoping for some clarity. But it wasn't clear at all. It was blurred and muddy like a painting dumped into the water. All I could see were the fuzzy outlines of the bathroom fixtures and a great blue blob sitting in the tub.

I tried again, getting some more success and opening my eyes to a clearer view of the room. The blue blob took shape and I soon got a full view of a lifeless blue body lying in the water.

They hadn't removed him from the building yet? Why was he still there?

I stepped closer, taking another look at the poor man now sinking with his face downturned into the water. He was just another soul suffering the consequences of their life choices. Reaching over, I lifted his chin from the water to see his face again. But it wasn't the same face anymore – it wasn't the same man.

Lying there, soaked through and covered in the same markings of a blue overdose, was a man in a dress uniform, a police officer, staring up at me with cold, lifeless silver eyes. I recognized him. Trembling, I looked at his nametag to confirm his identity: "Leone". It was Lieutenant Michael Leone of the SPD: my father.

I bolted from the room, stumbling over myself to get away from the corpse that shouldn't have been there.

My footing escaped me again, sending me reeling into the room, tumbling to the floor and coming to rest somehow next to the patch I'd dropped. I scrambled away from it, scooting myself back into the corner of the room, staring at the destroyed bathroom door.

"Bro," Emil's voice seeped through the walls in a hazy whisper, "it's okay. The stuff will make it feel so much better."

I was tripping out, seriously tripping out. Emil was in jail and my father had been dead for years. Had I really inhaled that much of it? Was I that gone already?

I closed my eyes, hoping it would go away, a tear running down my face. The voice of Emil grew louder behind that wall, laughing at me along with my father's voice starting to echo out of the bathroom.

"Bro, just do it already and take the shit," Emil said. "It'll make it all go away."

My father, feet dragging and shuffling across the floor, came to me – water sloshing in his wake. I opened my eyes, looking up at him, feeling so much smaller than him again. His cold, lifeless silver eyes stared through me.

"It helped me, kiddo."

Looking at the patch on the floor, I was soon surrounded by the people I knew, twisted and distorted. Dulaf, Lucian and my father stood there lifeless and warped. Even Max was there, towering over us, staring at me with his one remaining eye. They murmured around me, trying to make me pick up the patch again. Their voices became a steady stream of noise beginning to overwhelm me. I covered my ears and tried to seal them out.

I threw my head back and screamed, "Stop it! Leave me alone!!"

They went silent and I opened my eyes to see they'd gone. Only one person stood with me now.

He was shorter than me, silver plates and a cape resting across broad shoulders. We shared the same dark hair, the same blue-green eyes. He carried a broad sword at his side and wore silver gauntlets and greaves under an intricately decorated cloak draping him in shadow, only small points of light coming off the highly polished gear. He smiled at me and reached out his hand.

I took it, shaking as the light from the window grew brighter while the sun rose at his back. I felt warm, safe and secure as I rose to my feet.

And then he nodded to me, speaking in a soft but strong voice, "You are not worthy."

His smile turned to a frown and his grip tightened on my hand, overpowering me and pulling me closer. With a quick motion he rolled up my sleeve and slapped the patch against my forearm. I didn't have time to react before a surge rushed through my body and sent me spinning away from him.

"What," I stammered, "what the hell did you just do?!"

He didn't answer, frowning and backing away. Staring at him in shock, my mind clouded and everything began to burn with energy. I looked back at my arm, staring at the patch as it started to bubble and boil over like a pot on a stove. Within moments it expanded around my forearm in an explosion of liquid silver.

I screamed as it surged across me and threw me to the floor, tendrils whipping from the mass to grab at my flesh and pull me into its expanding core. I fought with it, digging my feet into the floor, trying to pull myself free. But with every inch I gained it just threw more tendrils out at me. It spread across the floor around me and started to drag me in, my gear melting into molten slag around my body as it was absorbed into the blob.

The man, Leo, stood over me and the growing mass, watching me fall into it. Looking up into his face, I watched it change from the strangely familiar visage to a new form I'd never seen before. Backlit and shadowed, a smile crossed this new face.

"Rufus will destroy you."

I looked into the light as the tendrils closed around me, outstretching a hand to the sun in the distance. And as the light faded, I heard Rufus' sinister laugh as everything went dark…

***

I sat up in bed, screaming in panic and raking my fingers across my arms to peel the mass from myself in that moment between nightmares and the waking world. It took a moment to realize I was in my room. The sunlight outside was casting a narrow shred of light on me through the gaps in my curtains. Lifting a hand to block out the light, I glanced at the clock to see it was nine thirty in the morning.

Sighing in relief, I dropped my head back to my pillow, resting a forearm across my face to cover my eyes. I caught a glimpse of something on my arm. The darkness on my forearm brought a cold chill up my spine. Fearing that part of the dream was true, I slowly turned my arm to the light so I could see what it was. Thankfully, it was only the scribbling of Janice's number and address, just now beginning to fade.

I hadn't heard from her since the night I'd attached my badge to my foot and tried to swallow them both whole. I could figure why she'd be upset. Looking back on the date, I brought the work with me the whole time. The timing couldn't have been worse.

Encountering Emil alone, on this case especially, didn't do me much good. Finding these drugs and my father's dealer attached to it bothered me, even if I tried to control it. It was gnawing at me now as I realized how deep the rabbit hole went.

Knowing that Rufus knew my father, his "problem", I realized how the man pulled those strings. He found a man that gave him trouble, like my father, and pulled him down to their depths. I thought about the creature in my dream, Rufus' emissary, and those words spoken through a twisted grin: "Rufus will destroy you."

Whatever the killer was doing, it wasn't just a mindless beast. There was a cunning, brutal nature to the way it used people's identities to somehow get closer to them and whatever else it wanted. I needed to know my enemy and knew I'd probably never get back to sleep. So I stood from my bed and staggered into the next room with the old worn out furniture, starting my day on three hours of sleep, hearing that haunting laugh again.

Chapter 19
Altered Thinking

Rufus was a piece of work. I spent a good part of my morning looking into the man and everything that happened around him. There was a world of information about him, most of it written in journal format by an anonymous observer. Water-stained, decaying old sheets of paper scanned in with typed transcripts on the Oracle hand-link detailed a very long life.

He was, as far as the old journals stated, involved in every major uprising from the French Revolution to the American Civil War. Earlier than that, there were stories of him taking part in the Gothic invasions of Rome, fabricating evidence against the Knights Templar, instigating parts of the Spanish Inquisition, and generally just being a *swell* guy. He'd slipped up a few times, like becoming enamored with the premise of an "Übermensch" in the early 20th century. But siding with the wrong team didn't seem to bother him much.

While the humans around him always had their own motivations, he seemed to follow a pattern. He wanted to keep humans disorganized and he wanted to find all of the Alters he could. Even his flirtation with eugenics was to root out Alters in the genome. And as his associates toppled, he somehow survived to later do it again. But worse than that, a tendency to place himself on both fronts of any conflict worried me.

Did he really have a mole in the Force?

With the Shifter running around I could picture it possibly happening, especially if the Shifter was already in the force somehow. Genetic tests were always done to new recruits to identify what risk they might have with equipment assignments. But if someone were killed and then instantly replaced by a duplicate I don't think anyone would notice. There would be little way to tell outside of the Oracle or friends noticing. Really, it meant it could have happened when they were new to the force and no one, including the Oracle, really knew them well enough. That had some pretty heavy implications given Rufus has been down there since the headquarters was built.

The real irony was Rufus had played me. For every action I could take I was in turn playing into his hand at that moment. If I ignored what he implied and didn't look into it I was probably not looking at something I should have been. On the other hand, if I did look into it, I was probably looking the wrong way as he slipped something by me. In the end I just couldn't win, only minimize the damage.

After depressing myself for most of the morning, it felt like time to take a break and maybe have some breakfast. Hell, I was hungry and fatalistic enough to try my hand at the only thing I had in my refrigerator. Fetching the crappy toaster waffles once again, I popped them into the old busted toaster.

I sat on my stool, watching my hand-link and thinking about what I could do from there. I'd been working on it for hours and finding the hole only getting deeper. The man was everywhere and nowhere all at once. He believed himself to be a freedom fighter and so did a lot of other people. As much as he was a cutthroat criminal, he was always claiming to do it for the good of his kind. And here I was looking like the bully even to people like Janice.

I glanced at my phone not far from the hand-link and idly cycled through the messages on it hoping to see her name pop up. Given the time, knowing her general hours were probably like mine, I resisted the urge to call her first. Maybe later I could try again, but it would only wake her up and probably piss her off at a time like this.

Putting the phone down, I looked between it and the hand-link. The two of them stood almost in opposition of each other. One would let me call Janice and the other showed me exactly why I shouldn't. What he'd said before about my parents became so much clearer looking at the two devices.

I'd just started to get to know Janice and he was already standing between us. From what he'd said, he'd helped destroy what my parents had too. Maybe, I thought, it was for the best to just let go.

Like mom did…

As the thought crossed my mind I smelled something burning and looked up to see thick-black smoke billowing out of the top of the old toaster. Frantically darting from my stool I yanked the power and ran to the fire extinguisher across the kitchen. Spraying it down, snuffing out the flames, I stood there watching the damn thing smolder under the foam.

Too cold or burnt, nothing that came out of the thing was ever something in between. It, like the case, was fucking with me. For a moment, I considered taking a hammer to the old toaster before deciding it was too much of a hassle.

Walking back over to the phone and hand-link, I realized there was something I could actually do about the Rufus situation. Someone had been talking to him to get information in and out of that room, whoever it was had a high chance of being "the one". I picked up the phone and called Dulaf, asking her to put her group to the task. Having gotten that out of the way, I dragged myself to my room, collapsing into bed again and giving in to a brand new set of nightmares.

Before I knew it the alarms went off and the sun was setting again, leaving me feeling like a member of the undead myself.

Obviously, my daily visit to Ahab's was a must at that point. Feeling exhausted and a little paranoid, the only thing that was going to push me through the day was enough caffeine to make an elephant jittery. Maybe I'd even consider what I'd begun to think of as the "Dulaf Special".

Standing in line was more uncomfortable than usual to say the least. Everyone I'd seen before felt like a completely different person. People I'd known for years, or at least remembered, could have been someone completely different. I didn't remove my visor at all; I just watched everyone like a hawk – especially the uncomfortable ones. Every flicker of yellow, every averted gaze had a weight behind it that just wasn't there before.

Dulaf snuck up on me during that time, weaving her way through the line like a viper ready to strike. I'd left her with at least a day's worth of footage to go through and honestly didn't expect to hear from her so soon. But now that she'd been to the coffee shop once before it was only a matter of time before she did it again. I just wasn't expecting her to move in on me while I was half-dead and watching for the bogeyman.

"Hi there, Nate!" she exclaimed, slapping my back and

sending me reeling. "How're you doing today?"

I lifted my visor, watching her cringe at the horrible mess beneath.

"That bad, huh?" she asked.

I could've probably called in one of my sick days and taken a breather. But as I lowered my visor again and watched the auras light up before me I remembered why that was out of the question. There were so many yellowing figures with us, too many to be ignored or considered useful, just enough to make me suspect everyone in the room.

"Well, it could be worse," she said, turning to face the front of the line and look away from the pathetic mess I'd become. "Speaking of worse, actually, I found out who visited Rufus' level before you."

"Speaking of worse" was enough to make me dread asking the obvious: "Who was it?"

"He's only had two visitors in the last two weeks, three visits total," she murmured, taking out a handful of photos, "if you don't count the guards or maintenance crews that get a debriefing every time they leave."

She shuffled the photos in her hands idly, skirting around the point and stalling. Her ears were pulled back, eyes turned straight ahead instead of my direction. She was obviously nervous about something in those photos.

"Come on, Dulaf," I said, frustrated, "tell me who the other person was."

A saddened look in her big green eyes made me feel a pang of doubt. Ear-tips lowered and lower-lip quivering, she looked like someone who'd watched a beloved pet die.

"Lucian," she said sadly. "Lucian was the last person to see him before you."

I'd heard people say the news "floored" them before but I'd never really understood the expression. How could someone be "floored" by words? Well, with the shock, doubt, rage and confusion hitting me all at once I couldn't help having my legs suddenly give out on me. Was it not for Dulaf's hand catching my sleeve as I stepped back I think I really would have been on the floor.

"Lucian?" I stammered. "How could it be Lucian? He helped

put the man in there in the first place!"

Dulaf shook her head and reeled me back in by the sleeve clutched in her hand.

I couldn't believe it: the idea the man who'd brought me into the organization could have any connection to this was so unreal to me. Worse, there was a possibility the real Lucian was dead and gone, replaced by the Shifter. My heart sank; the man was like a second father to me. Regardless of how it happened, there was something that had been done to him or by him that could not be forgiven.

"I just can't believe it," I said breathlessly, looking to the floor for some sense of stability and balance.

"I'm sorry Nate, sweetie," she said solemnly, "aside from your visits there wasn't anyone else."

I almost missed that. No, I heard it, I just hadn't registered it right away. "Visits" was the word she used, plural.

"Visits?"

"Yeah, aside from the two times you went in, it was just Lucian."

I went from weakened and stupefied to a state of rage that couldn't even begin to be expressed in a public place without psychological exams and forced leave. No, because of where I was standing, I had to swallow that bitter pill and force it down. And as it went down, I flashed to another bitter revelation.

"Back so soon," I repeated to myself, remembering Rufus' introduction to me.

Dulaf, sounding far more confused than I was, echoed, "Back so soon?"

I placed a shaking hand on her shoulder and pointed as I stammered, "That's what he said to me when I got there, 'back so soon'."

"Well yeah," she said, "you'd been there only…"

Dulaf's ears shot up and her eyes grew wide, her mouth hanging open as she stared at me, whispering, "No way."

"They stole my face," I snapped at her. "That damned Shifter stole my face!"

Dozens of eyes turned my way in surprise. The normally quiet ACTF agent suddenly yelling in the middle of the line was a red flag for them. Dulaf responded with the kind of cold stare you'd give an unruly dog or child. I realized I'd been squeezing her shoulder a little too tightly as I looked into those angry emerald eyes and released my grip on her.

"Sorry Dulaf," I whispered, remembering where I was again. "I just can't believe they could take my face and I wouldn't even know it."

"It has to be someone in direct contact with you, then."

"Yeah," I groaned, "meaning it could still be tied to Lucian."

"But with all of the drugs in their system the Shifter would have to be glowing bright yellow," she said. "Wouldn't you have noticed that with him?"

I considered that for a moment, wondering if it would even be possible to miss that kind of thing. Having looked around and taken a new interest in the yellow shades of the spectrum, I knew it wouldn't be easy to miss and yet wouldn't be hard to ignore. But, thinking back on Hale's office, I realized if Lucian were glowing even half as brightly as Thompson I would have seen it right then and there.

"Yeah, you're right," I said. "There's no way I could have missed it."

The line continued the march forward and we, like anyone else acclimated to the culture, followed it without any thought, acting in reflex to keep our place. And so I found myself looking at the darkened blue aura, the shielded figure I'd looked at so many times before and realized the one thing that could have prevented me from noticing.

"Unless they could control their body chemistry," I said, growling slightly at Trey across the counter, seeing our game in a whole different light.

He was the only Alter I'd ever known that could disguise his type. And, looking into his smiling face, I could only imagine how useful that kind of skill would be for a Shapeshifter. Though, worse, the thought he could have been the one and yet still be smiling at me enraged me all over again.

His aura was always blue, guarded, and I could never determine just what he was. It was all in good fun before that became a liability. I'm sure it was unfair of me to jump straight to thinking about Trey, even unreasonable, but it wasn't impossible and that was the thing weighing heaviest on my mind at the time. Dulaf glanced at me, a gesture I only noticed out of the corner of my eye as I focused on the increasingly suspect smile behind the counter.

"Don't do it," Dulaf murmured.

"I know what I'm doing," I whispered.

"No," she said, stepping closer to me and tugging my sleeve, "you really don't."

But I didn't hear her, I didn't want to. Someone had stolen my face, possibly even Lucian's face. A killer, a thief and a drug dealer had walked around with my face on and the only man whose race I couldn't identify was standing right across from me. It was stupid, probably more than I realize even now, but when that line cleared I stepped forward, reached across that counter and grabbed Trey's shirt fast enough that even Dulaf couldn't catch me.

"Show me your aura!" I yelled at him, shocking everyone around us.

"What the hell is your problem man?!" Trey yelled back, grabbing my wrists and trying to pry them loose.

"I want to know what you are," I snarled at him, not realizing I had the guy nearly half across the counter. "Show me what you are!"

"Dude!" Trey cried out, finally loosening the grip enough to regain his footing. "It's just a game!"

"It's not a game anymore, Trey!" I seethed. "Refusing to identify yourself to an agent is illegal, you know!"

Trey looked as shocked as you'd expect. I can't blame him for it, I'd gone nuts. I admit that now. But at the time I only knew one thing: someone committed crimes wearing my face. I felt paranoid, betrayed, and – worse than that – scared. Someone I was investigating had gotten close enough to do this and suddenly everything I thought was harmless seemed so sinister.

Regardless of reasons, I know I was wrong now and, luckily, Dulaf knew I was wrong right then.

She snatched away my visor with one hand and grabbed the wrist still holding onto Trey with the other. With a quick jerk she pried me off of him and turned me to face her while she put the visor on herself.

I snapped again, "What the hell are you doing?"

191

Staring at me with the visor on, she calmly replied, "Reigning you in for your own good before this ends up online."

"My own good?" I grumbled. "What the hell do you know about what's for my own good?!"

She ignored my ramblings and turned back to Trey, asking, "Are you okay?"

He nodded, keeping a wary eye on me. Surely, seeing me without the visor helped my case a little. I must have looked horrible enough to partially explain my stupidity. He relaxed, straightening out his shirt a bit while looking around the room of gawkers.

Embarrassment is a funny thing. Of all the people standing there, the one person who should have been embarrassed for being a jackass, me, was completely unfazed by it. Meanwhile, the other two did their best to avert their eyes from the rest of the crowd pretending nothing happened.

Dulaf tugged me down to her level by the sleeve, whispering, "The visor information was making you paranoid. Trey's not a Shifter."

"Shifter?" Trey repeated, "No way man, I'm nothing close to that."

Dulaf was right: taking off the visor was putting things back into perspective. Without the auras, I looked into Trey's eyes and saw my friend again. Try as they might, a Shifter could never keep up the act as long as I've known the people I trusted. I started to feel that embarrassment creep over me. I sheepishly nodded to Trey and quietly apologized, reaching out my hand across the counter.

He looked at it for a moment, hesitating, then took it and said, "And, even if I was one, man, I wouldn't have done anything to a girl you were dating."

"A girl I was dating?" I asked, "What does that mean?"

He stared at me for a second with a hesitant look. It was somewhere between confused and wary as he watched me, possibly looking for a sign I was joking or going over the deep end again. "Janice," he said, lowering his voice so he wouldn't be overheard, "as far as I heard, a Shifter emptied her accounts yesterday."

Words escaped me again. Really, there was only one that felt fitting: "Damn."

Chapter 20
Silent History

I tried to call Janice six times without an answer. It was possible she was dodging the call, considering how it ended the last time we spoke. I imagine that's also why Trey found out before I did. After all, I'd tried to patch up a really awkward situation with flowers and a cheesy card.

But I also imagined she was spending her night trying to salvage what was left of her life. I was tired, steamed and paranoid all over again despite Dulaf's best effort to calm me down by playfully punching me in the shoulder until I agreed to smile. Smiling wasn't something I was prepared to do that night, even if Dulaf was slowly bruising my shoulder into oblivion.

One thing I knew was the longer I left the Shifter out there, the worse it was going to get. I couldn't just sit back and wait for evidence to lead me in the right direction. I needed to go and find him based on what I already had. Staking out every coffee shop in the area occurred to me for a bit. But yellow tinted auras were way too common to be useful.

Instead, I needed to use a little logic. Well, the closest I could get to logic in my paranoid and sleep deprived state. The first thing I knew to be true was I'd been copied by someone.

Now, that shouldn't have been such a big deal, a lot of other people who'd had their identities stolen were going to the same places. But the thing none of those people had in common with me was the badge. My badge was a visual and digital marker, extremely difficult to duplicate without being in direct contact with it for a lengthy period of time. Yet, somehow, the Shifter had a duplicate of it, or of another official badge, that allowed them to just waltz in without a moment of resistance from the security.

Having the duplicate meant only one thing to me: it was either someone I knew very well, or someone I work with. And, despite not wanting to, that meant I had to look at the people who fit both of those criteria exactly. Sadly, that meant I had to start with Lucian.

It didn't have to be Lucian, just someone close enough to copy him and get close to me. Bill Thompson's history alone wasn't enough to condemn him, even if it wasn't unheard of for a self-hating Alter to lead those mobs. But his aura was uniquely yellow when I saw him in City Hall. And, considering it, he was missing in action and had been quite a few times according to Lucian.

Regardless, for sanity alone, I had to check Lucian first.

Unfortunately, the first thing I had to do was lose the hearse. The patrol cars weren't meant to blend in: their shape and color were blatantly recognizable. So if I was going to try to investigate Lucian I needed to exchange it with something. Walking out of Ahab's, I looked down the street and realized just who I needed to go to – unfortunately. Sitting in front of my apartment building was a beat up 2012 electric car from the good old days, when people were still burning oil like a million rolling bonfires.

The paint was chipped and faded, the battery didn't hold a charge worth a damn and it was made before solar paints or power relay networks so it needed to be plugged in. I'd seen it a dozen times before, sitting out there hooked up to a series of extension cords. I could never figure out why someone would keep the piece of crap. It barely counted as a car by today's standards.

Ironically, now I needed it.

To the car's credit, it wasn't one of the ugly creampuffs painted in horrible neon green colors. My grandfather had one like that in his garage when I was a kid. Can't remember what it was called anymore, just that it looked like an ugly bubble on wheels. But this one at least looked like a real car, a rare thing back in those days. It could have even passed for a modern car if not for the fact it looked like it'd rolled through three decades of bird crap and rain.

As I considered how likely someone would expect me to be driving around in something like that, I found myself at a loss for who exactly owned it. The people in my building were fairly eccentric: from the opera singing Werewolf on the third floor to my landlady whom I was fairly certain was a Witch. Of course, she also listened to new age music and lit incense, so she could have just been a hippy out of her generation. And, who knows, maybe it was both.

I took the hand-link and made a quick sweep of the license plates. Every shot I took was added to the pile of evidence, time-stamped and given a quick analysis. Used on a car, it tells you what kind of vehicle it is and who the plates belong to. Of course, it also lets you know if a car's been stolen and people have been caught on more than one occasion by driving a little too close to an ACTF agent.

But my hunch was right – the car was registered to "Barbara Zdunk". It belonged to the landlady I rarely spoke to outside of when it was time to pay the rent. I didn't really even know her full name before that, just referring to her as "Babs" like everyone else that lived there. Maybe I would have known her name had I actually devoted some time to get to know her, or anyone else in the building really.

Babs isn't a bad person to be around, just a little strange. From someone in my line of work that speaks volumes. But every time I handed her a check it was like standing to the gateway of some sort of otherworldly realm filled with the smell of burning incense and the sound of music from a distant land.

Avoiding her wasn't something I did because she was strange, though. I knew she was odd, but everyone was. I avoid a lot of people who know my profession to avoid conflict. I hear so much criticism from Alter-rights activists, human power fanatics and people who just hated the UN. I suppose adding a possible anti-authoritarian pacifist Witch was a bit too much.

Heading inside, I realized just how many assumptions I'd made about the woman.

But when she answered the door her small, frail face lit up as though she were seeing a good friend. She was so tiny in so many ways, from the way her thin fingers gripped the door to the way she peeked around it as though she were using it as a shield. For a moment, I looked into her hazel eyes and saw my grandmother behind those bifocal glasses. In fact, thinking on it now, that might've been another reason I avoided Babs.

Grandma stayed with me for so many years, even through the times where I beat on people for a living. She was by my side right up to the time a pale visitor named Lucian showed up and asked me to fight for something other than profit. Then, she stood behind me despite what happened to her son. But now she'd been gone for a couple years.

Guess at the time, being the mess I was, I was feeling pretty nostalgic.

I hesitated as the shaking but energetic voice brightly said, "Oh, Officer Leone! How can I help you, sweetie?"

It was the second time I'd been called sweetie that day. Dulaf did it on and off over the years, but when Babs did it I felt awkward all of a sudden. Grandma called me that, even up to the last time I spoke to her. And hearing it invoked memories of a hospital room and that last sunset I saw with the only one I could have really called family. It was strange how it hit me just then, leaving me stuttering and stumbling over myself as I tried to think of how to ask her for what I needed. I must have looked like a jackass.

But she took my hand as I stammered, careful to avoid the plating on my gloves like someone who'd experienced a silver burn at an agent's hand. She guided me in and said with the warmest tone, "Oh sweetie, you look just awful. Come in, sit down."

I couldn't help it after the dreams I'd had through my long day. I wandered in with her, taking note of the dashiki she wore and the old memorabilia of the days of my great grandfather's time. Peace emblems, mementos of Woodstock and images of long lost civil rights activists adorned her walls like a museum to long forgotten eras. She didn't seem that old, a generation younger at least. But in the end that probably meant she was far older than any of them could be.

Witches are a unique breed, walking the thin line between mortals and the divine. If pressed they have abilities that could make an Oracle or Succubus look like an amateur. But, unlike those types, a Witch is neither an active or passive A-type. Instead, they share the realm of Were-creatures and their kind: weaving from one form to another as the world effects them. Every transformation meant great power and a period of renewed youth and vitality. Used often enough, Witches had an ability no other on Earth possessed: the ability to choose.

A Witch could choose to be mortal, choose to be "normal" and avoid the conflict of the world outside. Yet, watching her as she helped me to a seat on a couch older than anything else in the room, I wondered how often Babs had chosen another life altogether. How often had she chosen the power over the peace? Maybe she'd chosen to be herself and not care of the outside world, like the tie-dye wearing people of the era she adopted so well.

I nearly sank into that couch, with overstuffed down cushions that were clearly reupholstered with modern materials. The old wood frame reflected the style of a time I couldn't quite place, its little asymmetries telling me it was probably hand carved. The thing was older than anything else in the room, some piece she'd somehow preserved as everything else fell apart. But, however hard it was to keep intact, a very tired part of me understood the effort – I could have slept on that thing for days.

"You look horrible, young man," she murmured to me, stroking her fingers lightly through my hair, sweeping it away from my face. "Is it about your rent?"

"What?" I asked.

"You don't usually come unless you're here to pay the rent," she said, smiling. "So is it about the rent?"

"Oh, no ma'am," I said quickly, "I just wanted to ask you about your car."

I started to feel the creeping shame again. I really didn't want to ask such a big favor from a near-stranger, especially not one who was inspiring nostalgia I couldn't entirely explain. The disrupted sleep and the case had me thinking a lot about family lately. I found myself remembering the last words my grandmother said to me on a cold winter day, looking out at the last sunset of her life: *you're always so alone.*

A reedy voice brought me to attention as Babs offered me a cup of tea.

"What was that?" I asked. "I didn't make it out."

"I said you usually don't come here except to pay the rent," she replied, sitting next to me and forcing the cup into my hands. "You're usually a bit of a loner."

The nostalgia faded when looking at the outstretched arm. Old burns stretched from the wrist to the sleeve. Behind those colors, Babs had a much more colorful history than I was giving her credit for.

The academy devoted entire classes to Witch hunts. It was long believed the people who started the trials were either delusional or hateful. But when we realized just what exactly a Witch was it became readily apparent just what happened in those days. There were real Witches, they just didn't know which were which, including the Witches themselves.

When a Witch's powers emerge, even they aren't entirely sure what's going on. In fact, sometimes they completely black out, a second personality taking over as they act on pure instinct. A person witnesses a Witch, they tell the others then the person they went back to looks completely normal. But if she looks normal, then obviously that means Witches could look like anyone. That's usually where the blood bath began.

Ironically, if a Witch is aware of the powers, burning at the stake or hanging wouldn't stop them: a fact illustrated by the old burn scars along my landlady's arm. I wondered if she had been caught in a house fire or if she was really old enough to be in a place that would try such a thing.

"I can see you're wondering," she said, the faded remnants of a long forgotten accent creeping into her voice, "just how old I am."

Blushing slightly, I replied, "Maybe just a bit, ma'am."

"Don't worry," she said with a light smile. "I don't mind telling anyone that I'm over two hundred."

"So the burns," I said, voice trailing off.

"The eighteen hundreds were an interesting time," she said, nodding.

"I'm sorry," I said quietly.

"For what?" she asked. "You weren't there and if you were I imagine I'd be in much prettier shape today."

I didn't know how to take that. Did she mean the ACTF? If she did, it was probably true we wouldn't allow a Witch hunt in the first place. Or did she mean me personally? I guess, either way, it would have still been true. At the very least, I would have gotten the Puritan suntan right next to her. Either way, it was one of the few times I heard someone say kind things about the work I did. Suddenly, I felt bad avoiding this sweet old lady and the cloud we sat on.

"So, what was it about that old hunk of junk out there?" she asked, patting my arm.

I looked at my arm and the antique cup in my hands, feeling it'd be rude to mention I'd just had more coffee than my bladder would forgive me for. I took a sip anyway, washing down that bit of pride I needed to swallow to say, "I need to borrow it, ma'am."

An awkward pause followed as she took a sip from her cup. The burning sensation rose in my cheeks again. I could only picture how audacious it must have seemed. And, as short as that sip actually was, I felt the silence needed to be filled.

"For an important case," I nervously added.

She lowered her cup and glanced my way, smiling as she asked, "Now was that so hard?"

And I, with my mastery of the English language, responded, "Huh?"

"Of course you can borrow it," she said happily, getting up to her feet and wandering to a bowl filled with keys on the far end of the apartment. "I know you wouldn't ask if you didn't really need it."

She smiled again, pushing her glasses up to get a good look at me. "It looks like it hurt to ask anyway."

She sat down again, patting my knee with an assuring slap, shaking the keys in her other hand. "You know, you worry too much about little things like this."

"Oh really?" I asked, eyebrow raised at the assumptions starting to go the other way.

All she did was laugh, carefully turned my hand over and dropped the keys into my palm. Laying the end of her shirt over the hand to avoid the plates, she closed my hand around the keys and squeezed. Still smiling, she patted my forearm with her unprotected hand and said, "I don't take new tenants without finding out who they are."

"Like background checks?" I asked.

She tilted her head a little and nodded with a smug expression. A flash of brilliant green crossed her hazel eyes, a light flaring across them.

"In a manner of speaking," she said with a mischievous

smirk that seemed far too young for a woman of her apparent age.

"So," I stumbled on the question, "you're an active user?"

"Hah, not nearly as active as I used to be," she said. "Though I do take peeks from time to time, I don't use them long enough for 'her' to get out."

"Her?"

She leaned in with the wicked little grin on her face and patted my chest, saying, "The fun one."

I leaned back from the grin and a sudden familiar vibe. "The fun one?"

"The fun me," she replied, winking.

Suddenly she reminded me more of Dulaf or Janice than my grandmother, making it all very awkward again. I supposed if you have the potential to live longer than any other human around you, it required a bit of eternal youth to cover the age. Though, that thought made me wonder. Did Dulaf or Janice have a story like Babs'? What were their 1800s like?

"I vet my tenants pretty carefully," she said as her eyes returned to a human shade. "I check you, the real you, and I deal with people based on that."

I looked at the keys in my hand and nodded to her. I'm sure I should have resented the violation of privacy. But I guess recent events desensitized me to those sorts of breeches now. Instead, I felt a little honored someone could measure me so fully and still take me in.

"You think so?" I asked quietly.

"I learned a long time ago," she said brightly, "you surround yourself with people that you can trust. Like the Werewolf that eats tofu or the boy trying to redeem his father's mistakes."

She reached up and put a frail hand on my cheek, the paper-thin skin cold to the touch yet still comforting. "Now go do your thing, sweetie, and fight that good fight. But please, no high speed chases. It's an old car."

"I'm sorry I have to borrow it," I said, "but I really don't have a lot of choices."

"I know," she said with a wicked tone, "do you think you would have thought about it if you hadn't walked past that giant cable I plugged into it as you staggered on out of here this afternoon?"

It was then that I'd realized I'd been secretly played by a Witch. She'd read what I needed before I even did and placed a suggestion on me much as Rufus did. Luckily, for once, the manipulator was a friendly face working in my favor. I lifted the keys and nodded with a nervous little smile while I got up and stepped out. "I'll try my best, ma'am."

As the door closed, I walked away feeling a little better than I had all day. Whatever was going on around me, at least one person knew where my heart was. Maybe she was naïve, believing the best in her tenants. But I've yet to meet someone who would let a stranger borrow a car. She must have known me better than I realized.

And she was right: I have no idea how I could have missed that big-ass power cable on the way out.

Chapter 21
"Friendly" Inquisition

I tried to call Janice again after getting the old car moving. No answer, no word at all about what happened or how she was. Helpless was probably the best word to describe how I was feeling. But I didn't have time to think about it.

Babs' car wasn't exactly the most graceful thing ever. In fact, I quickly realized if I expected to get it back I was probably going to have to push it by the end of the night. Aside from the fact it rolled, it really did very little else. Even turning on the lights was enough to drain the battery irrevocably. How anyone managed to stay sane driving a pure electric car before improved batteries was beyond me, I could barely fathom owning one without Aurorastin cells and solar paint. Still, I'd survive so long as it got me where I needed to go.

The first possible location on the Lucian hit-parade was going to be Hale's home – wherever the hell he lived. Though, as you can imagine from the way I just said it, I had no clue where the hell the man lived. So I needed to figure that out… in a car that narrowly predated universal installation of GPS and a power supply this side of a potato battery. So my first stop was a gas station with public WiFi where I could figure it the old fashioned way: running web searches and trying to figure out which "B. Hale" was most likely to be an attorney.

I could have called Dulaf and asked for her to check through the system for me. But with what had been happening, especially with the fact my identity had been compromised by someone who managed to get a replica badge or, worse, a real badge, I couldn't afford to risk a potential target being tipped off by a hit to the system. In fact, if by the off chance the guy had managed to get his hands on a complete ACTF identity he could have been driving one of our cars as far as I knew.

Browsing through addresses in a corner of the parking lot that someone had apparently used as a urinal, I paused on that thought and looked at Babs' car. The license plates would be automatically read by an ACTF car. The question was whether they could connect Babs with me. It might have been a long shot, but the Shifter clearly already knew more about me than I knew about them.

Standing there, saturating in the scent of a drunk's piss, I paddled the idea back and forth of wrecking the plates so they couldn't be scanned. I mean, sure, it would have meant needing to replace Babs' plates, but it'd be less likely for my cover to be blown. Eventually the fact I was already a rolling bulls-eye for regular red and blues made me realize I couldn't just wreck the things without expecting to be made into a public display. Fortunately, I knew an old trick I learned watching my "friend" Emil.

Finding a grocery store and grabbing some glitter and glue, I scan proofed my plates with a quick sparkle job. Applying the stuff generously, the letters on the plates now shimmered like a stripper. Was it effective? Sometimes. Was it illegal? Slightly. And, most importantly, was it stupid looking? Most definitely.

But I'd seen the trick in action while working with Lucian. We'd been hunting for Emil's car out in the middle of the midnight rush hour on the tip he had a trunk full of silver bullets. After a few hours of circling through town we realized we'd passed one car twenty times without ever getting a clean scan. The glitter he'd painted across the plates refracted the light used to scan them. It would have been a brilliant move if he hadn't parked in the same place for six hours solid waiting on a client that never came. But, had he been smart enough to move the car, I knew from experience that it could keep the Oracle confused for at least six hours – more than enough time for what I needed to do. It even made me feel slightly grateful to have known Emil.

It was a feeling that quickly passed.

There were a couple of Hales in the city that could have been Ben. Gambling that I knew the guy's personality a bit, I took a shot. His office didn't have photos of friends and family, so I figured he didn't have a large house. He was an elected official thinking of going for a far more cutthroat office, so I figured he had some cash too. He seemed to like serene things, so probably away from the middle of town. Of the list I'd compiled, only one address seemed to fit those criteria.

The drive through town was a harrowing experience as I realized just how useless the old batteries were. The lights couldn't be turned on without draining them and in the time it took me to travel the short distance I needed to go there were several moments I had to duck the police. Though I wasn't driving particularly recklessly, it wouldn't take long to notice me with my lights off in the dead of night like some sort of nut job. Sure, I could try to come up with a really great bullshit excuse for driving without the lights. But given the animosity between our organizations I had to ask myself: would they ever let me live down driving this shitty car? Worse, would they let me go without informing the ACTF? I had to make sure they didn't get the chance.

I found myself driving by a condo sitting against the backdrop of Lake Washington reflecting the moonlight above. The collection of cars parked nearby confirmed my hunches on who was inside. The car in the driveway had the body of a classic sports car from the era before everything had gone electric but the design of the wheels told me it'd been converted with electric motors. This was a very expensive car compared to the car immediately next to it – a generic black economy model for a guy making chump change. But more importantly, even if it made all my nifty deduction less impressive, was that Lucian's patrol car was parked out at the curb.

The cheapest car at the house probably belonged to Mr. Thompson who, after my encounter with Trey, brought up some interesting questions when I considered him. He was in security, had access to several legal buildings and access to Lucian, which gave him the chance to do any number of identity switches. He could have gotten a good look at the badge, become Lucian, become someone else in the station through Lucian and eventually made his way to me. Lord knows his aura was bright enough for it, even visible from the street as I coasted by.

Watching the figures pass the windows of the house, I considered what my next move would be. With Lucian being the last person to talk to Rufus that I could confirm wasn't me, I needed to think of a way to investigate him properly. I couldn't just stalk him the whole night, even with the old car to cloak my movements for the time being. Besides the fact the car wouldn't survive a whole night, I'd be sure it'd get spotted eventually, and even then I wouldn't likely find any real evidence. I needed a more direct route.

But the drive-by still served a purpose. If they were with Benjamin Hale, they weren't at home. Luckily, as I pointed out to Anubis, the ACTF didn't exactly require warrants. I just didn't want the slippery shit to notice what I was doing. With one last glance at the yellow form of Thompson through the window, I drove away as quickly as possible in Babs' old car.

Lucian's home was the first place to go. I'd been there a few times even before becoming his devotee. It was a relatively small one story house in a quiet neighborhood with an unassuming exterior and blinds that likely never opened. I'm not sure his neighbors would have known what he was besides an agent that sometimes brought some kid home with him. Several times he'd taken me to this little house towards the edge of the city and helped polish my skills from street thug to professional. Beyond the unassuming house, the back yard featured a crude duplicate of the gauntlet the academy ran us through. At the time I resented being forced through drills when I'd already graduated. Now, I found myself sitting in his driveway considering the idea the man who trained me that hard could have been a double agent.

It didn't add up even if we were the only two seen going there and he was the person who had the most time to copy me. But that meant a worse possible fate, something I couldn't just leave alone to protect myself. There was a chance somewhere inside the man's house there was evidence he wasn't the same man I'd known back then. There was even a chance I could find him there, dead. Either way, I couldn't just sit in the driveway forever. I stepped out and walked up to the front door.

I decided to hit Lucian's house first for a number of reasons. The first of which was the fact that with the car I was driving I needed to hit the furthest distance first in case I ran out of power later and had to get the thing towed back. Lucian's house wasn't exactly sitting in the center of Seattle. In fact, his house was further from my apartment building than Hale's was in the exact opposite direction. Even then I could see the battery was on its way to going dead in no time and cursed myself for even bothering with trying to get to Hale's before the others.

The second reason was I knew the man. I'd known him since before I'd even joined the force. He recruited me, trained me and taught me how to be an agent. If anyone was going to recognize he'd been replaced, it would've been me. Of course, that familiarity was a bit of a double-edged sword here.

As my mentor, Lucian was probably the closest thing I'd had to a father in the years since my real one died. If he was gone too I don't know how I'd really react. And if he wasn't I'd have to figure out why he'd been talking to a man like Rufus. The thought of getting that answer made standing at his door and breaking in an uncomfortable situation.

Luckily, the third reason was that he was a Vampire. And that meant, despite the fact he was old enough to tune out some Vampire quirks, the man had no locks on his doors. Technically, it wasn't really "breaking in". Hell, I even had the code to his security system provided he didn't change it on me.

In fact, funny enough, the fact I could just walk right through the front door was my first piece of evidence. If he were a Shapeshifter and not the Vampire I'd always known him to be I'd imagine "Lucian" would have put locks in eventually.

Vampires are the worst when it came to the locked door problem. Alters of certain breeds require permission to enter other people's homes; Vampires, disturbed people they are, are unable to enter anything without some sort of authority granted to them – even their own homes. The need for a sense of order and structure to appease their obsessive-compulsive disorders was profound. Funny enough, that's also why so many of them have problems stepping onto "holy ground" too. They simply don't feel invited.

But the Shifter, despite the "always invited" plates on their lab doors, would probably never feel the security to leave anywhere good without locks. They didn't have the same compulsion the Vampires suffered from, so the idea they wouldn't use locks just to keep up appearances was unlikely. Still, hearing the warning chimes of the alarm, I knew it wasn't entirely impossible. So I made a mental note of the fact, entered quickly, and disarmed the alarm.

As I turned away from the alarm I was surrounded in the hallmarks of a Vampire's disorders. The spare shoes just inside the house were lined up according to function and color. In fact, everything was ordered like that. There wasn't a speck of dust, misplaced item, or a slanted picture frame in the whole house as far as I could see. With the white and beige interior, you'd think you'd see some dirt, but there was nothing. It was more like a house on display than one that had been lived in.

Usually you can feel the way someone lives by walking into their home, the way things are naturally supposed to flow there. You can tell when people don't have kids by the fact they have the expensive breakable objects on the table. You can tell when they do have kids by the way they keep those same objects on the highest shelf you can find. But in Lucian's house you couldn't get an impression of anything: it was like a hospital or a morgue the way the mostly black and white interior was so pristine and untouched. I felt like I'd walked into a shrine for a dead man.

Of course, that's exactly how it should have been.

Lucian's house had surprisingly few reflective surfaces. He's never had a problem with looking into his reflection as long as I've known him. In fact, sadly, I was well aware that the man was a little vain. I stopped believing the reflection myth the day I watched my mentor play with his hair in a mirror for nearly half an hour one evening.

But what few reflective surfaces there were in his house weren't broken. Everything remotely shiny in the drug lab had been destroyed if it wasn't somehow useful to the process. If the Shifter who'd done that had been living in this house, in Lucian's house, they wouldn't have left those surfaces untouched for long.

Everything was in order, Lucian's order, and nothing was out of place. But if that were the case, I was left with another possibility that no one had been in the house. If someone had stolen the identity they didn't necessarily need to live in the man's home and Lucian had always been the one to pick me up so I wouldn't have noticed he wasn't at home.

The easiest way to confirm he'd been living there was to go to the one room that was time sensitive: the kitchen. I was a bit unsure of walking into a Vampire's kitchen. While I knew some of the basics of what would be there, I could never quite put together the image of a bloodsucker's cooking utensils. Did they have drawers full of straws? Did they make blood pudding? I wasn't exactly sure I wanted to know.

But I really wasn't left with any other choice, everything else was checking out. The only thing that could possibly have been a bad marker would be if the kitchen had somehow been abandoned.

I'm not delusional enough to think looking into a regular person's kitchen and finding spoiled food would be an indication they were gone. Being a twenty-something male myself I'm well aware that sometimes there's no time during what seems like an incredibly busy life to go shopping or dump out the crap. Of course, during the daytime when I'm not working I really, really like to sleep and that just gets in the way of so much. These were but a few of the reasons why I was so happy to live just down the block from a coffee shop and that I never actually ate "dinner" so much as a soggy breakfast and a really elaborate lunch. If I ate the food from my kitchen, I'd likely die. But I digress.

The point behind looking into the man's kitchen and finding spoiled food in there was that, while I am a pig, I lack a Vampire's OCD. For Lucian, on the other hand, spoiled food would give reason for involuntary convulsions.

I swallowed my personal disgust and marched into the kitchen. It was surprisingly normal at first. Anytime I'd been to the kitchen of a person on a case it was typically covered in blood from knife attacks or strange torture rituals being carried out on the kitchen table. Really, it was a bit disappointing just how ordinary the damn thing was. But there was one location I know wouldn't let me down: the fridge.

I reached for the refrigerator, grabbed the handle, took a deep breath and reminded myself I'd known the man for years. I pictured what I knew would be on the inside, closed my eyes, took a few cleansing breaths and went for it.

When I opened my eyes I saw the blood packs lining racks all along one side of the fridge. It wasn't nearly as bad as I'd expected, looking more like he'd just stored red juice in a very strange way. But I was shocked by what I found on the other side of the fridge, opposite the crimson wall of blood.

"Oh wow, cake."

And that was it; that was the most unexpected element of my entire venture into his house: cake. Really, the house was so perfectly normal I began to feel silly and strange about suspecting him in the first place. There was no real evidence for it aside from his conversation with Rufus and that in itself didn't amount to much. Or at least it wouldn't have if I was fully awake and well-rested. That night I was a victim of my own stupidity and sleep deprivation.

But the exercise did provide me with something. Lucian was off the list, firmly, and I was now free to deal with other suspects with a clear mind. Thompson felt likely, even if I hardly knew him, just due to his proximity to Lucian and the fact he lit up yellow as the sun. But then, who could say it wasn't Dulaf, one of her tech boys, Joe the guard or one of the people I nailed at the warehouses. Really, getting Lucian off the list cleared my head and opened me to the possibilities that it could have been anyone I'd directly encountered for longer than an hour in the last few weeks.

That wasn't a cool concept. But Lucian's devil's food cake made it easier to swallow.

Chapter 22
Other Angles

I paid for my sins; the cake wasn't as delicious as it looked. In fact, it had blood in it. So after half an hour of purging the horrible taste from my mouth and avoiding everything in his house remotely looking red, I managed to calm myself and get back to work.

I should have been elsewhere, investigating something solid, but I had nothing. My leads, my information, were all entirely circumstantial and inconclusive. I sat in Lucian's living room, which was probably not the smartest thing a man ever did while breaking and entering, and considered what I did have.

Considering the Shifter stole my identity, I assumed they were someone I knew. Lucian had visited Rufus once before but there was no way to confirm whether or not that was Lucian or the Shifter. Even if I asked him, he could lie about it whether he was the real one or not. But then who else could it have been?

Dulaf was an option. She was the one helping me the most and somehow knew Trey wasn't the Shifter. That could have meant she's more observant than me or it could have meant she was the Shifter herself. Still, that would have been far too convenient, especially considering the number of leads she let me have without slapping my hands and shaking me off. She could have faked matched fingerprints right off the bat and covered her ass, leaving me to go on a wild goose chase for some other entity and leaving herself high and dry.

Trey was another option, being the man I could never identify. It seemed impossible for someone to hide their identity that well without having the ability to shift their features slightly. But Dulaf vouched for him and even scolded me for suspecting him. So either she was wrong or I was and, given our levels of experience, I'd figure I was the more likely candidate. Still, the fact a man was a standing, smiling question mark that I saw every single day was enough to make me wonder. Not to mention the fact his last name was Thompson, a strange coincidence.

And then there was Bill Thompson himself. I couldn't shake the feeling the man couldn't be trusted. His aura was bright yellow the last time I saw him and he was positioned in a place where he could have easily taken Lucian's identity. Not to mention he had confirmed himself to be a screaming lunatic fairly recently. But then, why was it absolutely necessary to grab Lucian's identity? In theory, he really didn't need it.

I knew the Shifter had to be in close contact with those whose faces it stole, but I'd never really thought about how the theft actually occurred. And then I figured out my truly boneheaded move.

I'd assumed something I shouldn't have: that the Shifter had been stalking me in a single form for a prolonged period of time. In truth, if they wanted to get to me, they could have come at me a dozen times over in a half dozen faces and pulled off the same trick. They could have been all of my friends or none of them. They could have simply been sitting at the same table in the coffee shop every single day and then just waited for me to sit at the same table *I* sat at every single day. In fact, that could have been how he got every single one of the identities in that shop.

But, if that were the case, I was back to square one with a brand new problem. It was bad enough the Shifter could have robbed me of my identity, but to think it could have snagged Lucian's was more troubling. Though, that was better than Lucian being in contact with Rufus and having been the mole after all.

Of course, Rufus was going to know I'd be going this direction with my thinking. So what could I have done?

I needed to scratch Lucian and Thompson off the list once and for all. If I could confirm both of them were clean then I knew at least anyone around them was likely clean too. For every person I knocked off the list I could scratch off dozens out of the possible millions. And I'd confirmed Lucian was alive and well by eating his nasty cake. I just needed to confirm Thompson's identity.

Since I didn't know Thompson's home address I was going to have to follow him. Luckily, I still had enough of a charge in Babs' car to stalk him for a while, so long as he parked often. I climbed into the car and started my way back towards City Hall, where I imagined the trio would be for the night. They would have had time to get there by then given how long I spent upchucking blood cake.

When I saw Thompson before, I noticed he didn't seem to be around Hale during his cases, probably under orders not to stay too close. Lucian was waiting outside Hale's office and Thompson showed up after the three of us were already walking away. I had the impression the two of them weren't supposed to stick around until Hale left the courthouse and the safety of a building crawling in cops and bailiffs.

If an attorney comes in with armed guards it could come off looking like there were a reason for him to be scared. It could be an image concern or Hale could just have a problem with accepting help. But whatever the reason, I knew that as long as Hale was in the court there was a high probability Mr. Thompson would periodically walk away, possibly even leave the courthouse. This would have been my best bet since going inside the courthouse would have left me wide open to being spotted by Lucian.

The big problem with spotting a car like Thompson's at a place like the Seattle Municipal Court was the fact it's the busiest courthouse in the State of Washington. This meant I had to find one of the most common cars in the country parked in the busiest parking structure attached to a courthouse in the Cascadia region. There are a lot of sayings like "needle in a haystack", "a drop in the ocean" or "a grain of sand on the beach". But I propose a new one: "a black car in a parking garage".

The four most common colors of car throughout the history of cars have typically been black, white, red and silver. Now, picture how high those statistics spiked once black paint was made solar reactive so it could actually power your air conditioner on a hot day. Then picture that over half the people having court hearings after nightfall had tinted windows required. It was like being surrounded by Feds while I drove around in a little old lady's car.

Though at the time I was glad to have borrowed the car I did. Even though there were other ACTF cars parked on the lot and I theoretically could have blended in, we made sure every unit could be readily identified on sight. Aside from the fact Lucian would probably recognize someone sitting in an ACTF car instead of going inside to testify, it wouldn't take him that long to spot the unit number.

Still, driving in the clunker I was overwhelmed by just how out of place the thing felt. My one saving grace was Lucian would never expect a car junky like me to be sitting in a 2012 with flower decals on the hubcaps. Actually, I was surprised while looking at the rest of the cars that I was even sitting in it myself. Babs' powers of persuasion were apparently strong enough to make me do things I wouldn't have considered normally, which left some question about why I always paid my rent early.

If I'd been in the hearse I would have found the man's car easily. It would have read his license plates and then told me exactly which one it was. But in Babs' car, I have to admit, I was a little at a loss. If I'd been smarter I would have written the man's plate numbers down before driving on by, especially once I noticed it was a black car. Unfortunately, blood cake and a few other oversights had shown me I wasn't exactly smart that night.

At a loss, I realized I'd gone as far as I could without help while staying off the grid. I'd brought my cell phone with me, usually a no-no on duty, because I'd been trying to call Janice for most of the night to make sure she was okay. But as I wandered the garage like a lost child I realized I could use it to call someone else.

"Hey, Dulaf, it's Nate," I said quietly, trying not to sound defeated. "Do you mind doing me a favor?"

"I think I've already done a couple favors for you tonight," she whispered with an agitated hiss. "You do realize when you don't call in or plug into the Oracle system that people start to wonder where an agent goes, right?"

"Crap!" I exclaimed, "I forgot to punch in!"

"Damn right you did," she said. "I told them you were sick and that I confirmed it myself."

"I'm sorry, Dulaf," I said, cringing at her tone. "I wasn't thinking."

"No you weren't," she snapped. "Where are you anyway?!"

I hesitated, feeling stupid for having done so much wrong in one night. "I need to get Bill Thompson's license plate number so I can tail his car when he leaves the Municipal Court."

"Who's Bill Thompson?" she asked, raising her voice slightly.

"Right now, a suspect I have to scratch off the list for the Shifter," I said. "He works for Benjamin Hale as a bodyguard to supplement Lucian."

She laughed. I couldn't see her at the time but I could picture it from all the times I'd seen it before. If she were sitting in her chair she was probably leaning back in it by now, spinning slowly in it with her head hanging back over the rest, just letting it all out. Dulaf was never one for covering her "happy" moments.

"Oh my god," she exclaimed, giggling, "They need a supplement for Lucian?"

"Yeah," I said, "hard for me to believe too."

"Lucian," she giggled, "Mr. Moody-Super-Vampire?"

I had to give her that. The idea anyone would need more security than a fully blood-loaded and Helios carrying Lucian was a bit silly in some regards. But I already know why they "needed" Thompson: "It's a political thing, neutrality between the races."

As her giggles subsided I heard the sound of caster wheels skating across a smooth floor. She rode her chair through the lab to get to the computers, refusing once again to simply get up. You could find her doing it at all hours of the night if you cared to look: skating through on her rolling chair, bouncing from one side of the lab to the other like a ping pong ball with pointy ears occasionally going "wee!"

"Okay, checking out the files on this Thompson," she said. The caster wheels gave way to a light thump as she came to a stop against the desk.

I found a parking space while waiting and slumped in my seat, hoping not to be spotted in the ridiculous car. Listening to the sound of the tapping keys I started to imagine the visual of Dulaf typing away. Her fingers were like lightning, the fastest typist in the department. I only imagined court recorders getting more words per minute.

Of course, that made me think of Janice, whom I still

couldn't get in contact with.

I zoned out watching people walk by the car in the rear-view mirror, thinking about how I could try to contact her. I knew where she lived so I could just go to see her. But I wouldn't have been able to do that for hours and by now she was probably already working herself, somewhere in one of the two courthouses in the area. I'd never asked her which one she actually worked in, probably just assuming she was in the Municipal Court since most Alter cases happen there. There were a few county cases involving Alters, probably held in the older courthouse on the opposite side of City Hall. But when you think "Alter Court" you think "Municipal".

Wandering through these thoughts I suddenly became much more aware of every woman that walked by the car and the idea one of them could be Janice herself. There were some who looked remotely similar: the way they wore their hair, their eye color, sometimes even little features like the shape of their nose. Watching them almost made me miss the numbers Dulaf rattled off to me. In fact, I really only caught a P, 3 and a Q: a more useless jumble of symbols never seen.

"What was that again?" I asked.

Dulaf made an annoyed click of her tongue and replied, "Fell asleep didn't you?"

It wasn't the best thing to admit to, but it was better than the obvious skirt chasing comments I'd get from her if I admitted the actual truth. So I relented and quietly said, "Sorry about that."

She repeated the numbers and this time I wrote them down. I activated my badge and she entered in a report I was feeling better and came in after a couple hours of rest. It was stupid of me to try to avoid the Oracle system without looking like I was missing in action. Though she definitely saved my ass by saying she'd confirmed I was ill. I considered for a moment and said what needed to be said: "Thank you."

"It's just a license number," she said.

"I mean for covering my ass."

There was surprised silence after I said it. But she replied in a gentle tone, "Not a problem."

Nodding, I was about to hang up so I could go about stalking Thompson. I even put the phone down and had my finger over the button when I heard her cry, "Wait!"

"What's up?" I asked.

The quick fall of fingers across the keyboard came through the phone as I lifted it back to my ear. Hurriedly she asked, "Remember Daniel Cho?"

Just hearing the name made me feel uneasy as I asked, "What about him?"

"He's dead."

Chapter 23
Lost Youth

Daniel Cho was a very unlucky man. In the period of only a couple weeks he'd had his identity stolen, used in the process of illegal activities, been put on a short list for possible suspects, and then murdered. To say he had a really bad month was an understatement and as I walked into his apartment, the third agent to arrive, I realized just how bad a hand he'd been dealt.

His penthouse was in shambles. Photos of family and friends were strewn about the floor with their frames shattered, glass fragments littering the hardwood floors which bore inexplicable gouges. His furniture, including a few expensively upholstered chairs, was toppled over or broken in front of a flat-screen television embedded in his wall, now shattered like a windowpane.

The two agents there before me were taking careful pictures of every part of the apartment as I lingered in the door and watched them go to work. We needed to make sure the entire scene was documented before we started making any attempt to deal with it and that meant everything had to be photographed before we could even touch the poor man in the corner.

I recognized the agents, Devotee Timothy Richards and Lancer Alicia Nguyen, and they were doing a pretty good job of things without me. Richards was a little younger than me, fresh out of the clerics only a few months ago and a little twitchy from time to time. On the other hand, Nguyen was seasoned, one of the few crossovers we ever had. Once upon a time, Nguyen was a typical red and blue police officer working the regular beats; now she was one of us and could probably hardly talk to some of her old coworkers without a tense moment. She was in her 40s, by my guess, but maintained that Alter-like youthful appearance that so many Asian women could manage.

She spotted me over her hand-link and gave me a light nod. "Weren't you sick, Leone?"

With a system like the Oracle, news travels fast, so I

expected her to throw that one at me. "I got better."

"Well we've got this one covered," she said. "You can go home and recoup some more if you'd like. You look like hell."

I wasn't sure how to take that but figured it was best to just go with the flow and try not to argue. Instead, I said, "Cho was involved in one of my investigations."

She waved me in with a sweeping gesture and an understanding nod. "We've covered most of the room but don't touch the body yet."

I followed her directions, trying to avoid walking over anything that might have not been photographed yet. Just in case, I pulled out my own hand-link and started recording everything in front of me.

The room smelled of blood and the subtle stench of a fresh corpse. Dried stains ran across the walls and floor with a seemingly random splattering and smearing. At points there were subtle hints of footprints in the red marks, vague impressions of two pairs of shoes. Both sets were men's of the same basic size and design. Given the fact Daniel was dressed for work the prints were probably from dress patent leather shoes, size eight from what I could tell by looking.

But one set of prints featured a slight irregularity in the shape of the heel. There was a corner missing, a minor chip to what would otherwise have been a perfectly straight line. But the other footprints didn't feature this or any sign of wear at all. Every line from the footprint was visibly perfect. At least, they were as perfect as you could get in a bloodstain.

Given the fact the blood was probably Danny's, I imagined the one with the fewest footprints through the blood would have been him since they were both moving in the same direction. Danny was running, likely bleeding on the floor ahead of and beneath him while trying to get away from the person I imagined to be the Shifter.

I was fairly sure it was the Shifter – it was the only thing that made sense. Daniel was a lawyer, so I'm sure he made enemies somewhere. And there was even something to be said about the idea someone could have mistaken him for the drug dealer like I had recently. But to have him be victimized so clearly by the Shifter in the last couple of weeks and then killed in such a brutal fashion spoke of an abrupt situation and a crime of familiarity.

Most crimes between strangers are just as cold and uninvolved as the people themselves. If someone who doesn't know you wants to kill you they make it quick and try to get the hell out of there. If this had been someone who didn't know him, or someone who had been provoked by his legal practice, they would have probably just killed him at the door and left. Also, they would have probably shot or stabbed him. But this didn't look like a stabbing and if he were shot it would have been called in long before the stains could dry.

The stains gave me some strange questions and also painted a loose, incomplete picture of what happened in that room. The heels of both sets of prints were firmly planted, not lifting like they would be if there were running or excited chasing involved, meaning as Daniel staggered away the Shifter simply stalked him slowly like some sort of animal. Also, the prints of the Shifter seemed lighter, less firmly imprinted into the stains, despite doing the most actual stepping through the blood. It was almost like the Shifter weighed less than the already small Cho while still wearing exactly the same shoes.

When I reached the body I photographed what was left of his face. He was in a horrible state, slumped against the wall, sleeve torn from his jacket and stains across his shirt in a spattering formation as if he coughed it out while his chin was to his chest. The arm with the torn sleeve was covered in glass cuts and a nasty gash across his wrist and forearm that probably produced most of the blood on the floor. But, as an Alter, that didn't necessarily kill him.

It's a little different judging things like time and cause of death on many races of Alter. Their immune system and metabolism are so powerful the body often destroys itself rapidly after death, especially depending on the cause. In fact, the myth of vampire-like creatures burning in the sunlight was the most accurate picture someone could paint of the process. Their bodies eat themselves apart and leave behind a dried out husk full of blackened holes. Unfortunately, Cho's body had done a pretty good job of breaking down most of the evidence.

Nguyen must have seen me examining him and guessed my next question. Calmly, she said, "He's been dead for two days."

220

I looked it over and came to the same conclusion. Even if it was different than a human's decay there were still patterns to see. Daniel's face was withered like it had been drained of all fluids, patches of his skin blackened like scorch marks. The scorching was flaked though, ulcers forming in the center of them like rust eating through a pan. These skin patterns on an active Alter not suffering from an allergic reaction meant the body had been eating itself for at least forty-eight hours. But the patches were too small to be any longer than sixty hours.

"Yeah," I murmured half-heartedly. "But how could the neighbors not notice all this noise, the smell and the fact he was missing for two days?"

I looked back at Nguyen and saw a knowing look, an almost sly expression as if I was missing something completely obvious. It took me a moment, but I realized she knew what my case was and that I should have put it together. Clearly, there was an obvious answer that would support my entire theory.

"They didn't notice he was gone because they saw him leave," I said.

She nodded, replying, "And no one was around to hear it because the tenants downstairs were on vacation."

"So," I paused, looking back at Daniel, "the killer has been preparing to do this to him for a while or just accidentally struck at the perfect time."

I turned and walked away from Daniel, taking in the rest of the room now that everything had been documented. With what I could see, I reconstructed the events in my mind.

Daniel let the Shifter in. Either it had come to the door or he had come in with it. Either way, it was someone he knew and was comfortable with because there was no sign of forced entry at the door. The Shifter wasn't in Danny's form yet, of course, but was wearing shoes identical to his, brand new at that, likely a way we'd find the footprints. This meant they didn't want their previous form identified. More than likely they intended to use the previous form again.

Once they were inside, a spilled bottle of scotch with the cap sitting on a counter told me he offered the person a drink. Not only were they someone he knew, they were a friend. The Shifter had taken several identities in the place where he worked due to the court's proximity to one of the coffee shops on the map. But to pinpoint just who to be, there was a sign the Shifter had been studying him personally for quite a while.

As he turned his back to start pouring the drink, the Shifter grabbed a lamp not far from where they were standing and smashed it across the back of his head. It shattered, the glass falling to the floor around them. However, he was still alert despite the injury to his head and he turned to fight back. There was a struggle in the room and Daniel managed to defend himself fairly well despite the surprise attack, otherwise there wouldn't be quite so much damage.

Eventually, despite his best efforts, Daniel was losing ground, likely from the blood loss and confusion he was suffering. The Shifter continued on, shoved him into the corner and, with a large, heavy object, hit him in the chest, collapsing his ribs and causing him to cough up the blood that splattered across the front of his shirt and likely the Shifter's own clothes. I knew it was a blunt object because, looking closer at Daniel, it was impossible to miss the fact his torso had an obvious deformation under the shirt. The dent showed a lot of force, breaking the ribs and caving in the torso along one side.

Combined with the blood loss from his arm and the injuries to his head, that hit to the chest was probably the last straw. Daniel collapsed into the corner, supported by the wall for a moment, before sliding down to a sitting position. He stared out at the attacker, confused by what had happened and unable to piece it together beyond the agony he was in. As he stared at the person he thought was his friend, he either slowly bled out or asphyxiated. Either way, I imagine his last moments were terrifying and baffling. He had no idea why his friend had done this to him as he gasped for air to no avail. He had no idea what had happened as the world faded to black.

"Do we have any idea what the murder weapon was?" I asked.

Richards opened a closet door, the bloody surface of a bowling ball catching my attention almost immediately. The ball was custom, sitting next to the bag that probably came with it, Cho's name written across both in gold lettering. However, Cho's blood was now splattered across the name on the ball, giving an idea on how it came in contact with him. The finger holes were facing out as the ball collided with his ribcage, probably catching some of the same mess as the man's own shirt, suggesting it was delivered with a bowling grip.

This brought up a new link to the chain. The killer knew Cho – a busy, high-paid lawyer – bowled. So, somewhere in the middle of the scuffle they opened the closet door, pulled out the ball and used it to cave in his ribcage. This wasn't just a matter of studying; this was a complete profile of the man.

I stared at his corpse a while longer and tried to think of just why someone would need to go to such great lengths to kill him. When I met him, he didn't seem to be all that unusual. He was a lawyer, but there were dozens of Alter lawyers out there. Not only that, but as far as I knew, Cho wasn't involved in anything particularly major thanks to a rather protective wolf pack. He didn't seem like the type of person to even be on Rufus' radar, let alone on his hit list.

No, Cho's death likely wasn't ordered. It was a means to an end at best and a cover up at worst. A cover up would have been important in so many ways because the list of things a Shifter would have to hide is fairly short and damning. Maybe Cho had figured out their true identity or realized what they were doing. Then again, if it were a means to an end, what end could that have been? Either prospect left new questions and the renewed hope of some answers.

"Any signs of a motive?" I asked, receiving a pair of baffled headshakes.

Nguyen went about her evidence gathering and finally stopped to take a closer look at Daniel's body while Richards wandered away from that corner, likely to get some fresh air or just step back to take in the whole picture. I remember what it was like to be new to it all and to see things like this. You never really get used to the really horrible scenes, but the first couple of times are always the roughest. The stench of what could only be described as old cooked pork and the metallic smell of blood were usually the most overwhelming. I remember choking on the air several times, more so than I did when I found that blue lab.

But he didn't look sick. Richards had the same color to his face he had when I'd walked in and stood straight and clear as though he were firmly in control of his body. He looked around the room, brow furrowed in thought, lips pursed together like he was about to chew on the bottom one in contemplation.

Eventually, he lifted his chin and asked in an energetic but confused tone, "Why did they stay here for a whole day after doing all this?"

And the man had a point. It was hard enough to sit in the room with the body for longer than fifteen minutes. Someone would have had to tolerate it for more than a day to be able to walk out the next morning with Cho's face. And, as rare as Shifters are, it was easy to overlook why they'd stay. But there was only one reason for a Shifter to stay so long at the crime scene.

"Heavy change," I muttered while scouring the room for more.

Nguyen nodded in agreement. "They require time."

Unlike movies or fairytales, Shifters don't simply wave a hand and take a whole new face effortlessly. No, shifting requires precise control of one's own body and the ability to tolerate the process of reshaping into something new. The more they changed, the longer it took.

Looking at the footprints, this made me realize that when they first entered they were lighter than Cho after all. They must have been sitting in the apartment, watching him wither, trying to duplicate every facet of what he was before they could leave. But then that meant if they wanted to return to what they were it would take at least a day to do that.

A quick glance to Nguyen and Richards and I realized that we'd all come to the same revelation. If the body was that drastically changed and required time to change back, then the fact they left that morning meant one thing that escaped me, and apparently them, until just that moment.

"He still looks like Cho, doesn't he?"

We shared a nod and I bolted out the door.

Chapter 24
Lost Assailant

If you were willing to spend a day copying someone's face and then another day trying to get rid of it, you would be doing it for more than just a chance to walk out and buy yourself a couple hours, right?

"Of course" is the only answer I could possibly think of. I couldn't fathom the idea that you could dedicate to something so entirely and only need it for three minutes. Then again I was driving an old beat up car with flower decals that I readily just proved to myself I didn't need. Obviously, if the Shifter was stuck as an Asian man, he wouldn't be able to go around as either Lucian, a man as white as you can get without actually being dead, or Thompson, a man with the facial features of a cheese grater. After going to all the trouble of grabbing a car to tail those two, I no longer needed it.

Funny how that worked out.

But I couldn't afford to waste even a minute to go back for my good car; I needed to find "Cho" as soon as possible. I used my hand-link to throw an APB onto the system for an Asian male in his mid-thirties with dramatic weight loss and a yellow-green tinted aura. Finally starting to remember some of my academy classes on Shifters, I remembered the green now, a sign of rapid, natural chemical adjustments in the body. This was useful for spotting angry Werewolves and the like but I'd totally forgotten about the Shifter link until I found myself trying to pick an Asian male out of the crowds in Seattle.

With the hand-link out, it occurred to me to make another search. After a quick lap around the apartment building just before leaving, I realized Cho had suffered another crime in his already horrendous week: his car had been stolen. The Shifter took his face, took his life and took his wheels. Sure, killing him was horrendous, but something about stealing a dead man's car felt… insulting. Regardless, it gave me another lead as I ran a search for Cho's car.

It paid off. The Oracle pinged it in the parking structure next to the Municipal Courthouse. Cross-referencing the name against the system, I even found the docket with his name still on it. I had my chance.

I wasn't as wary of the garage this time, nearly speeding to find the parking space and ignoring the fact Lucian's car was sitting only a couple spaces away. I even got out of the car in front of a couple red and blues without worry of embarrassment.

There were some snickers from the officers but I didn't care anymore. Of the things I could be mocked for, flower decals couldn't be any worse than Wolfendown. But I was about to bust a person who couldn't theoretically be caught on forensics. It was a time-sensitive situation with a potential to lose my suspect entirely after twenty-four hours instead of the standard forty-eight most homicide cases had. I just wondered how much could be changed on his face in the time he had.

The aura wasn't going to help too much without a similarity to Cho's face either. Everyone in the waiting room had a yellow aura of some shade, even the lawyers – leaving me to look for the greens instead. The green was much rarer in the crowd, only visible in a Werewolf and his girlfriend bickering in the corner. I was in a hurry, probably too much of one in hindsight, and couldn't stop to take a good look around the whole room. Instead, I was just waiting for some flash of color recognition from any angle I could get and hoping the face on the other side looked remotely like a "Cho".

I did a quick change to the settings on my hand-link and had it project a display across my visor. Names floated over the heads of everyone in the room that had a pending case and numbers flashed across the badges of all the jurors standing with them.

Amusing side-note, the people who were there for Jury Duty had greater degrees of red in their spectrum than the people actually there for a specific case. Now, mind you, a lack of red doesn't mean they were "calm", but it does mean that the jurors were a lot more pissed off about being there. And most of the lawyers in the room had hints of a deep blue, showing, like Trey, they were either guarded or trying to deceive someone. So, in the end, I knew my visor worked right at the very least.

But there was nothing in the room. Most of the people on the docket were still there, sitting, waiting for their time in court like cattle being left to consider their fate. Some of them were going to get milked by fines and, judging by their auras, they weren't exactly feeling wrongfully accused. But there were still a few names missing, possibly people already in court. I checked the court room assignments for those names, took one last look at the rainbow of happy-happy people and made my way out of there as quickly as possible.

The population of red and blues in the court was still amazingly high for the time of night. Sometimes the jurisdictions were a little fuzzy in a place or two, especially for traffic violations. But a few of them were oddly relaxed as if they had no reason to be there at all, like they were sitting and waiting for the freak show. Part of me was a little annoyed by their presence. But among them I spotted something far more interesting out by a window.

His aura was yellow and green in a way that made him look like an Amazonian parrot from a distance. So vibrant was the aura that I had to slide the visor down to look beyond the colors. What I saw was absolutely perfect. It was an Asian male in his mid-thirties around Danny's height while looking somewhat underweight like he'd been sick. Even the shoes matched as I glanced down at his patent leather uniform oxfords. He was exactly what I was hoping to find except for one detail: he was wearing a police uniform.

Surrounded by red and blues and realizing the man directly in front of me was probably "the guy" was a bit of a conflicting moment for me. On the one hand, I had him in my sights. On the other hand, this is how code 88s got started. If I approached him alone I'd probably end up caught in gunfire or exchanging variations of mace with my fellow officers. But if I brought along some ACTF agents with me we'd probably be running to Canada before the end of the week.

The only thing I could think of was to goad him into making the first move and hoping for the best. I pushed the visor back up and made my way over to him, keeping a careful eye on everything around me just in case he wasn't alone. As I put away the hand-link I stroked the grip of my Helios to reaffirm I'd managed to remember the thing in my hazy stupor of a night.

He didn't seem to notice me, too caught up in conversation with other officers as they stood by the window looking out over the city street beyond. I kept my distance, stopping about ten feet from them and making a quick nervous push at the bridge of my shades to make sure the visor was still firmly anchored to my face. If I'd learned anything since joining the ACTF it was the power of the visor. Useful as it may have been, the best feature was the fact every single Alter in the world knew what it meant on some base level… including the man I mentally referred to as "Officer Cho" in my head.

The conversation broke and stumbled for a minute, "Officer Cho" glancing my way out of the corner of his eye while trying not to break character. But the other officers took the liberty of doing that for him.

"Hey, you," one of them barked. "You got a problem?"

I stared him down as I would any other threatening presence and replied, "Not a bit, just want to talk to your friend there."

"Talk about what, Fang-bitch?"

"Fang-bitch" was a bit like I'd suddenly dropped my pants – everyone needed to look. At least a dozen pair of eyes were fixed on me and analyzing my every movement. Like a great red flag it had marked me and pointed out I was not one of them. But, fortunately, Lucian had taught me how to deal with it.

"Speaking of Fangs," I said as calmly as possible, "did you know he's one?"

"The hell did you just say?" the man I now considered "Fang-bitch" asked with a red face.

"I said your friend is an Alter," I said, taking off my visor to look him in the eye, "and I want to talk to him."

He growled and took an expression of total disgust at a sickening truth. "Sergeant Chen's been on the force for twelve years, punk. You have no right to be questioning him!"

"Just one problem," I said, "that's not Chen."

Fang-bitch's face was priceless as we stared each other down. Whatever brain he had in his head was now misfiring with the conflicting information. Either he'd just been talking to an imposter, making him look stupid, or he was going to pretend he didn't know what the visors do, which would have also made him look stupid. Really, it was a bit of a pickle he'd put himself in. I would have even felt for him if he wasn't a bit of a dick about it beforehand.

But some of Fang-bitch's friends had some slightly different reactions. While he looked like he'd just sucked on a lemon, his buddies were a combination of confusion, doubt and possible belief; one of them even took the opportunity to peer at "Chen" and analyze him. I recognized that man to be Ramirez.

Tension is a funny thing: even if it doesn't make sense it can still build, sometimes especially if it doesn't make sense. The police were gathering around me like a building storm cloud while "Chen" started to back out of the center of the situation slowly along the wall. I realized just why the Shifter took the shape they had: they were trying to use the blue wall against me. And, through that blue wall, we exchanged an uneasy, knowing glance.

I'd found him.

He was backing away and the rest were moving in. Subtly, I started to unhook the banshee from the back of my belt. I don't know if anyone saw it, but if they did they didn't move on me. My hope was that, if I was going to have to deal with the police, I could at least deal with them in a way that didn't involve having to actually shoot any of them. But "Fang-bitch" was too eager to get up in my face, standing only inches in front of me.

"Can I help you?" I asked him, dripping in sarcasm that I probably should have curbed a little.

"You Fang-bitches shouldn't even be in this country," he said to me, snarling. "When have you ever done anything to help *real* people over those freaks?!"

Now, I'm not sure if it was the way he was standing in my face or if it was the way he exclaimed "real people" and "freaks" the way he did, but I was fairly pissed off at that point and replied to his question with one of my own: "Breath mint, asshole?"

He growled and shoved me. It presented the perfect opportunity for "Chen" to run for it and let Fang-bitch hold me back. And, looking out of the corner of my eye, I saw "Chen's" back turn as he ran clear, the other officers too distracted to notice.

Seeing "Chen" flee, I reacted in a way I probably shouldn't have: I shoved Fang-bitch back.

The next few seconds were a blur as the man took out his nightstick and tried to hit me with it. There were two problems with that. First, the fact he lost his cool so fast spoke volumes about his personality. Second, when he swung that stick at me, a no-no in the first place, it was all reflex from there.

Grabbing his wrist behind the stick's grip, I redirected the swing off to the side and pushed it out past me as I spun around. The next thing he could see was my opposite elbow ramming into his face like he owed me money. He spun around and banged his head across the nearby window. The glass cracked as the man's head bounced and the other cops rushed me, dragging me away as if I took the first shot.

The ruckus gave "Chen" a chance to clear out while I struggled against the pack of cops holding my arms. But it also meant none of them actually noticed the banshee I was holding. I got one hand free, twisted the end and dropped it before punting the thing at Fang-bitch. There was a confused pause from the ones who hadn't seen a banshee yet and a panicked series of dives from the ones who had.

Ear piercing shrieks ran through the halls and caused an uproar back in the packed waiting room I just came from. I felt bad for some of them, especially for the Werewolves who could already hear better than most humans. But, as the cops around me were disoriented, stunned or, in the case of Fang-bitch, hurled a few feet by the sudden shockwave, I made a run for the fleeing "Chen".

As I ran down the corridor and listened to the sound of the screaming banshee I couldn't help but consider what I might have set off. While they had taken the first swing at me they were on less shaky ground than my group. They were the traditional, established police from the standing government of the area. Meanwhile, I was some guy who was essentially a UN peacekeeper. I just pissed on their turf.

I ran down the hallway and caught sight of the Shifter shoving his way through the crowd to the nearest exit. He was having some trouble, meeting with the resistance of people who were suffering the effects of the banshee even though we were a good hundred feet from where I dropped it by then. Thankfully, they held him for the few seconds I needed to catch up and pull my Helios.

I leveled it at the back of his head, flipping on the guide like marking where the shot would hit. We don't often use it, usually you can just see your target through the visor, but the guide is a low powered ultraviolet light meant to let the Alter know they were dead in the sights. He froze, feeling the heat of the light across the back of his head, and raised his hands slowly.

The banshee started cutting out as I kept the gun leveled at "Chen's" head and a pair of cops came running down the hall after me when it finally died away completely. I glanced over my shoulder as they pulled Tasers that were likely going to be fired into my ass real soon if I couldn't convince them "Chen" was a Shapeshifter.

"Hold it!" I cried, raising a hand, keeping the Helios steady with the other. "This man's not who you think he is; he's a Shifter that's suspected of involvement in narcotics, identity theft and murder. Please let me handle this!"

Looking back, I realized it was Ramirez again. He paused and gestured to the other, both lowering their weapons. It was a quiet, unspoken allowance, the first real sign of real trust between our departments I'd seen in some time. And, honestly, the fact they were willing to do that after what I'd done said a lot about them.

Having gotten a second gesture of trust from Ramirez in a week, I turned my attention back to "Chen" and called out to him, "I don't know what your real name is but we'll be sure to find out later. For now, you have the right to remain silent."

I stepped closer to him and reached out, getting ready to take his wrist and bring it around behind his back.

That hand never reached his wrist though. Instead, he spun around to face me as soon as my foot came in contact with the floor behind him. He turned, glared at me and swung a kick for my face in a single fluid motion.

I want to say that as the Shifter made his move and kicked me that it was futile, that my training kicked in as it did with Fang-bitch and everything moved in slow motion as I instinctively countered or weaved out of the way. But that would be a lie.

In truth, my experience was limited to a flash of leather, the smell of bubblegum on the bottom of the shoe and everything tasting like copper while I fell to the ground. I learned a lesson as everything faded in and out of black while I tried to shake the sensation that the room was spinning. The lesson was simple but important to remember from then on: Shifters are amazingly fast. Also, getting kicked in the face with a leather shoe hurts way more than any other material.

I heard Ramirez and the second cop cry out for him to give himself up and the pop of Tasers being fired over me in the Shifter's direction. I don't know if they hit, I was still too dazed to have any clue about it. But as I lifted my head again I watched "Chen" run for the window in a sprint and jump through it, shattering the glass and sailing out over the city street.

I pushed myself up and staggered after him, hardly aware of what was happening as I moved toward the broken window. Looking outside, I watched as the Shifter stood on the sidewalk across the street, people scattered around him like they'd seen him fall from the sky itself, and then turn to run into the crowd that was growing around the peculiar sight. Without my visor, I soon lost him in the dark of the night and the glow of the city lights as he weaved through the sea of people below.

Chapter 25
Offering Insight

Ramirez proved he was decent once again, smoothing things over with the others that caught up to us and corroborating my claim that "Chen" was an Alter. Not that there was really much doubt after the three of us explained "Chen" had cleared a city street from a few floors up, landed on his feet and ran off. But there were a few holdouts, Fang-bitch most specifically. Thankfully, Ramirez outranked him too, leaving me free and clear to walk away from what was an otherwise incredibly embarrassing situation.

I walked out of that building with a sore face and a bruised ego. Nothing like picking a fight with a cop over a suspect you lost anyway to leave you feeling sheepish. It wasn't an easy walk either as I was still dazed by the kick to the face but was too stubborn to admit I was hurting. I probably needed to get it checked out by the medical team back at the station, or at least by someone at a free clinic. Something told me it wasn't serious enough to really worry about but I still knew the mark on my face was going to be a beautiful sight in twenty-four hours.

Walking through the parking garage, I passed several red and blues that weren't looking too pleased with me. I avoided eye contact, even though I had my visor on, and skulked back to my hippy relic car. When I slipped in I laid low in the seat for a bit waiting for some of the other officers to head on by. I didn't have any real reason to be hiding from them, but I didn't have any reason to hold my head high either.

"That was dumb luck," a voice said from behind me.

I jumped, turning to look into the back seat. Lucian stared back coldly, arms crossed.

"Nathaniel," he said solemnly, "did you just decide to make an ass of yourself today or was it a natural process?"

I hate to admit it but I actually considered the question seriously for a minute. "Natural process, I think."

Leaning back in the seat, Lucian laughed. "I figured as

much. You don't look like a man who just planned to get kicked in the face."

I hesitated for a moment on "planned to get kicked in the face". Though he was laughing at me, I couldn't be sure he was actually mocking me. Strange as it may have seemed, part of me was sure he had a story where someone actually did.

"Why would anyone plan to get kicked in the face?" I asked, resting my forehead against the steering wheel.

"Make it believable?" he remarked. "So what exactly just happened back there?"

The steering wheel was cool against my forehead, helping with the headache I had since tasting the bottom of "Chen's" shoe. I didn't even lift my head away from it when replying to Lucian – just rolling it over onto its side instead – resting against my temple where the pressure was really starting to build.

"I found the Shifter," I said quietly, trying not to aggravate my headache. "The guy killed Cho, made his way to the courtrooms for some reason and took the identity of a cop after we found the body. He was probably trying to use the other cops as a shield."

Lucian chuckled again, a little less abrasively this time, and leaned forward in the seat, resting his elbows on the front seats while looking approximately in my eyes. His aura was a shade of light blue normally reserved for children and their caretakers, making me wonder how he looked at me right then. Supposedly every lancer feels their devotee is like family. But Lucian has always been there for me. Since the day he first offered me a position in the academy, he quietly held my hand every time I walked into trouble. Seeing the aura, I realized I might have been worrying the man a little.

"It's okay," I murmured, "I'm fine."

He closed his eyes and nodded with a single slow dip. It wasn't a grand gesture, but it was enough for me. As he opened his eyes again he extended the arm resting behind me and patted my back gently. I couldn't help but feel like he was comforting a kid that'd blown a game. But what he said next was a bit unexpected.

"You fucked up, kid," he said with a smirk. "But, don't worry, the fact is you probably did what most people would have done."

"Really?" I asked.

"Not that it's a good thing to do," he said with a minor cringe.

That wasn't reassuring: "you're an idiot, just like the rest of us". But I couldn't fault his logic. Thinking about it, there was very little doubt everyone in the force would have reacted the same way once someone started calling them fang-bitch and took the first swing. I guess that's probably a big part of why the Code 88s happen in the first place. But it didn't exactly make me feel any better or more reassured about what happened. Were it not for Ramirez, the whole lot of us would be running for Vancouver and we both knew it.

Still, I couldn't just sit there and mope. If we sat there talking about the number of ways I screwed up the situation we would be there forever in that little flower decaled car and then I'd have to push it home. But then, that thought brought up a whole new question.

"How'd you know I was using this car?"

Lucian smirked into the rear view mirror. "Your car wasn't here, I knew you were in the building and this was the least like you and the only one with sparkling plates."

Busted for being the only one who was actively unlike me had to be the definition of wasted effort.

"Who were you tailing?" he asked quietly, the smirk fading away to be replaced with the eerie calm of his normal expression.

I stared into the mirror at his face and wondered just how honest I should be about it all. There was a lot to ask him, starting with his apparent conversation with Rufus. Surely it was the logical and intelligent thing to do. Of course, I wasn't much of either for most of the night so I wasn't quite sure if that was really the logical and intelligent thing to do. Regardless, I bit the bullet in the most sarcastic way possible.

"Who puts blood in cake?" I asked.

He subtly frowned, an eyebrow raised. To my surprise, the next words out of his mouth weren't "you don't trust me". Instead he asked, "You ate my cake?"

Of everything that had just been said in so few words, it was amazing that was the thing he ended up responding to. He wasn't offended I suspected him or curious why he was on the list, just annoyed I ate his cake. Or, at least, that's what he made it out to be.

"It was disgusting," I said, trying my best to recreate the expression I had after taking the first bite, realizing the creamy stuff wasn't fudge or something similar.

"Well then, you've been punished," he said, settling back into his seat.

We stared into the mirror at each other, silently, and seemed to be waiting for someone to break the slowly rising feeling of dread. Each of us had a question we needed to ask, each of us had a reason not to ask it. His question was more to the point, more important, because it represented a possible shift in the nature of our relationship, the idea that maybe we weren't going to be allies, or friends, anymore. I'm sure that all sounds very quaint to a lot of people but it was still important enough to me that I didn't want to hear it.

But I didn't get my wish. Despite my best hopes he asked in a quiet, solemn tone, "Did you find anything?"

I looked over my shoulder to answer, feeling he deserved to be looked in the eye for something like that. It was hard to do, much harder than I think it should have been considering all I said was "No".

The tension eased after saying it and we shared a quiet moment where I could feel the whole situation start to resolve itself. Somehow the idea he had been talking to Rufus wasn't important in that quiet moment. Surely, if it were, I wouldn't have felt so much better. But it needed to be asked anyway.

"Have you talked to Rufus?"

A silent nod was his response, no clarification, no explanations, just a single bob of the head as though it didn't require a story behind it. Maybe it didn't, maybe it was just a simple situation, but I needed to press for that information anyway. "Why?"

"The same reason why I sent you to him," Lucian said calmly, letting his eyes close as he rested his head back. "He's an informant and I needed to ask him a question."

Suddenly, I realized how ridiculously blind I was. I'd always asked him one question before and always received the same cryptic answers. Now, sitting in that ridiculous car with him, I knew he actually passed it to me like some sort of torch.

"Rufus is your source?"

Once again, all I got was a profound nod. But that was enough.

Lucian sent me on my way after that, informing me I looked like crap and I needed to go home. After the night I'd had, I couldn't exactly disagree with the man. I drove the little car through town and back to the station so I could check in with the doctors down in the clinic. They patched me up, put me back on my feet and told me exactly the same thing so many others and my own gut had been telling me all night: "Go home."

And so, I did.

Thankfully the trip from the station to my apartment isn't a long distance – something I used to think was luck, but now suspected might have been Babs. Really, this was a great thing because that car wasn't going to cooperate any longer than another three blocks. Even as I pulled into the usual spot I found the lights dimming and felt the thing suddenly coast for the last few feet. I almost didn't even feel the need to hit the brakes.

There was a whine, a whistle and the feeling of the car settling in as the electricity from the brakes gave the woefully underpowered motors their last hurrah. It really almost sounded like the damn thing was crying and making one last effort to live at any cost. I climbed out, said my goodbyes to "ugly" and walked back inside with the keys and one hell of a headache.

My head was swirling a bit after getting some time to settle. The pain had kept me semi-focused, but as I walked up the stairs and made my way back to Babs' apartment the sleep deprivation and headache became disorienting. Were it not for the fact the doctors had looked at my head and determined it was a brick of some sort, I would have thought I had broken something.

The look on Babs' face when I handed over the keys told me I looked worse than I felt. She offered me some herbal remedies and sent me on my way back to my apartment, warning me not to fall down despite the fact I lived right across the hall. And, of course, she was prophetic once again as I found myself spinning half way through the door.

When I made it back inside, I nearly kissed the floor and

crawled my way to the couch I'd known as the "landing pad" since my early days. It was one of the rarely used pieces of furniture in my apartment anymore: my grandmother's couch still sitting there next to the other pieces of furniture that went unused. Regardless of what happened, a long night meant falling face-first into that couch instead of pushing my way through to the bedroom.

It's an old thing, passed onto me through my family and used since back when the damn thing was still trendy. My grandmother owned it, then my mother and then my grandmother again when mom left and dad… left. When I moved out of her house, grandma gave it to me as she felt the person who'd slept on it most in their life was me. Sadly, I think the couch was one of the only things in my apartment I had any emotional connection to.

When I go to work, I can look at the memorial wall and remember Leo and a dozen or so others to follow him. I can trace the lines of my family through generations that stood for something until a minor hiccup in my childhood. But I realized then, lying face down over a stain almost as old as me, that I didn't even have photos of my family lying around like other people.

Instead, I kept mementos that did little more than take up space, cold reminders of what used to be. They were things that I couldn't feel attached to, memories I didn't want to remember. Glancing around the room, I wondered why I kept any of it around. But without it, aside from my complete lack of organization, the apartment would remind me of Lucian's house in just how impersonal and sparse it really was.

Suddenly, I knew what it was about the Shifter that offended me. They weren't just involved with something that had taken my father from me – they were trying to take everything I had left. Make me question myself and you have only annoyed me; make me question my friends and you're playing with my lifelines. Lucian, Dulaf and Trey: they're stable factors in my life that I could depend on entirely before this person had arrived on the scene. And then, as I was down, they kicked me again by going after Janice, whom I'd only recently gotten to know in any way that I'd wanted to.

Janice: I still hadn't reached her after all the efforts. It was nearly dawn, so surely she'd be home by now. I pushed myself up and crawled to the far end of the couch, reaching for my phone despite my body telling me to just sit still for a while longer.

Though, when I picked it up I saw there was a surprise waiting for me. My voice-mail, normally empty and ignored, had a message. Flashing there was a small indicator that hadn't been there before. Janice finally called back.

I listened to her message, which was something along the lines of "sorry I missed you all night but I had more important things to deal with."

I could have been annoyed by the way she brushed me off and then sent me a message only to brush me off again. But I couldn't have been happier to hear someone's voice. She was okay, roughed up, but okay. The message was a couple hours old by the time I noticed and I wasn't entirely sure if she'd still be awake since I could see the light of the dawn reflecting off the windows across the street. But, on the off chance she could be, I had to try.

It didn't ring for long yet seemed like an eternity. Anticipation for whether or not she would pick up the phone built as I wondered the questions anyone with a bit of insecurity has had while on the phone: is she checking the caller ID? Is she avoiding me? Is she screening her calls? I don't even remember how many times it rang; I just knew it was longer than I was comfortable with. Not that it was hard to achieve at the time.

The sleepy, nasally congested voice finally responded, "Hello?"

"Janice, it's Nate."

"Nate? What're you doing calling so early?"

She was ticked but it was a good kind of ticked, at least in my opinion. You don't get angry at people for calling early if you've been feeling alone the whole time. At least you don't as far as I understand the world. So I smiled to myself and replied, "I've been calling all night, this is the first time you picked up."

There was some sniffing and coughing as she tried to clear her throat. "Sorry, I've been scrambling to close all of my accounts and get reports on what happened."

"Yeah, I heard," I said, "that's why I've been calling."

She surprised me then, her voice getting stronger as she snapped, "Well you should have been focusing on something else!"

"Like what?" I asked.

"Like," she paused, the difficulty to breathe obvious over the phone now, "I don't know, something else, something work related."

"Trust me," I said, chuckling, "I got my timecard punched."

"What's that supposed to mean?"

I rolled over to take the pressure off that side of my face once I remembered it, saying, "You'll know when you see it, I have something of a mark."

A light giggle came across the phone, one that really made my day. Sure, she was laughing at my pain but at least she was laughing. Choking back the snickers she apologized, "Sorry, sorry, I really shouldn't be laughing about that. Is it bad?"

"Eh, I'll live," I said, rolling over onto my back entirely now that I'd realized the blood rush was making my face throb, "provided it doesn't horrify you."

"Did you break anything?" she asked.

"Only my pride," I replied, "as far as I know."

"I'm sorry," she said in a quiet, almost mournful tone.

"What would you be sorry for?" I asked.

A brief silence fell over the other end of the phone again, then a sniff before she continued, "For not calling you back sooner – I should have."

"You were busy, Janice," I said. But just then the thoughts of the Shifter came back to me and I realized she was stuck in the middle just like Danny had been. And Danny, did she even hear about him?

Hesitating, I asked, "Did you hear about Daniel Cho?"

"Danny?" She asked, "What about him?"

What could I tell her? She'd just become the next victim on a long list of victims and her friend had died after becoming one himself. But I'd already stepped too far into it to back out, just by implying something had happened to him. I couldn't avoid it.

"He," I started to say, pausing to search for the right words and not finding any. "We found his body today."

240

The phone went silent again, even her strained breathing stopping for a moment as if the wind were knocked out of her entirely. Eventually, she asked only one thing: "How?"

Chapter 26
Working Juxtaposition

Janice took the news as well as anyone could have imagined. But while the question of how was heavy on her mind, the question of why was heavier on mine. We stayed up for a good couple of hours talking about Danny and how he'd never done anything to anyone. In fact, he sounded like a really decent guy.

In the past, all public defenders in the Seattle area were non-profit and worked strictly for the government. But the system changed when the Alters came on the scene. The public defender agencies would have had to work twenty-four hours a day. It was necessary to bring in all resources possible. Volunteers had to come to defend the Alters from a legal system that wasn't sure what to do with them.

Danny was one of the good guys. He didn't work strictly for the state and he didn't *have* to work for them either. In fact, his private practice was with one of the best firms in the state and probably on the west coast altogether. He made six figures easily a year and didn't have to take up the low-paying jobs of the state to make ends meet or bolster his reputation. He just wanted to help people who couldn't afford it otherwise.

"I'm sorry for doubting him," I said quietly.

Janice fell silent again, making me feel nervous. But before long she said, "I wasn't being fair to you. If things had gone differently maybe he'd still be alive."

Truer words never spoken. There was a lot that could have gone differently. Had I gone after Daniel instead of Anubis, there would have been a chance I could have done something to help him. Instead, I found out days later that I'd missed a shot to prevent worse from happening.

"I'm sorry I couldn't help anyway," I said.

Her voice rose with a quiver as she asked, "What if they did it because you found him?"

A chill ran over me as I thought of that. I'd already considered they'd gone after Janice because of her connection to me, but what about Danny? If they were toying with me it wouldn't be out of the question. In fact, it seemed like Rufus' kind of play.

"I don't know," I said. "I have to investigate what happened to Danny and see if there was any other motive."

There were a few more sniffs on the other side, possibly trying to stifle the urge to cry out loud. "I hope this is all over soon," she said with a shaking voice.

"Yeah, I hope so too," I said, feeling an ache in my chest from the sounds on the other end.

We both went quiet again and I stared into the ceiling waiting for something to break that empty, hollow feeling growing in the silence.

"I think I need to get some sleep now," she said finally.

I glanced out the window, seeing a well-lit street outside and realizing it was well into the morning hours. "Yeah, I could probably use some too."

We said our goodbyes then I hung up and stared into the ceiling again. I needed to get to sleep before I spent the next day as a zombie like the last. But my mind was racing now. Even in the old comfortable couch I'd slept on so many times before I couldn't relax enough to drift away.

"Maybe something to eat," I mumbled to myself, rising to my feet. I took off my jacket and tossed it across the back of the couch, dragging myself into the kitchen and hoping there was something worthwhile.

Unfortunately, I forgot my kitchen was a death-trap and my fridge had slowly turned into a horror show. Months of neglect had fostered an interesting variety of sights and smells. I want to say that I would have cleaned it on another day, but the crime scene spoke for itself. Giving up on the fridge, I searched the freezer and cupboards for anything else. Despite my best efforts, all I could find were a loaf of bread and my old friends the frozen waffles. Having tired of the soggy waffles, I reached for the loaf of bread that somehow managed to escape the ravages of mold and time.

"Sounds like toast," I muttered, turning to the toaster behind me.

Staring at it, seeing the burn marks and the fire extinguisher

243

on the counter next to it, I remembered it set itself on fire. Obviously, fire was a sign that the old girl was probably ready for pasture. But, some small part of me wondered if it would still work even now. I couldn't tell if it was misplaced nostalgia or some deep-seated need for toast, but I needed to know if it might still turn back on.

I reached out and carefully plugged it in, then promptly got shocked for my efforts.

"Fuck!" I yelled, likely loud enough to be heard across the hall. I pulled my gloves out of my pocket and put them on again, yanking the plug back out. At first, I didn't even understand why I'd been stupid enough to even try it. But, looking out at the furniture, I realized I was wrong earlier: there *was* a connection to this stuff.

Staring at the thing, I felt a strange grief for the fact it was most definitely dead. They weren't pictures, but these objects were all I had of family. This toaster was only one of two things I had of my mother and now it was dead.

I'd been faced with these kinds of moments for most of the week. I'd been sulking and lingering in memories of what the blue had done to my family and the new knowledge Rufus had set us down that path. And now I stood holding a broken relic of that era. I could have continued sulking.

Instead, I went to the hardware store.

I didn't go to buy a new toaster. I went to buy some wood, a few nails and some household chemicals mostly used for cleaning. It was an innocuous collection of materials that I'm sure had been bought together plenty of times before without any problem. However, me, I had strange intentions for it that not many would have guessed.

The toaster, for all I hated it, was a symbol for me. I'd held onto that thing for years because it was something that belonged to my mother. And, as much as I fooled myself into believing otherwise, that still meant something to me. It deserved a proper send-off.

For decades the nerd community has found various ways to honor their old electronics. Sometimes this involved sledgehammers, throwing things off of rooftops or running them over. Other times this has involved elaborately staged recreations of scenes from movies where office guys would destroy their equipment. But me, I chose something a little more old school.

They call it a Viking funeral.

After a few minutes of driving around, I'd found a quiet spot by the harbor where no one was around and assembled my materials. I nailed the boards together into a pretty rudimentary box, placed the toaster in it, then mixed the chemicals I'd bought and poured them into the busted appliance. I then placed it on the water and set it adrift.

Using the chemicals from the hardware store I set the old bastard ablaze on the water. It was immature, irresponsible and illegal. But watching the old thing burn was strangely cathartic. It was almost a relief to see it go out like that – maybe because it wasn't happening in my kitchen.

I watched the fire rolling on the surface of the water, thinking about how I let a lot of my personal opinions and private crap get in the way since I found that first patch. I couldn't entirely let go of my issues, I don't think anyone could. But I'd taken a lot of wrong turns being reactionary. I needed to let go of some things even if they still bothered me. It was kind of weird, finding clarity in that fire, but I guess I just needed to really vent somehow.

"Time to pull my head out of my ass," I murmured, sitting on the hood of my car and watching the fireball sink into the water. "If I can help it, Danny, you're going to be their last victim."

***

That night, strangely better rested than I had been in days, I stood in Daniel's office. Though Danny was somewhere in his 30s at the time of his death, his office spoke of an old soul. His furniture was mostly vintage, the centerpiece a desk that was either an antique or custom made to look like one. An old pen and inkwell kit sat on the desk next to his computer and a collection of photos. On one wall he even had a bookcase full of old leather-bound legal books which were probably well out of date. Approaching them and smelling the genuine leather and the distinct smell of old book pages, I was pretty sure he wasn't keeping them around for reference.

245

Through the photos of his family I could also see a guy that'd been surrounded in friends and family his whole life before and after the change. He'd become a different creature and yet, unlike so many others, he kept his family intact as if nothing had happened at all. There was no reason to hurt this man or kill him. If the Shifter wasn't an Alter himself I would have assumed this was a hate crime of some sort.

Not that there was any proof someone hated the man. His employees gathered around outside his office door saying tearful goodbyes as I entered the room. I didn't know what to say to them or even how to react. But I'm glad I didn't try to ignore them, because one of them said exactly what I needed to hear.

"And I just talked to him yesterday," she said in a stammering, weeping voice.

Bingo. The reason for killing Daniel Cho was somewhere in that office – or at least it was before the Shifter had gotten to it. Janice didn't know what it was, neither did his staff, but the Shifter had come into the office for some reason. All I needed to do was figure out where he'd been while passing through.

Everything was spotless, not a sign of evidence tampering anywhere. Given how much of a mess was made in Cho's apartment compared to his office I could tell there was a deliberate nature this time. This wasn't quick or messy – this was planned and acted on slowly and calmly. It was probably why they took his face in the first place. His bookshelves were in perfect order, nothing missing, his filing cabinets, a rare sight in the modern day, still locked.

"If you need to get into that," his secretary said from the doorway, "I can get you the key."

"He didn't hold onto it himself?" I asked.

"Oh no," she replied, going to her own desk to get it, "Danny would have lost it."

As she returned with the key, I asked, "Did Danny ask for this yesterday?"

She shook her head, suggesting the Shifter would have to take her identity to get in without anyone suspecting. Still, after taking a snapshot of her to make sure she wasn't on the hit-list wall, I looked through the cabinet and found nothing out of place there either. Case files, clientele and even some vanity folders of old newspaper clippings from the few papers that still existed for guys like Danny – all there and without any sign anyone had rifled through them.

I had the secretary double-check since I had no idea the full range of what was supposed to be in there. She checked the digital catalogue of everything in the cabinet, scanning the tags on folders and the digital paper sheets. She confirmed it, the room was pristine.

"If they were after files, it wasn't the physical copies," she murmured.

It wasn't that they necessarily had to get at those copies. The only reason why offices like this keep copies at all is in case of some horrible system failure or a targeted hack. But the fact they even had physical copies made getting at those copies the easiest route. So if the Shifter had gone after their files at all, they had to get into Daniel's system without being noticed, which was comparatively harder. Yet again, they'd have to have done pretty detailed research on the man.

"Did he access the system yesterday?" I asked.

His secretary sat down and logged into the system when I asked. In moments, she started the database and brought it up only to find…absolutely nothing. Not that it was like that right away, for a moment it looked like everything was there. But in an instant, with almost no warning, the system corrupted and crashed.

"Oh my god," she said in shock, "it's entirely gone!"

Watching the computer files scramble and break down, I realized what they had done on that system the day before. They took Daniel's face to put a virus on his computer and the system's database. Why?

"Did you keep anything in the computer that you couldn't keep in a physical copy?" I asked, peering over her shoulder as it continued to break down before our eyes.

"His daily planner, appointments, scheduled cases," she said quickly, rattling off the list before looking up, "things that changed at a moment's notice."

"So," I said, "they didn't want us knowing what his schedule was supposed to be."

Cho's secretary furiously looked through every part of the

network for any sign that a copy of the files had survived. All gone, every one, and the sound of her frustration brewed under the surface as every blank folder was met with a small grunt and the occasional hammering of her fingers against the keyboard.

She looked back up from it and snapped, "They destroyed every damn copy of it, the whole thing!"

I nodded, asking, "Any physical copies or copies off the network?"

"No, even my tablet was networked in," she said. "Though, the courts would have duplicates of his schedule for all of his cases."

"So the courts would have it?" I asked, walking for the door.

"Yeah, I can put in a few calls to get it from them," she said, still staring at the monitor in shock and disgust.

"Good," I said. "Could you transfer them to the ACTF headquarters then?"

I looked back for a response. She just looked around the room slowly taking the scene in. A tear rolled down her cheek while she stared frustrated at her surroundings. She wiped it away and picked up a photo of Danny's family off his desk. With a quick wipe she cleared dust from the old wood frame and handled it carefully. The others outside had the same sort of expressions, expressions I'd seen before.

"Are you going to be okay?" I asked from the door.

She nodded lightly – a half-hearted gesture I knew meant "no" but couldn't be said aloud. I returned the gesture to her and the others, then continued walking out.

The last thing I heard from the room as I left the building was memorable and apt: "Get the bastard."

I nodded, agreeing with the sentiment and word choice entirely. Though there was one minor semantic difference for me. The Shifter had crossed into bastard territory long ago. He'd been eluding me because of his abilities and the fact he had been playing me with Rufus' help. What he'd done now was cross from a simple bastard to a sloppy bastard – just where I needed him.

I went to the courthouses, not wanting to wait for the broken staffers to gather together the fragments of Cho's schedule like a scattered puzzle. I'd asked them to send it in, but I didn't expect them to do it quickly and knew it would probably just be easier to go straight to the source. If anything, it was busy work to keep them from falling apart while facing the questions of how, why and what was to come.

I bypassed the lobby area this time, going around so I could try to avoid any repeat encounters with Fang-bitch and the gang. I knew I could handle myself, but I had a feeling my shiner and his limp would be enough to give both of us ammo that didn't need to be loaded. It was fine just going to the office without that little encounter.

Lucian was there when I arrived, standing with a nervous clerk. The clerk was trying to sort through something, showing some of the same frustrations Cho's secretary had no more than half an hour earlier. Immediately my mind jumped to the worst-case scenario: they hit the courts too.

I walked up next to Lucian and gave him a quick glance, nodding at the clerk and asking, "What's up?"

"Well, there's a mess involving Daniel Cho," Lucian said, unintentionally causing part of my brain to implode.

"His schedule didn't disappear from the records, did it?"

Lucian shook his head and crossed his arms, staring at the clerk with me now as we both loomed over the poor guy and his keyboard. "Unfortunately his schedule was pretty heavily weaved into everyone else's. He was set up to defend a couple of people over the course of the next month and that's caused a bit of a domino effect through everyone's routine."

"Wow," I quietly mused, "the guy was that integral around here?"

"Yeah, I'd say he was," Lucian replied. "It's not something that'd be easy to see. But, because of the way legal offices would have to shuffle resources, taking him down was enough to cause trouble all over the place. Cases were delayed, clients were passed to other lawyers, public defenders were shuffled around – it's like your Shifter took him out just to screw with everyone else."

"Like a black hole," I murmured.

"Yeah," he said, "and it sucks like one too."

The bad pun would have made me cringe and did make the clerk groan, but I'd gotten used to the man over the years.

Truthfully, it wasn't the worst he'd made.

"So why are you here then?" I asked.

"Hale's schedule went to hell like the rest," he said, turning away from the clerk and smirking at me, "So he wants to use the downtime to announce you-know-what."

"You know what?" I whispered. "You don't mean..."

"Yeah," he replied, "he's going through with it."

I considered how one man's loss was like a thread unraveling the whole sweater. Not only did it affect his staff but everyone else, right on up to Benjamin Hale himself. Daniel Cho's death rippled through the area around him like a wave and then the Shifter erased his records to hide something that ripple caused. But, if it was intentional, what did it change and why was it necessary?

"It's a pain in the ass too," Lucian said. "I have to figure out how to protect the guy while he's standing out in the open for that damned press conference."

And that answered my question.

Why an Alter would want to take a shot at Hale was beyond me. But if it was a set-up, it was a perfectly executed one requiring one hell of an eye for detail. A plan like that wasn't something anyone just cooked up, especially not by some random hitman. This was the work of a very intelligent or obsessed man.

Unfortunately, I happened to know someone who fit the bill.

Chapter 27
Rufus' Barathrum

"Welcome back Agent Leone," the curate in the ninth level said with a broad smile as I stepped out of the elevator. "Three times so soon? You must like him."

I looked at the grinning face, imagining the same behind the dark visors of the others' helmets. After the way I left the last time, timid and shaken, they were clearly a little smug about my return. So I took a little bit of satisfaction in saying, "Or you guys just couldn't spot a Shifter the first time."

That sinking feeling was easy to register throughout the room. Suddenly, I was the one that had the smirk on my face as I marched on through to the next door.

The mood on the other side was different, colder than before. There was a sense something had been happening there since the last visit. It was hard to tell what exactly that may have been at first, walking down the dark corridor to the central room. But as the glass house inside the holding area became visible it was all too obvious what the problem was.

The walls, once completely pristine and clear for all to see through, had now become completely covered in carvings in the glass of such complexity that at least one whole wall had clouded from the intricacy of them.

They weren't simple shapes either, not random words or phrases. Instead, they looked like something out of archaic science texts. Alchemical formulas, drawings of human anatomy, Latin phrases of biological concepts and other endlessly confusing elements that seemed weaved together as if it had some greater purpose. Had the man gone insane? I doubted that sincerely. Was he trying to tell us something? That was a bit more likely.

"Couldn't take the scissors from him?" I asked while standing next to the patrolling guard of the vault.

He quickly responded with a chilling remark: "Feel free to try sir."

"Is it at least double layered?" I asked, examining the cracks and gouges closer.

"Triple," he said before looking over and murmuring, "thank god."

And that was why he had done it: to show us he could. He had been carving these things into the wall of his cell, knowing no one would try to stop him. It was a message, maybe a layered one at that, to everyone that would come to see him from then on. To me, that message was clear: "Your security is inadequate."

He'd tried to give me this impression before when I was leaving, commenting to me that he could get information outside. And in the time I had been gone he went to drive the point home not just for me but for everyone that could come to see him in the future. The reason for his lavish surroundings was a matter of human rights. We couldn't lock him in a tiny cell for life if he could potentially live forever. It was more humane to simply kill him. But the compromise we had made to keep this man alive also compromised our ability to truly control his surroundings.

I tried to take in as much of the carvings as possible and took note that every inch of certain walls were used, as though he flew while scrawling across the wall all the way to the ceiling. Troubling to me was the fact I recognized some of the information from our systems. Even saw the chemical formula for Aurorastin and simplified illustrations of the A-type cell. And yet, despite using every inch of all other surfaces, the alcove was untouched aside from that first chip to the doors.

As I stood in that alcove, I expected to see him grinning like a maniac. But instead I heard that same music again drifting around so peacefully against the backdrop of the now frosted glass. Meanwhile, he calmly sat on the floor of the room of dominos, sorting through a new box and adding to the elaborate arrangement he'd been working on for what had to be forever.

"You love the domino effect, don't you?" I asked calmly, absently tapping the corner of my visor to make sure it was still there.

He looked up from them with a sleepy glance and gave me a shitty little smirk. "They're beautifully logical, easily learned but hard to master."

"Like people?" I asked, crossing my arms and leaning against the wall of the alcove.

"Indeed, like people. If you know how to line them up just right you can make the most elaborate things happen. But if you make the smallest mistake you could potentially lose it all. A piece too far away from the next, an angle just off so that what would have been a glancing blow becomes pure air and then you'd lose it all. Unless, of course, you know how to set it up so that no strike goes to waste and you tap the true potential of every link in the chain."

Thin, nimble fingers rolled a domino as he spoke – flipping end over end as he manipulated it effortlessly in his hand. As he finished speaking he presented the domino he had been rolling and held it in front of his face, grinning vibrantly behind it.

"This one is you," he said through a toothy grin.

I stared at the little black and white tile in his fingers and thought about how he'd just rolled it around so easily. Obviously, the man thought he could play me from early on. He'd been succeeding too. Had he played the others the same way?

"Which one is Daniel Cho?" I asked.

He laughed, putting down the box carefully and standing up as cautiously as he could to avoid tapping any of the tiles. It was ominous he felt the need to stand for that question and yet didn't seem surprised at all. He was expecting it, meaning he expected the conversation and had planned for me to get as far as I had.

With a slow, meticulous pace he made his way out of the field of dominos and behind an inner wall, decorated as the outer walls had been. Centered in this divider was a demon's mask with horns and flames, invoking an image of some devil in the deepest reaches. The eyes and mouth of these overlapped Rufus' face as he stood behind it to stare at me, showing the detail he'd taken to stage this moment as he said, "So I see you understand what I did with Cho."

"Do you know how lucky you are we haven't executed you yet?" I asked, glaring from behind my visor even though he couldn't see it.

"Luck?" he chuckled, "Your organization needs me and you know it. Unfortunately for you, that means I can control you and your coworkers under your own noses."

He was trying to goad me into playing his game, reply the way he wanted me to, part of his staging to give himself a dominant edge he thought he had over me. But I wasn't about to give him the satisfaction as I looked at his smug face behind the elaborately carved wall. I ignored his taunts and pressed on.

"Is Hale next?" I asked.

"Probably," he said, frowning, "I haven't decided how I want to finish playing with you."

"Is it going to be during his press conference?" I asked, ignoring the continued taunts.

He threw back his head and laughed before snapping his eyes back in my direction, barking, "I've set up a dozen opportunities to take a shot at the man."

"So we'll just lock him away until we take down your Shifter," I said.

The smirk behind the demonic mask grew as I said that. Cheerfully, he replied, "He won't let you do that."

"Lucian's the head of his security," I said matter-of-factly.

He promptly asked in a snide tone, "But there's another working for him, a human, correct?"

I couldn't respond to his question for multiple reasons but I didn't have to. Details like that and the things engraved into his walls confirmed those information networks were better than I thought. He was aware of the outside world in a way that shouldn't have been possible from his place. Either the Shifter made frequent visits or they had found a way to transfer great deals of information without the guards noticing.

"He's acting politically already and right now disappearing would be career suicide," Rufus continued arrogantly. "He hired a human for appearances; he'll continue to act for appearances."

"Then I just have to nail your guy before the conference," I said, turning away.

"And then I win," he called out with a raised voice.

I was conflicted by that statement. Part of me wanted to throw it back in his face and tell him he couldn't. Another part wanted to walk away and not give him the satisfaction of playing with me again. But a final part wanted to know what exactly that meant. Unfortunately, curiosity won against reason under the guise of being "thorough".

"How the hell do you win by having your assassin stopped?" I said, nearly growling.

He chuckled and said, "At this point I win no matter how this plays out. If you don't stop the assassination, our people have a martyr to galvanize them. I'm sure you'd try to announce the truth but everyone would 'know' what 'really' happened. They'd be furious and start to side with people like me."

I looked over my shoulder, regaining my composure to ask, "And if I succeed and stop your hitman?"

"Sympathy votes," he declared happily, "for the world's first Alter to take office despite a world trying to stop him."

He moved around the wall now and made his way to the door, saying, "It wouldn't take long for me to get someone who supported my causes to take a similar position."

I turned to watch him come, trying not to show just how disturbed I was about the concept, and replied, "It's not about the win, is it? It's about the progression."

A few more steps and we were standing face to face again across those cracked doors. We stared each other down for a moment even though he couldn't see my eyes. Thankfully, I thought to check his hands this time and saw he didn't have something to carve with. But he didn't need the scissors to spook me this time. All he needed were the right words.

"Have fun," he said calmly, gesturing with a guiding wave, "trying to stop progress."

Chapter 28
Intimidare Apparatus

The challenge to stop progress was a ploy I quickly rejected when I left the ninth level. He wanted to leave the impression he couldn't be stopped. But even if he were right, the least I could do was minimize the damage. I needed to find the Shifter before they could take that shot at Hale. An open door was a better prospect than a riot.

I'd been following the people up to that point, the stupidest and least productive method of hunting an unmarked Shifter in hindsight. But now that I knew the next target was going to be Hale there was a brand new trail to follow. Hale, being an Empyreal, would be a hard target to hit. In fact, he'd be hard to kill period.

Throughout history the Empyreal have been revered as celestial beings sometimes known as "angels", "divas", "bodhisattvas" and countless other names. They've long been known for seemingly supernatural powers gained as they mature and a tendency to shine slightly in the light, a side effect of a strange form of photosynthesis. They have the aggressive immune system of an active type but the passives' lack of allergies. Eventually, some stories say they don't even need their bodies.

But they're far from perfect, more along the lines of stubbornly alive, and there have been ways to kill them in the past. It's just harder to do than for most Alters where you could easily turn their strengths against them. No, killing an Empyreal, even a young undeveloped one like Hale, required a special kind of offensive. They had to treat him less like a person and more like a tank. So I didn't need to find the Shifter anymore – I needed to find their weapon.

There aren't a whole lot of options for weapons designed specifically to kill Alters that could be purchased by a civilian. In fact, almost all anti-Alter weapons are illegal in civilian hands in most countries signing the ACTF pact. But there's always ways around limitations and always a loophole or two.

Obviously, the basics weren't going to cut it, so I didn't have to try to keep track of something like garlic pellets or someone melting silverware into bullets. They were going to need a professional, military-grade weapon that could put a dent into an Empyreal big enough to prevent the body from recovering. Furthermore, it had to do it in one shot because they weren't going to get many more than that. This presented very few options really, so few that I couldn't even think of one myself. Thankfully, I had a ballistics expert to defer to.

"Just the legal ones?' Dulaf asked, eyebrow raised, finger tapping her chin.

"Well," I said, trailing off to consider for a moment, "the ones someone could get into the country."

He ears folded back and her brow furrowed while she let her head lean over the back of the chair. Staring at the ceiling, she slowly spun, the gears in her head almost visibly turning while she considered all the little variables of the question. What could kill an Empyreal? What could be transported through town without being noticed? Could anything legal be modified to do the job? It was like running a Boolean search through a pointy-eared computer.

"The Salma Fattore," she said with an excited squeak, sitting up again. "It's got the power, it's relatively quiet and it can be taken apart to fit into a briefcase."

Salma Fattore: a name I'd heard long ago, one that I could only vaguely remember but didn't like the sound of.

"It was designed in the middle of a rash of early Code 88s," she said, turning to her computer and bringing up the files, "just after the first signing of the charter. Some nations had problems with protests and had to kick out Alters en masse."

Specs for the weapon flashed onto her screen. Not liking what I saw over her shoulder, I sank into the chair next to her.

"The F-421 Salma Fattore – their favorite at the time," she muttered. "They called it the 'Corpse Maker'."

A brutal weapon, I could see it was just a heavily modified anti-materials gauss rifle with a .50 caliber round. For something that could apparently fit in a briefcase, it certainly didn't look like it. The magnetic coils replacing the gunpowder meant the barrel didn't have to be a solid pipe. Worse, it didn't have to use heavy metals either, meaning it could pass through a metal detector.

"Some greedy bastard saw the Code 88s as a chance to turn a profit," she said with a small growl to her voice. "They even made specialized ammunition to rip people apart. It was even set up to ionize the air so it wouldn't make as much noise when it breaks the sound barrier. You wouldn't hear it until someone was screaming or blowing apart."

"Can anyone even buy one of these?" I asked in shock.

"Not in this country," she said quietly, looking concerned. "But it's not illegal to own one if you get it shipped in."

And there it was, the Alter screw-job: protect the Alters so far as the treaty requires then screw the details. Dulaf began the search for anyone ordering one in the last couple of months and found a very short list. Even extending the search, only three organizations that had ever ordered one in the area and two of them were right inside Fangtown. In fact... one of them was us.

Seeing that, the two of us reacted in harmony: "Son of a bitch."

After a quick look through the system for acquisitions I went upstairs to an area I rarely visited. Most agents spend an extraordinary amount of time down in the base floors where the offices, information networks, forensic labs and Acheron subbasements lie. Above were the offices for the Commissioner and legal counsels, the oracle hub and the R&D department. With any luck, none of them were places we ever needed to be.

R&D is no man's land for the most part. Populated by Dwarves, Gnomes and a handful of assorted crazies with a similar taste for experimentation, R&D is often the area of science gone right by way of wrong. They were never people who asked the question "why" but rather "what if?" It showed in what they created: from Vesperadin jackets to Helios guns, the really good toys originated in these rooms.

Dulaf was one of them not long ago and her personality still reflected in the environment, possibly vice-versa. As I walked through I was greeted with an explosion that nearly made me require new pants and the near-drunken laughter of men like I'd gotten lost and walked into a crazy frat party. The air was filled with smoke almost as thick as the bathrooms of a public school. But the fans soon kicked on, roaring to life, and sucked the air clear to reveal the researchers huddled around while busting a gut.

"Holy shit," one of the gravelly voiced Dwarves said with a tear in his eye. "We should have killed two birds with one stone and tested the damn helmet too."

The others nodded, reaching down to help an even smaller man with an extraordinarily large head, a Gnome, to his feet. At their feet as they scattered once again was a large rifle looking similar to the SOL's with a little extra weight to the casing.

I looked at it, wondering what the hell they could be doing with a weapon like that, and asked, "Is that the Salma Fattore?"

And, to my surprise, one of the Dwarves bellowed back, "Used to be!"

The room burst into laughter again and a couple of researchers carefully picked up the rifle from the floor, checking it for damage. They showed more care than they had for their coworker, who was now sitting in the corner with an icepack to his head.

"Who's responsible for it?" I demanded. "I have to talk to them now!"

The room fell silent under my harsh tone and soon one of them spoke from the far back of the lab. It was a small, feminine voice entirely unlike the rough and scratchy sounds of the deceptively intelligent morons playing with their toys in the front of the lab. But, despite being gentler, the voice carried a commanding tone as it said, "Back here, kid!"

Being called kid wasn't something I was particularly fond of, barely tolerating it for Lucian. But to hear it come from someone who had been responsible for the purchase of a weapon like that made me cringe. At least I could take solace in the fact it wasn't the Shifter waiting for me behind the curtain like some twisted version of the Wizard of Oz.

Well, at least I hoped.

Instead, I found a Dwarven woman in a lab coat – which I had to admit was a unique sight to me. Dwarves have an interesting look in general. It's not the height that draws your attention: they're definitely not the shortest type of common

Alter – a title held by either the Gnomes or Brounies depending on who you ask. Instead, the most distinctive thing about the Dwarves is their build. They're walking bricks with beards and there's no way around that fact. Even before going active they're easily spotted.

But female Dwarves are interesting in their own way. They shared the height of their male counterparts but much softer and rounded, curvy really. They shared the gene for hair but it wasn't like the old myth of Dwarven women with beards. They always had such full, bouncy hair that grew almost wildly. And hers was no different aside from the color, a platinum white matching the coat.

Sitting on a stool, she spun around to face me, bifocals resting on elf-like ears and the bridge of her small nose, making her already big, blue eyes look larger than they already were. I don't know what her age was since I got completely conflicting concepts from the bright white hair vs. the rounded cheeks. But just from the way she said "kid" I assumed she was at least nearing the age of someone like Babs.

"Doctor Arianna Locklin," she announced with an assured tone. "I ordered that crude weapon."

"Agent Leone," I said, "and I want to know what you're doing with that thing, Dr. Locklin."

She turned away and gave a subtle nod to a screen of figures and charts that didn't make much sense. Without a word of explanation she brought up more of the data: a video file showing a mannequin dressed in an ACTF uniform. With the click of a button there was a loud bang as the mannequin was ripped apart by the projectile.

Looking back, seeing me dumbfounded by the image, she answered casually, "Testing."

The sight of mannequin parts scattering in slow motion as an ACTF badge tumbled through the air was… horrifying. Pieces of ballistic gel and Vesperadin danced through the air, being carried on the shockwave of whatever forces had gone off. Even the remnants of now fragmented armor inserts bounced off the walls of their testing chamber and fluttered about like black confetti. And yet Locklin was smiling.

"What the hell were you testing?" I asked in shock. "And

why are you smiling?"

"Survivability rates," she replied calmly. "I've been using them for the production of a newer jacket design."

As the pieces continued to flutter around on the screen it was hard to imagine there being a way to stop that kind of hit. How was anyone supposed to put up a defense against a weapon of pure overkill? And how could I prevent such a shot from killing Hale? I needed to sit down badly.

"You look a bit faint," Locklin said, hopping off her chair and offering it to me. "Sit, sit."

The stool she was sitting on was a bit shorter than typical. But that was fine so long as my knees felt like jelly. It just kept going, just kept rolling on as the pieces continued to bounce in the frame-by-frame analysis of the forces inflicted on the poor artificial sap. What would it have done to a real agent? What kind of horror would that have been?

"The tests look promising though," she said. "The new jacket managed to save the poor bastard."

I looked over, still half lost in my trance, and asked, "Wouldn't happen to be going into production soon, would it?"

She shook her head and said, "Only one prototype right now."

"Great," I groaned. "We're so screwed."

"I take it your Shifter friend has one of these?" She asked, taking off her glasses and cleaning them gently with a small cloth.

"I didn't know the R&D was aware of that, Dr. Locklin."

She smiled and put the glasses back on. "Nonsense, Agent Leone, I've been aware of the Shifter case for quite a while. Dulaf is quite a gossip, you know. It only makes sense that's why you'd come here all of a sudden."

"So everyone knows I'm being played by a Shifter?" I asked.

She shook her head and reached over to the computer, shutting down the video and putting an end to the endless shrapnel and splattered artificial flesh.

I also shook my head as it finally went away, saying breathlessly, "I can't believe someone would do that."

"Do what?" she asked.

I gestured at the screen. "Cause someone that kind of bodily harm over some drug connections."

"I don't know, I feel bad for them," she said. "The Shifters, I mean."

"Why?" I asked.

"They've always been in pain, even when they were human, haunted by image problems," she said. "Could you imagine being able to become anything you want to become, looking in that mirror and still seeing nothing but imperfections no matter what you tried?"

She pulled up a chair next to me. "It would probably drive you mad."

I hadn't thought of it, but it would drive someone insane. Combined with the strains of breaking and mending your bones, subjecting yourself to hormonal shifts, it was no wonder these people would resort to drugs. They could probably put on the best front in the world, keep anyone from knowing what was happening, but would still be broken inside. They'd have no sense of identity, no sense of worth and, sadly, no sense of hope. And now someone like that was coming into possession of a brutal weapon.

"I guess I can feel some sympathy," I muttered, "but there's another two out there."

She looked up surprised and asked, "Shifters?"

"No," I replied, "Fattores."

Locklin plucked the glasses from her face again, rubbing her eyes from inevitable strain of staring at monitors all day, then looked at me with concern. Suddenly, she smiled and said, "At least two of them are accounted for. I ordered the second one for a museum of Alter history being built a couple blocks from the Crepusculum Forum."

I couldn't believe she would hand such a thing over to civilians. But before I could say a word she raised a hand and said, "Stripped down to just the case of course."

"Good," I said with a sigh of relief. "The last thing we need is another one of those damn things."

She nodded in agreement and added, "I even converted the one we had as soon as it stopped serving its purpose."

"What did you do to that thing anyway?" I asked.

"The coils and power supply are similar to the mechanisms

in the Helios guns," she said. "So I tried to see what would happen if I converted it into a heavier rifle for the SOL teams."

I nodded lightly in thanks, stood up, and starting out the room, saying, "I need to hunt down the third, then."

Her small hand reached up and caught my sleeve, stopping me before I could get far. "Wait a minute," she said, "I might be able to help."

She hopped off the stool and hurried to a table covered in old parts, picking one from the group and presenting it to me with an excited look.

"When I was doing the tests on these weapons, I found a few weaknesses that could be exploited," she said. "The scopes naturally link up to GPS satellites for trajectory and distance calculations, computer assisted targeting."

It took a moment for what she was implying to sink in. But, once it did, it was brilliant.

"So the Oracle could track it," I declared as if it was some sort of personal "Eureka" moment for me.

She nodded quickly and said, "In fact, there'd be a minute or two from the time of assembly to the moment it would be ready to fire. They'd be waiting for the power cell and computer to get their acts together."

"It's a small window," I said. "But it'd definitely let us know when to make Hale get down at the very least."

She nodded, putting the scope from the gun in my hand and closing my fingers around it. "Hopefully you can catch that poor soul before they get in any deeper."

I nodded, feeling a pang of sympathy for the person I'd been hunting down for the first time since I started. It didn't make sense: I knew they were violent and they represented aspects of society I loathed. But for a moment, after hearing Locklin talk about them, I couldn't think of them as the evil creature I'd been painting them as. Walking out, I realized how much more sympathetic I probably would have been if I changed the way they had.

Pausing, I looked back and asked Locklin, "Do you miss anything about being mainstream?"

Her brow furrowed while she took a thoughtful, melancholy look. She removed her glasses one last time and lowered them as the tension faded from her face. Then, with a small, bright smile, she jovially said to me, "I used to be one of the taller children growing up. But now I'm brilliant. So I don't think I miss it as much as I consider it a fair trade."

Holding up the scope, I nodded in agreement and chuckled. "I'm lucky you made the trade, right now."

I turned and walked out of the lab, knowing how to find my target when they made their move and hoping I'd be prepared for round two. Leaving, I watched the researchers continue about their work and realized just how many times those people had helped a human like me put a stop to another Alter. It was humbling.

And then I heard Locklin faintly as she said to herself, "I wish more people could look at it like that."

Chapter 29
Lenis Formositas

Leaving Locklin's lab, I used the night to coordinate with the security detail of Hale's conference. The ground forces would keep watch on the vicinity while a few patrolling officers and agents checked the rooftops. We weren't going to have enough people to try to cover every angle. But with the warning signal from the system we'd be able to have the ground level security pull Hale down. On top of that, we arranged to have Locklin's jacket taken to the scene. We couldn't be sure it would work, but it was better than nothing.

After relaying this information to the people in the detail I took the opportunity to look into the location of the third Fattore. Finding it was in a store in Issaquah and that it had been delivered some time ago, I knew it was moot to look for the Shifter there. Though, I was fairly tempted to kick down their door for selling the thing. Apparently, they passed the damn thing off as "hunting equipment" to get past restrictions.

Still, as tempting as it was to consider raising hell, I couldn't justify it. Legally they'd simply played the system without actually violating it. And that was really the government's fault.

I spent a great deal of time filling out paperwork and sorting my thoughts. Then the next night, realizing I couldn't do anything else until the Shifter made their move, I went patrolling for the first time since my promotion. There were no leads to track or dead ends to frustrate me. In fact, it was a pretty quiet night with only two domestic disputes and a drunk human, upset that a succubus didn't want to "eat his soul".

My job had been less intimate; the people had become faceless since the whole thing with the Shifter started. But sitting behind that wheel and watching the world roll by without having a specific place to go was an almost relaxing experience. It wasn't as productive as the rest may have been, but something got done and I reconnected with the locals in a small way.

One thing that did bother me during my strangely relaxed

shift was looking up every time I passed through the Forum. I'd crossed paths with Janice's apartment several times that night, looking up at her windowless walls and wondering what she was doing.

The urge to step out and just go to visit her grew with every pass and I anxiously started to wait for the end of my shift. Something was gnawing at me that I couldn't shake. It was a feeling like something was wrong or I wasn't going to see her again.

If that was the case, it was understandable. I was getting ready to face down what had to be the most terrifying weapon I'd ever seen handled by a person who had previously shown me to be lightning fast. A little bit of fear for one's own life was understandable even in the best-case scenario of getting the drop on the target.

And, as far as danger to Janice went, Daniel was alone and unseen for a day before he was discovered in his apartment. The Shifter used Daniel's death to move Hale's schedule. How could anyone be sure Janice, a court reporter, couldn't be used to get closer too?

I can't be entirely sure if that was what was going through my head at the moment. All I really know is I wanted to see her again and couldn't wait for the chance. In fact, I decided that visiting her was the last official task of my shift.

The city grew peaceful as the night continued on and my shift drifted into the blissful window of time between the rushes. As dawn approached the world grew quiet and people started to disappear from the streets. It was too late for the majority of Alters, too early for the humans. So I found myself rolling down the quiet streets and taking in the mix of golden light from the skies mingling with the murals of Fangtown as they started to fade from sight. There was time to stop by her place.

I drove along for one last pass through the city, planning my route to end up in the Forum. My shift was nearly finished and there wasn't any harm in finally acting on the feeling I'd been trying to ignore the entire night. I parked in a space that wouldn't have been available any other time of the day and strolled into the apartment building with a nervous spring in my step.

The interior was a bit more active than the exterior – people coming home from their long nights to their little corners of the mausoleum-like building. Music pounded through the lower floors, emanating from the basement apartment, as the sound of a couple Werewolves baying at an unseen moon echoed from the depths. The floor vibrated beneath annoyed feet and muted groans from other tenants were drowned out by the wild roar below.

One tenant looked at me in my uniform and said, frustrated, "Please tell me you're here for them!"

"Sorry," I said with a chuckle and a shrug.

He groaned and rolled his eyes before stamping his feet a few times, trying to get their attention below. With a sigh he watched me walk by and demanded, "What are you here for, then?"

I looked back with an amused grin, starting to enjoy the music, and gestured with a thumb upstairs, "Janice Gray."

"She's not in trouble, is she?" he asked.

"Nah," I replied, "just making sure she's doing okay."

"Ah yeah, she was pretty sick for a while," he said. "It was good to see her come out again after a couple days there."

It gave me a bit of pause. She'd been missing for "a couple days" before anyone saw her? Flashes of Daniel ran through my mind as I whirled about to look at the man again, calling out "Wait!" before he could go back inside.

"Did you say a couple days?" I asked.

"Yes," he said, nodding. "I hadn't seen her until tonight, not since she mentioned her identity was stolen."

The sounds of the building quickly melted away as I sprinted up the stairs two at a time, leaving a bewildered man behind. There wasn't time to explain to him what was going through my mind, nor was there any reason to bring them into the middle of it. But that gut feeling I'd been trying to shake reacted violently with the new information he'd given me.

Her floor was quiet, out of range of the raucous music and surrounded by neighbors that were either gone or long since asleep. It was peaceful, really, before my pounding on her door ripped through the silence like a shockwave. I refrained from calling for her, but continued to beat on it with a fist while peering through her eyehole in hopes of catching a glimpse

267

inside. If I woke anyone up they didn't come to see what was happening. Which was good, because I was about to break into her apartment.

Kicking in the door was too extreme if there wasn't a confirmation. Panicked as I was, she would have skinned me if she were alive and well. But, luckily, a Vampire like Lucian needed an underling that could open locked doors for him from time to time. He may have been old enough to ignore the feeling when necessary, but that threshold was still a wall to him. I quickly got to work on Janice's lock, hearing that momentarily satisfying click of the tumbler opening.

Unfortunately, Janice, standing behind me at the time I did that, heard it too.

"What the hell are you doing?" she asked without warning.

I practically jumped through her door as she spoke. In fact, I went past the threshold and took several stumbling steps inside before looking back at her. But, even though I was busted, I couldn't be more relieved to see her.

Though, she didn't look like her usual self for once: a bit feverish, in fact. The tone of her voice on the phone the last time we talked was nasal and weak. Now, I could see why: Janice had obviously been sick.

Undoubtedly the stress didn't do anything to help her recovery. Identity thefts and the death of Daniel couldn't have helped her sleep any. And then she came home to find me picking her lock as though she were a suspect. I expected her to explode.

She didn't react much at all, though. She walked inside, put her purse down, closed the door and headed to her couch as though nothing had happened. It worried me just how calm she was as she sat down with a heavy thump, as though her body were dead weight. It worried me more that she didn't look my way after finally coming to a rest.

"I thought something happened," I said quietly.

She lifted her head my way finally and nodded. She didn't reply, just waved me over and patted the seat next to her. I guess that counted. When I came over and sat down she still didn't say anything to me, just leaned on me and quietly sighed.

"Are you okay?" I asked, hesitating to put an arm around

her.

She shook her head, closed her eyes and said, "Not really."

"Suppose you wouldn't be," I said, "with everything that's been going on."

Her eyes opened again and she looked up at me, reaching up to pull off the visor I'd forgotten to take off in my hurry. Quietly, as I saw her without the mess of auras showing me cold meds and a low-grade fever, she asked, "Are you getting any closer?"

Even in the state she was in, her eyes were hypnotic. Tearful, they were sparkling more than was even natural for an Alter. It was hard not to feel sympathy for her. I just wanted to tell her everything was going to be okay even if I didn't feel that way myself. I just wanted to make her feel better.

"I guess," I started to say, realizing it didn't sound too confident. "I'm getting a lot closer."

She didn't seem too thrilled by that and I wasn't going to get into much more detail. I couldn't tell her how well armed the Shifter was or that the very thing that could kill me was my only solid lead. I couldn't tell her that it scared the crap out of me and I wasn't entirely sure I'd be back. She didn't need to hear it and I didn't need to say it out loud. Instead, I repeated myself. "I've almost got him."

She let out a sad, world-weary sigh and settled against me. "It's such a mess," she said.

"Yeah," I replied, "I guess it is."

I put my arm around her shoulders finally and squeezed her lightly while she continued to sink against me. It didn't take long to realize she was falling asleep. Though I couldn't see outside her apartment with the lack of windows, I realized the sun was rising as I looked at the nearest clock. The day was beginning for people outside and coming to an end for the two of us. Exhausted and stressed from a couple of harsh days, it wasn't worth moving her at the time. In fact, getting comfortable there, I drifted off with her on the couch.

Chapter 30
Duras Lumen

The couch grew steadily uncomfortable throughout the morning, especially in full uniform with armor plate inserts. I woke up repeatedly in different positions with a new ache or pain. But every time I woke I looked over and saw her sleeping rather comfortably, curled up on the couch with her head against me. It was hard to get up and just walk away when she'd been having such a hard time.

That didn't help me much, though. Her couch was styled like a futon with a wood frame that just happened to find its way under my neck whenever I managed to close my eyes. I twisted, turned and wiggled into as many variations of the same position as possible, never quite finding the right way to do it without disturbing her.

But it did me some good to be there despite the discomfort. There weren't any strange dreams or odd thoughts through the day. Not to say it was a peaceful rest, obviously. But it wasn't as bad as it had been since the whole mess started. I didn't think about the drugs, the murders or the faceless people running wild through the city. All I thought of was putting a stop to it for her and all the other victims out there.

With that thought on my mind I gave up on sleep, slipping out from under her with the greatest of care. If it weren't for youth and conditioning I probably would have moved like a mummy at that moment. But the crimp in my neck wasn't quite as bad as it could have been. A small blessing, I suppose.

I wandered into her bathroom, using the only mirror in the apartment to examine the beautiful shiner still on my face. The swelling had gone down considerably and it now looked like just one large bruise across my cheek. I've had worse and it was starting to heal. But it was a stark reminder of how fast the Shifter was. If it weren't for the fact I was surrounded by police at the time it could have been far worse.

"Looking good," I muttered sarcastically.

I turned to walk out, stopping as a crack caught my eye. It was small, hardly noticeable until I turned just right. Standing there, entranced by it, I stroked my fingers along the length of it. Thoughts of the Shifter were starting to get heavier on my mind. The idea I might never stand in this apartment again started to trouble me.

But I pushed it aside, leaving to find desperately needed aspirin.

The apartment was silent and dark even in the middle of the day thanks to a lack of windows. My eyes were adjusting slowly at first and it was almost tempting to put on the visor just to make my way around before deciding to just follow the walls. Thankfully, given the quiet and lack of fur on the furniture, I was fairly sure she didn't have a pet for me to kick in the dark – though it still felt too soon to ask if she shed herself.

I wandered into her kitchen to find it had a television and a small bottle of aspirin on the counter. Picking it up, I found it was a little light, likely used for her illness and after a night of gracefully accepting my feet stomping all over hers in good humor a few nights ago. Opening it, I confirmed it was empty and turned to search for another.

I flipped on the TV, hovering my fingers over the volume control to make sure it wouldn't blast her off the couch. It was fine, quiet really, as the afternoon news played through. Somehow, despite every shift and sudden awakening, we'd slept a full eight hours by my best estimate.

Fishing through her drawers I found a lot of plastic forks, assorted batteries and screwdrivers. The girl was almost as disorganized as me and yet managed to decorate her apartment so much better. Just about everything was in those drawers aside from what I was looking for. Cluttered messes greeted me in every drawer, including one holding a pack of cigarettes I didn't know she smoked next to a set of nicotine patches I'd never seen her use.

"I'll be damned," I whispered to myself, picking up the pack to take a closer look at it. Lifting the pack was the best thing I did that day: the aspirin bottle was lying underneath with a pack of mint-flavored gum that explained the lack of cigarette breath. The pack went back where it belonged and the bottle came with me as I sat down on a stool in front of her TV and watched the same twits talk about pointless crap all over again.

The news was about the same as it always is: celebrities getting arrested, people going to rehab, the First Lady's fashion choices and, of course, politicians perfecting the art of stupid human tricks. The anchors are always so chipper about these things, never really caring about what's going on except for that little moment where they make their serious face. I didn't think they really meant it, but they had to fake it while reporting that apparently everything, including breathing, causes cancer.

My father was an avid news follower. Every day he sat down and, despite having been in the middle of all of it, told me what was happening in the world required our attention. He was right, one day, when the Alters revealed themselves. It was really the last thing I could clearly remember him being right about.

The thoughts of my father stopped my hands around the aspirin cap. Normally I kept the concept of the minor painkillers separate from the things he became so familiar with in the last years of his life. But my chest tightened while thinking about it that time, sitting in her kitchen with a tiny bottle of pills.

"You're losing it again, dude," I sighed to myself before finally opening the bottle and swallowing a couple tablets.

Dad was definitely right, though. Even though the news was mostly drivel, watching it every day is probably the only thing to really ground someone in the reality of things happening beyond your personal circles. At one time in history every little event in someone's life must have seemed so much more profound. Now we have the benefit of watching people tell us the rest of the world was apparently on fire. Life could still get worse according to the news. But that night it stopped casting its lens on the world outside and turned squarely back towards me.

The anchor, in the same chipper, happy little voice, announced quite brightly to the camera, "City Attorney Benjamin Hale has called a press conference tonight. A recent rumor of his plans to run for Mayor has resurfaced and it's believed that's the topic of tonight's conference."

"Tonight, huh," I muttered, looking at the time and considering how much I had left.

I stood to get ready, looking at the other wall of the kitchen and seeing a small corkboard with photos pinned to it. I walked over, seeing Daniel's smiling face as he held an arm around Janice. Thinking about him again, I felt the weight of the situation. And, right next to him, I saw a photo of Hale, smiling on just as brightly as Daniel. She had a lot of friends at work, all of them in serious danger.

Stages had been set, players moved into place and the curtain was ready to draw. I walked out of the kitchen, shutting off the TV on the way. She was still sound asleep and looking somewhat better. A good morning's rest did her a lot of good it seemed. I stroked her hair lightly and walked out, stopping to watch her for a moment as she slept.

A thought of the corkboard and the events of the last few days crossed my mind. The little details of her apartment felt more important as my thoughts wandered. A sinking feeling started to pass over me as I lingered on images like the crack in the mirror and the photos on the wall. Shaking it off, I stepped outside, muttering to myself, "Damn."

It was a nice, sunny day outside – perfect weather for an outdoor press conference. Not that being indoors would have stopped the Shifter from making a move since it was far too easy to jump out a window or fire the Fattore through a wall. Lucian said Hale made the decision to do it on the steps of City Hall because he wanted people to see he was unafraid and to make a link between him and the building.

It was a political bullshit move, but I guess it was also probably in everyone's best interests. If he'd forced the Shifter to fire through a wall there was nothing to stop others from getting in the way of the bullet. Maybe, if anyone had to die, it would only be one of the parties involved and not a bystander. Maybe the devastation of that weapon could be reduced to one person instead of many.

Then again, maybe Hale was an idiot with good intentions.

But I couldn't stop the conference from happening any more than I could order the tide not to come in. there was nothing left to be done but be prepared to hunt down the signal and hope I could get there in time. I traveled through town and did my best not to feel too anxious.

Everyone was there fairly early, preparing cameras and

273

getting spots. Hours before the conference was even supposed to start there were little power plays being made for the best location. If you got in closer to the podium, he might take your question sooner. On the other hand, if you were out in the nosebleed sections you might as well turn to the curb and call for a ride. They knew this and I watched them shuffle around like the world's most boring mosh-pit to pass my time.

Observing the area, bustling with mid-day activity, there weren't many angles I could picture using as a sniper. He was going to be standing on the steps of City Hall, close to the building itself where he would only be exposed on the west side. Standing about where he would, I could see out at all the buildings around and realized just how many obstructions there were for most rooftops. Trees, smaller buildings and overhangs obscured angles that could be used but were too uncertain for someone to be confident in a single shot.

That's all anyone would have: one shot. If they missed the first time it would be over before they could get off a second. Either Hale would be dragged out of the line of fire or the crowd would become chaos. And if I were the one to take that one shot I estimated I would have taken it from the roof of the King County Courthouse.

Walking through the courthouse, it was easy to see just how ballsy the move was. If my hunch was right then the Shifter was going to be walking right through a building that actually housed the county Sheriff among other things, with active cases bringing dozens of officers along to testify for superior court. Even I felt a little bit nervous walking through those halls after what I'd done with "Fang-bitch" a few days before.

I found the place buzzing with activity even as sunset approached, even this courthouse accommodating the Alters and their schedules. Quite a few of the human personnel were leaving in a hurry, probably a bit daunted by the idea the whole block was about to become Alter central. Not just because of Hale's announcement just around the corner but the inevitable sunset rush as the world changed shifts.

The building, despite being built over a century ago, has been renovated extensively since being made a landmark. With all the time and funding put into the place, the interior looked about as modern as the municipal court only a couple blocks away. But there was a sense of history in the old walls left behind from several retrofits. There was a sense in the building that many people had met a fate there, whether it was justice or a miscarriage of justice – I was standing in a building of fate.

I'll admit it: I was getting philosophical while running off to stare down a gun called the "Corpse Maker".

But I stifled that crap as I approached the path up to the roof. I don't know how long the small stairwell has been there, but it had to be the dingiest part of the building. In the years since the Alter revelation everything had long ago gone solar. Without a doubt this path had been used to place the solar panels up on the roof of the building like so many others in the country. And yet the rails were coming loose from the walls and the door ahead of me was showing signs of water damage from the wonderful Seattle raining season.

The roof itself was quiet, serene and almost entirely removed from the activity below. I could hear car horns and the shouts of reporters still fighting for their places remained a distant whisper. But the winds easily muffled those pesky noises from below to leave me alone with my thoughts and the endless rows of Aurorastin panels angled out toward the western horizon as the sun began to set.

It was at that moment my hand-link vibrated, letting me know the system found the signal. Ground units probably sprang to action, Lucian probably grabbed Hale and Thompson probably wasn't even aware what the hell was going on. Meanwhile, I lifted my hand-link and hoped the GPS would tell me I was right. And my hunch was right: I was standing on the same roof the gun was positioned on. I turned to the east carefully and tried to make out where they were past the angling panels.

My visor took a second to adjust as I stared directly into the reflection of the sunset in the distance that momentarily became the only thing I could see. But as it cleared and the sun disappeared behind the taller buildings beyond, I found myself lost in the endless sparkle of the panels as they started to gently glow in the dark. The energy they'd collected through the day now illuminated the rooftop for me fairly well, revealing the hooded figure on the far side.

The Shifter, the drug dealer and assassin was kneeling before me, unaware of my presence. Apparently they were left on their own as far as it came to knowing where I was and what we were doing. For once, I was allowed the element of surprise I'd been lacking for the entirety of our little dance.

Leveling my gun toward the back of their head, I called out, "ACTF, step away from the rifle!"

The Shifter froze, shoulders tensing and entire body going into an alert state I recognized from the split second before I tasted Chen's shoe. Had I not been several yards away I'm sure I would be repeating the experience all over again. But, with the gun trained on them and a good distance between us, there was nothing really to do.

This was good, because that feeling I had after the corkboard and the cracked mirror told me just what was coming next. I tightened my grip on the gun and exhaled, dreading what I had to say: "Turn around, Janice."

She looked over her shoulder and my hands shook slightly. It was traumatic to see her on that rooftop. The photos on her wall, the cracked mirror, and the cigarettes to cover up nicotine patch purchases: I was hoping the feeling was wrong. But she was there, I was there, and it had to be dealt with.

"Hands off of the weapon," I commanded again with the firmest tone I could muster, "and back away from it slowly."

"I can't do that," she said quietly.

Hearing her voice confirmed my fears. I pushed it aside the best I could and pleaded, "Put it down, Janice."

She glanced down, then lifted her chin again and said in a pitiful tone, "I'm sorry."

She tensed, a frown quickly flashing across her face and her hands tightening around the grip of the rifle. With a quick twist she lifted it from the tripod she'd set up and whipped it around my direction. But this wasn't going to be like the time when she was Chen. I fired a round into her knee and stopped her momentum cold before she could complete the motion. As much as it pained me, I wasn't about to come to the fight using the crowd control setting.

She didn't make a sound when I did it. She barely did anything but slump over the gun, shaking. Obviously she was on blue and completely without pain. But I can only imagine what was going through her mind right then. This probably wasn't how it was supposed to happen.

"Let go of the gun," I demanded.

A low, exasperated sigh left her and suddenly her teeth were clenched. With another quick motion, completely ignoring the injury to her scorched knee, she whipped the gun my direction again.

Unlike our last encounter, my training kicked in during this swift motion. In the academy they call it the crucifix: the arrangement of five shots you have to take to stop an extremely dangerous Alter. I fired two shots across the chest, one in the forehead and two down the center. It was meant to hit any redundancies and make sure they couldn't fight through it or regenerate past it. But, as the light flashed across my eyes, all I noticed were her screams.

The series of shots set her on fire, the heat of repeated blasts igniting her clothes like a candle and sending her falling back engulfed. I lowered my gun, probably out of shock, and soon regretted the move. With a click of the trigger, the F-421 went off.

The shot was nearly silent, just a buzz and a flash, but the sound of dozens of Aurorastin panels exploding as it ripped through them was like a rain of glass. Unsurprisingly, I saw a flash of the ballistic gel bouncing off Locklin's test chamber in the split second it took for everything to go black.

Chapter 31
Crepusculum Finis

Locklin's prototype jacket wasn't quite perfect, but it was enough. Though I doubt she knew I took it instead of Hale, it prevented me from exploding like so much ballistic gel. While I was far from being in good shape afterwards, I was alive… sort of. The sleeve was tattered, blood running down my arm as it throbbed and pulsed with the feeling of being pierced and possibly broken. My visor was gone, probably hurled from the roof with an impressive velocity of its own. And my body stung in ways that let me know, at the very least, I wasn't dead.

The commotion below was understandable with the roof of the King County Courthouse exploding with a display of glowing shards flying through the air. And when other agents arrived, they likely found the burning remains of a woman clutching a vile weapon. But what they didn't find was me. I'd left on a more important matter.

I probably shouldn't have moved without medical treatment and most people who saw me on the street as I staggered along looked stunned by my broken form. But I had to go to Janice's apartment. I had to know the truth.

That thing on the roof, despite my hunch, couldn't have been her. It couldn't have been the woman that slept through the day on the couch with me. I woke up before her and saw her lying peacefully on the couch as I left. But I needed to confirm that with my own eyes.

The streets of Fangtown were brighter than ever, possibly due to blood loss. The people were oblivious to the things that had happened within walking distance despite likely hearing the roar of shattering panels with their heightened hearing. But all knew from my face and the blood down my arm that it had to be something profound.

A few Werewolves, in the first night of their monthly transformation by the look of their hair growth, heckled me as I staggered by. My ears were ringing too badly to even hear what they were saying clearly. But I could tell from the looks on their faces that they weren't too fond of the uniform and thought themselves lucky to see one of my "pack" so severely injured. Fortunately, my left arm was the injured one and I carried my gun in the right.

We quickly came to an understanding.

The rest of the people weren't all too concerned with the plight of one agent. Though some stopped to look at the trail of blood I left in my wake, the majority of them were simply curious why I was walking like a drunk. A couple cell-phones were flicked out. Though, I couldn't be sure if they were filming or calling for help.

Along the way I spotted some faces that seemed vaguely familiar walking the streets, including Trey as he walked into a Zomboner Club arm in arm with a pair of women that seemed to be clearly under his trance.

Weakly, I muttered to myself, "Incubus."

A week ago they'd all been suspects to me. Now I knew they were all legitimate, which was a feeling I came to appreciate despite the plethora of negative ones throughout my body.

When I finally came to the Forum I wasn't entirely sure just how much blood I'd lost but everything was clearly fuzzier than usual. The normally crisp images of the bright sunset colored murals now looked like the real thing on a hazy day. The sparkling water looked like a colorful blob. And the people looked like shadows moving across the twilight hours – phantoms on the border between life and death.

I staggered into Janice's building, the pounding music from before now sounding like the rapid beats of my pulse filling my ears. My head throbbed, my eyes burned and my arm slowly started to go numb in a way I knew couldn't have been good. But still I went up those stairs to see her face and tell her I'd gotten the beast that stole her sense of security from her.

I reached the door and limply slapped the back of my gun wielding hand against it to knock. But the door swung open on its own from the tap to reveal a darkened room. I staggered inside and heard the crunch of glass under my boot. My knees seemed to melt away and my body collapsed to the floor in fatigue.

As I drifted off, the sight of her bathroom mirror, shattered, slowly faded from view. It was the last thing I saw before passing out to the sound of beeping from the emergency beacon in my badge.

Chapter 32
Aftermath

I awoke to a beeping sound similar to the beacon but more distant than before. I opened my eyes, the fuzzy image of an omega pack hanging over me, the steady flash of light coming off a monitor behind it. I groaned at the sight of it, numb to whatever pain I should have been in. I rolled my head across the pillow, too weak to lift it, and saw the vague image of someone standing at the foot of my bed.

As my vision cleared I saw into the smiling face of the Grim Reaper looming over me. The doctor had been watching me like a hawk… or a vulture.

But another shadow moved out of the corner of my eye, soon leaning over me and blocking that toothy grin from view.

"Hey," Dulaf said quiet yet happily, "you're awake!"

"Barely," I whispered, straining to see her through the bright lights shining into my blurry eyes.

"We weren't sure how long it was going to be," she said, frowning, ears folded back. "You lost a lot of blood."

I glanced up at the omega pack above as she said that, quietly fuming over seeing it.

"Don't do that," she murmured, stroking my head lightly. "We had to save your life."

"And Janice?" I asked.

The frown deepened as she said, "We found you in her apartment. They scoured the place."

"Did you find her?" I asked weakly.

"Nate, her DNA was all over that apartment," Dulaf replied sadly. "It matched the body."

I stared at her, a hollow feeling in my chest. I'd really done it. I really killed her. I would have cried if not for a hand resting on my head at that moment, brushing some hair from my face.

"Why do you always hover over me?" I muttered. "I'm not worth it."

She stared at me quietly, stroking my cheek before pulling

her hand away. "You know, I put a lot of effort into looking and sounding like I belong. But, truthfully, Lucian and I are so far removed from here we can't even start to describe how unreal it is to live this long."

I looked at her, seeing a strange serenity in normally energetic eyes. I asked, "What does that have to do with hovering over me?"

"Sometimes, we need something to feel more secure in this time," she said, sitting down again. "We've been doing this long before Alters were anything more than legend, before there was even an organization like this one."

I groped around the edge of the bed, eventually finding the control to raise the back and prop myself up. She lifted her head to meet my gaze and smiled in a sad, distant way.

"Back then, when we started, there was this boy from Tuscany," she said sadly. "He irritated me and tormented me. But he put his life on the line to help our people. He was an orphan, but he found strength in being with us and fought by our side."

"Leo?" I whispered.

She nodded, lowering her head and fidgeting in her seat. "He was my best friend back then, even if he was a jerk. He was brave, strong and made sure everything he did was the right thing."

"I got that impression," I said, sighing.

"Centuries later," she continued, patting my knee, "Lucian brought in this scrappy little cage fighter. He was an orphan with the same eyes, the same spirit. It was like he came back from the dead."

"Really?" I asked, looking into her eyes.

"Really!" she exclaimed. "I admit, I take old grudges out on you, tease you like I did with him. Hell, I probably tease you just to get back at him sometimes. You're so much like him."

I thought back on the image of that man from my dreams and the name on the wall. Listening to her speak about him, I couldn't help but think about my dad and wonder if we might have been cursed. Looking at her hand on my knee, I asked, "How did he die?"

She stared at me, lifting her hand to my cheek, her lip

starting to quiver, her ears sinking. "Rufus had him killed."

"So… it's the family legacy," I said, leaning away from her hand.

The hand clenched by my face and she stood again, leaning over the bed. She wiped away a tear and smiled at me again. Her voice rose with a strong, confident tone as she said, "I never met Michael. But I've met you and I remember Leo. You are so much like that boy from Tuscany. I know I can trust the Leone family."

Looking up, the feeling I got from her was completely different than normal. She seemed so… calm.

"Rufus corrupts people," she said quietly. "He doesn't control through power or fear. He controls by learning the rules of the game and preying on weaknesses. He uses indirect tactics to make people fall into line and finds ways to turn people on each other. It's how he got to Leo and why he sent a drug dealer to your father."

"And sent Janice to me," I said.

Her smile grew into a beautiful, peaceful expression. "He was trying to make you hesitate and doubt yourself."

"It worked," I said, lowering my head.

She laughed. "Boy was it working for a while there."

Leaning in, she kissed my forehead. "But you're still alive."

The gesture left me stunned. I watched her step back and walk out. Sitting in that room felt like an eternity afterwards. But eventually my stubborn pride made me get up.

The doctor would have likely been pissed, smiling at me even while furious, but he didn't see me leaving. I just couldn't sit there any longer. I needed to go somewhere else. So I wandered to the nerve center after fetching a few important articles like my pants.

Sitting in the shared office in the central room was strangely lonely that night. I'd come in without permission from the doctor, probably something I shouldn't have done, and sat behind the desk I'd used for most of the case. Thoughts of everything that happened were running through my head and I felt the same hollow feeling I had when shooting Max finally set in. Only now it was mixed with a complete sense of failure and loneliness, despite Dulaf's efforts.

Janice was still dead.

"Were you ever real to me?" I asked to the open air, receiving only the cold hum of monitors in return. "Or was it just a show?"

Thinking back on the last moments we sat together before it unraveled, it was hard to ignore the fact it could have been stopped right there. If I just hadn't left or if I had just put the pieces together before it was too late, she'd still be alive. For all the time and effort I put into following the strings, chemicals and reports I missed the important parts – I missed her. I failed to do anything to stop it or to quietly convince her to help me stop it.

"Is it my fault?" I whispered, resting my head on the desk. "Do you blame me? I tried to stop it, tried to figure it out before it could get there. I really did."

The lights flickering over me caught the corner of my eye. For an instant, I felt she was somehow there.

"But it wasn't enough, was it?" I said breathlessly. "I'm so sorry. I should have done something else or done it all faster. If only I'd been... better."

The realization I was talking to myself fell over me and the pit I'd been feeling grew, like the air in my lungs had moved into my throat and just wouldn't leave. I knew nothing was there but I couldn't fight the feeling away. I couldn't swallow or do anything to just make that feeling stop.

Was I crazy, talking to no one?

"Look at me now," I whispered into the surface of the desk as a surrogate person, "They promote me and I end up burning toasters and sobbing to a desk. I didn't even freak out like this when dad died."

I could have stopped what happened to him too. I was just a kid, but I could have tried harder to make him see we were there. And after it was over for him, all I ever heard were people telling me how it was part of some greater plan. They told me he'd been taken from us to a better place. But if it was part of a greater plan for this to keep on happening then it was in that plan for me to keep failing.

They were comforted by the idea that someone else was responsible for what happened. Sadly, they were right, but it wasn't who they thought. And as for who they were hoping was in control, it seemed they didn't much care which side won.

"If you're watching," I growled, lifting my head and resting it in my free hand, "screw you and your games."

I don't know why I expected an answer then, but I received none. All I heard was the cold, empty noise of a room without natural life. All I felt was the realization I was talking to ghosts that weren't there and a desk that couldn't understand.

"Though, if you can hear this," I whispered, "I guess telling you off is a mistake too."

"You did the right thing," Lucian said behind me, shocking me out of my trance. "Even if it was hard, it was the right thing to do."

I glanced back, absently wiping at my face in case there was a tear I didn't expect, saying, "I could have saved her, man. She was right there. I could have done something. It didn't have to end up like that."

He stared at me, walking to another desk and pulling up a chair, straddling it and resting his chin on his arms while looking at me from across the glass desktop. We'd made eye contact before, but this time it felt different. For the first time, I think I truly saw eye-to-eye with my mentor.

"Nate," he said in a quiet, solemn tone, "Do you remember the first time you walked into that lab in New Skids?"

I nodded, thinking back on the wall of photos and the acrid urine-like smell. "It was pretty bad…"

"That was her life," he said. "A room full of chemicals and broken glass. Every day she looked into a mirror and she saw a monster that was horrible enough she couldn't stand to see it anymore. So she broke the mirrors, took the drugs and tried to wash away that feeling of fear and anger she couldn't escape."

"I didn't see it," I said, shaking my head.

"Most people don't," he replied.

Something about the implication angered me, but I think I managed to control my tone when I asked, "What's your point?"

"My point, Nate, is that this is why we wear those visors. It's not to let us see the people better. It's to let us see past them better. You looked at her and you saw a beautiful face and a dazzling smile. But that blinded you to the shards of glass littering the floor in her wake."

285

I sat up again and leaned back. "So, what, do I just stop being human?"

He lifted his head and looked at me with a sympathetic, saddened face. "No, I think you need to be more than just human. You need to be more than just an Alter. I think we all have to make that mental jump to being an agent."

He stood up on that note, walking around the desk and ruffling my hair as my father once did. Part of me wondered if I'd failed them or if I'd succeeded in what he'd just told me to do. Did putting the mission ahead of myself count for being "more than human"?

I looked up at him and asked, "Did it ever happen to you?"

He lifted his gaze and looked out across the offices past me with a light frown. "A long time ago, I had a good friend who went bad on me. He started to call himself Letum, Death, because he said his 'resurrection' had taught him so much. I was too blind to realize what he was becoming."

The tone of his voice was haunting and telling. I could almost hear the words he wasn't saying and started to realize why Lucian would disappear to "find himself" so many times. Even if it wasn't obvious, my gut told me what he meant and I felt the driving need to ask one last question: "What happened to him?"

An extraordinarily cold look crossed his face as he glanced down at me, squeezing my shoulder tightly and essentially confirming my guess. With a frigid, halting voice he responded, "Let's just say he stopped using that name…and I started something I've yet to fully take ownership of."

He removed his hand from my shoulder and began to walk away while I sat there and considered what exactly those cryptic words meant. What had Lucian started that he wasn't taking responsibility for? For the first time since I met him, I felt as though I truly didn't know him at all. Worse, I realized I may have fallen into the same sort of trap he had.

It came back to me as Lucian was leaving that I had taken an active part in something that might have been bigger than I realized. Rufus told me the domino he was placing in his array was supposed to represent me. So, if that was true, what chain of events did I trigger on that rooftop?

I called out before he could leave the room. "Lucian! How do you think he managed to communicate out of the station before he had Janice?"

He looked back at me with a thoughtful expression and shrugged his shoulders, saying, "Maybe there was no 'before Janice'."

"And what if that's true?" I asked. "What if she's been infiltrating this place the whole time and no one noticed?"

"Then you just cut Rufus off from the outside world," he replied with a hushed chuckle and restrained smile.

We exchanged half-hearted nods and I watched him turn the corner at the far end. I think, right then, we both knew it couldn't have been that simple. Rufus wasn't concerned enough about her welfare for Janice to have been his only link to the outside world. She probably wasn't even his first backup. The man was known to cover his bases.

The next day the doctor released me after informing me the bone in my arm had been reinforced with carbon fiber and that I should probably expect arthritis eventually. It was a pleasant enough exchange. But I just wanted to go home.

I walked down the street, deciding not to drive for once after all that time spent glaring at people behind a windshield. Besides, my arm was in a sling.

It was a nice evening anyway. The Alters were out and about with something of a buzz from the announcement one of their own was going to run for office soon. A poster of Hale was already up against the wall of a few buildings I passed, hastily thrown together on someone's printer.

I stopped at Ahab's, stepping inside without my uniform for the first time in a long time, seeing more of those posters against the walls as I walked on through.

"Nate!" Trey said happily. "I heard what happened, I'm glad to see you're okay!"

Sighing and smiling lightly, I nodded and reached across the counter to offer my hand. "I'm sorry for how I was acting before, I shouldn't have suspected you. You could have filed a complaint or pressed charges. I'm surprised the video didn't end up everywhere."

He looked down at my hand, hesitated, took it and shook it

287

firmly. "Tight community, I told everyone why you weren't yourself," he said, "and I know I haven't been fair to you with that game we've played."

Still holding his hand, I smiled a little bigger than before. Leaning in, I whispered across the counter, "Incubus."

He laughed and patted my hand, "Dulaf tell you?"

"I saw you outside the Zomboner," I said, relieved to be right for once.

He laughed harder and slapped my shoulder, making me wince a bit despite the drugs they'd used to numb it. Brightly he said, "This one's on me then!"

I watched him get my usual and leaned on the counter while I waited, taking out a couple tablets for the arm. I stared at them down in my palm and then decided that little tap wasn't going to kill me. I put the tablets back in the bottle and looked up at him again, asking, "Why'd you hide it for all those years anyway?"

He put the cup on the counter and whispered to me, "How hard do you think it'd be to get a first date if women knew I was a literal predator? It's hard enough when they're keeping an eye out for the other kinds of predator."

Staring at him, I couldn't fault the man's logic.

I shook my head and took my order, waving and walking out of the shop. On the way I stopped and looked at Janice's usual table, a pair of Dryad girls sitting where she would have been. They were glancing through fashion magazines, whispering about how skinny the models were.

I grunted quietly to myself, sipped my coffee and walked on by.

When I arrived to my apartment I did what I could to open the door and still hold onto my coffee with just one hand. For a moment I considered various ways to go about it. But in the end the easiest was to turn around and knock lightly on Babs' door with my knuckle.

She opened her door, saw my arm in the sling and gasped at it. "Oh dear boy!" she exclaimed. "Are you okay?"

I smiled sheepishly and replied, "I've had better days. Can you help me open my door?"

She nodded, opened it for me and helped me on through. I thanked her, did my best to bow without dropping coffee on myself and watched her close the door on her way out.

As she left, I walked over to my TV and turned it on manually for the first time in what had to be eons. I even noticed some dust across the panel that shouldn't have been there. A news report for Hale flashed onto the screen, the poster I'd been seeing waved around by cheering Alters while news anchors began to downplay the event.

I'd obviously missed the man's speech, but I imagine it was a hell of a good one.

I backed away from the TV and looked around at the furniture in the room, wondering if I should just keel over onto my old friend the couch. But something told me it wasn't time to go falling onto a bad shoulder. I walked through the room carefully, listening to the report behind me and thinking of someone else who was likely watching the same report.

Deep beneath the station, far from the eyes of that cheering public, a man sat in a cold, dark cell at the bottom of a prison. And, though we were separated by several tons of rock, steel and a few city blocks, I could almost see what he was doing right at that moment. I could see the dim glow of a television in a darkened cell as it cast across his pale face and the glyphs he'd carved into the glass walls beyond. I could hear the same anchor echoing off the walls of the vault.

And, I swear, I could hear Rufus laughing from the shadows as he watched his puppets dance.

But me? I sat in the recliner that'd been sitting in the corner of my living room for the first time since I moved it in. I sank into the old, ragged chair and thought about how uncertain the future could be. But, watching those people smile and cheer, I thought of a man who said we needed to watch over them.

And I relaxed there, letting myself sink into it, surrounded in the faint memories of the smell of cheap cologne and pine trees.

About the author

A longtime fan of science fiction and fantasy, **Jeremy Varner** has been writing speculative fiction for most of his life in one form or another. First introduced to the genre through his father, a huge fan of sci-fi and fantasy from the days when that wasn't very cool, some of his earliest memories formed around watching aliens, creatures of legend, and robots of all shapes and sizes. It wasn't long before Jeremy wanted to create his own worlds and tell his own stories. From fan-fiction to original works that he dare not ever show the public, Jeremy's childhood notebooks were littered with fantastic worlds inspired by the works of greats.

It was during a particularly rough time that Jeremy realized that he didn't want to just dream anymore. After years of treating it as his secret, geeky hobby, Jeremy eventually decided to take his work professional and bring his own quirky brand of world building to the real world he was often escaping. **Shards of Glass**, originally released in 2011, was his debut novel and the first book of the **Agent of Argyre** series – a series he hopes will someday inspire someone else to take the same journey.

These books are dedicated to lost loved ones, dear friends, and the people that introduced him to these wonderful worlds.

You can find more about Jeremy through his website, blog and twitter account at:

Website: JeremyVarner.com
Twitter: @JDVarner

Acknowledgements

Shirley Allen
Jean Cox
Kristopher Cox
Rebecca Cox
Earlaine Hunter
Sean O'Dell

Dawn Prato
Christi Sawyer
Andrew Schiffbauer
Gerald Varner
Karen Varner